Andrew Lang

The True Story Book

Andrew Lang

The True Story Book

ISBN/EAN: 9783744747820

Printed in Europe, USA, Canada, Australia, Japan

Cover: Foto ©Andreas Hilbeck / pixelio.de

More available books at **www.hansebooks.com**

THE
TRUE STORY BOOK

EDITED BY

ANDREW LANG

With *NUMEROUS ILLUSTRATIONS* by *L. BOGLE,*
LUCIEN DAVIS, H. J. FORD, C. H. M. KERR, and LANCELOT SPEED

THIRD EDITION

LONDON
LONGMANS, GREEN, AND CO.
AND NEW YORK: 15 EAST 16th STREET
1894

DEDICATION

TO FRANCIS MacCUNN

You like the things I used to like,
    The things I'm fond of still,
The sound of fairy wands that strike
    Men into beasts at will;

The cruel stepmother, the fair
    Stepdaughter, kind and leal,
The bull and bear so debonair,
    The trenchant fairy steel.

You love the world where brute and fish
    Converse with man and bird,
Where dungeons open at a wish,
    And seas dry at a word.

That merry world to-day we leave,
    We list an ower-true tale,
Of hearts that sore for Charlie grieve,
    When handsome princes fail,

Of gallant races overthrown,
    Of dungeons ill to climb,
There's no such tale of trouble known,
    In all the fairy time.

There Montezuma still were king,
    There Charles would wear the crown.
And there the Highlanders would ding
    The Hanoverian down:

In Fairyland the Rightful Cause ·
Is never long a-winning,
In Fairyland the fairy laws
Are prompt to punish sinning :

For Fairyland's the land of joy,
And this the world of pain,
So back to Fairyland, my boy,
We'll journey once again !

INTRODUCTION

It is not without diffidence that the editor offers *The True Story Book* to children. We have now given them three fairy books, and their very kind and flattering letters to the editor prove, not only that they like the three fairy books, but that they clamour for more. What disappointment, then, to receive a volume full of adventures which actually happened to real people! There is not a dragon in the collection, nor even a giant; witches, here, play no part, and almost all the characters are grown up. On the other hand, if we have no fairies, we have princes in plenty, and a sweeter young prince than Tearlach (as far as this part of his story goes) the editor flatters himself that you shall nowhere find, not in Grimm, or Dasent, or Perrault. Still, it cannot be denied that true stories are not so good as fairy tales. They do not always end happily, and, what is worse, they do remind a young student of lessons and schoolrooms. A child may fear that he is being taught under a specious pretence of diversion, and that learning is being thrust on him under the disguise of entertainment. Prince Charlie and Cortés may be asked about in examinations, whereas no examiner has hitherto set questions on 'Blue Beard,' or 'Heart of Ice,' or 'The Red Etin of Ireland.' There is, to be honest, no way of getting over this difficulty. But the editor vows that he does not mean to teach anybody, and he has tried to mix the stories up so much that no clear and consecutive view of history can possibly be obtained from them ; moreover, when history does come in, it is not the kind of history favoured most by examiners. They seldom set questions on the conquest of Mexico, for example.

That is a very long story, but, to the editor's taste, it is simply the best true story in the world, the most unlikely, and the most romantic. For who could have supposed that the new-found world of the West held all that wealth of treasure, emeralds and gold, all those people, so beautiful and brave, so courteous and cruel, with their terrible gods, hideous human sacrifices, and almost Christian prayers? That a handful of Spaniards, themselves mistaken for children of a white god, should have crossed the sea, should have found a lovely lady, as in a fairy tale, ready to lead them to victory, should have planted the cross on the shambles of Huitzilopochtli, after that wild battle on the temple crest, should have been driven in rout from, and then recaptured, the Venice of the West, the lake city of Mexico—all this is as strange, as unlooked for, as any story of adventures in a new planet could be. No invention of fights and wanderings in Noman's land, no search for the mines of Solomon the king, can approach, for strangeness and romance, this tale, which is true, and vouched for by Spanish conquerors like Bernal Diaz, and by native historians like Ixtlilochitl, and by later missionaries like Sahagun. Cortés is the great original of all treasure-hunters and explorers in fiction, and here no feigned tale can be the equal of the real. As Mr. Prescott's admirable history is not a book much read by children (nor even by ' grown-ups ' for that matter), the editor hopes children will be pleased to find the ' Adventures in Anahuac ' in this collection. Miss Edgeworth tells us in *Orlandino* how much the tale delighted the young before Mr. Prescott wrote that excellent narrative of the world's chief adventure. May it please still, as it did when the century was young !

The adventures of Prince Charlie are already known, in part, to boys and girls who have read the *Tales of a Grandfather*, for pleasure and not as a school book. But here Mrs. McCunn has treated of them at greater length and more minutely. The source, here, is in these seven brown octavo volumes, all written in the closest hand, which are a treasure of the Advocates' Library in Edinburgh. The author is Mr. Forbes, a bishop of the persecuted Episcopalian Church in Scotland. Mr. Forbes collected his information very carefully, closely comparing the narratives of the various actors in the story. Into the boards of his volumes are fastened a scrap of the Prince's tartan waistcoat, a rag from his sprigged calico dress, a bit of his brogues—a twopenny treasure that has been wept and prayed over by the faithful. Nobody, in a book for children, would have the heart to tell the tale of the Prince's later years, of a moody, heart-broken, degraded exile. But, in the hills and the isles, bating a little wilfulness and foolhardiness, and the affair of the broken punch-bowl, Prince Charles is a model for princes and all men, brave, gay, much-enduring, good-humoured, kind, royally courteous, and considerate, even beyond what may be gathered from this part of the book, while the loyalty of the Highlanders (as in the case of Mackinnon, flogged nearly to death) was proof against torture as well as against gold. It is the Sobieski strain, not the Stuart, that we here admire in Prince Charles ; it is a piety, a loyalty, a goodness like Gordon's that we revere in old Lord Pitsligo in another story.

Many of the tales are concerned with fighting, for that is the most dramatic part of mortal business. These English captives who retake a ship from the Turks, these heroes of the *Shannon* and the *Chesapeake*, were doubtless good men and true in all their lives, but the light of history only falls on them in war. The immortal Three Hundred of Thermopylæ would also have been unknown, had they not died, to a man, for the sake of the honour of Lacedæmon. The editor conceives that it would have been easy to give more ' local colour ' to the sketch of Thermopylæ : to have dealt in description of the Immortals, drawn from the friezes in Susa, lately discovered by French enterprise. But the story is Greek, and the Greeks did not tell their stories in that way, but with a simplicity almost bald. Yet who dare alter and ' improve ' the narrative of Herodotus ? In another most romantic event, the finding of Vineland the Good, by Leif the Lucky, our materials are vague with the vagueness of a dream. Later fancy has meddled with the truth of the saga. English readers, no doubt, best catch the charm of the adventure in Mr. Rudyard Kipling's astonishingly imaginative tale called ' The Best Story in the World.' For the account of Isandhlwana, and Rorke's Drift, ' an ower-true tale,' the editor has to thank his friend Mr. Rider Haggard, who was in South Africa at the time of the disaster, and who has generously given time and labour to the task of ascertaining, as far as it can be ascertained, the exact truth of the melancholy, but, finally, not inglorious, business. The legend of ' Two Great Cricket Matches ' is taken, in part, from Lillywhite's scores, and Mr. Robert Lyttelton's spirited pages in the ' Badminton ' book of Cricket. The second match the editor writes of ' as he who saw it,' to quote Caxton on Dares Phrygius. These legends prove that a match is never lost till it is won.

Some of the True Stories contain, we may surmise, traces of the imaginative faculty. The escapes of Benvenuto Cellini, of Trenck, and of Casanova must be taken as the heroes chose to report them ; Benvenuto and Casanova have no firm reputation for veracity. Again, the escape of Cæsar

Borgia is from a version handed down by the great Alexandre
Dumas, and we may surmise that Alexandre allowed it to
lose nothing in the telling ; he may have ' given it a sword
and a cocked hat,' as was Sir Walter's wont.   About Kaspar
Hauser's mystery we can hardly speak of ' the truth,' for
the exact truth will never be known.   The depositions of the
earliest witnesses were not taken at once ; some witnesses
altered their evidence in later years ; parts of the records of
Nuremberg are lost in suspicious circumstances.   The Duchess
of Cleveland's book, *Kaspar Hauser*, is written in defence of
her father, Lord Stanhope.   The charges against Lord Stanhope, that he aided in, or connived at, the slaying of Kaspar,
because Kaspar was the true heir of the House of Baden—are
as childish as they are wicked. But the Duchess hardly allows
for the difficulties in which we find ourselves if we regard
Kaspar as absolutely and throughout an impostor. This, however, is not the place to discuss an historical mystery ; this
' true story ' is told as a romance founded on fact ; the hypo-
thesis that Kaspar was a son and heir of the house of Baden
seems, to the editor, to be absolutely devoid of evidence.

To Madame Von Platt Stuart the author owes permission to quote the striking adventures of her father, or of her
uncle, on the flooded Findhorn.   The *Lays of the Deer
Forest*, which contain this tale in the volume of notes, were
written by John Sobieski Stuart, and by Charles Edward
Stuart, and the editor is uncertain as to which of those
gentlemen was the hero of these perilous crossings of the
Highland river.   Many other good tales, legends, and studies
of natural history and of Highland manners may be found in
the *Lays of the Deer Forest*, apart from the curious interest
of the poems.   On the whole, with certain exceptions, the
editor has tried to find true stories rather out of the beaten
paths of history ; the narrative of John Tanner, for instance,

is probably true, but the book in which his adventures were published is now rather difficult to procure. For 'A Boy among the Red Indians,' 'Two Cricket Matches,' 'The Spartan Three Hundred,' 'The Finding of Vineland the Good,' and 'The Escapes of Lord Pitsligo,' the editor is himself responsible, as far as they do not consist of extracts from the original sources. Miss May Kendall translated or adapted Casanova's escape and the piratical and Algerine tales. Mrs. Lang reduced the narrative of the Chevalier Johnstone, and did the escapes of Cæsar Borgia, of Trenck, and Cervantes, while Miss Blackley renders that of Benvenuto Cellini. Mrs. McCunn, as already said, compiled from the sources indicated the Adventures of Prince Charles, and she tells the story of Grace Darling ; the contemporary account is, unluckily, rather meagre. Miss Alleyne did ' The Kidnapping of the Princes,' Miss C. A. Hutton the ' Story of Kaspar Hauser.' Miss Wright reduced the Adventures of Cortés from Prescott, and Mr. Rider Haggard has already been mentioned in connection with Isandhlwana.

Here the editor leaves *The True Story Book* to the indulgence of children, explaining, once more, that his respect for their judgment is very great, and that he would not dream of imposing *lessons* on *them*, in the shape of a Christmas book. No, lessons are one thing, and stories are another. But, though fiction is undeniably stranger and more attractive than truth, yet true stories are also rather attractive and strange, now and then. And, after all, we may return once more to Fairyland, after this excursion into the actual workaday world.

CONTENTS

PLATES

THE earliest event of my life which I distinctly remember (says John Tanner) is the death of my mother. This happened when I was two years old, and many of the attending circumstances made so deep an impression that they are still fresh in my memory. I cannot recollect the name of the settlement at which we lived, but I have since learned it was on the Kentucky River, at a considerable distance from the Ohio.

My father, whose name was John Tanner, was an emigrant from Virginia, and had been a clergyman.

When about to start one morning to a village at some distance, he gave, as it appeared, a strict charge to my sisters, Agatha and Lucy, to send me to school; but this they neglected to do until afternoon, and then, as the weather was rainy and unpleasant, I insisted on remaining at home. When my father returned at night, and found that I had been at home all day, he sent me for a parcel of small canes, and flogged me much more severely than I could suppose the offence merited. I was displeased with my sisters for attributing all the blame to me, when they had neglected even to tell me to go to school in the forenoon. From that time, my father's house was less like home to me, and I often thought and said, ' I wish I could go and live among the Indians.'

One day we went from Cincinnati to the mouth of the Big Miami, opposite which we were to settle. Here was some cleared land, and one or two log cabins, but they had been deserted on account of the Indians. My father rebuilt the cabins, and inclosed them with a strong picket. It was early in the spring when we arrived at the mouth of the Big Miami, and we were soon engaged in preparing a field to plant corn. I think it was not more than ten days after our arrival, when my father told us in the morning, that, from the actions of the horses, he perceived there were Indians lurking about in the woods, and he said to me, ' John, you

B

must not go out of the house to-day.' After giving strict charge to my stepmother to let none of the little children go out, he went to the field, with the negroes, and my elder brother, to drop corn.

Three little children, besides myself, were left in the house with my stepmother. To prevent me from going out, my stepmother required me to take care of the little child, then not more than a few months old ; but as I soon became impatient of confinement, I began to pinch my little brother, to make him cry. My mother, perceiving his uneasiness, told me to take him in my arms and walk about the house; I did so, but continued to pinch him. My mother at length took him from me to nurse him. I watched my opportunity, and escaped into the yard ; thence through a small door in the large gate of the wall into the open field. There was a walnut-tree at some distance from the house, and near the side of the field where I had been in the habit of finding some of the last year's nuts. To gain this tree without being seen by my father and those in the field, I had to use some precaution. I remember perfectly well having seen my father, as I skulked towards the tree ; he stood in the middle of the field, with his gun in his hand, to watch for Indians, while the others were dropping corn. As I came near the tree, I thought to myself, 'I wish I could see these Indians.' I had partly filled with nuts a straw hat which I wore, when I heard a crackling noise behind me; I looked round, and saw the Indians; almost at the same instant, I was seized by both hands, and dragged off betwixt two. One of them took my straw hat, emptied the nuts on the ground, and put it on my head. The Indians who seized me were an old man and a young one; these were, as I learned subsequently, Manito-o-geezhik, and his son Kish-kau-ko.

After I saw myself firmly seized by both wrists by the two Indians, I was not conscious of anything that passed for a considerable time. I must have fainted, as I did not cry out, and I can remember nothing that happened to me until they threw me over a large log, which must have been at a considerable distance from the house. The old man I did not now see ; I was dragged along between Kish-kau-ko and a very short thick man. I had probably made some resistance, or done something to irritate this last, for he took me a little to one side, and drawing his tomahawk, motioned to me to look up. This I plainly understood, from the expression of his face, and his manner, to be a direction for me to look up for the last time, as he was about to kill me. I did as he directed, but Kish-kau-ko caught his hand as the tomahawk was descending, and prevented him from burying it in my brains. Loud talking ensued between the two. Kish-kau-ko presently raised

a yell: the old man and four others answered it by a similar yell, and came running up. I have since understood that Kish-kau-ko complained to his father that the short man had made an attempt to kill his little brother, as he called me. The old chief, after reproving him, took me by one hand, and Kish-kau-ko by the other and dragged me betwixt them, the man who had threatened to kill me, and who was now an object of terror to me, being kept at some distance. I could perceive, as I retarded them somewhat in their retreat, that they were apprehensive of being overtaken ; some of them were always at some distance from us.

It was about one mile from my father's house to the place where they threw me into a hickory-bark canoe, which was concealed under the bushes, on the bank of the river. Into this they all seven jumped, and immediately crossed the Ohio, landing at the mouth of the Big Miami, and on the south side of that river. Here they abandoned their canoe, and stuck their paddles in the ground, so that they could be seen from the river. At a little distance in the woods they had some blankets and provisions concealed ; they offered me some dry venison and bear's grease, but I could not eat. My father's house was plainly to be seen from the place where we stood ; they pointed at it, looked at me, and laughed, but I have never known what they said.

After they had eaten a little, they began to ascend the Miami, dragging me along as before.

It must have been early in the spring when we arrived at Sau-ge-nong, for I can remember that at this time the leaves were small, and the Indians were about planting their corn. They managed to make me assist at their labours, partly by signs, and partly by the few words of English old Manito-o-geezhik could speak. After planting, they all left the village, and went out to hunt and dry meat. When they came to their hunting-grounds, they chose a place where many deer resorted, and here they began to build a long screen like a fence ; this they made of green boughs and small trees. When they had built a part of it, they showed me how to remove the leaves and dry brush from that side of it to which the Indians were to come to shoot the deer. In this labour I was sometimes assisted by the squaws and children, but at other times I was left alone. It now began to be warm weather, and it happened one day that, having been left alone, as I was tired and thirsty, I fell asleep. I cannot tell how long I slept, but when I began to awake, I thought I heard someone crying a great way off. Then I tried to raise up my head, but could not. Being now more awake, I saw my Indian mother and sister standing by me, and perceived that my face and head were wet. The old woman and her

daughter were crying bitterly, but it was some time before I perceived that my head was badly cut and bruised. It appears that,
after I had fallen asleep, Manito-o-geezhik, passing that way, had
perceived me, had tomahawked me, and thrown me in the bushes ;
and that when he came to his camp he had said to his wife, ' Old
woman, the boy I brought you is good for nothing ; I have killed
him ; you will find him in such a place.' The old woman and her
daughter having found me, discovered still some signs of life, and
had stood over me a long time, crying, and pouring cold water on
my head, when I waked. In a few days I recovered in some
measure from this hurt, and was again set to work at the screen,
but I was more careful not to fall asleep ; I endeavoured to assist
them at their labours, and to comply in all instances with their
directions, but I was notwithstanding treated with great harshness,
particularly by the old man, and his two sons She-mung and Kwo-
tash-e. While we remained at the hunting camp, one of them put
a bridle in my hand, and pointing in a certain direction motioned
me to go. I went accordingly, supposing he wished me to
bring a horse : I went and caught the first I could find, and in this
way I learned to discharge such services as they required of me.

I had been about two years at Sau-ge-nong, when a great council
was called by the British agents at Mackinac. This council was
attended by the Sioux, the Winnebagoes, the Menomonees, and
many remote tribes, as well as by the Ojibbeways, Ottawwaws, &c.
When old Manito-o-geezhik returned from this council, I soon
learned that he had met there his kinswoman, Net-no-kwa, who, notwithstanding her sex, was then regarded as principal chief of the
Ottawwaws. This woman had lost her son, of about my age, by death ;
and, having heard of me, she wished to purchase me to supply his place.
My old Indian mother, the Otter woman, when she heard of this,
protested vehemently against it. I heard her say, ' My son has
been dead once, and has been restored to me ; I cannot lose him
again.' But these remonstrances had little influence when
Net-no-kwa arrived with plenty of whisky and other presents.
She brought to the lodge first a ten-gallon keg of whisky, blankets,
tobacco, and other articles of great value. She was perfectly
acquainted with the dispositions of those with whom she had to
negotiate. Objections were made to the exchange until the con-
tents of the keg had circulated for some time ; then an additional
keg, and a few more presents, completed the bargain, and I was
transferred to Net-no-kwa. This woman, who was then advanced

in years, was of a more pleasing aspect than my former mother.
She took me by the hand, after she had completed the negotiation
with my former possessors, and led me to her own lodge, which
stood near. Here I soon found I was to be treated more indul-
gently than I had been. She gave me plenty of food, put good
clothes upon me, and told me to go and play with her own sons
We remained but a short time at Sau-ge-nong. She would not
stop with me at Mackinac, which we passed in the night, but ran
along to Point St. Ignace, where she hired some Indians to take
care of me, while she returned to Mackinac by herself, or with one
or two of her young men. After finishing her business at
Mackinac, she returned, and, continuing on our journey, we arrived
in a few days at Shab-a-wy-wy-a-gun.

The husband of Net-no-kwa was an Ojibbeway of Red River,
called Taw-ga-we-ninne, the hunter. He was seventeen years
younger than Net-no-kwa, and had turned off a former wife on
being married to her. Taw-ga-we-ninne was always indulgent and
kind to me, treating me like an equal, rather than as a dependent.
When speaking to me, he always called me his son. Indeed, he
himself was but of secondary importance in the family, as everything belonged to Net-no-kwa, and she had the direction in all
affairs of any moment. She imposed on me, for the first year,
some tasks. She made me cut wood, bring home game, bring
water, and perform other services not commonly required of the
boys of my age ; but she treated me invariably with so much kindness that I was far more happy and content than I had been in the
family of Manito-o-geezhik. She sometimes whipped me, as she
did her own children : but I was not so severely and frequently
beaten as I had been before.

Early in the spring, Net-no-kwa and her husband, with their
family, started to go to Mackinac. They left me, as they had
done before, at Point St. Ignace, as they would not run the risk of
losing me by suffering me to be seen at Mackinac. On our return,
after we had gone twenty-five or thirty miles from Point St.
Ignace, we were detained by contrary winds at a place called
Me-nau-ko-king, a point running out into the lake. Here we encamped with some other Indians, and a party of traders. Pigeons
were very numerous in the woods, and the boys of my age, and the
traders, were busy shooting them. I had never killed any game,
and, indeed, had never in my life discharged a gun. My mother
had purchased at Mackinac a keg of powder, which, as they thought

it a little damp, was here spread out to dry. Taw-ga-we-ninne had a large horseman's pistol; and, finding myself somewhat emboldened by his indulgent manner toward me, I requested permission to go and try to kill some pigeons with the pistol. My request was seconded by Net-no-kwa, who said, 'It is time for our son to begin to learn to be a hunter.' Accordingly, my father, as I called Taw-ga-we-ninne, loaded the pistol and gave it to me, saying, ' Go, my son, and if you kill anything with this, you shall immediately have a gun and learn to hunt.' Since I have been a man, I have been placed in difficult situations; but my anxiety for success was never greater than in this, my first essay as a hunter. I had not gone far from the camp before I met with pigeons, and some of them alighted in the bushes very near me. I cocked my pistol, and raised it to my face, bringing the breech almost in contact with my nose. Having brought the sight to bear upon the pigeon, I pulled trigger, and was in the next instant sensible of a humming noise, like that of a stone sent swiftly through the air. I found the pistol at the distance of some paces behind me, and the pigeon under the tree on which he had been sitting. My face was much bruised, and covered with blood. I ran home, carrying my pigeon in triumph. My face was speedily bound up ; my pistol exchanged for a fowling-piece; I was accoutred with a powder-horn, and furnished with shot, and allowed to go out after birds. One of the young Indians went with me, to observe my manner of shooting. I killed three more pigeons in the course of the afternoon, and did not discharge my gun once without killing. Henceforth I began to be treated with more consideration, and was allowed to hunt often, that I might become expert.

Game began to be scarce, and we all suffered from hunger. The chief man of our band was called As-sin-ne-boi-nainse (the Little Assinneboin), and he now proposed to us all to move, as the country where we were was exhausted. The day on which we were to commence our removal was fixed upon, but before it arrived our necessities became extreme. The evening before the day on which we intended to move my mother talked much of all our misfortunes and losses, as well as of the urgent distress under which we were then labouring. At the usual hour I went to sleep, as did all the younger part of the family; but I was wakened again by the loud praying and singing of the old woman, who continued her devotions through great part of the night. Very early on the following morning she called us all to get up, and put on our moccasins, and be ready to move. She then called Wa-me-gon-a-biew to her, and said to him, in rather a low voice, 'My son, last night I sung and prayed to the Great Spirit, and when I slept, there came to me one like a man, and said to me, "Net-no-kwa, to-morrow you shall eat a bear. There is, at a distance from the path you are to travel to-morrow, and in such a direction" (which she described to him), "a small round meadow, with something like a path leading from it; in that path there is a bear." Now, my son, I wish you to go to that place, without mentioning to anyone what I have said, and you will certainly find the bear, as I have described to you.' But the young man, who was not particularly dutiful, or apt to regard what his mother said, going out of the lodge, spoke sneeringly to the other Indians of the dream. 'The old woman,' said he, 'tells me we are to eat a bear to-day; but I do not know who is to kill it.' The old woman, hearing him, called him in, and reproved him; but she could not prevail upon him to go to hunt.

I had my gun with me, and I continued to think of the conversation I had heard between my mother and Wa-me-gon-a-biew respecting her dream. At length I resolved to go in search of the place she had spoken of, and without mentioning to anyone my design, I loaded my gun as for a bear, and set off on our back track. I soon met a woman belonging to one of the brothers of Taw-ga-we-ninne, and of course my aunt. This woman had shown little friendship for us, considering us as a burthen upon her husband, who sometimes gave something for our support; she had also often ridiculed me. She asked me immediately what I was doing on the path, and whether I expected to kill Indians, that I came there with my gun. I made her no answer; and thinking I must be not far from the place where my mother had told Wa-me-gon-a-biew to leave the path, I turned off, continuing carefully to regard all the directions she had given. At length I found what appeared at some former time to have been a pond. It was a small, round, open place in the woods, now grown up with grass and small bushes. This I thought must be the meadow my mother had spoken of; and examining around it, I came to an open space in the bushes, where, it is probable, a small brook ran from the meadow; but the snow was now so deep that I could see nothing of it. My mother had mentioned that, when she saw the bear in her dream, she had, at the same time, seen a smoke rising from the ground. I was confident this was the place she had indicated, and I watched long, expecting to see the smoke; but, wearied at length with waiting, I walked a few paces into the open place, resembling a path, when I unexpectedly fell up to my middle in the snow. I extricated myself without difficulty, and walked on; but, remembering that I had heard the Indians speak of killing bears in their holes, it occurred to me that it might be a bear's hole into which I had fallen, and, looking down into it, I saw the head of a bear lying close to the bottom of the hole. I placed the muzzle of my gun nearly between his eyes and discharged it. As soon as the smoke cleared away, I took a piece of stick and thrust it into the eyes and into the wound in the head of the bear, and, being satisfied that he was dead, I endeavoured to lift him out of the hole; but being unable to do this, I returned home, following the track I had made in coming out. As I came near the camp, where the squaws had by this time set up the lodges, I met the same woman I had seen in going out, and she immediately began again to ridicule me. ' Have you killed a bear, that you come back so soon, and walk so fast? ' I thought to myself, ' How does she know that I have killed a bear? ' But I passed by her without saying anything, and went into my mother's lodge. After a few minutes, the old woman said, ' My son, look in that kettle, and you will find a mouthful of beaver meat, which a man gave me since you left us in the morning. You must leave half of it for Wa-me-gon-a-biew, who has not yet returned from hunting, and has eaten nothing to-day.' I accordingly ate the beaver meat, and when I had finished it, observing an opportunity when she stood by herself, I stepped up to her, and whispered in her ear, ' My mother, I have killed a bear.' ' What do you say, my son? ' said she. ' I have killed a bear.' ' Are you sure you have killed him? ' ' Yes.' ' Is he quite dead? ' ' Yes.' She watched my face for a moment, and then caught me in her arms, hugging and kissing me with great earnestness, and for a long time. I then told her what my aunt had said to me, both going and returning, and this being told to her husband when he returned, he not only reproved her for it, but gave her a severe flogging. The bear was sent for, and, as being the first I had killed, was cooked all together, and the hunters of the whole band invited to feast with us, according to the custom of the Indians. The same day one of the Crees killed a bear and a moose, and gave a large share of the meat to my mother.

One winter I hunted for a trader called by the Indians Aneeb, which means an elm-tree. As the winter advanced, and the

weather became more and more cold, I found it difficult to procure
as much game as I had been in the habit of supplying, and as was
wanted by the trader. Early one morning, about mid-winter, I
started an elk. I pursued until night, and had almost overtaken
him; but hope and strength failed me at the same time. What

clothing I had on me, notwithstanding the extreme coldness of the
weather, was drenched with sweat. It was not long after I turned
towards home that I felt it stiffening about me. My leggings were
of cloth, and were torn in pieces in running through the bush. I
was conscious I was somewhat frozen before I arrived at the place
where I had left our lodge standing in the morning, and it was now

midnight. I knew it had been the old woman's intention to move, and I knew where she would go; but I had not been informed she would go on that day. As I followed on their path, I soon ceased to suffer from cold, and felt that sleepy sensation which I knew preceded the last stage of weakness in such as die of cold. I re-doubled my efforts, but with an entire consciousness of the danger of my situation; it was with no small difficulty that I could prevent myself from lying down. At length I lost all consciousness for some time, how long I cannot tell, and, awaking as from a dream, I found I had been walking round and round in a small circle not more than twenty or twenty-five yards over. After the return of my senses, I looked about to try to discover· my path, as I had missed it; but, while I was looking, I discovered a light at a dis-tance, by which I directed my course. Once more, before I reached the lodge, I lost my senses; but I did not fall down; if I had, I should never have got up again; but I ran round and round in a circle as before. When I at last came into the lodge, I immediately fell down, but I did not lose myself as before. I can remember seeing the thick and sparkling coat of frost on the inside of the pukkwi lodge, and hearing my mother say that she had kept a large fire in expectation of my arrival; and that she had not thought I should have been so long gone in the morning, but that I should have known long before night of her having moved. It was a month before I was able to go out again, my face, hands, and legs having been much frozen.

There is, on the bank of the Little Saskawjewun, a place which looks like one the Indians would always choose to encamp at. In a bend of the river is a beautiful landing-place, behind it a little plain, a thick wood, and a small hill rising abruptly in the rear. But with that spot is connected a story of fratricide, a crime so un-common that the spot where it happened is held in detestation, and regarded with terror. No Indian will land his canoe, much less encamp, at '*the place of the two dead men.*' They relate that many years ago the Indians were encamped here, when a quarrel arose between two brothers, having she-she-gwi for totems.[1] One drew his knife and slew the other; but those of the band who were present, looked upon the crime as so horrid that, without hesitation or delay, they killed the murderer, and buried them together.

As I approached this spot, I thought much of the story of the two brothers, who bore the same totem with myself, and were, as I

---

[1] The totem is the crest of the Indians.

supposed, related to my Indian mother. I had heard it said that, if any man encamped near their graves, as some had done soon after they were buried, they would be seen to come out of the ground, and either re-act the quarrel and the murder, or in some other manner so annoy and disturb their visitors that they could not sleep. Curiosity was in part my motive, and I wished to be able to tell the Indians that I not only stopped, but slept quietly at a place which they shunned with so much fear and caution. The sun was going down as I arrived; and I pushed my little canoe in to the shore, kindled a fire, and, after eating my supper, lay down and slept. Very soon I saw the two dead men come and sit down by my fire, opposite me. Their eyes were intently fixed upon me, but they neither smiled nor said anything. I got up and sat opposite them by the fire, and in this situation I awoke. The night was dark and gusty, but I saw no men, or heard any other sound than that of the wind in the trees. It is likely I fell asleep again, for I soon saw the same two men standing below the bank of the river, their heads just rising to the level of the ground I had made my fire on, and looking at me as before. After a few minutes, they rose one after the other, and sat down opposite me; but now they were laughing, and pushing at me with sticks, and using various methods of annoyance. I endeavoured to speak to them, but my voice failed me; I tried to fly, but my feet refused to do their office. Throughout the whole night I was in a state of agitation and alarm. Among other things which they said to me, one of them told me to look at the top of the little hill which stood near. I did so, and saw a horse fettered, and standing looking at me. 'There, my brother,' said the ghost, ' is a horse which I give you to ride on your journey to-morrow; and as you pass here on your way home, you can call and leave the horse, and spend another night with us.'

At last came the morning, and I was in no small degree pleased to find that with the darkness of the night these terrifying visions vanished. But my long residence among the Indians, and the frequent instances in which I had known the intimations of dreams verified, occasioned me to think seriously of the horse the ghost had given me. Accordingly I went to the top of the hill, where I dis-covered tracks and other signs, and, following a little distance, found a horse, which I knew belonged to the trader I was going to see. As several miles travel might be saved by crossing from this point on the Little Saskawjewun to the Assinneboin, I left the canoe, and, having caught the horse, and put my load upon him, led him towards the trading-house, where I arrived next day. In all subsequent journeys through this country, I carefully shunned ' the place of the two dead '; and the account I gave of what I had seen and suffered there confirmed the superstitious terrors of the Indians.

I was standing by our lodge one evening, when I saw a good-looking young woman walking about and smoking. She noticed me from time to time, and at last came up and asked me to smoke with her. I answered that I never smoked. ' You do not wish to touch my pipe ; for that reason you will not smoke with me.' I took her pipe and smoked a little, though I had not been in the habit of smoking before. She remained some time, and talked with me, and I began to be pleased with her. After this we saw each other often, and I became gradually attached to her.

I mention this because it was to this woman that I was afterwards married, and because the commencement of our acquaintance was not after the usual manner of the Indians. Among them it most commonly happens, even when a young man marries a woman of his own band, he has previously had no personal acquaintance with her. They have seen each other in the village ; he has perhaps looked at her in passing, but it is probable they have never spoken together. The match is agreed on by the old people, and when their intention is made known to the young couple, they commonly find, in themselves, no objection to the arrangement, as they know, should it prove disagreeable mutually, or to either party, it can at any time be broken off.

I now redoubled my diligence in hunting, and commonly came home with meat in the early part of the day, at least before night. I then dressed myself as handsomely as I could, and walked about the village, sometimes blowing the Pe-be-gwun, or flute. For some time Mis-kwa-bun-o-kwa pretended she was not willing to marry me, and it was not, perhaps, until she perceived some abatement of ardour on my part that she laid this affected coyness entirely aside. For my own part, I found that my anxiety to take a wife home to my lodge was rapidly becoming less and less. I made several efforts to break off the intercourse, and visit her no more ; but a lingering inclination was too strong for me. When she perceived my growing indifference, she sometimes reproached me, and sometimes sought to move me by tears and entreaties ; but I said nothing to the old woman about bringing her home, and became daily more and more unwilling to acknowledge her publicly as my wife.

About this time I had occasion to go to the trading-house on Red River, and I started in company with a half-breed belonging to that establishment, who was mounted on a fleet horse. The distance we had to travel has since been called by the English settlers seventy miles. We rode and went on foot by turns, and the one who was on foot kept hold of the horse's tail, and ran. We passed over the whole distance in one day. In returning, I was by myself, and without a horse, and I made an effort, intending, if possible, to accomplish the same journey in one day; but darkness, and excessive fatigue, compelled me to stop when I was within about ten miles of home.

When I arrived at our lodge, on the following day, I saw Mis-kwa-bun-o-kwa sitting in my place. As I stopped at the door of the lodge, and hesitated to enter, she hung down her head; but Net-no-kwa greeted me in a tone somewhat harsher than was common for her to use to me. 'Will you turn back from the door of the lodge, and put this young woman to shame, who is in all respects better than you are? This affair has been of your seeking, and not of mine or hers. You have followed her about the village heretofore; now you would turn from her, and make her appear like one who has attempted to thrust herself in your way.' I was, in part, conscious of the justness of Net-no-kwa's reproaches, and in part prompted by inclination; I went in and sat down by the side of Mis-kwa-bun-o-kwa, and thus we became man and wife. Old Net-no-kwa had, while I was absent at Red River, without my knowledge or consent, made her bargain with the parents of the young woman, and brought her home, rightly supposing that it would be no difficult matter to reconcile me to the measure. In most of the marriages which happen between young persons, the parties most interested have less to do than in this case. The amount of presents which the parents of a woman expect to receive in exchange for her diminishes in proportion to the number of husbands she may have had.

I now began to attend to some of the ceremonies of what may be called the initiation of warriors, this being the first time I had been on a war-party. For the first three times that a man accompanies a war-party, the customs of the Indians require some peculiar and painful observances, from which old warriors may, if they choose, be exempted. The young warrior must constantly paint his face black; must wear a cap, or head-dress of some kind; must never precede the old warriors, but follow them, stepping in their tracks. He must never scratch his head, or any other part of his body, with his fingers, but if he is compelled to scratch he must use a small stick; the vessel he eats or drinks out of, or the knife he uses, must be touched by no other person.

The young warrior, however long and fatiguing the march, must neither eat, nor drink, nor sit down by day; if he halts for a moment, he must turn his face towards his own country, that the Great Spirit may see that it is his wish to return home again.

. . . .

It was Tanner's wish to return home again, and after many dangerous and disagreeable adventures he did at last, when almost an old man, come back to the Whites and tell his history, which, as he could not write, was taken down at his dictation.[1]

[1] From *Tanner's Captivity.* New York, 1830.

CASANOVA'S ESCAPE

IN July 1755 Casanova di Seingalt, a Venetian gentleman, who, by reason of certain books of magic he possessed, fell under the displeasure of the Church, was imprisoned by order of the Inquisition in a cell in the ducal palace.

The cell in which he was imprisoned was one of seven called 'The Leads,' because they were under the palace roof, which was covered neither by slates nor bricks, but great heavy sheets of lead. They were guarded by archers, and could only be reached by passing through the hall of council. The secretary of the Inquisition had charge of their key, which the gaoler, after going the round of the prisoners, restored to him every morning. Four of the cells faced eastward over the palace canal, the other three westward over the court. Casanova's was one of the three, and he calculated that it was exactly above the private room of the inquisitors.

For many hours after the gaoler first turned the key upon Casanova he was left alone in the gloomy cell, not high enough for him to stand upright in, and destitute even of a couch. He laid aside his silk mantle, his hat adorned with Spanish lace and a white plume—for, when roused from sleep and arrested by the Inquisition, he had put on the suit lying ready, in which he intended to have gone to a gay entertainment. The heat of the cell was extreme: the prisoner leaned his elbows on the ledge of the grating which admitted to the cell what light there was, and fell into a deep and bitter reverie. Eight hours passed, and then the complete solitude in which he was left began to trouble him. Another hour, another, and another; but when night really fell, to take Casanova's own account,

'I became like a raging madman, stamping, cursing, and uttering wild cries. After more than an hour of this furious exercise, seeing no one, not hearing the least sign which could have made me imagine that anyone was aware of my fury, I stretched myself on the ground. . . . But my bitter grief and anger, and the hard floor on which I lay, did not prevent me from sleeping.

'The midnight bell woke me : I could not believe that I had really passed three hours without consciousness of pain. Without moving, lying as I was on my left side, I stretched out my right hand for my handkerchief, which I remembered was there. Groping with my hand—heavens ! suddenly it rested upon *another* hand, icy cold ! Terror thrilled me from head to foot, and my hair rose : I had never in all my life known such an agony of fear, and would never have thought myself capable of it.

'Three or four minutes I passed, not only motionless, but bereft of thought ; then, recovering my senses, I began to think that the hand I touched was imaginary. In that conviction I stretched out my arm once more, only to encounter the same hand, which, with a cry of horror, I seized, and let go again, drawing back my own. I shuddered, but being able to reason by this time, I decided that while I slept a corpse had been laid near me—for I was sure there was nothing when I lay down on the floor. But whose was the dead body ? Some innocent sufferer, perhaps one of my own friends, whom they had strangled, and laid there that I might find before my eyes when I woke the example of what my own fate was to be ? That thought made me furious : for the third time I approached the hand with my own : I clasped it, and at the same instant I tried to rise, to draw this dead body towards me, and be certain of the hideous crime. But, as I strove to prop myself on my left elbow, the cold hand I was clasping became alive, and was withdrawn—and I knew that instant, to my utter astonishment, that I held none other than my own left hand, which, lying stiffened on the hard floor, had lost heat and sensation entirely.'

That incident, though comic, did not cheer Casanova, but gave him matter for the darkest reflections—since he saw himself in a place where, if the unreal seemed so true, reality might one day become a dream. In other words, he feared approaching madness.

But at last came daybreak, and by-and-by the gaoler returned, asking the prisoner if he had had time to find out what he would like to eat. Casanova was allowed to send for all he needed from his own apartments in Venice, but writing-implements, any metal instruments whatever, even knife and fork, and the books he mentioned, were struck from his list. The inquisitors sent him books which they themselves thought suitable, and which drove him, he said, to the verge of madness.

C

He was not ill-treated—having a daily allowance given him to
buy what food he liked, which was more than he could spend.
But the loss of liberty soon became insupportable.   For months he
believed that his deliverance was close at hand ; but when November
came, and he saw no prospect of release, he began to form pro-

jects of escape.   And soon the idea of freeing himself, however wild
and impossible it seemed, took complete possession of him.
By-and-by he was allowed half an hour's daily promenade in
the corridor (galetas) outside his cell—a dingy, rat-infested place,
into which old rubbish was apt to drift.   One day Casanova noticed
a piece of black marble on the floor—polished, an inch thick and

six inches long. He picked it up stealthily, and without any definite intention, managed to hide it away in his cell.

Another morning his eyes fell upon a long iron bolt, lying on the floor with other old odds and ends, and that also, concealed in his dress, he bore into his cell. When left alone, he examined it carefully, and realised that if pointed, it would make an excellent spontoon. He took the black marble, and after grinding one end of the bolt against it for a long while, he saw that he had really succeeded in wearing the iron down. For fifteen days he worked, till he could hardly stir his right arm, and his shoulder felt almost dislocated. But he had made the bolt into a real tool; or, if necessary, a weapon, with an excellent point. He hid it in the straw of his armchair so carefully that, to find it, one must have known that it was there ; and then he began to consider what use he should make of it.

He was certain that the room underneath was the one in which on entering he had seen the secretary of the Inquisition, and which was probably opened every morning. A hole once made in the floor, he could easily lower himself by a rope made of the sheets of his bed, and fastened to one of the bed-posts. He might hide under the great table of the tribunal till the door was opened, and then make good his escape. It was probable, indeed, that one of the archers would mount guard in this room at night ; but him Casanova resolved to kill with his pointed iron. The great difficulty really was that the hole in the floor was not to be made in a day, but might be a work of months. And therefore some pretext must be found to prevent the archers from sweeping out the cell, as they were accustomed to do every morning.

Some days after, alleging no reason, he ordered the archers not to sweep. This omission was allowed to pass for several mornings, and then the gaoler demanded Casanova's reason. He answered, that the dust settled on his lungs, and made him cough, and might give him a mortal disease. Laurent, the gaoler, offered to throw water on the floor before sweeping it ; but Casanova's arguments against the dampness of the atmosphere that would result were equally ingenious. Laurent's suspicions, however, were roused, and one day he ordered the room to be swept most carefully, and even lit a candle, and on the pretence of cleanliness, searched the cell thoroughly. Casanova seemed indifferent, but the next day, having pricked his finger, he showed his handkerchief stained with blood, and said that the gaoler's cruelty had brought on so severe a cough that he had actually broken a small blood-vessel. A doctor was sent for, who took the prisoner's part, and forbade sweeping out the cell in future. One great point was gained; but the work could not begin yet, owing to the fearful cold. The prisoner would have been forced to wear gloves, and the sight of a worn glove might have excited suspicion. So he occupied himself with another stratagem—the creation, little by little, of a lamp, for the solace of the endless winter nights. One by one, the gaoler himself, unsuspectingly, brought the different ingredients: oil was imported in salads, wick the prisoner himself made from threads pulled from the quilt, and in time the lamp was complete.

The very unwelcome sojourn of a Jewish usurer, like himself captive of the Inquisition, in his cell, forced Casanova to delay his projects of escape till after Easter, when the Jew was imprisoned elsewhere.

No sooner had he left than Casanova, by the light of the lamp constructed with so much difficulty, began his task. Drawing his bed away, he set to work to bore through the plank underneath, gathering the fragments of wood in a napkin—which the next morning he contrived to empty out behind a heap of old cahier books in the corridor—and after six hours' labour, pulling back his bed, which concealed all trace of it from the gaoler's eyes.

The first plank was two inches thick; the next day he found another plank beneath it, and he pierced this only to find a third plank. It was three weeks before he dug out a cavity large enough for his purpose in this depth of wood, and his disappointment was great when, underneath the planks, he came to a marble pavement which resisted his one tool. But he remembered having read of a general who had broken with an axe hard stones, which he first made brittle by vinegar, and this Casanova possessed. He poured a bottle of strong vinegar into the hole, and the next day, whether it was the effect of the vinegar or of his stronger resolution, he managed to loosen the cement which bound the pieces of marble together, and in four hours had destroyed the pavement, and found another plank, which, however, he believed to be the last.

At this point his work was once more interrupted by the arrival of a fellow-prisoner, who only stayed, however, for eight days. A more serious delay was caused by the fact that unwittingly a part of his work had been just above one of the great beams that supported the ceiling, and he was forced to enlarge the hole by one-fourth. But at last all was done. Through a hole so thin as to be quite imperceptible from below he saw the room underneath. There was only a thin film of wood to be broken through on the night of his escape. For various reasons, he had fixed on the night of August 27. But hear his own words:

'On the 25th,' writes Casanova, 'there happened what makes me shudder even as I write. Precisely at noon I heard the rattling of bolts, a fearful beating of my heart made me think that my last moment had come, and I flung myself on my armchair, stupefied. Laurent entered, and said gaily:

'"Sir, I have come to bring you good news, on which I congratulate you!"

'At first I thought my liberty was to be restored—I knew no other news which *could* be good; and I saw that I was lost, for the discovery of the hole would have undone me. But Laurent told me to follow him. I asked him to wait till I got ready.

'"No matter," he said, "you are only going to leave this dismal cell for a light one, quite new, where you can see half Venice through the two windows; where you can stand upright; where——"

'But I cannot bear to write of it—I seemed to be dying. I implored Laurent to tell the secretary that I thanked the tribunal for its mercy, but begged it in Heaven's name to leave me where I was. Laurent told me, with a burst of laughter, that I was mad, that my present cell was execrable, and that I was to be transferred to a delightful one.

'"Come, come, you must obey orders," he exclaimed.

'He led me away. I felt a momentary solace in hearing him order one of his men to follow with the armchair, where my spontoon was still concealed. That was always something! If my beautiful hole in the floor, that I had made with such infinite pains, could have followed me too—but that was impossible! My body went; my soul stayed behind.

'As soon as Laurent saw me in the fresh cell, he had the armchair set down. I flung myself upon it, and he went away, telling me that my bed and all my other belongings should be brought to me at once.'

For two hours Casanova was left alone in his new cell, utterly hopeless, and expecting to be consigned for the rest of his life to one of the palace dungeons, from which no escape could be possible. Then the gaoler returned, almost mad with rage, and demanded the axe and all the instruments which the prisoner must have employed in penetrating the marble pavement. Calmly, without stirring, Casanova told him that he did not know what he was talking about, but that, if he *had* procured tools, it could only have been from Laurent himself, who alone had entrance to the cell.

Such a reply did not soften the gaoler's anger, and for some time Casanova was very badly treated. Everything was searched ; but his tool had been so cleverly concealed that Laurent never found it. Fortunately it was the gaoler's interest not to let the tribunal know of the discovery he had made. He had the floor of the cell mended without the knowledge of the secretary of the Inquisition, and when this was done, and he found himself secure from blame, Casanova had little difficulty in making peace with him, and even told him the secret of the lamp's construction.

Fortunately, out of the tribunal's allowance to the prisoner enough was always left, after he had provided for his own needs, for a gift—or bribe, to the gaoler. But Laurent did not relax his vigilance, and every morning one of the archers went round the cell with an iron bar, giving blows to walls and floor, to assure himself that there was nothing broken. But he never struck the ceiling, a fact which Casanova resolved to turn to account at the first opportunity.

One day the prisoner ordered his gaoler to buy him a particular book, and Laurent, objecting to an expense which seemed to him quite needless, offered to borrow him a book of one of the other prisoners, in exchange for one of his own. Here at last was an opportunity. Casanova chose a volume out of his small library, and gave it to the gaoler, who returned in a few minutes with a Latin book belonging to one of the other prisoners.

Pen and ink were forbidden, but in this book Casanova found a fragment of paper ; and he contrived, with the nail of his little finger, dipped in mulberry juice, to write on it a list of his library —and returned the volume, asking for a second. The second came, and in it a short letter in Latin. The correspondence between the prisoners had really begun.

The writer of the Latin letter was the monk Balbi, imprisoned in the Leads with a companion, Count André Asquin. He followed it by a much longer one, giving the history of his own life, and all that he knew of his fellow-prisoners. Casanova formed a very poor opinion of Father Balbi's character from his letters ; but assistance of some kind he must have, since the gaoler must needs discover any attempt to break through the ceiling, unless that attempt was made from above. But Casanova soon thought of a plan by which Balbi could break through . *his* ceiling, undis-covered.

'I wrote to him,' he relates, ' that I would find some means of sending him an instrument with which he could break through the roof of his cell, and having climbed upon it, go to the wall separating his roof from mine. Breaking through that, he would find himself on *my* roof, which also must be broken through. That done, I would leave my cell, and he, the Count, and I together, would manage to raise one of the great leaden squares that formed the highest palace roof. Once outside *that*, I would be answerable for the rest.

' But first he must tell the gaoler to buy him forty or fifty pictures of saints, and by way of proving his piety, he must cover his walls and ceiling with these, putting the largest on the ceiling. When he had done this, I would tell him more.

' I next ordered Laurent to buy me the new folio Bible that was just printed ; for I fancied its great size might enable me to conceal my tool there, and so send it to the monk. But when I saw it, I became gloomy—the bolt was two inches longer than the Bible. The monk wrote to me that the cell was already covered according to my direction, and hoped I would lend him the great Bible which Laurent told him I had bought. But I replied that for three or four days I needed it myself.

'At last I hit upon a device. I told Laurent that on Michaelmas Day I wanted two dishes of macaroni, and one of these must be the largest dish he had, for I meant to season it, and send it, with my compliments, to the worthy gentleman who had lent me books. Laurent would bring me the butter and the Parmesan cheese, but I myself should add them to the boiling macaroni.

' I wrote to the monk preparing him for what was to happen, and on St. Michael's Day all came about as I expected. I had hidden the bolt in the great Bible, wrapped in paper, one inch of it showing on each side. I prepared the cheese and butter ; and in due time Laurent brought me in the boiling macaroni and the great dish. Mixing my ingredients, I filled the dish so full that the butter nearly ran over the edge, and then I placed it carefully on the Bible, and put that, with the dish resting on it, into Laurent's hand, warning him not to spill a drop. All his caution was necessary : he went away with his eyes fixed on his burden, lest the butter should run over ; and the Bible, with the bolt projecting from it, were covered, and more than covered, by the huge dish.

His one care was to hold that steady, and I saw that I had succeeded. Presently he came back to tell me that not a drop of butter had been spilt.'

Father Balbi next began his work, detaching from the roof one large picture, which he regularly put back in the same place to conceal the hole. In eight days he had made his way through the roof, and attacked the wall. This was harder work, but at last he had removed six and twenty bricks, and could pass through to Casanova's roof. This he was obliged to work at very carefully, lest any fracture should appear visible below.

One Monday, as Father Balbi was busy at the roof, Casanova suddenly heard the sound of opening doors. It was a terrible moment, but he had time to give the alarm signal, two quick blows on the ceiling. Then Laurent entered, bringing another prisoner, an ugly, ill-dressed little man of fifty, in a black wig, who looked like what he was, a spy of the Inquisition.

Casanova soon learned the history of Soradici—for this was the spy's name—and when his new companion was asleep he wrote to Balbi the account of what had happened. For the present, evidently the work must be given up, no confidence whatever could be placed in Soradici. Yet soon Casanova thought of a plan of making use even of this traitor.

First he ordered Laurent to buy him an image of the Virgin Mary, holy water, and a crucifix. Next he wrote two letters, addressed to friends in Venice—letters in which he made no complaint, but spoke of the benevolence of the Inquisition, and the blessing that his trials had been to him. These letters, which, even if they reached the hands of the secretary, could do him no possible harm, he entrusted to Soradici, in case he should soon be set free ; exacting the spy's solemn oath, on the crucifix and the image of the Virgin, not to betray him, but to give the letters to his friends.

Soradici took the oath required of him, and sewed the letters into his vest. None the less, Casanova felt confident that he would be betrayed, and this was exactly what happened. Two days after the spy was sent for to the secretary, and when he returned to the cell, his companion soon discovered that he had given up the letters.

Casanova affected the utmost anguish and despair. He flung himself down before the image of the Virgin, and demanded vengeance on the monster who had ruined him by breaking so solemn a pledge. Then he lay down with his face to the wall, and for the whole day uttered no single word to the spy, who, terrified at his companion's prayer for vengeance, entreated his forgiveness. But when the spy slept he wrote to Father Balbi and told him to go on with his work the next day, beginning at exactly three o'clock, and working four hours.

The next day, after the gaoler had left them, bearing with him the book of Father Balbi in which the prisoner's letter was concealed, Casanova called his companion. The spy, by this time, was really ill with terror; for he believed that he had provoked the wrath of the Virgin Mary by breaking his oath. He was ready to do anything his companion told him to do, and weak enough to credit any falsehood.

Casanova put on a look of inspiration, and said:

' Learn that at break of day the Holy Virgin appeared to me, and commanded me to forgive you. You shall not die. The grief that your treachery caused me made me pass all the night sleepless, since I knew that the letters you had given to the secretary would prove my ruin—and my one consolation was to believe that in three days I should see you die in this very cell. But though my mind was full of my revenge—unworthy of a Christian—at break of day the image of the Blessed Virgin that you see moved, opened her lips, and said : " Soradici is under my protection : I would have you pardon him. In reward of your generosity I will send one of my angels in figure of a man, who shall descend from heaven to break the roof of the cell, and in five or six days to release you. To-day this angel will begin his work at three o'clock, and will work till half an hour before the sun sets, for he must return to me by daylight. When you escape you will take Soradici with you, and you will take care of him all his life, on condition that he quits the profession of a spy for ever." With these words the Blessed Virgin disappeared.'

At first even the spy's credulity would hardly be persuaded that Casanova had not dreamed ; but when at the appointed hour the sound of the angel working in the roof was really to be heard, when it lasted four hours, and ceased again as foretold, all his doubt vanished, and he was ready to follow Casanova blindly. The thought of once more betraying him never entered his mind ; he believed that the Blessed Virgin herself was on the side of his companion.

The angel would appear, Casanova told him, on the evening of October 31. And at the hour appointed Father Balbi, not looking in the least like an angel, came feet foremost through the ceiling. Casanova embraced him, left him to guard the spy, and himself ascending through the roof, crossed over into the other cell and greeted the monk's fellow-prisoner, Count André, who had all this time kept their secret, but, being old and infirm, had no desire to fly with them.

The next thing was to return into the garret above the two cells, and set to work to break through the palace roof itself. Most of this task fell to Casanova, till he reached the great sheet of lead surmounting the planks, and there the monk's help was necessary. Uniting their strength, they raised it till an opening was made wide enough to pass through. But outside the moonlight was too strong, and they would have been seen from below had they ventured on the roof. They returned into the cell and waited. Casanova had made strong ropes by tying together sheets, towels, and whatever else would serve. Now, since there was nothing to be done till the moon sank, he sat down and wrote a courteous letter to the Inquisition, explaining his reasons for attempting to escape.

The spy, too cowardly to risk his life in so daring a venture, and beginning to see that he had been imposed upon, begged Casanova on his knees to leave him behind, praying for the fugitives—and this Casanova was thankful to do, for Soradici could only have encumbered him. Father Balbi, though for the last hour he had been heaping reproaches on his friend's rashness, was less of a coward than the spy, and as the time had come to start he followed Casanova. They crept out on the roof, and began cautiously to ascend it. Half-way up the monk begged his companion to stop, saying that he had lost one of the packages tied round his neck.

' Was it the package of cord ? ' asked Casanova.

' No,' replied the monk, ' but a black coat, and a very precious manuscript.'

' Then,' said Casanova, resisting a sudden temptation to throw Balbi after his packet, ' you must be patient, and come along.'

The monk sighed, and followed. Soon they had reached the highest point of the roof, and here Balbi contrived to lose his hat, which rolled down the roof, failed to lodge in the gutter, and fell into the canal below. The poor fellow grew desperate, and said it was a bad omen. Casanova soothed him, and left him seated where he was, while he himself went to investigate, his faithful tool in his hand.

Now fresh difficulties began. For a long time Casanova could find no way of re-entering the palace, except into the cell they had quitted. He was growing hopeless, when he saw a skylight, that he was sure was too far away from their starting-point to belong to any of the cells. He made his way to it; it was barred with a fine iron grating that needed a file. And Casanova only had one tool !

Sitting on the roof of the skylight, he nearly abandoned himself to despair, till the bell striking midnight suddenly roused him. It was the first of November : All Saint's Day—the day on which he had long had a curious foreboding that he should recover his liberty. Fired with hope, he set his tool to work at the grating, and in a quarter of an hour he had wrenched it away entire. He set it down by the skylight, and went back for the monk. They regained the skylight together.

Casanova let down his companion through the skylight by the cord, and found that the floor was so far away that he himself dared not risk the leap. And though the cord was still in his hands, he had nowhere to fasten it. The monk, inside, could give him no help—and, not knowing what to do, he set out on another voyage of discovery.

It was successful, for in a part of the roof which he had not yet visited he found a ladder left by some workmen, and long enough for his purpose. Indeed, it seemed likely to be too long, for when he tried to introduce it into the skylight, it only entered as far as the sixth round, and then was stopped by the roof. However, with a superhuman effort Casanova, hanging to the roof, below the skylight, managed to lift the other end of the ladder, nearly, in the action, flinging himself down into the canal. But he had succeeded in forcing the ladder farther in, and the rest was comparatively easy. He climbed up again to the skylight, lowered the ladder, and in another moment was standing by his companion's side.

They found themselves in a garret opening into another room, well barred and bolted. But just then Casanova was past all exertion. He flung himself on the ground, the packet of cord under his head, and fell into a sleep of utter exhaustion. It was dawn when he was roused at last by the monk's despairing efforts. For two hours the latter had been shaking him, and even shouting in his ears, without the slightest effect !

Casanova rose, saying :

' This place must have a way out. Let us break everything— there is no time to lose ! '

They found, at last, a door, of which Casanova's tool forced the lock, and which led them into the room containing the archives or records of the Venetian Republic. From this they descended a staircase, then another, and so made their way into the chancellor's office. Here Casanova found a tool which secretaries used to pierce parchment, and which was some little help to them —for he found it impossible to force the lock of the door through which they had next to part, and the only way was to break a hole in it. Casanova set to work at the part of the door that looked most likely to yield, while his companion did what he could with the secretary's instrument—they pushed, rent, tore the wood ; the noise that they made was alarming, but they were compelled to risk it. In half an hour they had made a hole large enough to get through. The monk went first, being the thinner; he pulled Casanova after him—dusty, torn, and bleeding, for he had worked harder than Father Balbi, who still looked respectable.

They were now in a part of the palace guarded by doors against which no possible effort of theirs could have availed. The only way was to wait till they were opened, and then take flight. Casanova tranquilly changed his tattered garments for a suit which he had brought with him, arranged his hair, and made himself look— except for the bandages he had tied round his wounds—much more like a strayed reveller than an escaped prisoner. All this time the monk was upbraiding him bitterly, and at last, tired of listening, Casanova opened a window, and put out his head, adorned with a gay plumed hat. The window looked out upon the palace court, and Casanova was seen at once by people walking there. He drew back his head, thinking that he had brought destruction upon himself; but after all the accident proved fortunate. Those who had seen him went immediately to tell the authority who kept the key of the hall at the top of the grand staircase, at whose window Casanova's head had appeared, that he must unwittingly have shut someone in the night before. Such a thing might easily have happened, and the keeper of the keys came immediately to see if the news were true.

Presently the door opened, and quite at his ease, the keeper appeared, key in hand. He looked startled at Casanova's strange figure, but the latter, without stopping or uttering a word, passed him, and descended the stairs, followed by the frightened monk. They did not run, nor did they loiter; Casanova was already, in spirit, beyond the confines of the Venetian Republic. Still followed by the monk, he reached the water-side, stepped into a gondola, and flinging himself down carelessly, promised the rowers more than their fare if they would reach Fusina quickly. Soon they had left Venice behind them ; and a few days after his wonderful escape Casanova was in perfect safety beyond Italy.

ADVENTURES ON THE FINDHORN

THE following adventures in crossing the Findhorn are extracted from 'Lays of the Deer Forest,' by John Sobieski and Charles Edward Stuart (London, 1848).

I had lost my boat in the last speat; it was the third which had been taken away in that year, and, until I obtained another, I was obliged to ford the river. I went one day as usual; there was a dark bank of cloud lying in the west upon Beann-Drineachain, but all the sky above was blue and clear, and the water moderate, as I crossed into the forest. I merely wanted a buck, and, therefore, only made a short circuit to the edge of Dun-Fhearn, and rolled a stone down the steep into the deep, wooded den. As it plunged into the burn below, I heard the bound of feet coming up; but they were only two small does, and I did not 'speak' to them, but amused myself with watching their uneasiness and surprise as they perked into the bosky gorge, down which the stone had crashed like a nine-pounder; and, as their white targets jinked over the brae, I went on to try the western terraces.

There is a smooth dry brae opposite to Logie Cumming, called 'Braigh Choilich-Choille,'[1] great part of the slope of which is covered with a growth of brackens from five to six feet high, mixed with large masses of foxgloves, of such luxuriance that the stems sometimes rise five from a single root, and more than seven feet in height, of which there is often an extent of five feet of blossoms, loaded with a succession of magnificent bells. As we crossed below this beautiful covert, I observed Dreadnought suddenly turn up the wind towards it. I immediately made for the crest beyond where the bank rises smooth and open, and whence I had a free sweep of the summit and of both sides. I had just reached the top when the dog entered the thicket of the ferns, and I saw their tall heads stir about twenty yards before him,

---

[1] The woodcocks' brae, from the frequency with which they breed there.

followed by a roar from his deep tongue, and a fine buck bolted up the brae. I gave a short whistle to stop him, and immediately he stood to listen, but behind a great spruce fir, which then, with

many others, formed a noble group upon the summit of the terrace. The sound of the dog dislodged him in an instant, and he shot out through the open glade, when I followed him with the rifle, and sent him over on his horns like a wheel down the steep, and splash,

like a round shot, into the little rill at its foot. We brittled him
on the knog of an old pine, and rewarded the dog, and drank the
Dochfalla; when, having occasion to send the piper to the other
side of the wood, and being so near home, I shouldered the roe,
and took the way for the ford of Craig-Darach, a strong wide
broken stream with a very bad bottom, but the nearest then pass-
able.

As I descended the Bruach-gharbh, Dreadnought stopped and
looked up into a pine, then approaching the tree, searched it all
round with his nose. I scanned the branches, but could see nothing
except an old hawk's nest, which had been disused long ago; and
if it had not, I do not understand how it should be interesting to a
hound. The dog, however, continued to investigate the stump and
stem of the fir, gaze into the branches, turning his head from side
to side, and setting up his ears like a cocked-hat. I laid down the
buck, and unslung my double gun, and threw a stick at the nest,
when out shot a large pine-martin, and, like a squirrel, sprung
along the branches from tree to tree, till I brought him to the
ground. Dreadnought examined him with a sort of wrinkle in his
whiskers, and turned away, and sat down in dignified abstraction;
while I remounted the buck, and braced the martin to his feet with
the little 'ial-chas,' or foot-straps used for trussing the legs of the
roe. We then resumed our path for the ford.

As I descended through the Boat-Shaw, I heard a heavy sound
from the water, but when I came out from the birches upon the green
bank on its brink, I saw that the river had come down, and was just
lipping with the top of the stone, the sight of whose head was the
mark for the last possibility of crossing. As I looked upon its con-
tracting ring, I perceived that the stream was still growing; there
was no time to be lost, for the alternative now was to go round by
the bridge of Daltulich, a circuit of four miles; and I knew that,
before I reached the next good ford, the water would be a continuous rapid, probably six feet deep : I decided, therefore, upon trying
the chance where I was. Dreadnought, who had gone about
thirty yards up the stream to take the deep water in the pool of
Craig-Darach, had observed my hesitation with one leg out and one
in the water, and was standing on the point of the rock waiting the
result. As soon as I made another step he plunged into the river,
and in a few moments was rolling on the bank of silver sand
thrown up by the back-water upon the opposite side of the river.
As I advanced through the stream, he looked at me occasionally,

and I at him, and the beautiful smooth sand and green bank upon his side—for by that time I began to wish I was there too. I was then in pretty deep water for a ford, but still some distance from the deepest part; my kilt was floating round me in the boiling water, and the strong eddy, formed by the stream running against my legs, gulped and gushed with increasing weight. I moved slowly and carefully, for the whole ford was filled with large round slippery stones from the size of a sixty-pound shot to a two-hundred-weight shell. I stopped to rest, and looked back to the ford mark : it was wholly gone, and I saw only the broad smooth wave of water which slipped over its head. Ten paces more, and I should be through the deepest part. I stepped steadily and rigidly, but I wanted the use of my balancing limbs and the freedom of my breath; for the barrels of the double gun and rifle, which were slung at my back, were passed under my arms to keep them out of the water; and I was also obliged to hold the legs of the buck, which, loaded with the 'wood-cat,' were crossed upon my breast. At every step the round and slidering stones endangered my footing, rendered still more unsteady by the upward pressure of the water. In this struggle the current gave a great gulp, and a wave plashed up over my guns. I staggered downwards with the stream, and could not recover a sure footing for several yards. At last I secured my hold against a large fixed stone, and paused to rest. After a little I made another effort to proceed.

The water was now running above my belt, and at the first step which I made from the stone I found that it deepened abruptly before me. I felt that in six inches more that strong stream would lift me off my legs; and with great difficulty I gained about two yards up the current to ascertain if the depth was continuous, but the bottom still shelved before me, and, as I persisted in attempting it, I was turned round by the stream, the waves were leaping through the deep channel before me, and having no arms to balance my steps, I began to think of the bonnie banks on *either* side the river. In this jeopardy poor Dreadnought had not been unconcerned; at the first moment of my struggle he had gone down the great stony beach which lay before me, and, sitting down by the water, watched me with great anxiety, and at last began to whine, and whimper, and tremble with agitation. But when he saw me stagger down the stream, he rose, went in up to his knees, howled, pawed the water, and lapped the waves with impatience. Meanwhile I was obliged to come to a rest, with my left foot planted strongly against a stone, for the mere resistance to the pressure of water, which, rushing with a white foam from my side, was sufficient exertion without the weight of the buck and the two guns, which amounted to more than seventy pounds.

After a few moments' pause I made a last effort to reach the east bank; but it was now impossible, and I turned to make an attempt to regain the Tarnaway side. I was at least thirty yards lower down than when I entered the stream, and the water was rushing and foaming all round me; another stagger nearly carried me off my feet, and, in the exertion to keep them, a thick transpiration rose upon my forehead, my ears began to sing, and my head to swim, while, disordered in their balance, the buck and the guns almost strangled me. I looked down the channel; the water was running in a white, broken rapid into the black pool below, and swept with a wide, foaming back-water under the steep rock which turned its force. The soft green bank before me was sleeping beneath the shade of the weeping birches, where bluebells and primroses grew thick in the short smooth turf, and, though they had long shed their blossoms, the bright patches of their clusters were yet visible among the tall foxgloves, which still retained the purple bells upon their tops. The bank looked softer, and greener, and more inviting than ever it had done before; but my eyes grow dim and my limbs faint with that last struggle. I felt for my dirk knife, for a desperate rolling swim for life seemed now inevitable, and, steadying myself in the stream, I cut loose the straps of the buck and the slings of the guns, and retaining them only with my hands, held them ready to let go as soon as I should be taken off my legs. When they were free, I dipped my hand in the water, and laved it over my brow and face. The singing of my ears ceased, and my sight came clear, and I discovered that I had lost my bonnet in the struggle, and distinguished the white cockade dancing like a little ' cailleach ' of foam in the vortex of the pool below.

Being now *morally* relieved from the weight of the roe and guns—though resolved to preserve them to the last—I resumed my attempt for the west bank; but when I reached a similar distance to that which I had gained for the other, I found an equally deep channel before me, and that the diminished water by which I had been encouraged was only the shoaling of a long bank which extended with the stream. I now saw that before I joined my bonnet, which still danced and circled in the pool below, there was only one effort left—to struggle up the stream, and reach the point

D

from which I had taken the water. But this was a desperate attempt; for at every step I had to find a safe footing at the upper side of some stone, and then with all my strength to force myself against the current. But often the stones gave way, and, loosening from their bed, went rolling and rumbling down the rapid, and I was driven back several feet, to recommence the same struggle. The river also was still increasing, and the flat sand, which was dry when I left it, was now a sheet of water. While I was thus wrestling with the stream, I saw Dreadnought enter, not at his usual place in the pool, but at the tail, just above the run of the stream in which I was struggling. He came whimpering over, and

crossed about a yard or two above me; but instead of making for the bank, he turned in the water, and swam towards me. The stream, however, was too strong for him, and carried him down. I called and waved to the forest, and he turned and steered for its bank, but did not reach the shelving sand till he was well tumbled in the top of the rapid, out of which he only emerged in time to catch a little back-water, which helped him on to the shore. The attempt of the dog to reach me had passed while I rested: and when he gained the bank, I resumed my effort to make the shallower water.

Dreadnought's eye was turned towards me as he came dripping up the bank, and seeing me move forward, he ran before me to the water's edge, at the right entrance of the ford, whining, and howling, and baying, as if he knew as well as I that it was the place to make for. In a few steps the stones became less slippery, and the bottom more even, and I began to think that I might gain it, when, at the rocky point above, I saw a white mass of foam, loaded with brushwood, sticks, and rubbish, borne along by a ridge of yellow curdling water, at least two feet higher than the stream. I gathered all my strength, and made a struggle for the bank opposite to where I was. The water was already above my belt, and rushing between my arms as I bore up the guns. I felt myself lifted off my legs; again I held the ground. The green bank was only a few yards distant, but the deep water was close below, and the yellow foaming flood above. As I staggered on, I heard it coming down, crumpling up and crackling the dead boughs which it bore along. I stumbled upon a round stone, and nearly fell backward, but it was against the stream which forced me forward. I felt the spray splash over my head: I was nearly blind and deaf. I made a desperate effort with the last strength which I had left, and threw myself gasping on the bank.

Dreadnought sprang forward, jumped over and over me, whined, and kissed my face and hands, and tried to turn me over with his snout, and scratched and pawed me to make me speak; but I could not yet, and gasped, and choked, and felt as if my heart would burst. I lay, dripping and panting, with my arms stretched out on the grass, unable to move, except with the convulsive efforts of my breath. At last I sat up, but I could scarcely see: a thin gauzy cloud was over my eyes, a heavy pressure rung in my ears, my feet still hung in the water, which was now sweeping a wide white torrent from bank to bank, and running with a fierce current through both the pools below. The back-water, where my bonnet had danced, no longer remained; all was carried clear out in one long rush down to the Cluag. 'Benedictum sit nomen Domini!' I thought, as I crossed myself. I stretched out my hand, and plucked the nearest flowers, and smelled their sweet greenwood scent with inexpressible delight. I never thought that flowers looked so beautiful, or had half so much perfume, though they were only the pale wild blossoms of the fading year. I placed them in my breast, and have them still, and never look upon them without repeating—

'DE PROFUNDIS CLAMAVI AD TE, DOMINE!'

Such were the hazards on the fords of the Findhorn; but even by boat the struggle was sometimes no less arduous, though it enabled us to cross the water at a height otherwise impassable, of which the following passage is an example:—

One evening I was returning with the piper, and the old hound which had accompanied me at the ford. As we descended towards the pool of Cluag, where I had left the coble quietly moored in the morning, Dreadnought frequently turned and looked at me with hanging ears and a heavy cheerless eye; and when we came to the path which led down to the river he stopped, and dropped behind, and followed at my heel, though usually he trotted on before, and instead of waiting for the boat, took the water, which he preferred to the coble. When we came out from the trees upon the steep bank above the river, I understood his altered manner. From rock to rock the stream was running a white, furious, rushing torrent, and the little boat tugging and jibbing on her chain, and swinging and bobbing upon the top of the froth, like the leaves which danced upon the eddy. Dreadnought had heard the sound of the river, and knew what there was at work before us. The boat was moored near the throat of the pool, in the back-water of a little bay, now entirely filled with froth and foam up to the gunwale of the coble, which was defended by a sharp point of rock, from whose breakwater the stream was thrown off in a wild shooting torrent. Within the bay the reaction of the tide formed a quick back-water, which raised the stream without nearly two feet higher than the level within, and at times sucked the boat on to the point, where she was struck in the stem by the gushing stream and sent spinning round at the full swing of her 'tether.'

Donald looked at me. There was no alternative but the bridge of Daltullich, more than four miles about, with two bucks to carry, and ourselves well run since four o'clock in the morning. I stood for some moments considering the chances, and the manifest probability of going down the stream. Immediately after emerging from the little mooring bay there was a terrific rush of water discharged through the narrow throat of the pool, and raised to the centre in a white fierce tumbling ridge, for which the shortness of the pool afforded no allowance for working, while the little back-water, which, in ordinary cases, caught us on the opposite side, and took us into the bank, was lost in a flood, which ran right through the basin like a mill-lead. 'Can you swim, Donald?' said I mechanically. '*Swim*, Sir!' said he, who knew how often I had seen

THE FINDHORN.

him tumbled by the waves both in salt water and fresh. ' Oh yes, I know you can. But I was thinking of that stream.' ' Ougudearbh!' replied Donald : ' But it was myself that never tried it yon way!' ' And what do you think of her ? ' ' Faith, Thighearna, you know best—but if you try it, I shall not stay behind.'

We had often ridden the water together by day and night, in flood and fair ; and, narrow as the pool was, I thought we could get through it. We threw in a broken branch to prove the speed of the current, but it leaped through the plunging water like a greyhound, and was away in a moment down to the fierce white battling vortex of the Scuddach, where there was no salvation for thing alive ; a few moments it disappeared in the wild turmoil, and then came up beyond—white and barked, and shivered like a splintered bone. Donald, however, saw that I was going to try the venture, and he was already up the bank unlocking the chain without a word. The bucks were deposited in the stern of the boat, the guns laid softly across them, covered with a plaid, and Dreadnought followed slowly and sternly, and laid himself down with an air as if, like Don Alphonso of Castile, ' the body trembled at the dangers into which the soul was going to carry it.' I took the oars—there were no directions to be given—Donald knew how to cross the pool, and every other where we were used to ferry.

The boat's head was brought round to the stream, for it was necessary to run her into it with the impulse of the back-water to shoot her forward, or she would have been drawn back, stern foremost, into the eddy, where the jaw of the water, over the point of the rock, would have swamped us in an instant. Donald knelt at the bows, and held fast by a light painter till I cried ' Ready !' when the little shallop sprung from the rope, tilted away like a seabird, and glided towards the roaring torrent. I looked over my shoulder ; Donald was gripping the bows, his teeth set fast, but a gleam of light was in his eye as we plunged headlong into the bursting stream. A blow like the stroke of a mighty wooden hammer lifted the boat into the surf ; there was a crack as if her bows were stove in, and she shot shivering through the pool, filled with water to our knees, and sending the spray over us like a sheet. The rocks and trees seemed to fly away ; the roaring water spouted and boiled, as it lifted up the boat, which spun round like a leaf, with her starboard gunwale lipping with the waves ; but a few seconds swept us through the pool, and we were flying into the mad tum-

bling thunder of the rapid below. I kept the larboard bow to the
stream, and pulled with all my might; but I thought she did not
move, the eddy of the great mid-stream seemed to fix her in the
ridge of the torrent, and take her along with it; the oars bent like
willows to the strain, a boiling gush from below lifted her bows,
and threw her gunwale under the froth. I thought we were gone,
but I redoubled the last desperate strokes, and we shot out of the
foaming ridge towards the opposite bank, rolling, and leaping, and
plunging into the throat of the rapid. Donald sat like a tiger ready
for the spring, and as we neared the shore, bounded on the grass
with the chain. This checked the speed of the boat; I unshipped
the oars, and sprung out just as the coble came crash alongside the
bank, then swirling round, her head flew out to the stream, dragging
Donald along the grass after her. I jumped into the water, and
caught hold of the bow; for two minutes the struggle was doubtful
and she continued to drag us along: at last Donald reached the
stump of a tree, and, running round it, made a turn of the chain
and brought her up.

We sat down, and wiped our faces, and looked at each other in
silence. The incredibly short space of time which had elapsed
since we stood on the 'other side,' with the mysterious future
before us, and now to be sitting on ' this,' and call it the past, was
like a dream. The tumult, the flying shoot, the concussion at
parting and arriving, seemed like an explosion, as if we had been
blown up and thrown over. 'I don't think that boat will ever go
back again, Thighearna,' said Donald. 'Why not?' 'Did you
not feel her twist, and hear her split, when we came into the burst
of the stream?' replied Donald. 'I don't know,' said I; 'I felt
and heard a great many things, but there was no time to think
what they were.' 'Oh, it was not thinking that I was,' answered
Donald; ' but the water came squirting up in my face through her
ribs, and I held on by both bows, expecting at every stroke to see
them open and let me through.' We got up and examined the
boat's bottom; there was a yawning rent from the stem to the
centre; and part of the torn planks lapped one over the other by the
twist, the bows being only held together by the iron band which
bound the gunwale.

THE STORY OF GRACE DARLING

A CAREFUL reader of the 'Times' on the morning of Tuesday, September 11, 1838, might have found, if he cared to look, a certain paragraph in an obscure corner headed ' The Wreck of the "Forfarshire." ' It is printed in the small type of that period ; the story is four days old, for in those days news was not flashed from one end of the country to the other ; and, moreover, the story is very incomplete.

On the evening of Wednesday, September 5, the steamship ' Forfarshire ' left Hull for Dundee, carrying a cargo of iron, and having some forty passengers on board. The ship was only eight years old ; the master, John Humble, was an experienced seaman ; and the crew, including firemen and engineers, was complete. But even before the vessel left the dock one passenger at least had felt uneasily that something was wrong—that there was an unusual commotion among officials and sailors. Still, no alarm was given, and at dusk the vessel steamed prosperously down the Humber.

The next day (Thursday, the 6th) the weather changed, the wind blowing N.N.W., and increasing towards midnight to a perfect gale. On the morning of Friday, the 7th, a sloop from Montrose, making for South Shields, saw a small boat labouring hard in the trough of the sea. The Montrose vessel bore down on it, and in spite of the state of the weather managed to get the boat's crew on board.

They were nine men in all, the sole survivors, as they believed themselves to be, of the crew and passengers of the ' Forfarshire,' which was then lying a total wreck on Longstone, one of the outermost of the Farne Islands.

It was a wretched story they had to tell of lives thrown away through carelessness and negligence, unredeemed, as far as their story went, by any heroism or unselfish courage.

While still in the Humber, and not twenty miles from Hull, it was found that one of the boilers leaked, but the captain refused to put about. The pumps were set to work to fill the boiler, and the vessel kept on her way, though slowly, not passing between the Farne Islands and the mainland till Thursday evening. It was eight o'clock when they entered Berwick Bay; the wind freshened and was soon blowing hard from the N.N.W. The motion of the vessel increased the leakage, and it was now found that there were holes in all the three boilers. Two men were set to work the pumps, one or two of the passengers also assisting, but as fast as the water was pumped into the boilers it poured out again. The bilge was so full of steam and boiling water that the firemen could not get to the fires. Still the steamer struggled on, labouring heavily, for the sea was running very high. At midnight they were off St. Abbs Head, when the engineers reported that the case was hopeless; the engines had entirely ceased to work. The ship rolled helplessly in the waves, and the rocky coast was at no great distance. They ran up the sails fore and aft to try and keep her off the rocks, and put her round so that she might run before the wind, and as the tide was setting southward she drifted fast with wind and tide. Torrents of rain were falling, and in spite of the wind there was a thick fog. Some of the passengers were below, others were on deck with crew and captain, knowing well their danger.

About three the noise of breakers was distinctly heard a little way ahead, and at the same time a light was seen away to the left, glimmering faintly through the darkness. It came home to the anxious crew with sickening certainty that they were being driven on the Farne Islands. [Now these islands form a group of desolate whinstone rocks lying off the Northumbrian coast. They are twenty in number, some only uncovered at low tide, and all offering a rugged iron wall to any ill-fated boat that may be driven upon them. Even in calm weather and by daylight seamen are glad to give them a wide berth.]

The master of the 'Forfarshire' in this desperate strait attempted to make for the channel which runs between the Islands and the mainland. It was at best a forlorn chance; it was hopeless here; the vessel refused to answer her helm! On she drove in the darkness, nearer and nearer came the sound of the breakers; the fear and agitation on board the boat grew frantic. Women wailed and shrieked; the captain's wife clung to him, weeping; the crew lost all instinct of discipline, and thought of nothing but saving their skins.

Between three and four the shock came—a hideous grinding noise, a strain and shiver of the whole ship, and she struck violently against a great rock. In the awful moment which followed five of the crew succeeded in lowering the larboard quarter-boat and pushed off in her. The mate swung himself over the side, and also reached her; and a passenger rushing at this moment up from the cabin and seeing the boat already three yards from the ship, cleared the space with a bound and landed safely in her, though nearly upsetting her by his weight. She righted, and the crew pulled off with the desperate energy of men rowing for their lives. The sight of agonised faces, the shrieks of the drowning were lost in the darkness and in the howling winds, and the boat with the seven men on board was swept along by the rapidly-flowing tide.

Such was the story the exhausted boat's-crew told next morning to their rescuers on board the Montrose sloop. And the rest of the ship's company—what of them? Had they all gone down by the island crag with never a hand stretched out to help them?

Hardly had the boat escaped from the stranded vessel when a great wave struck her on the quarter, lifted her up bodily, and dashed her back on the rock. She struck midships on the sharp edge and broke at once into two pieces. The after part was washed clean away with about twenty passengers clinging to it, the captain and his wife being among them. A group of people, about nine in number, were huddled together near the bow; they, with the whole fore part of the ship, were lifted right on to the rock. In the fore cabin was a poor woman, Mrs. Dawson, with a child on each arm. When the vessel was stranded on the rock the waves rushed into the exposed cabin, but she managed to keep her position, cowering in a corner. First one and then the other child died from cold and exhaustion, and falling from the fainting mother were swept from her sight by the waves, but the poor soul herself survived all the horrors of the night.

It was now four o'clock; the storm was raging with unabated violence, and it was still two hours to daybreak. About a mile from Longstorie, the island on which the vessel struck, lies Brownsman, the outermost of the Farne Islands, on which stands the lighthouse. At this time the keeper of the lighthouse was a man of the name of William Darling. He was an elderly, almost an old man, and the

only other inmates of the lighthouse were his wife and daughter
Grace, a girl of twenty-two.   On this Friday night she was awake,
and through the raging of the storm heard shrieks more persistent
and despairing than those of the wildest sea-birds.   In great trouble
she rose and awakened her father.   The cries continued, but in the
darkness they could do nothing.   Even after day broke it was
difficult to make out distant objects, for a mist was still hanging
over the sea.   At length, with a glass they could discern the wreck
on Longstone, and figures moving about on it.   Between the two
islands lay a mile of yeasty sea, and the tide was running hard
between them.   The only boat on the lighthouse was a clumsily
built jolly-boat, heavy enough to tax the strength of two strong
men in ordinary weather, and here there was but an old man and
a young girl to face a raging sea and a tide running.dead against
them.   Darling hesitated to undertake anything so dangerous, but
his daughter would hear of no delay.   On the other side of that
rough mile of sea men were perishing, and she *could* not stay where
she was and see them die.

So off they set in the heavy coble, the old man with one oar, the
girl with the other, rowing with straining breath and beating hearts.
Any moment they might be whelmed in the sea or dashed against
the rocks.   Even if they got the crew off it would be doubtful if they
could row them to the lighthouse; the tide was about to turn, and
would be against them on their homeward journey; death seemed
to face them on every side.

When close to the rock there was imminent danger of their
being dashed to pieces against it.   Steadying the boat an instant,
Darling managed to jump on to the rock, while Grace rapidly rowed
out a little and kept the boat from going on the rocks by rowing
continually.   It is difficult to imagine how the nine shipwrecked
people, exhausted and wearied as they were, were got into the boat
in such a sea, especially as the poor woman, Mrs. Dawson, was in an
almost fainting condition; but finally got on board they all were.
Fortunately, one or two of the rescued crew were able to assist in
the heavy task of rowing the boat back to Brownsman.

The storm continued to rage for several days after, and the
whole party had to remain in the lighthouse.   Moreover, a boat-
load which had come to their rescue from North Shields was also
storm-stayed, twenty guests in all, so that the housewifely powers
of Grace and her mother were taxed to the utmost.

It is told of this admirable girl that she was the tenderest and

GRACE DARLING.

gentlest of nurses and hostesses, as she was certainly one of the most singularly courageous of women.

She could never be brought to look upon her exploit as in any way remarkable, and when by-and-by honours and distinctions were showered upon her, and people came from long distances to see her, she kept through it all the dignity of perfect simplicity and modesty.

Close to Bamborough, on a windy hill, lie a little grey church and a quiet churchyard. At all seasons high winds from the North Sea blow over the graves and fret and eat away the soft grey sandstone of which the plain headstones are made. So great is the wear and tear of these winds that comparatively recent monuments look like those which have stood for centuries. On one of these stones lies a recumbent figure, with what looks not unlike a lance clasped in the hand and laid across the breast. Involuntarily one thinks of the stone Crusaders, who lie in their armour, clasping their half-drawn swords, awaiting the Resurrection morning. It is the monument of Grace Darling, who here lies at rest with her oar still clasped in her strong right hand.

THE 'SHANNON' AND THE 'CHESAPEAKE'

AMONG the captains of British 38-gun frigates who ardently longed for a meeting with one of the American 44-guns, in our war with the United States, was Captain Philip Bowesbere Broke, of the 'Shannon.' The desire sprang from no wish to display his own valour, only to show the world what wonderful deeds could be done when the ship and crew were in all respects fitted for battle. He had put his frigate in fighting order, taught his men the art of attack and defence, and out of a crew not very well disposed and got together in a rather haphazard manner, had made a company as pleasant to command as it was dangerous to meet.

With this desire, in March 1813 Captain Broke sailed from Halifax on a cruise in Boston Bay. But to his disappointment two American frigates, the weather being foggy, left the harbour without his having a chance to encounter them. Two remained, however, and one of these, the 'Chesapeake,' commanded by Captain James Lawrence, was nearly ready for sea. When her preparations were complete, Captain Broke addressed to her commanding officer a letter of challenge, having previously sent a verbal message, which had met with no reply.

'As the "Chesapeake" appears now ready for sea,' began this letter, ' I request you will do me the favour to meet the "Shannon" with her, ship to ship, to try the fortune of our respective flags.'

He then gave an account of the 'Shannon's' forces, which were somewhat inferior to the 'Chesapeake's.' The 'Chesapeake' had 376 men, the 'Shannon' 306 men and 24 boys, and the American vessel also had the advantage in guns.

'I entreat you, sir,' Captain Broke concluded, 'not to imagine that I am urged by mere personal vanity to the wish of meeting the "Chesapeake," or that I depend only upon your personal ambition for your acceding to this invitation. We have both nobler motives. . . . Favour me with a speedy reply.. We are short of provisions and water, and cannot stay long here.'

This letter he entrusted to Captain Plocum, a discharged prisoner; but it so happened that before his boat reached the shore, the American frigate left it—Captain Lawrence having received permission from Commodore Bairbridge to sail and attack the 'Shannon' in response to Captain Broke's verbal challenge.

Some manœuvring between the two ships took place; but at last, in the evening of June 1, 1813, the 'Chesapeake,' with three ensigns flying, steered straight for the 'Shannon's' starboard quarter. Besides the ensigns, she had flying at the fore a large white flag, inscribed with the words: 'Sailors' Rights and Free Trade,' with the idea, perhaps, that this favourite American motto would damp the energy of the 'Shannon's' men. The 'Shannon' had a Union Jack at the fore, an old rusty blue ensign at the mizzen peak, and two other flags rolled up, ready to be spread if either of these should be shot away. She stood much in need of paint, and her outward appearance hardly inspired much belief in the order and discipline that reigned within.

At twenty minutes to six Captain Lawrence came within fifty yards of the 'Shannon's' starboard quarter, and gave three cheers. Ten minutes after the 'Shannon' fired her first gun, then a second. Then the 'Chesapeake' returned fire, and the remaining guns on the broadside of each ship went off as fast as they could be discharged.

Four minutes before six the 'Chesapeake's' helm, probably from the death of the men stationed at it, being for the moment unattended to, the ship lay with her stem and quarter exposed to her opponent's broadside, which did terrible execution. At six o'clock, the 'Chesapeake' and 'Shannon' being in close contact, the 'Chesapeake,' endeavouring to make a little ahead, was stopped by becoming entangled with the anchor of the 'Shannon.' Captain Broke now ran forward, and, seeing the 'Chesapeake's' men deserting the quarter-deck guns, he ordered the two ships to be lashed together, the great guns to cease firing, and Lieutenant Watt to bring up the quarter-deck men, who were to act as boarders. This was done instantly, and at two minutes past six Captain Broke leaped aboard the 'Chesapeake,' followed by twenty men, and reached her quarter-deck.

Here not an officer or man was to be seen. Upon the 'Chesapeake's' gangways, twenty-five or thirty Americans made a slight

E

resistance, but were quickly driven towards the forecastle. Several fled over the bows, some, it is believed, plunged into the sea, the rest laid down their arms and submitted.

Lieutenant Watt, with others, followed quickly. Hardly had he stepped upon the taffrail of the ' Chesapeake ' when he was shot through the foot by a musket ball ; but, rising in spite of it, he ordered one of the ' Shannon's ' 9-pounders to be directed at the ' Chesapeake's ' mizzen top, whence the shot had come. The second division of the Marines now rushed forward, and while one party kept down the Americans who were ascending the main hatchway, another party answered a destructive fire which still continued from the main and mizzen tops. The ' Chesapeake's ' main top was presently stormed by midshipman William Smith. This gallant young man deliberately passed along the ' Shannon's '' foreyard, which was braced up to the ' Chesapeake's ' mainyard, and thence into her top. All further annoyance from the ' Chesapeake's ' mizzen top was put a stop to by another of the ' Shannon's ' midshipmen, who fired at the Americans from the yardarm as fast as his men could load the muskets and hand them to him.

After the Americans upon the forecastle had submitted, Captain Broke ordered one of his men to stand sentry over them, and sent most of the others aft, where the conflict was still going on. He was in the act of giving them orders when the sentry called out lustily to him. On turning, the captain found himself opposed by three of the Americans, who, seeing they were superior to the British then near them, had armed themselves afresh. Captain Broke parried the middle fellow's pike, and wounded him in the face, but instantly received from the man on the pikeman's right a blow with the butt-end of a musket, which bared his skull and nearly stunned him. Determined to finish the British commander, the third man cut him down with his broadsword, but at that very instant was himself cut down by Mindham, one of the ' Shannon's ' seamen. Can it be wondered if all concerned in this breach of faith fell victims to the indignation of the ' Shannon's ' men ? It was as much as Captain Broke could do to save from their fury a young midshipman, who, having slid down a rope from the ' Chesapeake's ' foretop, begged his protection.

While in the act of tying a handkerchief round his commander's head, Mindham, pointing aft, called out :

' There, sir—there goes up the old ensign over the Yankee colours ! '

Captain Broke saw it hoisting (with what feelings may be imagined), and was instantly led to the 'Chesapeake's' quarter-deck, where he sat down.

That act of changing the 'Chesapeake's' colours proved fatal to a gallant British officer and four or five fine fellows of the 'Shannon's' crew. We left Lieutenant Watt just as, having raised himself on his feet after his wound, he was hailing the 'Shannon' to fire at the 'Chesapeake's' mizzen top. He then called for an English ensign, and hauling down the American flag, bent, owing to the ropes being tangled, the English flag below instead of above it. Observing the American stripes going up first, the 'Shannon's' people reopened their fire, and, directing their guns with their accustomed precision at the lower part of the 'Chesapeake's' mizzen mast, killed Lieutenant Watt and four or five of their comrades. Before the flags had got halfway to the mizzen peak, they were pulled down and hoisted properly, and the men of the 'Shannon' ceased their fire.

An unexpected fire of musketry, opened by the Americans who had fled to the hold, killed a fine young marine, William Young. On this, Lieutenant Falkiner ordered three or four muskets that were ready to be fired down the hold, and Captain Broke, from the quarter-deck, told the lieutenant to summon. The Americans replied, 'We surrender'; and all hostilities ceased. Almost immediately after Captain Broke's senses failed him from loss of blood, and he was conveyed on board his own ship.

Between the discharge of the first gun and the time of Captain Broke's boarding only eleven minutes had passed, and in four minutes more the 'Chesapeake' was completely his. As a rule, however, this good fortune did not attend our arms in the conflict with the American marine.

CAPTAIN SNELGRAVE AND THE PIRATES

IN the year 1719, I, being appointed commander of the 'Bird' galley, arrived at the River Sierra Leone, on the north coast of Guinea. There were, at the time of our unfortunate arrival in that river, three pirate ships, who had then taken ten English ships in that place. The first of these was the 'Rising Sun,' one Cochlyn commander, who had not with him above twenty-five men; the second was a brigantine commanded by one Le Bouse, a Frenchman, whose crew had formerly served with Cochlyn's under the pirate Moody; the third was a large ship commanded by Captain Davis, with a crew of near one hundred and fifty men. This Davis was a generous man, nor had he agreed to join with the others when I was taken by Cochlyn; which proved a great misfortune to me, for I found Cochlyn and his crew to be a set of the basest and most cruel villains that ever were.

I come now to give an account of how I was taken by them. It becoming calm about seven o'clock, and growing dark, we anchored in the river's mouth, soon after which I went to supper with the officers that usually ate with me. About eight o'clock the officer of the watch upon deck sent me word, 'He heard the rowing of a boat.' Whereupon we all immediately went on deck, and the night being very dark, I ordered lanterns and candles to be got ready, supposing the boat might come from the shore with some white gentlemen that lived there as free merchants. I ordered also, by way of precaution, the first mate, Mr. Jones, to go into the steerage to put things in order, and to send me twenty men on the quarter-deck with firearms and cutlasses, which I thought he went about, for I did not in the least suspect Mr. Jones would have proved such a villain as he did afterwards.

As it was dark, I could not yet see the boat, but heard the noise of the rowing very plain. Whereupon I ordered the second mate to hail the boat, to which the people in it answered, ' They belonged to the " Two Friends,'' Captain Elliot, of Barbadoes.' At this, one of the officers who stood by me said he knew that captain very well. I replied, ' It might be so, but I would not trust any boat in such a place,' and ordered him to hasten the first mate, with the people and arms, on deck. By this time our lanterns and candles were brought up, and I ordered the boat to be hailed again ; to which the people in it answered, ' They were from America,' and at the same time fired a volley of small shot at us, which showed the boldness of these villains. For there were in the boat only twelve of them, as I understood afterwards, who knew nothing of the strength of our ship, which was indeed considerable, we having sixteen guns and forty-five men on board. But, as they told me after we were taken, ' they depended on the same good-fortune as in the other ships they had taken, having met with no resistance, for the people were generally glad of an opportunity of entering with them.'

Which last was but too true.

When they first began to fire, I called aloud to the first mate to fire at the boat out of the steerage portholes, which not being done, and the people I had ordered upon deck with small arms not appearing, I was extremely surprised, and the more when an officer came and told me ' The people would not take arms.'

I went down into the steerage, where I saw a great many of them looking at one another, little thinking that my first mate had prevented them from taking arms. I asked them with some roughness why they had not obeyed my orders, saying it would be the greatest reproach in the world to us all to be taken by a boat.

Some of them answered that they would have taken arms, but the chest they were kept in could not be found.

By this time the boat was along the ship's side, and there being nobody to oppose them, the pirates immediately boarded us, and coming on the quarter-deck, fired their pieces several times down into the steerage, giving one sailor a wound of which he died afterwards.

At last some of our people bethought themselves to call out for quarter, which the pirates granting, their quartermaster came down into the steerage, asking where the captain was. I told him I had been so till now. On that he asked me how I durst order my people to fire at their boat out of the steerage.

I answered, 'I thought it my duty to defend my ship if my people would have fought.'

On that he presented a pistol to my breast, which I had but just time to parry before it went off, so that the bullet passed between my side and arm. The rogue, finding he had not shot me, turned the butt-end of the pistol, and gave me such a blow on the head as stunned me, so that I fell on my knees, but immediately recovering myself, I jumped out of the steerage upon the quarter-deck, where the pirate boatswain was.

He was a bloodthirsty villain, having a few days before killed a poor sailor because he did not do something as soon as he ordered him. This cruel monster was asking some of my people where their captain was, so at my coming upon deck one of them pointed me out. Though the night was very dark, yet, there being four lanterns with candles, he had a full sight of me; whereupon, lifting up his broadsword, he swore that no quarter should be given to any captain that defended his ship, at the same time aiming a full stroke at my head. To avoid it I stooped so low that the quarter-deck rail received the blow, and was cut in at least an inch deep, which happily saved my head from being cleft asunder, and the sword breaking at the same time with the force of his blow on the rail, it prevented his cutting me to pieces.

By good fortune his pistols, that hung at his girdle, were all discharged, otherwise he would doubtless have shot me. But he took one of them and endeavoured to beat out my brains, which some of my people observing, cried:

'For God's sake don't kill our captain, for we never were with a better man.'

This turned the rage of him and two other pirates on my people, and saved my life; but they cruelly used my poor men, cutting and beating them unmercifully. One of them had his chin almost cut off, and another received such a wound on the head that he fell on the deck as dead, but afterwards, by the care of our surgeon, he recovered.

Then the quartermaster, coming on deck, took me by the hand, and told me my life was safe, provided none of my people complained of me. I answered that I was sure none of them could.

By this time the pirate ship had drawn near, for they had sent their boat before to discover us; and on approaching, without asking any questions, gave us a great broadside, believing, as it proved afterwards, that we had taken their boat and people. So the quartermaster told them, through the speaking-trumpet, that they had taken a brave prize, with all manner of good victuals and fresh provisions on board.

Just after this, Cochlyn, the pirate captain, ordered them to dress a quantity of these victuals; so they took many geese, turkeys, fowls, and ducks, making our people cut their heads off and pull the great feathers out of their wings, but they would not stay till the other feathers were pulled off. All these they put into our great furnace, which would boil victuals for five hundred negroes, together with several Westphalia hams and a large pig. This strange medley filled the furnace, and the cook was ordered to boil them out of hand.

As soon as the pirate ship had done firing, I asked the quartermaster's leave for our surgeon to dress my poor people that had been wounded, and I likewise went to have my arm dressed, it being very much bruised by the blow given me by the pirate boatswain. Just after that a person came to me from the quartermaster, desiring to know what o'clock it was by my watch; which, judging to be a civil way of demanding it, I sent it him immediately, desiring the messenger to tell him it was a very good gold watch. When it was delivered to the quartermaster he held it up by the chain, and presently laid it down on the deck, giving it a kick with his foot, saying it was a pretty football. On which one of the pirates caught it up, saying he would put it in the common chest to be sold at the mast.

By this time I was loudly called upon to go on board the pirate ship, and there was taken to the commander, who asked me several questions about my ship, saying she would make a fine pirate man-of-war.

As soon as I had done answering the captain's questions, a tall man, with four pistols in his girdle and a broadsword in his hand, came to me on the quarter-deck, telling me his name was James Griffin, and we had been schoolfellows. Though I remembered him very well, yet having formerly heard it had proved fatal to some who had been taken by pirates to own any knowledge of them, I told him I could not remember any such person by name. On that he mentioned some boyish pranks that had formerly passed between us. But I, still denying any knowledge of him, he told me that he supposed I took him to be one of the pirate's crew because I saw him dressed in that manner, but that he was a forced man, and since he had been taken, though they spared his life, they had obliged him to act as master of the pirate ship. And the reason of his being so armed was to prevent their ill-using him, for there were hardly any among the crew but what were cruel villains. But he would himself take care of me that night, when I should be in the greatest danger, because many of their people would soon get drunk with the good liquors found in my ship.

I then readily owned my former acquaintance with him, and he turned to Captain Cochlyn and desired that a bowl of punch might be made. So we went into the cabin, where there was not chair, nor anything else to sit upon, for they always kept a clear ship, ready for an engagement. So a carpet was spread on the deck, on which we sat down cross-legged, and Captain Cochlyn drank my health, desiring that I would not be cast down at my misfortune, for my ship's company in general spoke well of me, and they had goods enough left in the ships they had taken to make a man of me. Then he drank several other healths, among which was that of the Pretender, by the name of King James the Third.

It being by this time midnight, my schoolfellow desired the captain to have a hammock hung up for me to sleep in, for it seemed everyone lay rough, as they call it, that is, on the deck, the captain himself not being allowed a bed. This being granted, and soon after done, I took leave of the captain, and got into my hammock, but I could not sleep in my melancholy circumstances. Moreover, the execrable curses I heard among the ship's company kept me awake, though Mr. Griffin, according to his promise, walked by me with his broadsword in his hand, to protect me from insults.

Some time after, it being about two o'clock in the morning, the pirate boatswain (that attempted to kill me when taken) came on board very drunk, and being told I was in a hammock, he came near me with his cutlass. My generous schoolfellow asked him what he wanted; he answered, 'To kill me, for I was a vile dog.' Then Griffin bade the boatswain keep his distance, or he would cleave his head asunder with his broadsword. Nevertheless, the bloodthirsty villain came on to kill me; but Mr. Griffin struck at him with his sword, from which he had a narrow escape; and then he ran away. So I lay unmolested till daylight.

I come now to relate how Mr. Simon Jones, my first mate, and ten of my men entered with the pirates. The morning after we were taken he came to me and told me that his circumstances were bad at home; moreover, he had a wife whom he could not love;

and for these reasons he had entered with the pirates and signed their articles. I was greatly surprised at this declaration, and told him I believed he would repent when too late. And, indeed, I saw

the poor man afterwards despised by his brethren in iniquity, and have been told he died a few months after they left Sierra Leone. However, I must do him the justice to own he never showed any disrespect to me, and the ten people he persuaded to enter with him remained very civil to me. But I learned afterwards from one of them that, before we came to Sierra Leone, Jones had said that he hoped we should meet with pirates, and that it was by his contrivance that the chest of arms was hid out of the way when we were taken. And when I called on the people in the steerage to fire on the pirate boat, Jones prevented them, declaring that this was an opportunity he had long wished for, and that if they fired a musket they would all be cut to pieces. Moreover, to induce them to enter with the pirates, he had assured them that I had promised to enter myself. So it was a wonder I escaped so well, having such a base wretch for my first officer.

As soon as the fumes of the liquor were out of the pirates' heads they went on board the prize, as they called my ship, and all hands went to work to clear it, by throwing over bales of woollen goods, with many other things of great value, so that before night they had destroyed between three and four thousand pounds worth of the cargo—money and necessaries being what they wanted. The sight of this much grieved me, but I was obliged in prudence to be silent.

That afternoon there came on board to see me Captain Henry Glynn, with whom I was acquainted, who resided at Sierra Leone, but though an honest, generous person, was on good terms with the pirates. He brought with him the captains of the two other pirate ships, and Captain Davis generously said he was ashamed to hear how I had been used, for their reasons for going a-pirating were to revenge themselves on base merchants and cruel commanders, but none of my people gave me the least ill character; and, indeed, it was plain that they loved me.

This was by no means relished by Cochlyn; however, he put a good face on it.

That night the boatswain came down into the steerage, where he had seen me sitting with the ship's carpenter, but since we happened to have changed places, and it had grown so dark he could not distinguish our faces, he, thinking I sat where he had seen me before, presented a pistol and drew the trigger, swearing he would blow my brains out. By good fortune the pistol did not go off, but only flashed in the pan; by the light of which the carpenter, observing that he should have been shot instead of me, it so provoked him that he ran in the dark to the boatswain, and having wrenched the pistol out of his hand, he beat him to such a degree that he almost killed him. The noise of the fray being heard on board the pirate ship that lay close to us, a boat was sent from her, and they being told the truth of the matter, the officer in her carried away this wicked villain, who had three times tried to murder me.

I had one bundle of my own things left to me, in which was a black suit of clothes. But a pirate, who was tolerably sober, came in and said he would see what was in it. He then took out my black suit, a good hat and wig, and some other things. Whereon I told him I hoped he would not deprive me of them, for they would be of no service to him in so hot a country, but would be of great use to me, as I hoped soon to return to England.

I had hardly done speaking, when he lifted up his broadsword and gave me a blow on the shoulder with the flat side of it, whispering in my ear at the same time:

' I give you this caution, never to dispute the will of a pirate; for, supposing I had cleft your skull asunder for your impudence, what would you have got by it but destruction ? '

I gave him thanks for his warning, and soon after he put on the clothes, which in less than half an hour after I saw him take off and throw overboard, for some of the pirates, seeing him dressed in that manner, had thrown several buckets of claret upon him. This person's true name was Francis Kennedy.

The next day, understanding that the three pirate captains were on shore at my friend Captain Glynn's, I asked leave to go to them, which was granted, and next day I went on board in company with them. Captain Davis desired Cochlyn to order all his people on the quarter-deck, and made a speech to them on my behalf, which they falling in with, it was resolved to give me the ship they designed to leave to go into mine, with the remains of my cargo, and further, the goods remaining in the other prizes, worth, with my own, several thousand pounds. Then one of the leading pirates proposed that I should go along with them down the coast of Guinea, where I might exchange the goods for gold, and that, no doubt, as they went they should take some French and Portuguese vessels, and then they might give me as many of their best slaves as would fill the ship; that then he would advise me to go to the island of St. Thomas and sell them there, and after rewarding my people in a handsome manner, I might return with a large sum of money to London and bid the merchants defiance.

This proposal was approved of, but it struck me with a sudden damp. So I began to say it would not be proper for me to accept of such a quantity of other people's goods as they had so generously voted for me. On which I was interrupted by several, who began to be very angry.

On this Captain Davis said: 'I know this man, and can easily guess his thoughts; for he thinks, if he should act in the manner you have proposed, he will ever after lose his reputation. Now I am for allowing everybody to go to the devil their own way, so desire you will give him the remains of his own cargo and let him do with it what he thinks fitting.'

This was readily granted; and now, the tide being turned, they were as kind to me as they had at first been severe, and we employed ourselves in saving what goods we could.

And through the influence of Captain Davis, one of the ships the pirates had taken, called the ' Bristol Snow,' was spared from burning—for they burned such prizes as they had no use for. And I was set entirely at liberty, and went to the house of Captain Glynn, who, when the pirates left the river of Sierra Leone, together with other English captains who had been hiding from the pirates in the woods, their ships having been taken, helped me to fit up the ' Bristol Snow ' that we might return to England in it. And we left the river Sierra Leone the 10th day of May, and came safe to Bristol, where I found a letter from the owner of the ship I had gone out with, who had heard of my misfortune, and most generously comforted me, giving money for my poor sailors and promising me command of another ship—a promise which he soon after performed.

I shall now inform the reader what became of my kind school-fellow, Griffin, and my generous friend Davis. The first got out of the hands of the pirates by taking away a boat from the stern of the ship he was in when on the coast of Guinea, and was driven on shore there. But afterwards he went passenger to Barbadoes in an English ship, where he was taken with a violent fever, and so died.

As for Davis, he sailed to the island Princess, belonging to the Portuguese, which is in the Bay of Guinea. Here the people soon discovered they were pirates by their lavishness; but the Governor winked at it, because of the great gain he made by them. But afterwards, someone putting it into his mind that if the King of Portugal heard of this it would be his ruin, he plotted to destroy Davis. And when, before sailing, Captain Davis came on shore with the surgeon and some others to bid farewell to the Governor, they found no Governor, but many people with weapons were gathered together in the street, who at a word from the Governor's steward fired at Davis and his men. The surgeon and two others were killed on the spot, but Davis, though struck by four shots, went on running

'SOME OF THE PIRATES . . . HAD THROWN SEVERAL BUCKETS
OF CLARET UPON HIM.'

towards the boat. But being closely pursued, a fifth shot made him fall; and the Portuguese, being amazed at his great strength and

courage, cut his throat that they might be sure of him. Thus fell Captain Davis, who, allowing for the course of life he had been unhappily engaged in, was a most generous, humane person.

THIS is the story of the greatest deed of arms that was ever done. The men who fought in it were not urged by ambition or greed, nor were they soldiers who knew not why they went to battle. They warred for the freedom of their country, they were few against many, they might have retreated with honour, after inflicting great loss on the enemy, but they preferred, with more honour, to die.

It was four hundred and eighty years before the birth of Christ. The Great King, as the Greeks called Xerxes, the Persian monarch, was leading the innumerable armies of Asia against the small and divided country of Greece. It was then split into a number of little States, not on good terms with each other, and while some were for war, and freedom, and ruin, if ruin must come, with honour, others were for peace and slavery. The Greeks, who determined to resist Persia at any cost, met together at the Isthmus of Corinth, and laid their plans of defence. The Asiatic army, coming by land, would be obliged to march through a narrow pass called Thermopylæ, with the sea on one side of the road, and a steep and inaccessible precipice on the other. Here, then, the Greeks made up their minds to stand. They did not know, till they had marched to Thermopylæ, that behind the pass there was a mountain path, by which soldiers might climb round and over the mountain, and fall upon their rear. As the sea on the right hand of the Pass of Thermopylæ lies in a narrow strait, bounded by the island of Eubœa, the Greeks thought that their ships would guard their rear and prevent the Persians from landing men to attack it. Their army encamped in the Pass, having wide enough ground to manœuvre in, between the narrow northern gateway, so to speak, by which the invaders would try to enter, and a gateway to the south. Their position was also protected by an old military wall, which they repaired.

The Greek general was Leonidas, the Spartan king. He chose three hundred men, all of whom had sons at home to maintain their families and to avenge them if they fell. Now the manner of the Spartans was this : to die rather than yield. However sorely defeated, or overwhelmed by numbers, they never left the ground alive and unvictorious, and as this was well known, their enemies were seldom eager to attack such resolute fighters.

Besides the Spartans, Leonidas led some three or four thousand men from other cities, and he was joined at Thermopylæ by the Locrians and a thousand Phocians. Perhaps he may have had six or eight thousand soldiers under him, while the Persians may have outnumbered them by the odds of a hundred to one. Why, you may ask, did the Greeks not send a stronger force? The reason was very characteristic. They were holding their sports at the time, racing, running, boxing, jumping, and they were also about to be engaged in another festival. They would not omit or put off their games however many thousand barbarians might be knocking at their gates. There is something boyish, and something fine in this conduct, but we must remember, too, that the games were a sacred festival, and that the Gods might be displeased if they were omitted.

Leonidas, then, thought that at least he could hold the Pass till the games were over, and his countrymen could join him. But when he found, on arriving at Thermopylæ, that he would have to hold two positions, the Pass itself, and the mountain path, of whose existence he had not been aware, then some of his army wished to return home. But Leonidas refused to let them retreat, and bade the Phocians guard the path across the hills, while he sent home for reinforcements. He could not desert the people whom he had come to protect. Meanwhile the Greek fleet was also alarmed, but was rescued by a storm which wrecked many of the Persian vessels.

Xerxes was now within sight of Thermopylæ. He sent a horseman forward to spy out the Greek camp, and this man saw the Spartans amusing themselves with running and wrestling, and combing their long hair, outside the wall. They took no notice of him, and he returning, told Xerxes how few they were, and how unconcerned. Xerxes then sent for Demaratus, an exiled king of Sparta in his camp, and asked what these things meant. 'O king!' said Demaratus, ' this is what I told you of yore, when you laughed at my words. These men have come to fight you for the

F

Pass, and for that battle they are making ready, for it is our country fashion to comb and tend our hair when we are about to put our heads in peril.'

Xerxes would not believe Demaratus. He waited four days, and then, in a rage, bade his best warriors, the Medes and Cissians, bring the Greeks into his presence. The Medes, who were brave men, and had their defeat at Marathon, ten years before, to avenge, fell on, but their spears were short, their shields were thin, and they could not break a way into the stubborn forest of bronze and steel. In wave upon wave, all day long, they dashed against the Greeks, and left their best lying at the mouth of the Pass. 'Thereby was it made clear to all men, and not least to the king, that men are many, but heroes are few.'

Next day Xerxes called on his bodyguard, the Ten Thousand Immortals, and they came to close quarters, but got no more glory than the Medes. Thrice the King leaped from his chair in dismay as thrice the Greeks drove the barbarians in rout. And on the third day they had no better fortune.

But there was a man, a Malian, whose name is a scorn to this hour; he was called Epialtes. He betrayed to Xerxes the secret of the mountain path, probably for money. He later fled to Thessaly with a price on his head, but returned to Anticyra, and there he was slain by Athenades. Then Xerxes was glad beyond measure when he heard of the path, and sent his men along the path by night. They found the Phocians guarding it, but the Phocians disgracefully fled to the higher part of the mountain. The Persians, disdaining to pursue them, marched to the pass behind the Spartan camp, and the Greeks were now surrounded in van and rear. But news of this had come to Leonidas, and his army was not of one mind as to what they should do. Some were for retreating and abandoning a position which it was now impossible to hold. Leonidas bade them depart; but for him and his countrymen it was not honourable to turn their backs on any foe. He sent away the soothsayer, or prophet, Megistias, but he returned, and bade his son go home. The Thespians, to their immortal honour, chose to bide the brunt with Leonidas. There thus remained what was left of the Three Hundred, their personal attendants, seven hundred Thespians, and some Thebans, about whose conduct it is difficult to speak with certainty, as accounts differ. Leonidas, on this last day of his life, did not wait to be attacked in front and rear, but, sallying into the open, himself assailed the Persians. They drove the barbarians

like cattle with their spears; the captains of the barbarians drove
them back on the spears with whips. Many fell from the path
into the sea, and there perished, and many more were trodden
down and died beneath the feet of their own companions. But
the spears of the Greeks broke at last in their hands, so they drew
their swords, and rushed to yet closer quarters. In this charge fell
Leonidas, 'the bravest man,' says the Greek historian, 'of men
whose names I know,' and he knew the names of all the Three
Hundred. Over the body of Leonidas fell the two brothers of
Xerxes, for they fought for the corpse, and four times the Greeks
drove back the Persians. Now came up the Persians with the
traitor Epialtes, attacking the Greeks in the rear. Now was their
last hour come, so they bore the body of the king within the wall.
There they occupied a little mound in a sea of enemies, and there
each man fought till he died, stabbing with his dagger when his
sword was broken, and biting, and striking with the fist, when
the dagger-point was blunted. Among them all, none made a
better end than Eurytus. He was suffering from a disease of the
eyes, but he bade them arm him, and lead him into the
thick of the battle. Of another, Dieneces, it is told that
hearing the arrows of the Persians would darken the sun, he
answered, 'Good news! we shall fight in the shade.' One man
only, Aristodemus, who also was suffering from a disease of the
eyes, did not join his countrymen, but returned to Sparta. There
he was scouted for a coward, but, in the following year, he fell at
Platæa, excelling all the Spartans in deeds of valour.

This is the story of the Three Hundred. The marble lion
erected where Leonidas fell has perished, and perished has the
column engraved with their names, but their glory is immortal.[1]

[1] Herodotus.

PRINCE CHARLIE'S WANDERINGS

CHAPTER I

THE FLIGHT

APRIL 16, 1746. It was an April afternoon, grey and cold, with gleams of watery sunshine, for in the wilds of Badenoch the spring comes but slowly, and through April on to May the mountains are as black and the moors as sombre and lifeless as in the dead of winter. In a remote corner of this wild track stood, in 1746, a grey, stone house with marsh-lands in front, severe and meagre as the houses were at that time in the Highlands. Upstairs in a room by herself a little girl of ten was looking out of the window. She had been sent up there to be out of the way, for this was a very busy day in the household of Gortuleg. The Master, Mr. Fraser, was entertaining the chief of his clan, old Lord Lovat, who, in these anxious days, when the Prince was at Inverness and the Duke of

Cumberland at Aberdeen, had thought fit to retire into the wilds of Badenoch, to the house of his faithful clansman.

Downstairs, the astute old man of eighty was sitting in his arm-chair by the fire, plotting how he could keep in with both parties and secure his own advantage whichever side might win. By some

strange infatuation the household at Gortuleg were cheerful and elate. A battle was imminent, nay, might have been fought even now, and they were counting securely on another success to the Prince's army. So the ladies of the family—staunch Jacobites every one of them (as, indeed, most ladies were even in distinctly

Whig households)—were busy preparing a feast in honour of the
expected victory. The little girl sat alone upstairs, hearing the din
and commotion and looking out on the vacant marsh-land outside.
Suddenly and completely the noise ceased below, and the child
seized her opportunity and crept downstairs. All was still in the
big living-room, only in the dim recess of the fireplace the old lord
was sitting, a silent, brooding figure, in his deep armchair. The
rest of the household, men and women, gentle and simple, were
all crowded in the doorway, breathlessly intent on something outside. Threading her way through them the child crept outside the
circle and looked eagerly to see what this might be. Across the
grey marshes horsemen were riding, riding fast, though the horses
strained and stumbled, and the riders had a weary, dispirited air.
'It is the fairies' was the idea that flashed through her brain,
and in a moment she was holding her eyelids open with her fingers,
for she knew that the 'good people,' if they do show themselves, are
only visible between one winking of the eyes and another. But
this vision did not pass away, and surely never were fairy knights
in such a sorry plight as was this travel-stained, dishevelled company
that drew rein at the door of Gortuleg.

The leader of the band was a young man in Highland dress,
tall and fair, and with that 'air' of which his followers fondly
complained afterwards that no disguise could conceal it. At the
sight of him, arriving in this plight at their doors, a great cry of
consternation broke from the assembled household. There was
no need to tell the terrible news: the Prince was a fugitive, a
battle had been lost, and the good cause was for ever undone!
It was no time for idle grieving, immediate relief and refreshment must be provided, and the Prince sent forward without
delay on his perilous flight. The ladies tore off their laces and
handkerchiefs to bind up wounds, and wine was brought out for the
fugitives. There is no certain account of Charles's interview with
Lord Lovat; we do not know whether the cunning old man turned
and upbraided the Prince in his misfortune, or whether the instincts
of a Highland gentleman overcame for a moment the selfishness of
the old chief. Anyway, this was no time to bandy either upbraidings
or compliments. Forty minutes of desperate fighting on the field
of Culloden that morning had broken for ever the strength of the
Jacobite cause. Hundreds lay dead where they fell, hundreds were
prisoners in the hands of the most relentless of enemies, hundreds
were fleeing in disarray to their homes among the mountain fast-

nesses. For the Prince the only course seemed to be flight to the West coast. There, surely, some vessel might be found to convey him to France, there to await better times and to secure foreign allies. A price was on his head, his enemies would certainly be soon on his traces, he dared not delay longer than to snatch a hasty meal and drink some cups of wine.

At Gortuleg the party broke up and went their several ways. The Prince was accompanied by the Irish officers of his household, Sir Thomas Sheridan, O'Neal, and O'Sullivan, gentlemen-adventurers who had accompanied him from France and whose advice in his day of triumph had often been injudicious. Let it be said for them that they were at least faithful and devoted when his fortunes were desperate. As guide went a certain Edward Burke, who, fortunately for the party, knew every yard of rugged ground between Inverness and the Western sea. During all the time that he shared the Prince's wanderings this Edward Burke acted as his valet, giving him that passionate devotion which Charles seems to have inspired in all who knew him personally at this time. Reduced now to a handful of weary, wounded men, the Prince's party continued their flight through the chilly April night. At two o'clock next morning they had passed the blackened ruins of Fort George. As dawn broke they drew rein at the house of Invergarry. But the gallant chief of the Macdonells was away, and the hospitable house was deserted and silent; the very rooms were without furniture or any accommodation, and the larder was bare of provisions. But wearied men are not fastidious, and without waiting to change their clothes, they rolled themselves up in their plaids on the bare boards, and slept the sleep of utter weariness. It was high noon before they woke up again—woke up to find breakfast unexpectedly provided, for the faithful Burke had risen betimes and drawn two fine salmon from the nets set in the river. Here for greater security the Prince and his valet changed clothes, and the journey was continued through Lochiel's country. The next stage was at the head of Loch Arkaig, where they were the guests of a certain Cameron of Glenpean, a stalwart, courageous farmer, whom the Prince was destined to see more of in his wanderings. Here the country became so wild and rugged that they had to abandon their horses and clamber over the high and rocky mountains on foot. In his boyhood in Italy the Prince had been a keen sportsman, and had purposely inured himself to fatigue and privations. · These habits stood him now in good stead; he could rival even the light-footed

Highlanders on long marches over rough ground; the coarsest and scantiest meals never came amiss to him; he could sleep on the hard ground or lie hid in bogs for hours with a stout heart and a cheerful spirit.

Here on the night of Saturday, the 19th, among the mountains that surround Loch Morar, no better shelter could be found than a shieling used for shearing sheep.

The next day, Sunday, the 20th, they came down to the coast and found refuge in the hospitable house of Borodale, belonging to Mr. Angus Macdonald, a clansman of Clanranald's. Nine months before, when the Prince had landed from France and had thrown himself without arms or following on the loyalty of his Highland friends, this Angus Macdonald had been proud to have him as his guest. One of his sons, John, had joined the Prince's army and had fought under his own chief, young Clanranald. This young man was at this time supposed to have been killed at Culloden, though in fact he had escaped unhurt. When the Prince, therefore, entered this house of mourning he went up to Mrs. Macdonald and asked her with tears in his eyes if she could endure the sight of one who had caused her such distress. ' Yes,' said the high-hearted old Highland-woman, ' I would be glad to have served my Prince though all my sons had perished in his service, for in so doing they would only have done their duty.' [1]

While resting here at Borodale, Charles sent his final orders to the remnant of his gallant army, which under their chiefs had drawn to a head at Ruthven. They were to disperse, he wrote, and secure their own safety as best they could; they must wait for better times, when he hoped to return bringing foreign succours. Heart-breaking orders these were for the brave men who had lost all in the Prince's cause, and who were now proscribed and homeless fugitives.

Charles and the handful of men who accompanied him had expected that, once safely arrived at the coast, their troubles would be over and the way to France clear. But at Borodale they learned that the Western seas swarmed with English ships of war and with sloops manned by the local militia. A thorough search was being made of every bay and inlet of the mainland, and of every island, even to the Outer Hebrides, and further, to remote St. Kilda! This disconcerting news was brought by young Clanranald and Mr.

[1] ' I had three sons, who now hae nane,
   I bred them toiling sarely,
   And I wad bare them a' again
   And lose them a' for Charlie !'

Æneas Macdonald of Kinloch Moidart, the Parisian banker who had accompanied Charles from France. The latter had just returned from an expedition to South Uist, where he had more than once narrowly escaped being taken by some vigilant English cruiser. It was impossible, he urged, for a ship of any size to escape through such a closely-drawn net; the idea of starting directly for France must be abandoned, but could the Prince escape to the outer islands and there secure a suitable vessel, he *might* be out upon the wide seas before his departure was discovered. It was therefore decided that the little party should cross the Minch in an open boat and make for the Long Island. For this expedition the very man was forthcoming in the person of the Highland pilot who had accompanied Mr. Macdonald to South Uist. This was old Donald MacLeod of Guatergill, in Skye, a trader of substance and a man of shrewdness and experience. In spite of being a MacLeod he was a staunch Jacobite, and had joined the Prince's army at Inverness. He had a son, a mere lad, at school in that place; this boy, hearing that a battle was likely to take place, flung aside his book, borrowed a dirk and a pistol, and actually fought in the battle of Culloden. More lucky than most, he escaped from the fight, tracked the Prince to Borodale, and arrived in time to take his place as one of the eight rowers whom his father had collected for the expedition. The boat belonged to the missing John Macdonald, for the Borodale family gave life and property equally unhesitatingly in the Prince's service.

On April 26, in the deepening twilight, the party started from Lochnanuagh. Hardly had they set out when they were overtaken by a terrible storm, the worst storm, Donald declared, that he had ever been out in, and he was an experienced sailor. The Prince demanded vehemently that the boat should be run on shore, but Donald, knowing the rock-bound coast, answered that to do so would be to run on certain death. Their one chance was to hold out straight to sea. It was pitch dark, the rain fell in torrents; they had neither lantern, compass, nor pump on board. Charles lay at the bottom of the boat, with his head between Donald's knees. No one spoke a word; every moment they expected to be overwhelmed in the waves or dashed against a rock, and for several hours the vessel rushed on in the darkness. 'But as God would have it,' to use Donald's words, ' by peep of day we discovered ourselves to be on the coast of the Long Isle. We made directly for the nearest land, which was Rossinish in Benbecula.'

Here they found only a deserted hut, low, dark, and destitute of window or chimney ; the floor was clay, and when they had lit a fire, the peat smoke was blinding and stifling. Still, they could dry their clothes and sleep, even though it were on a bed no better than a sail spread on the hard ground. Here they rested two days, and then found a more comfortable refuge in the Island of Scalpa, where the tacksman—although a Campbell—was a friend of Donald MacLeod's and received them hospitably.

CHAPTER II

ON THE LONG ISLAND

THE object of the expedition was, of course, to find some vessel big enough to carry the Prince and his friends over to France. Such ships were to be had in Stornoway, and Donald MacLeod, being a man well known in these parts, undertook to secure a vessel and pilot, under the pretence of going on a trading expedition to the Orkneys. The Prince and his party were to remain at Scalpa till Donald should send for them. On May 3 came the message that vessel and pilot were in readiness, and that they should come to Stornoway without a moment's delay.

Owing to the wind being ahead it was impossible to go by sea, and the Prince and his two Irish followers were forced to go the thirty miles to Stornoway on foot. No footpath led through the wastes of heavy, boggy moorlands, the rain fell with an even down-pour, and the guide stupidly mistook the way and added eight long Highland miles to the distance. They were thoroughly drenched, exhausted, and famished when Donald met them at a place a mile or two out of Stornoway. Having cheered their bodies with bread and cheese and brandy, and their souls with the hopeful prospect of starting the next day for France, he took them to a house in the neighbourhood, Kildun, where the mistress, though a MacLeod, was, like most of her sex, an ardent Jacobite. Leaving the Prince and his friends to the enjoyment of food, dry clothes, a good fire, and the prospect of comfortable beds for tired limbs, Donald went back to Stornoway in hopeful spirits to complete his arrangements for taking the Prince on board. Another twenty-four hours and the ship would have weighed anchor, and the worst difficulties would be left behind. But as soon as he entered

Stornoway he saw that something was wrong. Three hundred men of the militia were in arms, and the whole place was in an uproar. The secret had leaked out; one of the boat's crew, getting tipsy, had boasted that the Prince was at hand with five hundred men, ready to take by force what he could not obtain by good-will.

The inhabitants of Stornoway were all Mackenzies, pledged by their chief, Seaforth, to loyal support of the Government. It is eternally to their honour that all that they demanded was that the Prince should instantly remove himself from their neighbourhood. Not one amongst them seems to have suggested that a sum of 30,000*l.* was to be gained by taking the Prince prisoner. So complete was Donald's confidence in their honesty that he did not hesitate to say to a roomful of armed militiamen, ' He has only two companions with him, *and when I am there I make a third,* and yet let me tell you, gentlemen, that if Seaforth himself were here he durst not put a hand to the Prince's breast.' Donald doubtless looked pretty formidable as he said these words; at any rate, the ' honest Mackenzies ' had no sinister intentions, only they vehemently insisted that the party should depart at once, and, what was worse, absolutely refused to give them a pilot. In vain Donald offered 500*l.*; fear made them obdurate; and so, depressed and crestfallen, Donald returned to Kildun and urged the Prince to instant flight. But not even the fear of immediate capture could induce the three wearied men to set out again in the wet and darkness to plod over rocks and morasses with no certain goal. So Donald had to control his fears and impatience till next day.

At eight next morning they started in the boat, hospitable Mrs. MacLeod insisting on their taking with them beef, meal, and even the luxuries of brandy, butter, and sugar. The weather being stormy they landed on a little desert island called Eiurn, which the Stornoway fishermen used as a place for drying fish. Between some fish which they found drying on the rocks and Mrs. MacLeod's stores they lived in comparative luxury for the next few days. Ned Burke, the valet, was told off as cook; but he soon found that the Prince was far more skilful in the art of cookery than himself. It was his Royal Highness who suggested the luxury of butter with the fish, and who made a quite original cake by mixing the brains of a cow with some meal, giving orders to ' birsle the bannock weel, or it would not do at all.' Donald used to declare that in all his life ' he never knew anyone better at a shift than the Prince when he happened to be at a pinch.' Like many another unfortunate man, whether prince or peasant, Charles found unfailing comfort in tobacco. He seems to have smoked nothing more splendid than clay pipes, and 'as in his wanderings these behoved to break, he used to take quills, and putting one into the other and all into the end of the "cutty," this served to make it long enough, and the tobacco to smoke cool.'

Donald records another characteristic little trait of the Prince at this time. On quitting the island he insisted on leaving money on the rocks to pay for the fish they had consumed.'

In the meantime the situation was growing more and more dangerous. Rumours had got abroad that the Prince was in the Long Island, and the search was being actively pursued. Two English men-of-war were stationed near the island, and sloops and gunboats ran up every bay and sound, while bodies of militia carried on the search by land. These, from their intimate knowledge of the country, would have been the more formidable enemy of the two if many of their officers had not had a secret sympathy with the Jacobite cause and very lukewarm loyalty to the Government.

For several days the Prince's boat had been so constantly pursued that it was impossible for the crew to land. They ran short of food, and were reduced to eating oatmeal mixed with salt water, a nauseous mixture called in Gaelic, Drammach. At last they ran into a lonely bay in Benbecula, where they were free from pursuit. It is characteristic of the Prince's irrepressible boyishness that he and the boatmen here went lobster-hunting with great enjoyment and success.

Without help at this juncture the little party must either have starved or fallen into the hands of their enemies. Charles therefore sent a message to the old chief of Clanranald—the largest proprietor in South Uist—begging him to come and see him.

Nine months before, when the Prince had landed on that island on his way from France, the old gentleman had refused to see him, pleading old age and infirmity. His brother, Macdonald of Boisdale, had seen the Prince and had vehemently urged him to give up so hopeless a design and to return to France; and, when he found that all persuasion was in vain, had roundly refused to promise him any assistance from his brother's clan. And though young Clanranald

---

¹ In this he resembled his father, who, on leaving Scotland after the failure of 1715, sent money to Argyll to compensate the country folk whose cottages had been burned in the war; an act without precedent or imitation.

had, indeed, joined the Prince's standard, it was with many mis-givings and against his better judgment.

But now, in the hour of Charles's total abandonment and distress, this gallant family laid aside all selfish prudence. The old chief, in spite of age and ill-health, came immediately to the wretched hut where Charles had taken refuge, bringing with him Spanish wines, provisions, shoes, and stockings. He found the young man, whom he reverenced as his rightful king, in a hut as big as, and no cleaner than, a pig-stye, haggard and worn with hardship and hunger. 'His shirt,' as Dougal Graham, the servant, was quick to observe, 'was as dingy as a dish-clout.' That last little detail of misery appealed strongly to the womanly heart of Lady Clanranald, who immediately sent six good shirts to the Prince.

For the next three weeks Charles enjoyed a respite under the vigilant protection of Clanranald and his brother Boisdale. They found a hiding-place for him in the Forest-house of Glencoridale, a hut rather bigger and better than most. By a system of careful spies and watchers they kept the Prince informed of every move-ment of the enemy. It was the month of June—June as it is in the North, when days are warm and sunny and the evening twilight is prolonged till the early dawn, and there is no night at all. South Uist, beyond all other islands of the Hebrides, abounds in game of all kinds, and the Prince was always a keen sportsman. He delighted his followers by shooting birds on the wing, he fished (though it was only sea-fishing from a boat), and he shot red-deer on the mountains.

Once, when Ned Burke was preparing some collops from a deer the Prince had shot, a wild, starved-looking lad approached, and seeing the food, thrust his hand into the dish without either 'with your leave or by your leave,' and began devouring it like a savage. Ned in a rage very naturally began to beat the boy, but the gentle Prince interfered, and reminded his servant of the Christian duty of feeding the hungry, adding, 'I cannot see anyone perish for lack of food or raiment if I have it in my power to help them.' Having been fed and clothed the wretched boy went off straight to a body of militia in the neighbourhood and tried to betray the Prince to them. Fortunately, his appearance and manners were such that no one believed him, and he was laughed at for his pains. Out of at least a hundred souls, gentle and simple, who knew of the Prince's hiding-place, this 'young Judas' was the only one who dropped the slightest hint of his whereabouts.

Nor was it only among the Jacobite clans that Charles found devoted and vigilant friends.

The two most powerful chiefs in the North-west of Scotland were at this time MacLeod of MacLeod and Sir Alexander Macdonald of Mugstatt, or Mouggestot, in Skye. These two had, to the great disappointment of the Jacobites, declared for the Government, and had shown considerable zeal in trying to suppress the rising; but in the very household of Mugstatt Charles had a romantic and zealous adherent in the person of Lady Margaret, Sir Alexander Macdonald's wife. A daughter of the house of Eglintoun, she had been brought up in Jacobite principles, and now, in the absence of her husband, did all she could to help the Prince in his distress. Through the help of a certain Mr. Hugh Macdonald of Belshair she kept Charles informed of the enemy's movements and sent him newspapers. Towards the end of June the Government authorities were pretty certain that the Prince was hiding somewhere in the Long Island, and attention began to be concentrated on that spot. Two more English cruisers were sent there, under Captains Scott and Fergusson—men who had learnt lessons of cruelty from the greatest master of that art, the Duke of Cumberland—and militia bands patrolled the whole island. It was quite necessary to remove the Prince from Glencoridale, and the faithful Belshair was at once despatched by Lady Margaret to consult with Charles about his further movements. This Mr. Macdonald of Belshair arranged with Macdonald of Boisdale—one of the shrewdest as well as kindest of the Prince's friends—that they should meet at the Forest-house of Glencoridale. The meeting, in spite of hardships and danger and a worse than uncertain future, was a merry one. The two Highland gentlemen dined with the Prince (on 'sooty beef' and apparently a plate of butter!), and the talk was cheerful and free. Forgetful of the gloomy prospects of the Jacobite cause, and ignoring the victorious enemies encamped within a few miles of them, they talked hopefully of future meetings at St. James's, the Prince declaring that 'if he had never so much ado he would be at least one night merry with his Highland friends.' But St. James's was far enough off from Coridale, and in the meantime it became daily more certain that there was no longer safety for the Prince in Uist.

The pleasant life in the Forest-house had to be broken up, and for the next ten weary days the little party lived in their boat, eluding as well as they could their enemies by sea and by land.

Their difficulties were much increased and their spirits sadly disturbed by the fact that their generous friend Boisdale had been taken prisoner.

It is one of the most singular facts of the Prince's wanderings that as soon as he lost one helpful friend another immediately rose up to take his place. This time an ally was found literally in the enemy's camp. One of the officers in command of the militia in Benbecula was a certain Hugh Macdonald of Armadale, in Skye, a clansman of Sir Alexander's, but, like many another Macdonald, a Jacobite at heart. It is very uncertain how far he was personally responsible for the plan that was at this time being formed for the Prince's escape. Donald MacLeod and others of the Prince's party were certain that Charles had met and talked with him at Rossinish and had presented him with his pistols. This gentleman had a step-daughter, a certain Flora Macdonald, a girl of remarkable character, courage, and discretion. She generally lived with her mother at Armadale, in Skye, but just now she was paying a visit to her brother in South Uist. It is difficult to make out how or when or by whom the idea was first started that this lady should convey the Prince to Skye disguised as her servant, but it appears that she had had more than one interview with O'Neal on the subject. On Saturday, June 21, being closely pursued by the implacable Captain Scott, Charles parted with his faithful little band of followers in Uist, paying the boatmen as generously as his slender purse would allow. With two clean shirts under his arm and with only O'Neal as his companion he started for Benbecula. Arriving at midnight in a small shieling belonging to Macdonald of Milton, 'by good fortune,' as O'Neal puts it, 'we met with Miss Flora Macdonald, whom I formerly knew.' It is a little difficult to believe that young ladies of Miss Flora's discretion were in the habit of frequenting lonely shielings far from their homes at midnight, at a time when the whole country was infested with soldiers. Nor does the beginning of her interview with O'Neal sound like the language of surprise. 'Then I told her I brought a friend to see her; and she, with some emotion, asked me if it was the Prince. I answered that it was, and instantly brought him in.' Among all the stout Highland hearts which were ready to risk everything for him, Charles never found one more brave and pitiful than that of the girl who was introduced to him in this strange and perilous situation.

The plan was at once proposed to her that she should convey

the Prince with her to Skye disguised in female attire as her maid. Flora was no mere romantic miss, eager for adventure and carried away by her feelings. She was quite aware of the danger she would bring on herself, and more especially on her friends, by this course. It was with some reluctance that she at last gave her consent, but once her word was pledged she was ready to go to the death if need were, and threw all her feminine ingenuity into carrying out the scheme. They arranged that she was to go next day to consult with Lady Clanranald and to procure feminine attire as a disguise for the Prince. As soon as all was prepared they were to meet at Rossinish in Benbecula; in the meantime O'Neal undertook to come and go between the Prince and Miss Macdonald to report progress and convey messages.

The two men seem to have returned to a hiding-place in the neighbourhood of Glencoridale, and Miss Flora returned to Milton. She had to pass one of the narrow sea fords next day on her way to Ormaclade, the Clanranalds' house; this ford was guarded by a body of militia, and having no passport, she and her servant, Neil MacKechan, were taken prisoners. The situation was awkward in the extreme, and every hour's delay was an added danger. To her great relief she learned that the officer in command, who was expected that morning, was her stepfather, Mr. Hugh Macdonald. On his arrival he was (or affected to be) extremely surprised to find his stepdaughter a prisoner in the guard-room; but with a complaisance very remarkable in an officer of the Government, he drew her out passports for herself, for her servant Neil, and for a new Irish servant, Betty Burke, whom she desired to take with her to Skye. So great was Macdonald's interest in this unknown Betty that he actually wrote a letter to his wife in Skye recommending the girl.

' I have sent your daughter from this country,' he wrote, ' lest she should be frightened by the troops lying here. She has got one Betty Burke, an Irish girl, who, she tells me, is a good spinster. If her spinning pleases you, you may keep her till she spins all your lint.' In spite of the gravity of the situation, one cannot help thinking that Flora and her stepfather must have had a good deal of amusement concocting this circumstantial and picturesque falsehood.

As soon as she was set at liberty Flora went to Ormaclade, where Lady Clanranald entered heartily into the plan. Among her stores they chose a light coloured quilted petticoat, a flowered gown—

lilac flowers on a white ground, to be particular—an apron and a long duffle cloak. Fortunately Highland women are tall and large, for the Prince's height, 5 feet 10 inches, though moderate for a man, looked ungainly enough in petticoats.

It was Friday the 25th before the way was clear for Flora and Lady Clanranald to meet the Prince at the rendezvous at Rossinish in Benbecula. The four intervening days had been full of difficulties for Charles and O'Neal. The fords between the two islands were so well guarded that there was no chance of their being able to cross them on foot; they had no boat, and the hours were passing for them in an agony of suspense. At last they risked asking a chance boat which was passing to set them across, and accomplished the passage in safety. But when they did arrive at the hut at Rossinish,

cold, wet, and wearied, they found that a party of militia were encamped within half a mile, and that the soldiers came every morning to that very hut for milk. Charles was by this time accustomed to the feeling that he was carrying his life in his hands. At daybreak he had to leave the hut to make room for his pursuers, all day he had to lie in an unsheltered fissure of a rock, where the rain—the heavy, relentless rain of the West Highlands—poured down on him; if it did clear at all, then that other plague of the Highlands, swarms of midges, nearly drove him distracted. On Friday the militiamen moved off, and the way being clear, Lady Clanranald, Miss Flora Macdonald, and a certain Mrs. Macdonald of Kirkibost came to visit him and O'Neal in their hut, bringing the

female attire with them. These loyal ladies found their lawful
sovereign roasting a sheep's liver on a spit; but neither discomfort,
danger, nor dirt could do away with the courtly charm of his manner
or the fine gaiety of his address. He placed Miss Macdonald on
his right hand—he always gave his preserver the seat of honour—
and Lady Clanranald at his left, and the strange little dinner-party
proceeded merrily. But before it was finished a messenger broke
in to tell Lady Clanranald that the infamous Captain Fergusson
had arrived at Ormaclade, and was demanding the mistress of the
house with angry suspicion.

The Prince had now to part with O'Neal, in spite of the poor
fellow's entreaties to be allowed to remain with him. Miss Macdonald had only passports for three and the danger was urgent.
He was a faithful and affectionate friend, this O'Neal, if a little
boastful and muddle-headed. He could shortly afterwards have
escaped to France—as O'Sullivan did—in a French ship, if he had
not insisted on going to Skye to try to fetch off the Prince. He
missed the Prince, and fell into the hands of Captain Fergusson.

CHAPTER III

IN SKYE

On Saturday (June 26) the Prince put on his female attire for the
first time, and very strange he must have felt as he sat in flowered
calico on wet, slippery rocks, trying to keep himself warm beside
a fire kindled on the beach. It was eight in the evening when
they started, and the storm broke on them as soon as they were out
at sea. The whole party was distressed and anxious, apparently,
except Charles himself, who sang songs and told stories to keep up
the spirits of his companions. Long afterwards Flora Macdonald
loved to tell how chivalrously and considerately he looked after her
comfort on that dangerous journey.

Going round the north end of the Isle of Skye, they came ashore
close to Mugstatt, Sir Alexander Macdonald's place. That chief
was himself away at Fort Augustus with the Duke of Cumberland,
but his wife, Lady Margaret, who, as we have seen, was a staunch
friend to the Prince, was at home. Still in her position it was
most undesirable that Charles should present himself at her house.
Miss Macdonald and her servant Neil went up to the house—the

garden sloped down to the part of the shore where they had landed—leaving Betty Burke sitting on the boxes in her flowered gown and duffle cloak.

Miss Macdonald had good reason to congratulate herself on her prudence when she found Lady Margaret's drawing-room full of guests. Among these was Mrs. Macdonald of Kirkibost, but she was already in the secret ; Mr. Macdonald of Kingsburgh was also there, but he was a man of such a chivalrous spirit and so kindly in his disposition, that the secret would have been safe with him even if he had not been—as he was—a staunch Jacobite at heart. Far more formidable was a third guest, young Lieutenant MacLeod, a militia officer who, with a small body of men, was stationed at Mugstatt for the express purpose of examining every boat that might arrive from the Long Island. He certainly neglected this duty as far as Miss Macdonald's boat was concerned, possibly out of complaisance to her hostess, Lady Margaret, possibly because the young lady's careless demeanour disarmed all suspicion.

The situation was a most anxious one for Miss Macdonald ; she had to carry on an easy flow of chat with a young officer while all the time she could think of nothing but Betty Burke sitting on her box on the shore. Every moment was precious and nothing was being done.

At last, during dinner, she managed to confide the whole situation to Kingsburgh, and while she kept the lieutenant engaged, the latter left the room and sent for Lady Margaret to speak to him on business. (He was her husband's factor, and there was nothing to excite remark in his wanting a private talk with her.) On learning the news she for a moment lost her head, and screamed out that they were undone. But with much sense and kindness Kingsburgh reassured her, saying that if necessary he would take the Prince to his own house, adding, with a touch of his characteristic chivalry, that he was now an old man, and it made very little difference to him whether he should die with a halter round his neck or await a death which could not be far distant.

As for the immediate future, the first idea that occurred both to Lady Margaret and Kingsburgh was, ' Let us send for Donald Roy.' This Donald was a brother of the Macdonald of Belshair who had visited the Prince at Coridale. He had been ' out ' with the Prince's army, and was now living with a surgeon near Mugstatt, trying to recover from a serious wound in his foot received at Culloden. This Donald must have been a good fellow, popular, and liked by all ; for even in those dangerous times he seems to have lived on an intimate footing with the very militia officers who were sent to search for hidden Jacobites.

No man could have been more suited for Kingsburgh's purpose than Donald. Not only was he sensible, honourable, and brave, but as an acknowledged Jacobite he had less to lose if discovered, and as a young and amiable man his person could not fail to be acceptable to the Prince.

On his arrival he found Kingsburgh and Lady Margaret walking up and down the garden. ‘O Donald !’ cried the lady, ‘we are undone for ever !’ After much rapid, anxious talk, the three agreed that the safest place for the Prince would be the Island of Rasay. Old Rasay had been ‘out’ and was in hiding, his second son was recovering from a wound received at Culloden, and the eldest, though he had kept quiet from motives of prudence, was quite as keen a Jacobite as the other two. Their eagerness to serve the Prince could be relied on, and as the island had been recently devastated by the Government soldiers, it was not likely to be visited again.

Donald Roy undertook to see young MacLeod of Rasay and to make arrangements for meeting the Prince at Portree next day, while Kingsburgh promised to carry the Prince off with him to his own house and to send him next day under safe guidance to Portree. In this way, whatever happened, Lady Margaret would not be compromised.

So the garden conclave broke up, and the three separated. Lady Margaret returned to her drawing-room, where, poor woman, she sadly disconcerted Miss Macdonald by nervously going in and out of the room. However, the lieutenant seems to have been too much taken up with his companion to notice his hostess's demeanour. Donald Roy, in spite of his lame foot, set off for Portree in search of young Rasay, and old Kingsburgh hurried off to look for Charles, carrying refreshments with him. Not finding him on the shore below the garden, the old man walked on rather anxiously till, seeing some sheep running, he concluded that someone must have disturbed them, and went to the spot. A tall, ungainly woman in a long cloak started forward to meet him brandishing a big knotted stick. As soon as Kingsburgh named himself the Prince knew that he had found a friend, and placed himself in his hands with the frank confidence he always showed in dealing with his Highland followers, a confidence which they so nobly justified.

After the Prince had had something to eat and drink, the pair set out to walk to Kingsburgh, a considerable distance off. Unfortunately it was Sunday, and they met many country people returning from church, who were all eager to have a little business chat with Sir Alexander's factor. He got rid of most of them by slyly reminding them of the sacredness of the day, for the Prince's awkward movements and masculine stride made his disguise very apparent. 'They may call you the Pretender,' cried Kingsburgh, between annoyance and amusement, 'but I never knew anyone so bad at your trade.'

At the first stream they had to cross the Prince lifted his skirts with a most masculine disregard of appearances, and to mend matters, when he came to the next, let his petticoats float in the water with a most unfeminine disregard of his clothes.

Halfway on their road Miss Macdonald rode past them on horseback, accompanied by Mrs. Macdonald of Kirkibost and the latter's maid. 'Look, look,' cried that damsel, 'what strides the jade takes! I dare say she's an Irishwoman or else a man in woman's clothes.' Miss Macdonald thought it best to quicken her pace and make no reply.

She was already at Kingsburgh when the Prince and his host arrived there at about eleven o'clock. All the household were in bed. A message was sent up to Mrs. Macdonald to tell her of the arrival of guests, but she very naturally refused to get up, and merely sent her compliments to Miss Macdonald and begged she would help herself to everything she wanted. When, however, her husband came up to her room and gravely requested her to come down and attend to his guest, she felt that something was wrong. Nor did it allay her fears when her little daughter ran up crying that 'the most odd, muckle, ill-shaken-up wife' she had seen in all her life was walking up and down in the hall. Mrs. Macdonald entered the main room with some misgiving, and in the uncertain firelight saw a tall, ungainly woman striding up and down. The figure approached her and, according to the manners of the time, saluted her. The rough touch of the unshaven lip left no doubt on the lady's mind; her husband's guest was certainly a man in disguise, probably a proscribed Jacobite. She hurried out of the room and met Kingsburgh in the hall. It did not occur to this good woman to upbraid her husband for bringing danger on his family; her first question was, 'Do you think the stranger will know anything about the Prince?'

'My dear,' said Kingsburgh very gravely, taking her hands in his, '*this is the Prince himself!*'

'The Prince!' cried Mrs. Macdonald, rather overwhelmed, 'then we shall all be hanged!'

'We can die but once,' said her husband, 'could we ever die in a better cause?'

Then, returning to the homely necessities of the hour, he begged her to bring bread and cheese and eggs.

Bread and cheese and eggs to set before Royalty! This disgrace to her housewifery affected Mrs. Macdonald almost as feelingly as the danger they were in. The idea, too, of sitting down at supper with her lawful sovereign caused the simple lady the greatest embarrassment. However, she was prevailed upon to take the seat at the Prince's left hand, while Miss Macdonald had her usual place at his right. After the ladies had retired Charles lighted his 'cutty,' and he and Kingsburgh had a comfortable chat and a bowl of punch over the fire. Indeed, good food, good fires, and good company were such congenial luxuries after the life he had been leading, that Charles sat on and on in his chair, and the hospitable Kingsburgh had at last to insist upon his guest going to bed.

Hour after hour the Prince slept on next morning, Kingsburgh being unwilling to disturb the one good rest he might have for weeks; Miss Macdonald was growing impatient and Mrs. Macdonald anxious, and at last Kingsburgh consented to rouse him at about one o'clock. Portree was seven miles off, and had to be reached before dark. It was decided that the Prince might resume male attire *en route*, but in case of exciting suspicion among the servants he had still to masquerade as Betty Burke till he left the house. Mrs. Macdonald, her daughter, and Miss Flora all came up to assist at his toilet, for 'deil a preen could he put in,' as his hostess expressed herself. He laughed so heartily over his own appearance that they could hardly get his dress fastened. Before he left the room he permitted Flora Macdonald to cut off a lock of his hair, which she divided with Mrs. MacLeod. What is a still more touching proof of the devotion of these two good women is that they carefully took off the sheets of the Prince's bed, vowing that these should be neither washed nor used again till they should serve each of them as winding-sheets. Kingsburgh accompanied his guests part of the way, assisted Charles to change his dress in a little wood, and then, with tears, bade him farewell.

Flora Macdonald rode on to Portree by another road, leaving

her servant, Neil MacKechan, and a little herd-boy to act as guides to the Prince.

In the meantime, Donald Roy had been active in the Prince's service. At Portree he had met young Rona MacLeod of Rasay and his brother Murdoch, and, as he had expected, found them eager to face any danger or difficulty for their Prince. They had a cousin rather older than themselves, Malcolm MacLeod, who had been a captain in the Prince's army. He entered into the scheme as heartily as the other two, and only suggested prudently that Rona should leave the matter to himself and Murdoch, who were 'already as black as black can be.' But Rona was not to be baulked of his share of the danger and glory of serving the Prince, and vowed that he *would* go even if it should cost him his estate and his head. So with two stout faithful boatmen they arrived within a mile of Portree, drew up their boat among the rocks where it could be hid, and remained waiting for the Prince, while the night fell and the rain came down in sheets.

It had been arranged at Mugstatt that Donald Roy was to meet the Prince late on Monday afternoon in the one public-house that Portree could boast. This public-house consisted of one large, dirty, smoky room, and people of all kinds kept going in and out, and here Donald took up his post. Flora Macdonald was the first to arrive, and she, Donald Roy, and Malcolm MacLeod sat together over the fire waiting anxiously. It was already dark when a small, wet herd-boy slipped in and going up to Donald whispered that a gentleman wanted to see him. The poor Prince was standing in the darkness outside drenched to the skin. As soon as they were at the inn Donald insisted on his changing his clothes, and Malcolm at once gave him his own dry philibeg. Food they could get, and water was brought in an old, battered, rusty tin from which the Prince drank, being afraid of arousing suspicion by any fastidiousness. He also bought sixpennyworth of the coarsest tobacco, and nearly betrayed his quality to the already suspicious landlord by a princely indifference to his change, but Malcolm prudently secured the 'bawbees' and put them into the Prince's sporran.

Miss Flora now rose very sadly to go, as she had to continue her journey that night. The Prince kissed her and said farewell with much suppressed emotion, but with his usual hopefulness added that he trusted that they might yet meet at St. James's. These constant partings from so many faithful, warm-hearted friends were among the hardest trials of Charles's wandering life.

He seems to have clung with special affection to Donald Roy, and urged him again and again not to leave him, but to go with him to Rasay. Donald could only reply that the state of his wounded foot made it impossible.

This conversation took place as they plunged through wet and darkness from Portree down to the shore where the boat was lying. Malcolm MacLeod, who made a third in the little party, had a spirit as firm and a heart as warm as Donald's own, and before the end of the week the Prince was clinging with the same affection to this new friend.

The wild and desolate island of Rasay offered the Prince a comparatively secure hiding-place, and the three MacLeods had both the will and the power to protect him, and to provide a reasonable amount of comfort for him. But a kind of restlessness seems to have come over the Prince at this time. It was only by being constantly on the move that he could escape from anxious and painful thoughts. Possibly he may have felt a little insecure in the midst of the Clan MacLeod (though he had met nowhere with more devotion than that of the three cousins); he certainly seems to have bestowed far more affection and confidence on Malcolm than on the other two.

On Thursday he insisted on starting for Skye, in spite of the entreaties of the young MacLeods, nor would he turn back when a storm broke and threatened to overwhelm them. It was night before they landed at Trotternish, a night such as had become familiar to the Prince, dark and chill and pouring with rain. They made for a byre on the property of Mr. Nicholson of Scorobeck. Young Rasay went on in front to see that no one was there. 'If there had been anyone in it, what would you have done?' he asked the Prince rather reproachfully; for Charles's self-will and foolhardiness must at times have been very trying to those who were risking life and estate for him. In the byre they lighted a fire, dried their clothes, and slept for some hours. The next day, Rona being away, the Prince asked Murdoch if he would accompany him into the country of the Mackinnons in the south of Skye (the old chief of that clan had been in the Prince's army, and Charles felt that he would be safe amongst them). Murdoch's wound prevented his undertaking such a journey—it was thirty miles over the wildest part of Skye—but Malcolm could go, and his cousin assured the Prince that he could nowhere find a more faithful and devoted servant. So the pair set out in the morning for their wild tramp.

To prevent discovery the Prince affected to be Malcolm's servant, walked behind him, and, further to disguise himself, put his periwig in his pocket and bound a dirty cloth round his head—a disguise specially calculated, one would think, to excite attention. The two young men talked frankly and confidentially, making great strides in friendship as they went along. Once a covey of partridges rose, and, with a true British instinct for sport at all hazards,[1] the Prince raised his gun and would have fired if Malcolm had not caught his arm. They were careful to pass through the hostile MacLeod country at night, and at break of day arrived in Strath, the country of the Mackinnons. Malcolm MacLeod had a sister married to a Mackinnon, an honest, warm-hearted fellow who had followed his chief and served as captain in the Prince's army. To his house they directed their steps; Mackinnon himself was away, but his wife received her brother and his friend with the utmost kindness. The Prince passed for a certain Lewis Caw, a surgeon's apprentice (who was actually 'skulking' in Skye at the time), and acted his part of humble retainer so well that poor Malcolm was quite embarrassed; and the rough servant-lass treated him with the contempt Highland servants seem to have for their own class, if 'Lowland bodies.' Both the tired travellers lay down to sleep, and when Malcolm awoke late in the afternoon he found the sweet-tempered Prince playing with Mrs. Mackinnon's little child. 'Ah, little man,' he cried, in a moment of forgetfulness, 'you may live to be a captain in my service yet.' 'Or you an old sergeant in his,' said the indignant nurse, jealous of her charge's position.

Next day Malcolm went out to meet his brother-in-law. He had absolute confidence in Mackinnon's faithfulness and loyalty, but he feared that his warm-hearted feelings might lead him into indiscretions which would betray the Prince; and in spite of all warnings Mackinnon could not restrain his tears when he saw his Prince under his roof in such a wretched plight.

It was important that Charles should be at once taken to the mainland, and John Mackinnon went off at noon to the house of the chief of the Mackinnons to borrow a boat. This old man was a fine type of a Highland gentleman. It was his daily—probably his only—prayer that he might die on the field of battle fighting for his king and country. He was simple-minded, brave, and faithful, and though now between sixty and seventy, as active and courageous as any young man. John had received injunctions

---

[1] Charles, about 1713, introduced golf into Italy, according to Lord Elcho.

not to betray the Prince's presence in the neighbourhood to the laird, but to keep such a piece of news from his chief was quite beyond honest John's powers. Nothing would restrain the old man from going off at once with his wife to pay their homage to the Prince. Nor would he hear of anyone conducting Charles to the mainland but himself.

At eight o'clock that night the little party embarked. The Prince took a most affecting farewell of Malcolm MacLeod. With courtly punctilio he sent a note to Donald Roy to tell of his safe departure, then pressed ten guineas—almost his last—on his friend's acceptance, smoked a last pipe with him, and finally presented him with the invaluable ' cutty.'

CHAPTER IV

ON THE MAINLAND

To understand the Prince's proceedings for the next few weeks it is necessary to have a clear idea of the country which was the scene of his wanderings. From Loch Hourn (which opens opposite Sleat in Skye) on the north down to Loch Shiel on the south a little group of wild and rugged peninsulas run out into the Atlantic, called respectively Knoydart, Morar, Arisaig, and Moidart. Between these deep narrow lochs run far inland. Loch Nevis lies between Knoydart and Morar; Loch Morar, a freshwater loch, cuts off the peninsula of the same name from Arisaig, and this again is separated from Moidart by Lochs Nanuagh and Aylort, and Loch Shiel separates the whole group from Ardnamurchan in the south. The wild, inaccessible nature of the country, the deep valleys and many rocky hollows in the hills offered many hiding-places; but a glance at the map will show that a vigilant enemy by stationing men of war in all the lochs and drawing a cordon of soldiers from the head of Loch Hourn to the head of Loch Shiel, could draw the net so tightly that escape would be nearly impossible.

In these first days of July, however, the search was still chiefly confined to the Long Island and Skye, and Charles got a clear start of his enemies. On July 5, in the early morning, he and his faithful Mackinnons landed at a place named Mallach on Loch Nevis, and spent the next three days in the open. They were in a good

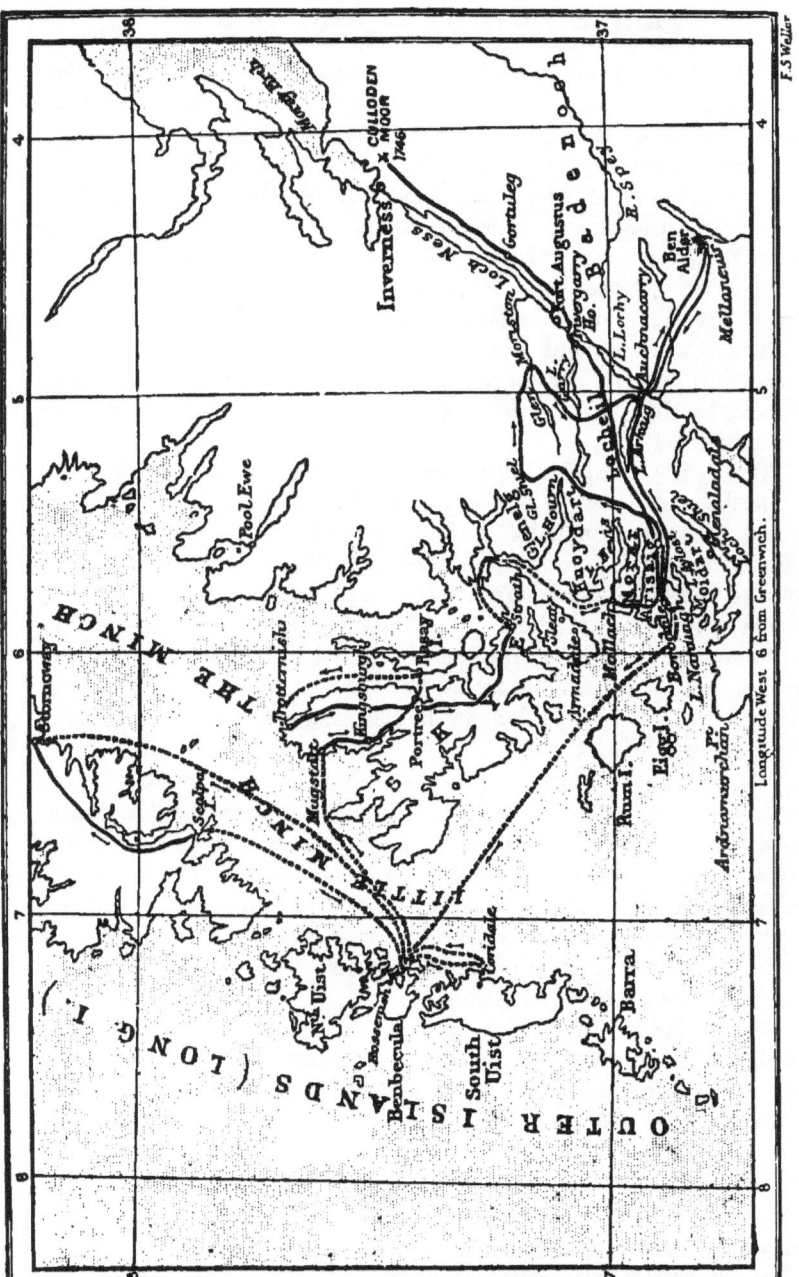

PRINCE CHARLIE'S WANDERINGS.

The black lines indicating land and the dotted lines sea journeys.

deal of perplexity as to their next movements, and when Charles learned that old Clanranald was staying in the neighbourhood, at the home of his kinsman Scothouse, he sent to ask his advice and help, expecting confidently to find the old faithful kindness that had helped him in Uist. But the old gentleman had had enough of danger and suffering in the Prince's cause; his son was a fugitive, his brother a prisoner, he himself was in hiding. The sudden appearance of Mackinnon startled him into a state of nervous terror, and he declared querulously that he could do no more nor knew anyone else who could give any help. Mackinnon returned indignant and mortified, but the Prince received the news philosophically, 'Well, Mr. Mackinnon, we must do the best we can for ourselves.'

It was the first rebuff he had met with; but a day or two later he found the same lukewarm spirit in Mr. Macdonald of Morar, a former friend. The poor man had had his house burnt over his head and was living with his family in a wretched hut, and probably thought that he had suffered enough for the cause. This desertion cut the Prince to the quick. 'I hope, Mackinnon,' he cried, addressing John, 'that you will not desert me too.' The old chief thought that the words were addressed to him. 'I will never leave your Royal Highness in the hour of danger,' he declared, with tears, and John's reply was no less fervent.

There was one house in the neighbourhood where the Prince could always count on a welcome whether he came at midnight, at cockcrow, or at noon, whether as a Prince on his way to win a crown or as a beggar with neither home nor hope. The hospitable house of Borodale was a mass of blackened ruins, but the laird— 'my kind old landlord,' as the Prince fondly called him—and his two sons had still strong hands, shrewd heads, and warm hearts ready for the Prince's service.

From Morar the Prince and the two Mackinnons walked through the summer night over the wildest mountain track and arrived at Borodale in the early morning. Old Angus was still in bed when they knocked at the door of the bothy where the family was living. He came to the door, wrapt in his blanket. When Mackinnon explained who it was that desired his hospitality, the old man's welcome came prompt and unhesitating. '*I* have brought him here,' said Mackinnon, 'and will commit him to *your* charge. I have done my duty, do you do yours.'

'I am glad of it,' said Angus, 'and shall not fail to take care of

him. I shall lodge him so securely that all the forces in Great
Britain shall not find him.'

So John Mackinnon, having done all he could, parted from the
Prince with the same affectionate sorrow that had marked the fare-
wells of all his faithful Highlanders. He was caught on his return to
Skye by the cruel Captain Scott, and five days later was brought
back to Lochnanuagh, a prisoner on board an English man-of-war.
Opposite the place where the ship cast anchor was a fissure in the

rock, and halfway up was what looked like a mere grassy bank. In
reality it was a small hut roofed with sods, so contrived that no
one unless he were in the secret would have suspected it of being
anything but a grassy slope. Here the Prince had spent the
preceding night, but as soon as the ship entered the loch he
betook himself to the hills. He was accompanied by old Borodale
and his son John—the young man who had been supposed to
have died at Culloden. A cousin of Borodale's, Macdonald of

Glenaladale, had always been a special friend of the Prince's. He joined him now in the wilds, resolved to share all his worst dangers, though he had to leave his wife and 'five weak pretty children' unprotected and living in a bothy, the only home the English soldiers had left them. The first plan these brave men concerted together was to carry the Prince into Lochiel's country, where young Clanranald had promised to provide him a hiding-place. On their way, however, they heard that a body of soldiers were approaching from Loch Arkaig, which completely blocked their way on that side. That same night old Borodale learnt that General Campbell with several ships was in Loch Nevis, Captain Scott was still in Lochnanuagh, and parties from these ships were searching every foot of ground in their neighbourhoods. At the same time troops had been landed at the head of Loch Hourn, and others simultaneously at the head of Loch Shiel. Between these two points the distance as the crow flies must be some twenty or five-and-twenty miles, but the wild mountainous nature of the country makes the actual distance far greater. In spite of all difficulties the Government troops in a few days had drawn a complete cordon from one point to the other. This cordon consisted of single sentinels planted within sight of each other who permitted no one to pass unchallenged. At night large fires were lighted, and every quarter of an hour patrolling parties passed from one to the other to see that all the sentinels were on the alert.

Charles's case was almost desperate. For several days he and his companions lived like hunted animals on the mountain-tops. They were frequently within sight of some camp of the enemy; more than once they had to go precipitately down one side of a hill because the soldiers were coming up the other. They changed their quarters at night, sometimes marching long miles merely to reach some mountain which having been searched the day before was less likely to be visited again. In the daytime the Prince could snatch a few hours of troubled sleep in some rocky hollow while the rest of the party kept guard. News of the enemy's movements was brought them occasionally by secret friends under cover of darkness, but even their approach was full of terror for the fugitives. Worst of all was their suffering from hunger. The soldiers devoured and destroyed what meagre stores the country could boast, and in spite of the generosity of the poorer clansmen no food could be had. For four days the whole party lived on a few handfuls of dry meal and some butter. On one occasion soldiers passed below their lair driving cattle. The Prince, who was starving, proposed to follow them, and ' lift ' some of the cattle in the night. His companions remonstrated, but he led the party himself, and secured the beef.[1] The guide, and indeed the leader of the little band, was a farmer, Donald Cameron of Glenpean. But for this man's daring courage and his intimate knowledge of the country the Prince must sooner or later have fallen into the hands of his enemies.

The circle was daily being drawn more closely round the prey, and daily the fear of starvation stared them in the face. Should they wait to die like driven deer or make one desperate effort to break through the toils that surrounded them, and either escape or die like men ? For brave men there could only be one answer to such a question. On the night of July 25 they determined to force their way through the cordon.

All that day the Prince had lain in closest hiding on a hill on the confines of Knoydart, not a mile from the chain of sentinels. He had slept some hours while two of the party had kept watch and the other two had gone and foraged for food, bringing back two dry cheeses as the result. (Old Borodale had gone back at this time ; the party consisted of his son John, Glenaladale and his brother, and Cameron of Glenpean.) All day parties of soldiers had been searching the neighbourhood, and now the sentinel fires were alight all along the line of defence. At nightfall the little band started, walking silently and rapidly up a mountain called Drumnachosi. The way was very steep, and the night very dark. Once crossing a little stream the Prince's foot slipped, he stumbled, and would have fallen down over a cliff had not Cameron caught one arm and Glenaladale the other and pulled him up. From the top of the hill they could see the sentinel fires close in front of them, and were near enough to hear the voices of the soldiers quite distinctly. Under cover of the friendly darkness they crept up another hill and came out opposite another fire. At a point midway between these two posts a mountain torrent had made a deep fissure on the side of a hill on the further side. Could they break through the line and reach this river-bed the overhanging banks, aided by the darkness of night, would conceal their figures, and following the stream they could cross over into wild broken

---

[1] The authority for this is an unpublished anecdote in Bishop Forbes's MS., *The Lyon in Mourning*.

country, where they could hide themselves. Donald Cameron, with a fine Highland gallantry, undertook to make trial of the way first. If he could reach the spot and return again to report 'all safe,' the rest of the party might make the attempt. It had all to be done in a quarter of an hour, for that was the interval at which the patrolling parties succeeded each other.

In dead silence they waited till the sentinels had past; then as stealthily and rapidly as a cat Cameron slipped down the hillside and disappeared into the darkness. The rest stood breathless, straining every nerve for the faintest sound ; no footfall or falling pebble broke the stillness, and in a few long, heavily-weighted minutes Cameron returned and whispered that all was well. It was two o'clock now and the darkness was growing thinner. They waited till the sentries had crossed again and had now their backs to the passage, then they all moved forward in perfect silence. Reaching the torrent, they sank on all fours and one after the other crept up the rocky bed without a sound. The dreaded cordon was passed, and in a short time they reached a place where they were completely hidden and could take a little much-needed rest.

Once clear of this chain of their enemies they turned northward to the Glenelg country. Their plan was to go through the Mackenzie's country to Poole Ewe, where they hoped to find a French vessel. But the next day they learned from a wayfaring man that the only French ship which had been there had left the coast. Seeing that that plan was fruitless, their next idea was to move eastward into the wilds of Inverness and wait there till the way should be clear for the Prince's joining Lochiel in Badenoch.

In Glen Sheil they parted with Cameron of Glenpean, and here too they had a curious adventure which might have proved seriously inconvenient to them. They had spent a whole hot August day hiding behind some rocks on a bare hillside, the midges had tormented them, and they were oppressed with thirst, but had not ventured from their hiding-place even to look for water. At sunset a boy appeared bringing quarts of goat's milk ; he was the son of a certain Macraw, a staunch though secret friend in the neighbourhood. Glenaladale at this time carried the fortune of the little party—some forty gold louis and a few shillings—in his sporran. He paid the lad for the milk, and in his hurry did not notice that he had dropped his purse. They had hardly gone an English mile before the loss was discovered, and Glenaladale insisted at all risks on going back to look for the purse. He and his cousin

did indeed find it lying at the expected place, but though some
shillings remained the louis were gone. It was midnight before
the indignant pair reached Macraw's house, and the family were
all asleep. They roused the master, however, and fairly told him
what had happened. No shadow of doubt seems to have crossed
the father's mind, no word of expostulation rose to his lips. ' Without a moment's delay he returned to the house, got hold of a rope
hanging there, and gripped his son by the arm in great passion,

saying, " You damned scoundrel, this instant get these poor gentlemen's money, or by the heavens I'll hang you to that very tree you
see there." The boy, shivering with fear, went instantly for the
money, which he had buried underground thirty yards from his
father's house.' This accident turned out most luckily for the
Prince. He and Glenaladale's brother while awaiting the other
two had hidden behind some rocks; shortly after they were hidden
they saw an officer and two soldiers *coming along the very path
they had intended to take.* But for the delay caused by their

H

companions going back they must have fallen into the hands of their enemies.

They now turned eastward, and after a long night's march found themselves in the wild tract of country called the Braes of Glenmoriston.

Here Charles was to find a new set of friends, different indeed from the chivalrous Kingsburgh and the high-bred Lady Margaret, but men who were as staunch and incorruptible as any of his former friends. These were the famous 'Seven Men of Glenmoriston,' men who had served in the Prince's army, and who now lived a wild, lawless life among the mountains, at feud with everything that represented the existing law and order. They have been described as a robber band, but that title is misleading. They were rather a small remnant of irreconcilable rebels who had vowed undying enmity and revenge against Cumberland and his soldiers. And indeed there was ample excuse for their hatred and violence in the cruelties they saw practised all round them. Sixty of their clansmen after surrendering themselves had been shipped off to the colonies, all their own possessions and those of their neighbours had been seized, and friends and kinsfolk had been brutally put to death.

Swooping down like mountain eagles on detached bands of soldiers, these seven men wreaked instant vengeance on oppressors and informers, and carried off arms and baggage in the face of larger bodies of the enemy. To these men, ignorant, reckless, and lawless, Charles unhesitatingly confided his person, a person on whose head a sum of thirty thousand pounds was set.

Four of these men were in a cave, Coraghoth, in the Braes of Glenmoriston, when Glenaladale brought Charles to see them. They had expected to see young Clanranald, and as soon as they saw the Prince one of their number recognised him, but had the presence of mind to address him as an old acquaintance by the name of 'MacCullony.' When the four knew who their guest really was, they bound themselves to be faithful to him by the dreadful Highland oath, praying ' that their backs might be to God, and their faces to the devil, and that all the curses the Scriptures do pronounce might come upon them and their posterity if they did not stand firm to the Prince in the greatest danger.'

For about three weeks Charles shared the life of these outlaws, sleeping in caves and holes of the earth, living on the wild deer of their shooting and the secret gifts of the peasantry. They did not understand his English, but the Prince was beginning to pick up a little Gaelic. He was able at least to improve their cooking and reprove their swearing, two services they liked afterwards to recall. Here too, as elsewhere on his wanderings, the Prince gained the hearts of all his followers by his gracious gaiety and plucky endurance of hardships. In the beginning of August his hopes had again turned to Poole Ewe, but learning for a second time that no French ship could land on the closely guarded coast, he and his friends determined to remain in the northern straths of Inverness-shire till the Government troops should withdraw from the Great Glen—the chain of lakes which now forms the Caledonian Canal—and thus leave the way clear into Badenoch, where Lochiel and Macpherson of Cluny were hiding.

A curious incident is supposed to have helped the Prince at this time. There had been among his Life Guards a handsome youth named Roderick Mackenzie, son of a jeweller in Edinburgh, who in face and figure was startlingly like the Prince. This lad was actually 'skulking' among the Braes of Glenmoriston at the time when the Prince was surrounded in Knoydart. A party of soldiers tracked him to a hut, which they surrounded. Flight was impossible, and the poor boy stood at bay. As he fell beneath their sword-thrusts he cried out, 'Villains, ye have slain your King.' Whether these words were a curious last flash of vanity, or whether he intended to serve the Prince by a generous act of imposture, can never be known. The soldiers at any rate believed that they had secured the prize. They carried off Mackenzie's head with them to Fort Augustus, and the authorities seem for some time to have been under the impression that it was indeed that of the Prince. Possibly it was owing to this that in the middle of August the Government rather relaxed their vigilance along the Great Glen. Charles was eager to press at once into Badenoch, but the wary outlaws would only consent to taking him to the Lochiel country, between Loch Arkaig, Loch Lochy, and Loch Garry. They travelled chiefly by night; the season was very wet, and the rivers were in flood, and they had to cross the River Garry Highland fashion in a line, with each man's arm on his neighbour's shoulder, for the water was running breast-high.

At this time the Prince's condition was as bad as at any period of his wanderings. His clothes were of the coarsest, and *they* were in rags. Lady Clanranald's six good shirts had long since disappeared ; it was as much as he could do to have a clean shirt once a fortnight. The provisions they carried were reduced to one peck of meal. In this state did the Prince arrive in the familiar country round Loch Arkaig. It was a year almost to the day since he had passed through that very country elate and hopeful at the head of his brave Macdonalds and Camerons. He was now a fugitive, ill-fed, ill-clad, with a price on his head ; the only thing that was un-changed was the faithful devotion of his Highlanders.

Cameron of Clunes and Macdonald of Lochgarry, or Lochgarie, though they were themselves ' skulking,' received the Prince with the utmost kindness and found a hiding-place for him in a hut in a wood at the south side of Loch Arkaig. Here the outlaws left him ; only one of their number, Patrick Grant, remained till the Prince should be supplied with money to reward their faithful service. From this place, also, John Macdonald and Glenaladale's brother returned to the coast, where they were to keep a careful look-out and to send the Prince news of any French ship which might appear.

Glenaladale still remained, but the Prince's thoughts were turn-ing more and more towards Badenoch, where his friend Lochiel was in comparatively secure hiding.

Among all the gallant gentlemen who risked life and estate in this rising there is no figure more attractive than that of the ' Gentle Lochiel.' He had for years before the rebellion been the mainstay of the Jacobite party. No man in the Highlands carried so much weight as he, partly from his position, but more from his talents and the charm of his character. ' Wise ' and ' gentle ' are the words that were applied to him, and with all the qualities of a high-bred gentleman he combined the simpler virtues of the High-land clansman—faithfulness, courage, and a jealous sense of per-sonal honour. From the very beginning he had seen the folly of the rising. But when he had failed to convince Charles of its hopelessness, he had thrown himself into the movement as if it had been of his own devising. Never did he afterwards reproach Charles by word or look for the ill-fated result.

He and his cousin, Macpherson of Cluny, were at this time hiding among the recesses of Benalder. The road to Inverness ran by within a few miles, and at a little distance lay Lord Loudoun's camp, but so great was the devotion of the clansmen, so admirable their caution and secrecy, that the English commander had not the slightest suspicion that the two most important Jacobite fugitives had for three months been in hiding so near to him.

Lochiel had been wounded in the feet at Culloden, and his lameness as well as his dangerous position prevented his going to look for the Prince. He had two brothers, one a doctor and the other a clergyman, both accomplished and bold men, who had also been involved in the Jacobite rebellion. Towards the end of August, news having come to Benalder that the Prince was living near Auchnacarry under the protection of Cameron of Clunes, the two Cameron brothers set off secretly for that country. The Prince with a son of Clunes and the faithful outlaw Patrick Grant were at this time living in a hut in a wood close to Loch Arkaig. It was early on the morning of August 25, the Prince and young Clunes were asleep in the hut, while Patrick Grant kept watch. He must have got drowsy, for waking with a start he saw a party of men approaching. He rushed into the hut and roused the Prince and his companion. Charles had long lived in expectation of such moments. He kept his presence of mind completely, decided that it was too late to fly, and prepared to defend himself. The fowling-pieces were loaded and got into position, and they very nearly received their friends with a volley. Dr. Cameron in his narrative describes the Prince's appearance thus : ' He was barefoot; had an old black kilt coat on and philibeg and waistcoat, a dirty shirt and a long red beard, a gun in his hand and a pistol and dirk at his side ; still he was very cheerful and in good health.'

Another week they all waited in the neighbourhood of Auchnacarry (the ruined home of the Lochiels). At last a message reached them from Benalder that the passes were free and that they might safely try to join Lochiel. Having parted with his devoted friend Glenaladale, who returned to the coast, the Prince, with Dr. Cameron and Lochgarry, arrived on August 30 at Mellaneuir, at the foot of Benalder. People in hiding have no means of discriminating their friends from their enemies at a little distance. Lochiel seeing a considerable party approaching believed that he was discovered and determined to make a good fight for it. He as narrowly missed shooting Charles as Charles had missed shooting Dr. Cameron the week before. When, however, he recognised the figure in the coarse brown coat, the shabby kilt, and the rough red beard, he hobbled to the door and wanted to receive the Prince on his knees. ' My dear Lochiel,' remonstrated Charles as he embraced him, ' you don't know who may be looking down from these hills.'

In the hut there was a sufficiency of mutton, beef sausages,

bacon, butter, cheese, &c., and an anker of whisky, and the Prince
was almost overwhelmed by such an excess of luxury. ' Now,
gentlemen,' he said with a cheerful air, ' now I live *like a Prince.*'
Charles's wardrobe was as usual most dilapidated, and Cluny's three
sisters set at once to work to make him a set of six shirts with
their own fair hands, doubtless sewing the most passionate loyalty
and infinite regret into their ' seams.'

The hiding-place where the Prince was now concealed was a
very curious hut contrived by Cluny in one of the inmost recesses
of the hills. It was called ' The Cage,' and was placed in a little
thicket on the rocky slope of a hill. The walls were formed by
actual growing trees with stakes planted between them, the whole
woven together by ropes of heather and birch. Till you were close
to the hut it looked merely like a thick clump of trees and bushes.
The smoke escaped along the rocks, and the stone being of a bluish
colour it could easily pass unnoticed. This hut could only hold
six persons at a time, so the party generally divided in this way:
one man cooked the food, four played cards, and the last man looked
on at the others and possibly smoked !

Probably they played cards and talked and jested over the daily
needs and hardships, and spoke little of the disastrous times that
lay behind them, or the doubtful hopes that lay before them.   Fearing lest the Prince might have to remain in hiding all winter the
ingenious Cluny began to fit up a subterranean dwelling, thickly
boarded up, where the party would have been in safety and shelter.
But in the meantime no efforts were lacking to find a means of
escape. Lochiel's brother, the clergyman, a man of great prudence,
went secretly to Edinburgh, and there procured a ship and sent it
round to a port on the East coast to await the Prince. Succour,
however, had come from another quarter; it was known to the
Prince and his followers that a certain Colonel Warren was fitting
out a couple of ships in France for the purpose of bringing off the
Prince, and daily they expected news of their arrival.   On
September 6 two ships, *L'Heureux* and *La Princesse*, appeared at
Lochnanuagh.   Old Borodale and his two sons immediately fled
to the hills, leaving a faithful servant to find out and report to them
who the strangers might be.   After nightfall, twelve French officers
came to the hut where they were hiding and told their errand.
Information was at once sent to Glenaladale, who undertook to go
to Auchnacarry and send on the news through Cameron of Clunes,
he himself not knowing where the Prince was hiding.   Any delay,

even of a few hours, might be fatal, as the presence of the French ships must sooner or later become known to the authorities at Fort Augustus. To his dismay Glenaladale failed to find Clunes, and only by an accident met with an old woman, who directed him to the place where the latter was hiding. A messenger was at once despatched, and he, happening by a curious chance to meet with Cluny and Dr. Cameron on a dark night in Badenoch, gave them his message, and an express was at once sent to the Cage. On September 13, at one in the morning, the party—which now included Cluny, Lochiel, Macpherson of Breakachie, and some others of the Prince's more important followers—set off for the coast. They travelled by night, remaining in concealment by day,

but so lonely was the country, so recklessly high were the Prince's spirits, that one whole day he amused himself by flinging up caps into the air and shooting at them.

Again he passed through the well-known country round Loch Arkaig, past Auchnacarry, the home of the Lochiels, which was lying in ruins, over the rugged hills where he had been hunted like a wild creature a few weeks before, down to the familiar waters of Lochnanuagh, back to the warm-hearted household of Borodale.

A considerable number of Jacobite gentlemen who had lain for months in hiding had been drawn to Lochnanuagh by the report of the landing of the French ships; amongst these were young Clanranald, Glenaladale, and Macdonald of Daleby. On the Prince's ship there sailed with him Lochgarry, John Roy Stuart, Dr.

Cameron, and Lochiel. 'The gentlemen as well as commons were seen to weep, though they boasted of being soon back with an irresistible force,' says the newspaper of the day. For the greater part they never came back, never saw again the homes they loved so well. Most were to spend a life of hope deferred and of desperate longings for home, as dependents on a foreign Court. Dr. Cameron was ten years later taken prisoner in London and executed, the last man who suffered as a rebel; Lochiel died two years after he left Scotland, a heart-broken exile. 'Weep ye not for the dead, neither bemoan him; but weep sore for him that goeth away, for he shall return no more nor see his native country.' [1]

---

[1] The authorities are Chambers's *Jacobite Memoirs*, selected from the MS. *Lyon in Mourning* ; Chambers's *History of the Rising of* 1745 ; Macdonald of Glenaladale's manuscript, published in *Blackwood's Magazine* ; Ewald's *History of Prince Charles Edward*, and the contemporary pamphlets anonymously published by Dr. Burton on information derived from Bishop Forbes, who collected it at first hand. Fastened on the interior of the cover of the *Lyon in Mourning* is a shred of the flowered calico worn by the Prince in disguise.

TWO GREAT MATCHES

THE University matches, between the elevens of Oxford and Cambridge, are the most exciting that are played at Lord's. The elevens have been so equal that neither University is ever more than one or two victories ahead of its opponent. The players are at their best for activity and strength, and the fielding is usually the finest that can anywhere be seen. But, of all University matches, the most famous are those of 1870 and of 1875, for these were the most closely contested.

In 1870 Cambridge had won for three years running. They had on their side Mr. Yardley, one among the three best gentlemen bats who ever played, the others being Dr. Grace and Mr. Alan Steel. In 1869, when Cambridge won by 58 runs, Mr. Yardley had only made 19 and 0. Mr. Dale and Mr. Money were the other pillars of Cambridge batting : they had Mr. Thornton too, the hardest of hitters, who hit over the pavilion (with a bat which did not drive !) when he played for Eton against Harrow. On the Oxford side were Mr. Tylecote (E. F. S.), a splendid bat, Mr. Ottaway, one of the most finished bats of his day, and Mr. Pauncefote. The Oxford team was unlucky in its bowling, as Mr. Butler had strained his arm. In one University match, Mr. Butler took all ten wickets in one innings. He was fast, with a high delivery, and wickets were not so good then as they are now. Mr. Francis was also an excellent bowler, not so fast as Mr. Butler; and Mr. Belcher, who bowled with great energy, but did not excel as a bat, was a useful man. For Cambridge, Mr. Cobden bowled fast, Mr. Ward was an excellent medium pace bowler, Mr. Money's slows were sometimes fortunate, and Mr. Bourne bowled slow round. Cambridge went in first, and only got 147. Mr. Yardley fell for 2, being caught by Mr. Butler off Mr. Francis. Mr. Scott's 45 was the largest score, and Mr. Thornton contributed 17, while Mr. Francis and Mr. Belcher divided the wickets. Oxford was only 28 runs better than Cam-

bridge, so that you might call it anybody's match. A good stand
was made for the first wicket, Mr. Fortescue getting 35, and Mr.
Hadow 17, but there was no high scoring. Mr. Butler got 18, which
is not a bad score for a bowler, but Mr. Stewart and Mr. Belcher,
who followed him, got ducks, and clearly the tail was not strong in
batting. The beginning of the Cambridge second innings was most
flattering to Oxford. When the fifth wicket fell, Cambridge had
but 40 runs, or twelve 'on.'

Tobin and Money, Fryer and Scott had made but 8 among them,

but Dale was in, and Yardley joined him. Mr. Dale was playing in
perfect style, and he needed to do so, for Mr. Francis was bowling
his best. Then came an hour and a half, or so, of sorrow for
Oxford. Mr. Butler was tried, and bowled eight overs for 8 runs,
but his arm was hurt, and he had to go off. He got Mr. Thornton's
wicket, but Oxford were playing, as Tom Sayers fought, with a
broken arm. Seven bowlers were put on, but the end of it was
that, after making the first 100 recorded in these matches, Mr.
Yardley sent a hard hit to Mr. Francis, who caught and bowled
him. Mr. Dale was splendidly caught at leg by Mr. Ottaway, off

Mr. Francis, with one hand over the ropes. He got 67 ; there was but one other double figure, Mr. Thornton's 11.

Oxford had to make 178 to win, and 178 is never easy to get, especially in a University match, where *so much depends on it*, and men are often nervous, as you shall see. Mr. Hadow came to grief, but Mr. Ottaway and Mr. Fortescue were not nervous bats. Mr. Ward bowled beautifully, but they got 44 and 69; it was 72 for one wicket, and Oxford were buoyant. At 86, however, the second wicket fell, and E. F. S. joined Mr. Ottaway. He put on 29, and Ottaway's defence was like a stone wall. Finally Mr. Ward bowled Mr. Tylecote; 25 to get and seven wickets to get them. It seemed all over but shouting. Another wicket fell for 1 ; 24 to get, and six wickets to fall. Mr. Hill came in, and played like a printed book, while Mr. Ottaway was always there. He played a ball to short leg, and Mr. Fryer held it so low down that Mr. Ottaway appealed. I dare say Oxford men in the pavilion distinctly saw that ball touch the ground, but the umpire did not; 17 to get, and four wickets to fall; but the last two wickets had scored exactly nothing in the first innings. But Mr. Francis could bat, and he stayed while Mr. Hill made 12, when he was l. b. w. to Ward, for a single. Four runs to get, and three wickets to fall! 'Mr. Charles Marsham's face wore a look that his friends know well.' Mr. Butler came in; he scored well in the first innings, and he could hit. Then came a bye. Four to get and three wickets to fall. Mr. Hill hit the next square, good for a 4, but Mr. Bourne got at it, and only a single was run. Three to get and three wickets to fall. *We did not get them !* Mr. Cobden, who had not done much, took the ball. Mr. Hill made a single to cover point. The next ball, to Mr. Butler, was well up on the off stump. Mr. Butler drove at it, Mr. Bourne caught it, and Mr. Belcher walked in, 'rather pale,' says Mr. Lyttelton, and if so, it was unusual. Mr. Belcher was of a ruddy countenance. He was yorked! he took a yorker for a half volley. Let us pity Mr. Stewart. If he could escape that one ball, the odds were that Mr. Hill would make the runs next over. Mr. Pauncefote had told Mr. Stewart to keep his bat immovable in the block-hole, but—he did not. Cobden scattered his bails to the breezes, 'and smash went Mr. Charles Marsham's umbrella against the pavilion brickwork.' Cambridge had won by two.

This is called Cobden's year, and will be so called while cricket

is played. But, in fact, Mr. Ward had taken six wickets for 29,
and these were all the best bats.

Mr. Butler's revenge came next year. He took fifteen wickets,
and made the winning hit. Oxford's revenge came in 1875. In
1874 Cambridge was terribly beaten. They went in on a good
wicket. Mr. Tabor, first man in, got 52, when a shower came. The
first ball after the shower, Mr. Tabor hit at a dropping ball of Mr.
Lang's, and was bowled. The whole side were then demolished by
Mr. Lang and Mr. Ridley, for 109, and 64 second innings, while
Oxford got 265 first innings. In 1876 Oxford had Mr. Webbe, an
admirable bat, as he is still; Mr. Lang, who had been known to
score; Mr. Ridley, a cricketer of the first class; Mr. Royle, the finest
field, with Mr. Jardine, ever seen; Mr. Game, who had not quite
come into his powers as a hitter, and Mr. Grey Tylecote, a good all-
round man; also Mr. Pulman, a sterling cricketer, and Mr. Buckland,
a very useful player all round. Cambridge had Mr. George Longman,
who could play anything but Mr. Ridley's slows; Mr. Edward
Lyttelton, one of the prettiest and most spirited bats in the world;
Mr. A. P. Lucas, whom it were superfluous to praise; Mr. Sims, a
hard hitter; Mr. W. J. Patterson, a renowned bat, and others. In
bowling, Oxford had Mr. Ridley, whose slows were rather fast and
near the ground. Being as tall as Mr. Spofforth, and following his
ball far up the pitch, Mr. Ridley was alarming to the nervous
batsman. He fielded his own bowling beautifully. Mr. Lang was
a slow round-arm bowler with a very high delivery, and a valuable
twist from either side. Mr. Buckland was afterwards better known
as a bowler; Mr. Royle could also deliver a dangerous ball; the fast
bowler was Mr. Foord Kelcey, but he, again, was lame, through an
accident to his foot. For Cambridge Mr. Sharpe and Mr. Sims
bowled. Lang and Webbe went to the wicket for Oxford, and made
a masterly stand, the ball being cut and driven to the ropes in all
directions. Mr. Webbe got 55, Mr. Lang 45, while Mr. Ridley contributed 21, Mr. Pulman 25, and Mr. Buckland 22. The whole
score was 200, 86 for the first wicket. Mr. Longman's 40 was the
best score for Cambridge, and Mr. Edward Lyttelton got 23; total
163. Mr. Lang got five wickets for 35, Mr. Ridley, Mr. Buckland,
and Mr. Foord Kelcey divided the other four. In the second
Oxford innings Mr. Sharpe got six wickets for 66, and the whole
score was but 137, in which Mr. Pulman's 30 was very useful; Mr.
Royle, Mr. Game, and Mr. Webbe got 21, 22, and 21, and Mr. Grey
Tylecote, not out, contributed an invaluable 12. The tail of the

THE BALL HIT THE MIDDLE STUMP

Cambridge side made 14 among them in the first innings, not an assortment of duck's eggs. Cambridge went in, with 175 to get, much like Oxford in 1870. An over was bowled before seven o'clock, and resulted in a four to leg. Sharpe and Hamilton, who went in last, first innings, went in first in the second, to avoid losing a good bat in the five minutes before drawing stumps. One doubts if it was worth Mr. Ridley's while to insist on that one over, but such is the letter of the law. The two victims, in any case, played rarely, Mr. Sharpe making 29 and Mr. Hamilton 11. Mr. Lucas, however, was bowled by Mr. Buckland for 5. Two for 26. Mr. Longman came in and drove off Mr. Lang and Mr. Ridley. Mr. Royle then took the ball, a fast change-bowler. He bowled three maidens, and then settled Mr. Sharpe (at 65), Mr. Blacker (at 67), and Mr. Longman at 76 (for 23), with a fine breaking shooter such as you seldom see now. Twenty years ago a large percentage of balls shot dead. Mr. Greenfield and Mr. Edward Lyttelton stuck together.

At 97, an awful yell went up; mid-on had missed Mr. Lyttelton, a low hard catch, but one which he would have taken nine times in ten. At 101, Mr. Campbell caught Mr. Greenfield off Mr. Royle, six down and 70 to get. Then Mr. Sims came in, and another yell was heard. Mid-on had given Mr. Lyttelton another let-off, an easy thing he might have held in his mouth. Mid-on wished that the earth would open and swallow him. Presently Mr. Lyttelton hit Mr. Buckland a beautiful skimming smack to square leg. Mr. Webbe was standing deeper, but, running at full speed along the ropes, sideways to the catch, he held it low down—a repetition of what he did unto Mr. Lyttelton when they played for Harrow and Eton. Mr. Lyttelton had scored 20, but not in his best manner. There were now three wickets to fall for 60; Oxford seemed to have the advantage. Sims and Patterson had added 14 (40 to win), when a heavy shower came down, lasted for an hour and a half, and left Oxford with a wet ball and a slippery ground. The rain, which favoured Oxford in 1874, when Cambridge collapsed, was now on the Cambridge side. Mr. Sims was determined to knock the runs off by a forcing game, and these were the right tactics. Then Ridley went on, and his first slow bowled Mr. Patterson clean. Mr. Macan came in, and got a single (13 to win). Then Mr. Sims hit Mr. Ridley over his head to the ropes for 4 (9 to win). Mr. Lang went on for Mr. Royle, a leg bye followed, and then a no-ball (7 to win). Mr. Lang then, in a moment of despair, as unusual measures were needed, bowled a full pitch right at Mr. Sims's head. Mr. Sims, naturally concluding that two more hits would finish the match, hit at it as hard as he could. Mr. Pulman was standing by the ropes ' in the country ' and the ball soared towards him ; would it cross the ropes ? would Pulman reach it ; he had a long way to run ? He reached it, he held it, and back went Mr. Sims. There remained Mr. Smith, in the same historical position as Mr. Belcher. There were six runs to get, and Mr. Macan, his companion, a good bat, was not yet settled. Some one in the pavilion said, 'His legs are trembling, Oxford wins.' Mr. Smith, unlike Mr. Belcher, stopped two of Mr. Ridley's slows, but not with enthusiasm. To the third he played slowly forward, the ball hit the middle stump, and Oxford won by six runs.

There was also a very good match in 1891. Cambridge was far the better team, and went in, second innings, for a small score. But Mr. Berkeley (left-hand medium) bowled so admirably that there were only two wickets to fall for the last run. Mr. Woods, however, was not nervous, and hit the first ball he received for 4 to the ropes. Still, I am inclined to think that, in these three matches, the bowling of Mr. Berkeley was the best, for he had very little encouragement, whereas, with 178 or so to get, a bowler has a good chance, and is on his mettle.

The moral is, don't poke about in your block-hole, but hit, and, when you bowl in an emergency, aim at getting wickets by any means, rather than at keeping down runs.

THE STORY OF KASPAR HAUSER

ON May 28, 1828, the town of Nuremberg, in Bavaria, presented a singularly deserted appearance, as it was Whit-Monday, and most of the inhabitants were spending their holiday in the country. A cobbler, who lived in Umschlitt Square, was an exception to the general rule, but towards four o'clock he, too, thought that he would take a stroll outside the city walls. When he came out of his door his curiosity was excited by a strange figure, which was leaning, as

if unable to support itself, against a wall near, and uttering a moaning sound. The figure was that of a young man of about seventeen, dressed in a grey riding suit, and wearing a pair of dilapidated boots; he held a letter in one hand.

The cobbler's curiosity led him to approach the strange figure, which moaned some incoherent sounds, and held out the letter in its hand. This was addressed 'To the Captain of the 4th

I

squadron of the 6th regiment of dragoons now stationed at Nuremberg'; and, as he lived quite near, the cobbler thought the surest
way of gratifying his own curiosity was to take the stranger
there. The poor creature stumbled and shuffled along behind his
guide, and reached the captain's house quite worn out. The
captain was not at home, but his servant, pitying the sufferings of
the stranger, gave him a sack of straw to lie on in the stable, and
brought him some bread and meat and beer. The meat and the beer
he would not touch, but ate the bread greedily and drank some
water ; he then fell fast asleep. Towards eight o'clock the captain
came home, and was told of his strange visitor, and of the letter he
had brought with him. This letter was written in a feigned hand,
and said that the writer, a poor labourer with ten children, had
received the boy in 1812, and had kept him shut up in his house for
sixteen years, not allowing him to see or know anything ; that he
could keep him no longer, and so sent him to the captain, who
could make a soldier of him, hang him, or put him up the chimney,
just as he chose. He added that the boy knew nothing and could
tell nothing, but was quick at learning. Enclosed was a letter
giving the date of the boy's birth (April 30, 1812), and purporting
to be written by the mother; but the writing, paper, and ink all
showed that the two letters were by the same person.

The captain could make nothing of this mysterious letter, but
went to the stable, where he found the stranger still asleep. After
many pushes, kicks, and thumps he awoke. When asked his
name and where he came from, he made some sounds, which were
at last understood to be, ' Want to be a soldier, as father was ; '
' Don't know,' and ' Horse home.' These sentences he repeated
over and over again like a parrot, and at last the captain decided
to send his new recruit to the police office. Here he was asked his
name, where he came from, &c., &c., but the result of the police
inspector's questioning was the same : the stranger repeated his
three sentences, and at last, in despair of getting any sensible reply
from him, he was put into a cell in the west tower of the prison
where vagrants were kept. This cell he shared with another
prisoner, a butcher boy, who was ordered to watch him carefully, as
the police naturally suspected him of being an impostor. He slept
soundly through the night and woke at sunrise. He spent the
greater part of the day sitting on the floor taking no notice of
anything, but at last the gaoler gave him a sheet of paper and a
pencil to play with. These he seized with pleasure and carried

them off to a seat; nor did he stop writing until he had covered the paper with letters and syllables, arranged just as they would be in a copy-book. Among the letters were three complete words, 'Kaspar Hauser,' and 'reiter' (horse soldier). 'Kaspar Hauser'

was evidently his name, though he did not recognise it when called by it.

The news of the strange arrival spread through the city. The guard-house, where he spent part of the day, was thronged by a curious crowd, anxious to see this strange creature, who looked at things without seeing them, who could not bear a strong light, who loathed any food but bread and water, and who, parrot-like, repeated a couple of phrases which he evidently did not understand, and one word, ' horse,' to which he seemed to attach some meaning. What they saw was a youth of about seventeen, with fair hair and blue eyes, the lower part of his face slightly projecting like a monkey's. He was four feet nine inches in height, broad-shouldered, with tiny hands and delicate little feet, which had never worn shoes nor been put to their natural use, for the soles were as soft as a baby's. He was dressed in grey riding-breeches, a round jacket, which had been made out of a frock-coat by cutting off the skirts, and wore a round felt hat bound with red leather. In his pockets were some rags, some tracts, a rosary, and a paper of gold sand.

Everyone who saw him and watched him came to the same conclusion, that his mind was that of a child of two or three, while his body was nearly grown up; and yet he was not half-witted, because he immediately began to pick up words and phrases, had a wonderful memory, and never forgot a face he had once seen, or the name which belonged to it. During the next two or three weeks he spent part of every day in the guard-room ; part with the family of the gaoler, whose children taught him to talk and to walk as they did their own baby sister. He was not afraid of anything ; swords were whirled round his head without his paying any attention to them ; he stretched out his hand to the flame of a lighted candle, and cried when it burnt him, and when he saw his face in a looking-glass, looked behind it for the other person. He was particularly pleased when anything bright or glittering was given to him. Whenever this happened he called out ' Horse, horse,' and made signs as if he wanted to hang it on to the neck of something. At last one of the policemen gave him a wooden horse, when his happiness was complete, and he spent hours sitting on the floor playing with this horse and the dozens of horses which were given to him by his visitors as soon as they heard of his liking for them.

Six or seven weeks passed in this way, and all this time the town council were discussing what they would do with him. At last they decided to adopt him as the ' Child of Nuremberg,' and to have him properly cared for and taught, so that, if possible, something of his past might be learned. He was taken away from the prison and put under the charge of Professor Daumer, whose interest in the youth led him to undertake the difficult task of developing his mind so that it might fit his body. The burgomaster issued a notice to the inhabitants that in future they would not be allowed to see Kaspar Hauser at all hours of the day, and that the police had orders to interfere if the curiosity of visitors led them to annoy Dr. Daumer and his household. He entered Dr. Daumer's house on July 18, 1828, and during the next five months made such astonishing progress that the delight of his teacher knew no bounds. In order to satisfy public curiosity the burgomaster published, in July, a short account of Hauser's previous life, gleaned from him by careful questioning. It was to this effect :—

'He neither knows who he is nor where he came from, for it was only at Nuremberg that he came into the world. He always lived in a hole, where he sat on straw on the ground ; he never heard a sound, nor saw any vivid light. He awoke and he slept, and awoke again ; when he awoke he found a loaf of bread and a pitcher of water beside him. Sometimes the water tasted nasty and then he fell asleep again, and when he woke up found he had a clean shirt on ; he never saw the face of the man who came to him. He had two wooden horses and some ribbons to play with ; was never ill, never unhappy in his hole; once only the man struck him with a stick for making too much noise with his horses. One day the man came into his room and put a table over his feet ; something white lay on the table, and on this the man made black marks with a pencil which he put into his fingers. This the man did several times, and when he was gone Kaspar imitated what he had done. At last he taught him to stand and to walk, and finally carried him out of his hole. Of what happened next Kaspar had no very clear idea, until he found himself in Nuremberg with the letter in his hand.'

At first sight this story seems quite impossible, but it is borne out by two or three things. Kaspar's legs were deformed in just such a way as would happen in the case of a person who had spent years sitting on the ground; he never walked properly to the end, and had great difficulty in getting upstairs. His feet showed no signs of use, except the blisters made by his boots and his walk to Nuremberg ; he could see in the dark easily and disliked light ; and finally, for several months after he came to Nuremberg, he refused to eat anything but bread and water, and was, in fact, made quite ill by the smell of meat, beer, wine, or milk.

For the first four months of his stay with Daumer, his senses of sight, taste, hearing, and smell were very acute. He had got past the stage in which he disliked light, and could now see much further than most people by day, without, however, losing his power of seeing in the dark; at the same time he could not distinguish between a thing and a picture of that thing, and could not for a long time judge distances at all, for he saw everything flat. His favourite colours were réd and yellow; black and green he particularly disliked; everything ugly was called green. He could not be persuaded that a ball did not roll because it wished to do so, or that his top did not spin of its own accord. For a long time he saw no reason why animals should not behave like human beings, and was much annoyed because the cat refused to sit up at table and to eat with its paws, blaming its disobedience in not doing as it was told. He further thought that a cow which had lain down in the road would do well to go home to bed if it were tired. His sense of smell was very keen, painfully so, in fact, for he was made quite ill by the smell of the dye in his clothes, the smell of paper, and of many other things which other people do not notice at all; while the smell of a sweep a hundred yards off on the other side of the road upset him for a week. On the other hand, he could distinguish the leaves of trees by their smell.

By November he had made sufficient progress to make it possible for Dr. Daumer to teach him other things besides the use of his senses: he was encouraged to write letters and essays, to use his hands in every way, to draw, to make paper-models, to dig in the garden, where he had a little plot of ground with his name in mustard and cress; in fact, to use his lately acquired knowledge. The great difficulty was to persuade him to eat anything but bread and water, but by slow degrees he learned to eat different forms of farinaceous food, gruel, bread and milk, rice, &c., into which a little gravy and meat was gradually introduced. By the following May he could eat meat without being made ill by it, but never drank anything but water, except at breakfast, when he had chocolate.

For the next eleven months he lived a happy, simple life with his friend and tutor, who mentions, however, that the intense acuteness of his senses was gradually passing away, but that he had still the charming, obedient, child-like nature which had won all hearts. In the summer, public interest was aroused by the news that Kaspar Hauser was writing his life, and the paper was eagerly looked forward to. All went well until October 17, when Kaspar was discovered senseless in a cellar under Dr. Daumer's house, with a wound in his forehead. He was carried upstairs and put to bed, when he kept on moaning, 'Man! man!—tell mother (Mrs. Daumer)—tell professor—man beat me—black sweep.'

For some days he was too ill to give any account of his wound, but at last said, that he had gone downstairs and was suddenly attacked by a man with a black face,[1] who hit him on the head; that he fell down, and when he got up the man was gone; that he went to look for Mrs. Daumer, and, as he could not find her, finally hid in the cellar to be quite safe. After this murderous attack it was no longer safe to leave him in Dr. Daumer's house, so when well again he was removed to the house of one of the magistrates, and constantly guarded by two policemen, without whom he never went out. He was not very happy here, and after some months was put under the charge of Herr von Tucher (June 1830), with whom he remained for eighteen months. At first the arrangement answered admirably; he was happy in his new home, his only trouble being that he was sent to the grammar school and put into one of the upper forms, where he had to learn Latin, a task which proved too hard for his brain. By this time his face had quite lost the brutish character it had when he came to Nuremberg, and its expression was pleasant, though rather sad. Unfortunately for himself, he was one of the sights of Nuremberg, was always introduced to any stranger of distinction who came to the town, and attracted even more attention than the kangaroo; so that even his warmest friends were obliged to admit that he was rather spoiled.

At the beginning of 1831, an Englishman, Lord Stanhope, came to Nuremberg, saw the foundling, was curiously interested in him, and wished to adopt him. Kaspar was very much flattered, and drew unfavourable comparisons between this Englishman who thought nothing too good for him, and his guardians, who were thinking of apprenticing him to a bookbinder. Lord Stanhope's kindness turned his head, and Herr von Tucher, after repeated remonstrances, resigned his guardianship in December 1831. With the full consent of the town council of Nuremberg, Lord Stanhope removed Kaspar to Ansbach, and placed him under the care of Dr. Mayer. It was generally supposed that this was only preparatory to taking him to England. Ample funds were provided for his maintenance, but the journey to England was again and again put off; and at last there were signs that Lord Stanhope was not quite satisfied with his new plaything. So much had been said about Kaspar's cleverness, that his new teachers were disappointed to find that his acquirements were about those of a boy of eight. They accused him of laziness and of deceit; and he, finding himself suspected

---

[1] Probably the man had tied a piece of black crape over his face as a mask.

and closely questioned as to everything he did, took refuge in falsehood. At last a government clerkship of the lowest class was procured for him, but great complaints were made of his inattention to his duties (mainly copying); he was unhappy, and, when on a visit to Nuremberg in the summer, made plans for the happy time when he should.be able to come back and live with his friends there. For the people of Ansbach, though making him one of the shows of the place, do not seem to have had that perfect belief in him shown by his earlier friends; while his new guardians expected a great deal too much from him. His chief friend in Ansbach was the clergyman who had prepared him for confirmation, who noticed, in November 1833, that he was very much depressed; but this passed away. On the afternoon of December 14, Kaspar came to call on the clergyman's wife, and was particularly happy and bright. Three hours afterwards he staggered into his tutor's house, holding his hand to his side, gasping out ' Garden—man—stabbed—give purse —let it drop—come—' and dragged the astonished Dr. Mayer off to a public garden, where a little purse was found on the ground. In it was a piece of paper, on which was written backwards in pencil these lines: 'I come from the Bavarian frontier. I will even tell you my name, " M. L. O."'

Kaspar was taken home and put to bed, when it was discovered that there was a deep stab in his left side. For some hours he was too ill to be questioned, but on the 15th he was able to tell his story. On the 14th, as he was coming out of the government buildings to go home to dinner, he was accosted by a man who promised to tell him who his parents were, if he would come to a spot in the public gardens. He refused, as he was going home to dinner, but made an appointment for that afternoon. After dinner he called on the clergyman's wife, and then went to the gardens, where he found the man waiting for him. The man led him to the Uz monument, which was at a little distance from the main path, and shut in by trees. Here he made him take a solemn oath of secrecy and handed him the little purse, which Kaspar, in his hurry to seize it, let drop. As he stooped to pick it up he was stabbed, and when he lifted himself up the stranger was gone. Then he ran home.

For two days he was not supposed to be in any danger, but fever set in; the doctors gave no hope of his recovery, and on the 17th he died.

His death caused great excitement, not only in Ansbach and

Nuremberg, but throughout all Germany. The question as to whether he was an impostor or not was hotly debated; those who favoured the former theory insisting that he had killed himself accidentally when he only meant to wound himself and so excite sympathy. Some of the doctors declared, however, that that was quite impossible, for the wound was meant to kill, and could only have been self-inflicted by a left-handed person of great strength, for it had pierced through a padded coat. A large reward (1,200*l.*) was offered for the capture of the assassin, but in vain; and the spot of the murder was marked by an inscription in Latin:

HIC

OCCULTUS

OCCULTO

OCCISUS EST

(Here the Mystery was mysteriously murdered).

The same idea is repeated on his tombstone. 'Here lies K. H., the riddle of the age. His birth was unknown, his death mysterious.'

His death was the signal for a violent paper-war between his friends and his enemies. It raged hotly for years; but his friends have never succeeded in proving who he was; why, after having been shut up for so long, he was at last set free; or why his death was, after all, necessary; while his enemies have utterly failed to prove that he was an impostor.[1]

---

[1] This is rather a picturesque than a critical story of Kaspar Hauser. The evidence of the men who first met him shows that he could then speak quite rationally. The curious will find a brief but useful account of him in the Duchess of Cleveland's 'Kaspar Hauser' (Macmillans. 1893.)

AN ARTIST'S ADVENTURE

NEARLY four hundred years ago, a boy was born in Italy who grew up to be one of the most accomplished artists of his own or any other age. Besides excelling as a sculptor, modeller, and medallist, he was a musician, an author, and an admirable swords-man; and popes, kings, and other great princes eagerly employed him, and vied with each other to secure his services. His name was Benvenuto Cellini.

Under Pope Clement VII. he took part in the defence of the Castle of St. Angelo, when it was besieged by the Constable de Bourbon, and the Pope reposed such confidence in Cellini that he was entrusted with the task of removing all the gems in the treasury from their settings, and concealing the stones in the thick folds of his clothing. However, I am not going to enlarge on Benvenuto's many talents, but to tell you of a wonderful adventure which befell him in the very Castle of St. Angelo he had helped to defend.

Those were lawless days, and Cellini was a man of fiery temper, to whom blows came more naturally than patience and forbearance. So it came to pass that, being told that a certain goldsmith named Pompeo had been spreading false reports about him, Benvenuto fell upon him one fine day in the very midst of Rome, and promptly stabbed him to death.

This might possibly have been overlooked, but a workman, jealous of Cellini's success and reputation, accused the artist to the reigning Pope, Paul III., of having purloined some of the jewels entrusted to his care during the siege, and Paul was not to be trifled with where the affairs of the treasury were concerned. Moreover, a near relation of the Pope's was Cellini's sworn enemy, and this sufficed to seal his fate.

So, when taking a walk one morning, Benvenuto suddenly found himself face to face with Crespino, the sheriff, attended by his band of constables. Crespino advanced, saying, 'You are the Pope's prisoner.'

'Crespino,' exclaimed Benvenuto, 'you must take me for some one else.'

'No, no,' replied Crespino, 'I know you perfectly, Benvenuto, and I have orders to carry you to the Castle of St. Angelo, where great nobles and men of talent like yourself are sent.'

Then he politely begged Benvenuto to give up his sword, and led him off to the Castle, where he was locked up in a room above the keep.

It was easy enough for Benvenuto to refute the accusations brought against him ; nevertheless he was kept prisoner, in spite of the intervention of the French ambassador, who demanded his liberty in the name of Francis I.

The governor of the Castle was, like Cellini, a Florentine, and at first showed himself full of kind attentions towards his countryman, allowing him a certain amount of liberty on parole, within the Castle walls. Growing suspicious later, he kept his prisoner closer, but after a time he restored him to comparative liberty.

When Benvenuto found how changeable the governor's humour was, he set himself to think over matters seriously. 'For,' he reflected, 'should a fresh fit of anger or suspicion cause him to confine me more strictly, I should feel myself released from my word, and it may be as well to be prepared.'

Accordingly he ordered some new coarse linen sheets to be brought him, but when soiled he did not send them back. When his servants asked for the sheets so as to have them washed he bade them say no more, as he had given them to one of the poor soldiers on guard, who would be sure to get into trouble if the matter were known. By degrees he emptied the straw out of his mattress, burning a little of it at a time in his fireplace, and replacing it with the sheets, which he cut into strips some inches wide. As soon as he thought these strips were long enough for his purpose, he told his servants that he had given all the sheets away, and that in future they had better bring him finer linen, which he would be sure to return.

Now it so happened that every year the governor was subject to a most distressing illness, which, for the time being, entirely deprived him of his reason. When it began to come on, he would talk and chatter incessantly. Each year he had some fresh hallucination, at one time fancying himself an oil-jar, at another a frog, and skipping about like one. Again, another time, he declared he was dead, and wished to be buried; and so, year by year, he was the victim of some new delusion. This year he imagined he was a bat, and as he walked about he uttered little half-smothered cries like a bat, and flapped his hands and moved his body as though about to fly. His faithful old servants and his doctors noticed this, and, thinking change of ideas and variety of conversation might do him good, they frequently fetched Benvenuto to entertain him.

One day the governor asked Benvenuto whether it had ever occurred to him to desire to fly, and, on being answered in the affirmative, he inquired further how he should set about it.

Benvenuto replied that the only flying creature it would be at all possible to imitate artificially was the bat, on which the poor man cried out, ' True, true, that's it, that's the thing.' Then turning round he said, ' Benvenuto, if you had everything you required for it, do you think you could fly ? '

' Oh, yes,' said the artist; ' if you will only leave me free to do it, I will engage to make a pair of wings of fine waxed cloth, and to fly from here to Prati with them.'

' And I, too,' exclaimed the governor; ' I could do it too, but the Pope has ordered me to keep you like the apple of his eye, and as I strongly suspect you're a cunning fellow, I shall lock you well up and give you no chance of flying.'

Thereupon, and in spite of all Benvenuto's entreaties and protestations, the governor ordered him to be taken back to prison and more carefully guarded than ever.

Seeing he could not help himself, Cellini exclaimed before the officers and attendants: ' Very well ! lock me up and keep me safe, for I give you due warning I mean to escape in spite of everything.'

No sooner was he shut up in his cell than he fell to turning over in his mind how this escape could be made, and began minutely examining his prison, and, after discovering what he thought would be a sure way of getting out, he considered how best he might let himself down from the top of this enormous donjon tower, which went by the name of 'Il Mastio.' He began by measuring the length of the linen strips, which he had cut and joined firmly together so as to form a sort of rope, and he thought there would be enough for his purpose. Next, he armed himself with a pair of pincers which he had taken from one of his guards who was fond of carpentering, and who, amongst his tools, had a particularly large and

strong pair of pincers, which appeared so useful to Benvenuto that
he abstracted them, and hid them in his mattress.

As soon as he thought himself safe from interruption, he began
to feel about for the nails in the ironwork of the door, but owing to
its immense thickness they were by no means easy to get at. However, he managed at length to extract the first nail. Then came
the question, how to conceal the hole left behind. This he contrived by making a paste of rusty scrapings and wax, which he
modelled into an exact representation of the head of a nail, and in
this way he replaced each nail he drew by a facsimile of its head
in wax.

Great care was required to leave just a sufficient number of
nails to keep the ironwork and hinges in their places. But
Benvenuto managed this by first drawing the nails, cutting them as
short as he dared, and then replacing them in such a way as to
keep things together, and yet to allow of their being easily drawn
out at the last moment.

All this was by no means easy to contrive, for the governor was
constantly sending some one to make sure that his prisoner was safe.

The two men who were specially charged with this duty were
rough and rude, and one of them in particular took pains to inspect
the whole room carefully every evening, paying special attention to
the locks and hinges.

Cellini lived in constant terror lest it should occur to them to
examine his bedding, where, besides the pincers, he had hidden a
long sharp dagger and some other instruments, as well as his long
strips of linen. Each morning he swept out and dusted his room
and carefully made his bed, ornamenting it with flowers which he
got the soldier from whom he had taken the pincers to bring him.
When his two warders appeared he desired them on no account to
go near or touch his bed, for fear of soiling or disturbing it. Sometimes, in order to tease him, they would touch it, and then he
would shout: ' Ah ! you dirty rascals ! Just let me get at one of
your swords and see how I'll punish you ! How dare you touch
the bed of such a man as I am ? Little care I about risking my
own life, for I should be certain to take yours. Leave me in peace
with my grief and trouble, or I will show you what a man can do
when driven to desperation ! '

These words were repeated to the governor, who forbade the
gaolers touching Cellini's bed, or entering his room armed. The
bed once safe, he felt as if all else must go right.

One night the governor had a worse attack than ever, and in a fit of madness kept repeating that he certainly was a bat, and that, should they hear of Benvenuto's escape, they must let him fly off too, as he was sure he could fly better at night and would overtake the fugitive. 'Benvenuto,' said he, 'is but a sham bat, but as I am a real bat, and he has been given into my keeping, I shall soon catch him again, depend on it.'

This bad attack lasted several nights, and the Savoyard soldier, who took an interest in Benvenuto, reported to him that the servants were quite worn out watching their sick master. Hearing this, Cellini resolved to attempt his escape at once, and set hard to work to complete his preparations. He worked all night, and about two hours before dawn he, with much care and trouble, removed the hinges from the door. The casing and bolts prevented his opening it wide, so he chipped away the woodwork, till at length he was able to slip through, taking with him his linen ropes, which he had wound on two pieces of wood like two great reels of thread.

Having passed the door he turned to the right of the tower, and having removed a couple of tiles, he easily got out on the roof. He wore a white doublet and breeches and white boots, into one of which he had slipped his dagger. Taking one end of his linen rope, he now proceeded to hook it carefully over an antique piece of tile which was firmly cemented into the wall. This tile projected barely four fingers' breadth, and the band hooked over it as on a stirrup. When he had made it firm he prayed thus : 'O Lord, my God, come now to my aid, for Thou knowest that my cause is righteous, and that I am aiding myself.' Then he gently let himself slide down the rope till he reached the ground. There was no moon, but the sky was clear, and once down he gazed up at the tower from which he had made so bold a descent, and went off in high spirits, thinking himself at liberty, which indeed was by no means the case.

On this side of the Castle the governor had had two high walls built to inclose his stables and his poultry-yard, and these walls had gates securely bolted and barred on the outside.

In despair at these obstacles Benvenuto roamed about at random, cursing his bad luck, when suddenly he hit his foot against a long pole which lay hidden in the straw. With a good deal of effort he managed to raise it against the wall and to scramble up to the top. Here he found a sharply sloping coping stone which made it impossible to draw the pole up after him, but he fastened a portion of

HE PREPARED TO ATTACK THE SENTRY

the second linen band to it, and by this means let himself down as he had done outside the donjon tower.

By this time Benvenuto was much exhausted, and his hands were all cut and bleeding; however, after a short rest he climbed the last inclosure, and was just in the act of fastening his rope to a battlement, when, to his horror, he saw a sentinel close to him. Desperate at this interruption, and at the thought of the risk he ran, he prepared to attack the sentry, who, however, seeing a man advance on him with a drawn dagger and determined air, promptly took to his heels, and Benvenuto returned to his rope. Another guard was near, but, hoping not to have been observed, the fugitive secured his band and hastily slid down it. Whether it was fatigue, or that he thought himself nearer the ground than he really was, it is impossible to say, but he loosened his hold, and fell, hitting his head, and lay stretched on the ground for more than an hour.

The sharp freshness of the air just before sunrise revived him, but his memory did not return immediately, and he fancied his head had been cut off and that he was in purgatory. By degrees, as his senses returned, he realised that he was no longer in the Castle, and remembered what he had done. He put his hands to his head and withdrew them covered with blood, but on carefully examining himself he found he had no serious wound, though on attempting to move he discovered that his right leg was broken. Nothing daunted, he drew from his boot his poniard with its sheath, which had a large ball at the end; the pressure of this ball on the bone had caused the fracture. He threw away the sheath, and cutting off a piece of the remaining linen band with his dagger, he bound up his leg as best he could, and then, dagger in hand, proceeded to drag himself along on his knees towards the gate of the town. It was still closed, but seeing one stone near the bottom, which did not look very huge, he tried to displace it. After repeated efforts it shook, and at length yielded to his efforts, so, forcing it out, he squeezed himself through.

He had barely entered Rome when he was attacked by a band of savage dogs, who bit and worried him cruelly. He fought desperately with his dagger, and gave one dog such a stab that it fled howling, followed by the rest of the pack, leaving Benvenuto free to drag himself as best he could towards St. Peter's.

By this time it was broad daylight, and there was much risk of discovery; so, seeing a water-carrier passing with his train of asses

laden with jars full of water, Benvenuto hailed him and begged he
would carry him as far as the steps of St. Peter's.

'I am a poor fellow,' said he, 'who have broken my leg trying
to get out of the window of a house where I went to see my lady-
love. As the house belongs to a great family, I much fear I shall
be cut to pieces if I am found here; so pray help me off and you
shall have a gold crown for your pains,' and Benvenuto put his
hand to his purse, which was well filled.

The water-carrier readily consented, and carried him to St.
Peter's, where he left him on the steps, from whence Benvenuto
began to crawl towards the palace of Duke Ottavio, whose wife, a
daughter of the emperor's, had brought many of Cellini's friends
from Florence to Rome in her train. She was well disposed towards the great artist, and he felt that beneath her roof he would
be in safety. Unluckily, as he struggled along, he was seen and
recognised by a servant of Cardinal Cornaro's, who had apartments
in the Vatican. The man hurried to his master's room, woke him
up, and cried: 'Most reverend lord, Benvenuto is below; he must
have escaped from the Castle, and is all bleeding and wounded. He
appears to have broken his leg, and we have no idea where he is
going.'

'Run at once,' exclaimed the Cardinal, 'and fetch him here,
to my room.'

When Benvenuto appeared the Cardinal assured him he need
have no fears, and sent off for the first surgeons in Rome to attend
to him. Then he shut him up in a secret room, and went off to try
and obtain his pardon from the Pope.

Meantime a great commotion arose in Rome, for the linen ropes
dangling from the great tower had attracted notice, and all the town
was running out to see the strange sight. At the Vatican Cardinal
Cornaro met a friend, to whom he related all the details of Benvenuto's escape, and how he was at that very moment hidden in a
secret chamber. Then they both went to the Pope, who, as they
threw themselves at his feet, cried, 'I know what you want with
me.'

'Holy Father,' said the Cardinal's friend, 'we entreat you to
grant us the life of this poor man. His genius deserves some
consideration, and he has just shown an almost superhuman
amount of courage and dexterity. We do not know what may be
the crimes for which your Holiness has seen fit to imprison him,
but if they are pardonable we implore you to forgive him.'

The Pope, looking somewhat abashed, replied that he had imprisoned Benvenuto for being too presumptuous; 'however,' he added, 'I am well aware of his talents and am anxious to keep him near me, and am resolved to treat him so well that he shall have no desire to return to France. I am sorry he is ill; bid him recover quickly, and we will make him forget his past sufferings.'

I am sorry to say the Pope was not so good as his words, for Benvenuto's enemies plotted against him, and after a time he was once more shut up in his former prison, from which, however, he was eventually delivered at the urgent request of the King of France, who warmly welcomed the great artist to his Court, where he spent some years in high honour.

THE TALE OF ISANDHLWANA AND
RORKE'S DRIFT

LTHOUGH but fourteen years have gone by since 1879, perhaps some people, if they chance to be young, have forgotten about the Zulus, and the story of our war with them; so, before beginning the tale of Isandhlwana and Rorke's Drift, it may be worth while to tell of these matters in a few words.

The Zulus live in South-Eastern Africa. Originally they were not one tribe but many, though the same blood was in them all. Nobody knows whence they came or who were their forefathers; but they seem to have sprung from an Arab or Semitic stock, and many of their customs, such as the annual feast of the first fruits, resemble those of the Jews. At the beginning of this century there arose a warrior king, called Chaka, who gathered up the scattered tribes of the Zulus as a woodman gathers sticks, and as of the frail brushwood the woodman makes a stout faggot, that none can break, so of these tribes Chaka fashioned a nation so powerful that no other black people could conquer it.

The deeds of Chaka are too many to write of here. Seldom has there been a monarch, black or white, so terrible or so absolute, and never perhaps has a man lived more wicked or more clever. Out of ' nothing,' as the Kafirs say, he made the Amazulu, or the ' people

of heaven,' so powerful, that before he died he could send out an
army of a hundred thousand men to destroy those whom he feared
or hated or whose cattle he coveted. These soldiers were never
beaten; if they dared to turn their back upon an enemy, however
numerous, they were killed when the battle was done, so that
soon they learned to choose death with honour before the foe in
preference to death with shame at the hands of the executioner.
Where Chaka's armies went they conquered, till the country was
swept of people for hundreds of miles in every direction. At
length, after he had killed or been the cause of the violent death of
more than a million human beings, in the year 1828 Chaka's own
hour came; for, as the Zulu proverb says, ' the swimmer is at
last borne away by the stream.' He was murdered by the princes
of his house and his body servant Umbopo or Mopo. But as he
lay dying beneath their spear thrusts, it is said that the great
king prophesied of the coming of white men who should conquer
the land that he had won.

' What,' he said, ' do you slay me, my brothers—dogs of mine
own house whom I have fed, thinking to possess the land? I
tell you that I hear the sound of running feet, the feet of a great
white people, and they shall stamp you flat, children of my
father.'

After the death of Chaka his brother Dingaan reigned who had
murdered him. In due course he was murdered also, and his
brother Panda succeeded to the throne. Panda was a man of peace,
and the only one of the four Zulu kings who died a natural death;
for though it is not commonly known, the last of these kings,
our enemy Cetywayo, is believed to have met his end by poison.
In 1873, Cetywayo was crowned king of Zululand in succession to
his father Panda on behalf of the English Government by Sir Theo-
philus Shepstone. He remained a firm friend to the British till Sir
Bartle Frere declared war on him in 1879. Sir Bartle-Frere made
war upon the Zulus because he was afraid of their power, and the
Zulus accepted the challenge because we annexed the Transvaal and would not allow them to fight the Boers or the Swazis.
They made a brave resistance, and it was not until there were
nearly as many English soldiers in their country armed with
breech-loading rifles as they had effective warriors left alive in it,
for the most part armed with spears only, that at length we conquered them. But their heart was never in the war; they defended
their country against invasion indeed, but by Cetywayo's orders

they never attacked ours. Had they wished to do so, there was nothing to prevent them from sweeping the outlying districts of Natal and the Transvaal after our first great defeat at Isandhlwana, but they spared us.

And now I have done with dull explanations, and will go on to tell of the disaster at Isandhlwana or the 'place of the Little Hand,' and of the noble defence of Rorke's Drift.

On the 20th of January, 1879, one of the British columns that were invading Zululand broke its camp on the left bank of the Buffalo river, and marched by the road that ran from Rorke's Drift to the Indeni forest, encamping that evening under the shadow of a steep-cliffed and lonely mountain, called Isandhlwana. This force was known as number 3 column, and with it went Lord Chelmsford, the general in command of the troops. The buildings at Rorke's Drift were left in charge of sixty men of the 2nd battalion 24th regiment under the late Colonel Bromhead, then a lieutenant, and some volunteers and others, the whole garrison being commanded, on the occasion of the attack, by Lieutenant Chard, R.E.

On January 21, Colonel, then Major, Dartnell, the officer in command of the Natal Mounted Police and volunteers, who had been sent out to effect a reconnaissance of the country beyond Isandhlwana, reported that the Zulus were in great strength in front of him. Thereupon Lord Chelmsford ordered six companies of the 2nd battalion 24th regiment, together with four guns and the Mounted Infantry, to advance to his support. This force, under the command of Colonel Glyn, and accompanied by Lord Chelmsford himself, left Isandhlwana at dawn on the 22nd, a despatch having first been sent to Lieut.-Colonel Durnford. R.E., who was in command of some five hundred friendly Natal Zulus, about half of whom were mounted and armed with breech-loaders, to move up from Rorke's Drift and strengthen the camp, which was now in charge of Lieut.-Colonel Pulleine of the 1st battalion 24th regiment. Orders were given to Colonel Pulleine by the general that he was to 'defend' the camp.

About ten o'clock that morning Colonel Durnford arrived at Isandhlwana and took over the command of the camp, which was then garrisoned by seven hundred and seventy-two European and eight hundred and fifty-one native troops, in all one thousand six hundred and twenty-three men, with two guns. Little did Lord Chelmsford and those with him guess in what state they would find that camp when they returned to it some eighteen hours later, or that of those sixteen hundred men the great majority would then be dead !

Meanwhile a Zulu 'impi' or army, numbering about twenty thousand men, or something more than one-third of King Cetywayo's entire strength, had moved from the Upindo Hill on the night of January 21, and taken up its position on a stony plain, a mile and a half to the east of Isandhlwana. The impi was made up of the Undi regiment, about three thousand strong, that formed its breast, or centre, the Nokenke and Umcityu regiments, seven thousand strong, that formed its right wing or horn, and the Imbonanbi and Nkobamikosi regiments, ten thousand strong, forming its left horn or wing. That night the impi slept upon its spears and watched in silence, lighting no fires. The king had reviewed it three days previously, and his orders to it were that it should attack number 3 column, and drive it back over the Buffalo, but it had no intention of giving battle on the 22nd, for the state of the moon was not propitious, so said the 'doctors'; moreover, the soldiers had not been 'moutied,' that is, sprinkled with medicines to 'put a great heart' into them and ensure their victory. The intention of the generals was to attack the camp at dawn on the 23rd; and the actual engagement was brought about by an accident.

Before I tell of this or of the fight, however, it may be as well to describe how these splendid savages were armed and disciplined. To begin with, every corps had a particular head-dress and fighting shields of one colour, just as in our army each regiment has its own facings on the tunics. These shields are cut from the hides of oxen, and it is easy to imagine what a splendid sight was presented by a Zulu impi twenty thousand strong, divided into several regiments, one with snow-white shields and tall cranes' feathers on their heads, one with coal-black shields and black plumes, and others with red and mottled shields, and bands of fur upon their foreheads. In their war with the English many of the Zulus were armed with muzzle-loading guns and rifles of the worst description, of which they could make little use, for few of them were trained to handle fire-arms. A much more terrible weapon in their hands, and one that did nearly all the execution at Isandhlwana, was the broad-bladed short-shafted stabbing assegai. This shape of spear was introduced by the great king Chaka, and if a warrior cast it at an enemy, or even chanced to lose it in a fight, he was killed when the fray was over. Before Chaka's day the Zulu tribes used light assegais, which they threw at the enemy from a distance, and thus their ammunition was sometimes spent before they came to close quarters with the foe.

Among the Zulus every able-bodied man was enrolled in one or other of the regiments—even the girls and boys were made into regiments or attached to them, and though these did not fight, they carried the mats and cooking pots of the army, and drove the cattle for the soldiers to eat when on the march. Thus it will be seen that this people differed from any other in the world in modern days, for whereas even the most courageous and martial of mankind look upon war as an exceptional state of affairs and an evil only to be undertaken in self-defence, or perhaps for purposes of revenge and aggrandisement, the Zulus looked on peace as the exceptional state, and on warfare as the natural employment of man. Chaka taught them that lesson, and they had learnt it well, and so it came about that Cetywayo was forced to allow the army to fight with us when Sir Bartle Frere gave them an opportunity of doing so, since their hearts were sick with peace, and for years they had clamoured to be allowed to ' wash their spears,' saying that they were no longer men, but had become a people of women. Indeed, had the king not done so, they would have fought with each other. It is a terrible thing to be obliged, year after year, to keep quiet an army of some fifty or sixty thousand men who are too proud to work and clamour daily to be led to battle that they may die as their fathers died. We may be sure that the heart of many a Zulu warrior beat high as in dead silence he marched that night from the heights of Upindo towards the doomed camp of Isandhlwana, since at last he was to satisfy the longing of his blood, and fight to the death with a foe whom he knew to be worthy of him.

Doubtless, also, the hearts of the white men beat high that night as they gathered round the fires of their camp, little knowing that thousands of Zulu eyes were watching them from afar, or that the black rock looming above them was destined to stand like some great tombstone over their bones for ever. Englishmen also are a warlike race, and there was honour and advancement to be won, and it would seem that but few of those who marched into the Zulu country guessed how formidable was the foe with whom they had to deal. A horde of half-naked savages armed with spears did not strike English commanders, imperfectly acquainted with the history and nature of those savages, as particularly dangerous enemies. Some there were, indeed, who, having spent their lives in the country, knew what was to be expected, but they were set down as 'croakers,' and their earnest warnings of disaster to come were disregarded.

Now let us return to the camp. It will be remembered that Colonel Glyn's force, accompanied by General Lord Chelmsford, had left at dawn. About eight o'clock a picket placed some 1,500 yards distant reported that Zulus were approaching from the north-east. This information was despatched by mounted messengers to Colonel Glyn's column.

Lieut.-Colonel Durnford, with his mounted natives and a rocket battery arriving from Rorke's Drift about 10 A.M., took over the command of the camp from Colonel Pulleine. According to the evidence of Lieutenant Cochrane given at the court of inquiry, Colonel Pulleine thereupon stated to Colonel Durnford the orders that he had received, to 'defend the camp,' and it would appear that either then or subsequently some altercation took place between these two officers. In the issue, however, Colonel Durnford advanced his mounted force to ascertain the enemy's movements, and directed a company of the 1st battalion 24th regiment to occupy a hill about 1,200 yards to the north of the camp.

Other companies of the 24th were stationed at various points at a distance from the camp. It may be well to explain here, that to these movements of troops, which, so far as can be ascertained, were made by the direct orders of Colonel Durnford, must be attributed the terrible disaster that followed. There are two ways of fighting a savage or undisciplined enemy; the scientific way, such as is taught in staff colleges, and the unscientific way that is to be learned in the sterner school of experience. We English were not the first white men who had to deal with the rush of the Zulu impis. The Boers had encountered them before, at the battle of the Blood River, and armed only with muzzle-loading ' roers,' or elephant guns, despite their desperate valour, had worsted them, with fearful slaughter. But they did not advance bodies of men to this point or to that, according to the scientific method; they drew their ox waggons into a square, lashing them together with ' reims ' or hide-ropes, and from behind this rough defence, with but trifling loss to themselves, rolled back charge after charge of the warriors of Dingaan.

Had this method been followed by our troops at the battle of Isandhlwana, who had ample waggons at hand to enable them to execute the manœuvre, had the soldiers even been collected in a square beneath the cliff of the mountain, it cannot be doubted but that, armed as they were with breech-loaders, they would have been able to drive back not only the impi sent against them, but, if necessary, the entire Zulu army. Indeed, that this would have been so is demonstrated by what happened on the same day at Rorke's Drift, where a hundred and thirty men repelled the desperate assaults of three or four thousand. Why, then, it may be asked, did Colonel Durnford, a man of considerable colonial experience, adopt the more risky, if the more scientific, mode of dealing with the present danger, and this in spite of Colonel Pulleine's direct intima- tion to him that his orders were 'to defend the camp'? As it chances, the writer of this account, who knew Colonel Durnford well, and has the greatest respect for the memory of that good officer, and honourable gentleman, is able to suggest an answer to the problem which at the time was freely offered by the Natal colonists. A few years before, it happened that Colonel Durnford was engaged upon some military operations against a rebellious native chief in Natal. Coming into contact with the followers of this chief, in the hope that matters might be arranged without bloodshed, Durnford ordered the white volunteers under his command not to fire, with the result that the rebels fired, killing several of his force and wounding him in the arm. This incident gave rise to an irrational indignation in the colony, and for a while he himself was designated by the un- generous nickname of 'Don't fire Durnford.' It is alleged, none can know with what amount of truth, that it was the memory of this undeserved insult which caused Colonel Durnford to insist upon advancing the troops under his command to engage the Zulus in the open, instead of withdrawing them to await attack in the comparative safety of a 'laager.'

The events following the advance of the various British com- panies at Isandhlwana are exceedingly difficult to describe in their proper order, since the evidence of the survivors is confused.

It would appear, however, that Durnford's mounted Basutos discovered and fired on a portion of the Umcityu regiment, which, forgetting its orders, sprang up and began to charge. Thereon, accepting the position, the other Zulu regiments joined the move- ment. Very rapidly, and with the most perfect order, the impi adopted the traditional Zulu ox-head formation, namely, that of a centre and two horns, the centre representing the skull of the ox. In this order they advanced towards the English camp, slowly and without sound. Up to this time there had been no particular alarm in the camp. The day was bright and lovely, with a hot sun tempered by a gentle breeze that just stirred the tops of the grasses, and many men seem to have been strolling about quite unaware of their imminent danger, although orders were given to collect the transport oxen, which were at graze outside the camp; not for the

CHARLES KERR

purpose of inspanning the waggons, but to prevent them from being captured by the enemy. One officer (Captain, now Colonel, Essex) reports that after the company had been sent out, he retired to his tent to write letters, till, about twelve o'clock, a sergeant came to tell him that firing was to be heard behind a hill in face of the camp. He mounted a horse and rode up the slope, to find the company firing on a line of Zulus eight hundred paces away to their front. This line was about a thousand yards long, and shaped like a horn, tapering towards the point. It advanced slowly, taking shelter with great skill behind rocks, and opened a quite ineffective fire on the soldiers. Meanwhile the two guns were shelling the Zulu centre with great effect, the shells cutting lanes through their dense ranks, which closed up over the dead in perfect discipline and silence. The attack was now general, all the impi taking part in it except a reserve regiment that sat down upon the ground taking snuff, and never came into action, and the Undi corps, which moved off to the right with the object of passing round the north side of the Isandhlwana hill.

On came the Zulus in silence, and ever as they came the two horns crept further and further ahead of the black breast of their array. Hundreds of them fell beneath the fire of the breech-loaders, but they did not pause in their attack. Ammunition began to fail the soldiers, and orders having reached them—too late—to concentrate on the camp, they retired slowly to that position. Captain Essex also rode back, and assisted the quartermaster of the 24th to place boxes of ammunition in a mule cart, till presently the quartermaster was shot dead at his side. Now the horns or nippers of the foe were beginning to close on the doomed camp, and the friendly natives, who knew well what this meant, though as yet the white men had not understood their danger, began to steal away by twos and threes, and then, breaking into open rout, they rushed through the camp, seeking the waggon road to Rorke's Drift.

Then at last the Zulu generals saw that the points of the horns had met behind the white men, and the moment was ripe. Abandoning its silence and slow advance, the breast of the impi raised the war-cry and charged, rolling down upon the red coats like a wave of steel. So swift and sudden was this last charge, that many of the soldiers had no time to fix bayonets. For a few moments the scattered companies held the impi back, and the black stream flowed round them, then it flowed *over* them, sweeping them along like human wreckage. In a minute the defence had become an utter rout. Some of the defenders formed themselves into groups and fought back to back till they fell where they stood, to be found weeks afterwards mere huddled heaps of bones. Hundreds of others fled for the waggon road, to find that the Undi regiment, passing round the Isandhlwana mountain, had occupied it already. Back they rolled from the hedge of Undi spears to fall upon the spears of the attacking regiments. One path of retreat alone remained, a dry and precipitous 'donga' or watercourse, and into this plunged a rabble of men, white and black, mules, horses, guns, and waggons.

Meanwhile the last act of the tragedy was being played on the field of death. With a humming sound such as might be made by millions of bees, the Zulu swarms fell upon those of the soldiers who remained alive, and, after a desperate resistance, stabbed them. Wherever the eye looked, men were falling and spears flashing in the sunshine, while the ear was filled with groans of the dying and the savage *S'gee S'gee* of the Zulu warriors as they passed their assegais through and through the bodies of the fallen. Many a deed of valour was done there as white men and black grappled in the death-struggle, but their bones alone remained to tell the tale of them. Shortly after the disaster, one of the survivors told the present writer of a duel which he witnessed between a Zulu and an officer of the 24th regiment. The officer having emptied his revolver, set his back against the wheel of a waggon and drew his sword. Then the Zulu came at him with his shield up, turning and springing from side to side as he advanced. Presently he lowered the shield, exposing his head, and the white man falling into the trap aimed a fierce blow at it. As it fell the shield was raised again, and the sword sank deep into its edge, remaining fixed in the tough ox-hide. This was what the Zulu desired; with a twist of his strong arm he wrenched the sword from his opponent's hand, and in another instant the unfortunate officer was down with an assegai through his breast.

In a few minutes it was done, all resistance had been overpowered, the wounded had been murdered—for the Zulu on the war-path has no mercy—and the dead mutilated and cut open to satisfy the horrible native superstition. Then those regiments that remained upon the field began the work of plunder. Most of the bodies they stripped naked, clothing themselves in the uniforms of the dead soldiers. They stabbed the poor oxen that remained fastened to the 'trek-tows' of the waggons, and they drank all the spirits that they could find, some of them, it is said, perishing through the accidental consumption of the medical stores. Then, when the sun grew low, they retreated, laden with plunder, taking with them the most of their dead, of whom there are believed to have been about fifteen hundred, for the Martinis did their work well, and our soldiers had not died unavenged.

All this while Lord Chelmsford and the division which he accompanied were in ignorance of what had happened within a few miles of them, though rumours had reached them that a Zulu force was threatening the camp. The first to discover the dreadful truth was Commandant Lonsdale of the Natal Native Contingent. This officer had been ill, and was returning to camp alone, a fact that shows how little anything serious was expected. He reached it about the middle of the afternoon, and there was nothing to reveal to the casual observer that more than three thousand human beings had perished there that day. The sun shone on the white tents and on the ox waggons, around and about which groups of red-coated men were walking, sitting, and lying. It did not chance to occur to him that those who were moving were Zulus wearing the coats of English soldiers, and those lying down, soldiers whom the Zulus had killed As Commandant Lonsdale rode, a gun was fired, and he heard a bullet whizz past his head. Looking in the direction of the sound, he saw a native with a smoking rifle in his hand, and concluding that it was one of the men under his command who had discharged his piece accidentally, he took no more notice of the matter. Forward he rode, till he was within ten yards of what had been the headquarter tents, when suddenly out of one of them there stalked a great Zulu, bearing in his hand a broad assegai from which blood was dripping. Then his intelligence awoke, and he understood. The camp was in the possession of the enemy, and those who lay here and there upon the grass like holiday makers in a London park on a Sunday in summer, were English soldiers indeed, not living but dead.

Turning his horse, Commandant Lonsdale fled as swiftly as it could carry him. More than a hundred rifle-shots were fired after him, but the Zulu marksmanship was poor, and he escaped untouched. A while afterwards, a solitary horseman met Lord Chelmsford and his staff returning : he saluted, and said, ' *The camp is in the possession of the enemy, sir !* ' None who heard those words will forget them, and few men can have experienced a more terrible shock than that which fell upon the English general in this hour.

Slowly, and with all military precaution, Lord Chelmsford and his force moved onward, till at length, when darkness had fallen, they encamped beneath the fatal hill of Isandhlwana. Here, momentarily expecting to be attacked, they remained all night amid the wreck, the ruin, and the dead, but not till the following dawn did they learn the magnitude of the disaster that had overtaken

our arms. Then they saw, and in silence marched from that fatal field, heading for Rorke's Drift, and leaving its mutilated dead to the vulture and the jackal.

Now let us follow the fate of the mob of fugitives, who, driven back from the waggon road by the Undi, plunged desperately into the donga near it, the sole avenue of retreat which had not been besieged by the foe, in the hope that they might escape the slaughter by following the friendly natives who were mixed up with them. How many entered on that terrible race for life is not known, but it is certain that very few won through. Indeed, it is said that, with the exception of some natives, no single man who was not mounted lived to pass the Buffalo River. For five miles or more they rode and ran over paths that a goat would have found it difficult to keep his footing on, while by them, and mixed up with them, went the destroying Zulus. Very soon the guns became fixed among the boulders, and one by one the artillerymen were assegaied. On went the survivors, hopeless yet hoping. Now a savage sprang on this man, and now on that; the assegai flashed up, a cry of agony echoed among the rocks, and a corpse fell heavily to the red earth. Still, those whom it pleased Providence to protect struggled forward, clinging to their horses' manes as they leaped from boulder to boulder, till at length they came to a cliff, beneath which the Buffalo rolled in flood. Down this cliff they slid and stumbled, few of them can tell how; then, driven to it by the pitiless spears, they plunged into the raging river. Many were drowned in its waters, some were shot in the stream, some were stabbed upon the banks, yet a few, clinging to the manes and tails of their horses, gained the opposite shore in safety.

Among these were two men whose memory their country will not willingly let die, who, indeed (it is the first time in our military history), have been decreed the Victoria Cross although they were already dead: Lieutenants Coghill and Melvill of the 24th regiment. One of these, Lieutenant Coghill, the writer of this sketch had the good fortune to know well. A kindlier-hearted and merrier young English gentleman never lived. Melvill and Coghill were swept away upon the tide of flight, down the dreadful path that led to Fugitives' Drift, but Melvill bore with him the colours of the 24th regiment that were in his charge as adjutant, not tied round his waist, as has been reported, but upon the pole to which they were attached. He arrived in safety at the river, but, owing to the loss of his horse, was unable to cross it, and took refuge upon a rock in mid-stream, still holding the colours in his hand. Coghill, whose knee was disabled by an accident and who had reached the Natal bank already, saw the terrible position of his friend and brother officer, and, though spears flashed about him and bullets beat the water like hail, with a courage that has rarely been equalled, he turned his horse and swam back to his assistance. The worst was over; safety lay before him, there behind him in the river was almost certain death ; but this gallant gentleman heeded none of these things, for there also were the colours of his regiment and his drowning friend. Back he swam to the rock through the boiling current. Soon his horse was shot dead beneath him, yet, though none knows how, the two of them came safe to shore. The colours were lost indeed, for they could no longer carry them and live, but these never fell into the hands of their savage foes : days afterwards they were searched for and found in the bed of the river. Breathless, desperate, lamed, and utterly outworn, the two friends struggled up the bank and the hill beyond. But Zulus had crossed that stream as well as the fugitive Englishmen. They staggered forward for a few hundred yards, then, unable to go further, the friends stood back to back and the foe closed in upon them. There they stood, and there, fighting desperately, the heroes died. Peace be with them in that land to which they have journeyed, and among men, immortal honour to their names !

They sold their lives dearly, for several Zulus were found lying about their bodies.

About forty white men lived to cross the river at Fugitives' Drift, and these, almost the only English survivors of the force at Isandhlwana, rode on, still followed by Zulus, to the provision depôt at Helpmakaar some fifteen miles away, where they mustered and entrenched themselves as best they were able, expecting to be attacked at any moment. But no attack was delivered, the Zulus being busily employed elsewhere.

Some little distance from the banks of the Buffalo, and on the Natal side near to a mountain called Tyana, stood two buildings erected by the Rev. Mr. Witt ; Rorke's Drift, from which No. 3 column had advanced, being immediately in front of them. One of these buildings had been utilised as a storehouse and hospital, and in 'it were thirty-five sick men. The other was occupied by a company of the 2nd 24th regiment, under the command of the late Lieut. Bromhead.[1]

On January 22, the ponts at Rorke's Drift were left in charge of Lieut. Chard, R.E., with a few men. About a quarter-past three on that day an officer of Lonsdale's regiment, Lieut. Adendorff, and a carbineer, were seen galloping wildly towards the ponts. On coming to the bank of the river, they shouted to Lieut. Chard to

---

[1] Col. Bromhead died recently.

take them across, and so soon as he reached them, they communicated to him the terrifying news that the general's camp had been
captured and destroyed by a Zulu impi. A few minutes later a
message arrived from Lieut. Bromhead, who also had learned the
tidings of disaster, requesting Lieut. Chard to join him at the
commissariat store. Mounting his horse he rode thither, to find
Lieut. Bromhead, assisted by Mr. Dolton, of the commissariat, and
the entire force at his command, amounting to about 130, inclusive
of the sick and the chaplain, Mr. Smith, a Norfolk man, actively
engaged in loopholing and barricading the house and hospital (both
of which buildings were thatched), and in connecting them by means
of a fortification of mealie bags and waggons. Having ridden round
the position, Lieut. Chard returned to the Drift. Sergeant Milne
and Mr. Daniells, who managed the ponts, offered to moor them
in the middle of the stream, and with the assistance of a few men
to defend them from their decks. This gallant suggestion being
rejected as impracticable, Lieut. Chard withdrew to the buildings
with the waggon and those under his command.

They arrived there about 3.30, and shortly afterwards an officer of
Durnford's native horse rode up, accompanied by about 100 mounted
men, and asked for orders. He was requested to send out outposts
in the direction of the enemy, and, having checked their advance as
much as possible, to fall back, when forced so to do, upon the buildings
and assist in their defence. Posts were then assigned to each man
in the little garrison, and, this done, the defensive preparations went
on, all doing their utmost, for they felt that the life of every one
of them was at stake. Three-quarters of an hour went by, and the
officer of Durnford's horse rode up, reporting that the Zulus were
advancing in masses, and that his men were deserting in the
direction of Helpmakaar. At this time some natives of the Natal
contingent under the command of Capt. Stephenson also retired,
an example which was followed by that officer himself.

Lieuts. Chard and Bromhead now saw that their lines of defence
were too large for the number of men left to them, and at once began
the erection of an inner entrenchment formed of biscuit boxes
taken from the stores. When this wall was but two boxes high,
suddenly there appeared five or six hundred Zulus advancing at a
run against the southern side of their position. These were soldiers
of the Undi regiment, the same that had turned the Isandhlwana
mountain, cutting off all possibility of retreat by the waggon road,
who, when they knew that the camp was taken, had advanced

to destroy the guard of Rorke's Drift. On they came, to be met presently by a terrible and concentrated fire from the Martinis. Many fell, but they did not stay till, when within 50 yards of the wall, the cross fire from the store took them in flank. Their loss was now so heavy that, checking their advance, some of them took cover among the ovens, cookhouse, and outbuildings, whence they in turn opened fire upon the garrison. Hundreds more rushing round the hospital came at full speed against the north-west fortification of sacks filled with corn. In vain did the Martinis pump a hail of lead into them: on they came straight to the frail defence, striving to take it at the point of the assegai. But here they were met by British bayonets and a fire so terrible that even the courage of the Zulus could not prevail against it, and they fell back, that is, those of them who were left alive.

By this time the main force of the Undi had arrived, two thousand of them, perhaps, and having lined an overlooking ledge of rocks, took possession of the garden of the station and the bush surrounding it, from all of which the fire, though badly directed, was so continuous that at length the little garrison of white men were forced back into their inner entrenchment of biscuit boxes. Creeping up under cover of the bush, the Zulus now delivered assault after assault upon the wall. Each of these fierce rushes was repelled with the bayonets wielded by the brave white men on its further side. The assegais clashed against the rifle barrels, everywhere the musketry rang and rolled, the savage war-cries and the cheers of the Englishmen rose together through the din, while British soldier and Zulu warrior thrust and shot and tore at each other across the narrow wall, that wall which all the Undi could not climb.

Now it grew dark, for the night was closing in; the spears flashed dimly, and in place of smoke long tongues of flame shot from the rifle barrels, illumining the stern faces of those who held them as lightning does. But soon there was to be light. If any had leisure to observe, they may have seen flakes of fire flying upwards from the dim bush, and wondered what they were. They were bunches of burning grass being thrown on spears to fall in the thatch of the hospital roof. Presently something could be seen on this roof that shone like a star. It grew dim, then suddenly began to brighten and to increase till the star-like spot was a flame, and a hoarse cry passed from man to man of: 'O God! the hospital is on fire!'

The hospital was on fire, and in it were sick men, some of whom could not move. It was defended by a garrison, a handful of men, and at one and the same time these must bear away the sick to the store building, and hold the burning place against the Zulus, who now were upon them. They did it, but not all of it, for this was beyond the power of mortal bravery and devotion. When the thatch blazed above them, room after room did Privates Williams and Hook, R. and W. Jones, and some few others hold with the white arm—for their ammunition was spent—against the assegais of the Zulus, while their disabled comrades were borne away to the store building beneath the shelter of the connecting wall. One of them lost his life here, others were grievously wounded, but, dead or alive, their names should always be remembered among their countrymen, ay! and always will. Yet they could not save them every one; the fire scorched overhead and the assegais bit deep in front, and ever, as foes fell, fresh ones sprang into their places, and so, fighting furiously, those few gallant men were thrust back, alas! leaving some helpless comrades to die by fire and the spear.

It would be of little use to follow step by step all the events of that night. All night long the firing went on, varied from time to time by desperate assaults. All night long the little band of defenders held back the foe. All were weary, some of them were dead and more wounded, but they fought on by the light of the burning hospital, wasting no single shot. To and fro went the bearded clergyman with prayers and consolations upon his lips, and a bag of cartridges in his hands, and to and fro also went Chard and Bromhead, directing all things. By degrees the Englishmen were driven back, the hospital and its approaches were in the hands of the foe, and now they must retire to the inner wall of the cattle kraal. But they collected sacks of mealies and built two redoubts, which gave them a second line of fire, and let the Zulus do what they would, storm the place they could not, nor could they serve it as they had served the hospital and destroy it by fire.

At length the attacks slackened, the firing dwindled and died, and the dawn broke, that same dawn which showed to General Lord Chelmsford and those with him all the horror of Isandhlwana's field. Here also at Rorke's Drift it revealed death and to spare, but for the most part the corpses were those of the foe, some four hundred of whom lay lost in their last sleep around the burning hospital, in the bush, and beneath the walls of corn-sacks; four hundred killed by one hundred and thirty-nine white men all told, of whom thirty-five were sick when the defence began. The little

band had suffered, indeed, for fifteen of them were dead, and twelve
wounded, some mortally, but seeing what had been done the loss
was small. Had the Zulus once won an entrance over the last
entrenchment of biscuit boxes not a man would have remained
alive. Surely biscuits were never put to a nobler or a stranger use.

The daylight had come and the enemy vanished with the night,
retreating over a hill to the south-west. But, as the defenders
of Rorke's Drift guessed, he had no intention of abandoning his
attack. Therefore they knew that this was no time to be idle.
Sallying out of their defences they collected the arms of the dead
Zulus, then returned, and began to strip the roof of the store of its
thatch, which was a constant source of danger to them, seeing that
fire is a deadlier foe even than the assegai. They were thus engaged when again the Zulus appeared to make an end of them.
Once more the weary soldiers took up their positions, and a while
passed. Now they perceived that the Undi, which had been
advancing, slowly commenced to fall back, a movement that they
were at a loss to understand, till a shout from those who were
engaged in stripping the roof told the glad news that English troops
were advancing to their relief.

These were the remains of No. 3 column, moving down from
Isandhlwana. Little did the general and these with him expect to
find a soul living at Rorke's Drift, for they also had seen the sullen
masses of the Undi retreating from the post, and the columns of
smoke rising from the burning hospital confirmed their worst fears.
What then was their joy when they perceived a Union Jack flying
amidst the smoke, and heard the ring of a British cheer rising
from the shattered walls and the defences of sacks of corn! Forward galloped Col. Russell and his mounted men, and in five
minutes more those who remained of the garrison were safe, and
the defence of Rorke's Drift was a thing of the past; another
glorious page ready to be bound into that great book which is
called 'The Deeds of Englishmen.'

Nearly six months passed before all the dead at Isandhlwana
were reverently buried. Strange were the scenes that those saw
whose task it was to lay them to their rest. Here, hidden by the
rank grass, in one heap behind the officers' tents, lay the bodies of
some seventy men, who had made their last stand at this spot;
lower down the hill lay sixty more. Another band of about the
same strength evidently had taken refuge among the rocks of the

mountains, an l defended themselves there till their ammunition was
exhausted, and their ring broken by the assegai. All about the
plain lay Englishmen and Zulus, as they had died in the dread
struggle :—here side by side, amidst rusted rifles and bent assegais,
here their bony arms still locked in the last hug of death, and
yonder the Zulu with the white man's bayonet through his skull,
the soldier with the Zulu's assegai in what had been his heart. One
man was found, who, when his cartridges were spent, and his rifle

was broken, had defended himself to the end with a tent-hammer that
lay among his bones, and another was stretched beneath the precipice,
from the crest of which he had been hurled.

Well, they buried them where they were discovered, and there
they sleep soundly beneath the shadow of Isandhlwana's cliff.

And now a few words more, and this true story will be finished.
We conquered the Zulus at last, at a battle called Ulundi, where they
hurled themselves in vain upon the bullets and bayonets of the

British square. To the end they fought bravely for their king and country, and though they were savages, and, like all savages, cruel when at war, they were also gallant enemies, and deserve our respect. The king himself, Cetywayo, was hunted down, captured, and sent into captivity. Afterwards, there was what is called a ' popular movement' on his behalf in England, and he was sent back to Zululand, with permission to rule half the country. Meanwhile, after the conclusion of the war, our Government would not take the land, and a settlement was effected, under which thirteen chiefs were put in authority over the country. As might have been expected, these chiefs fought with each other, and many men were killed. When Cetywayo returned the fighting became fiercer than ever, since those who had tasted power refused to be dispossessed, until at last he was finally defeated, and, it is believed, poisoned by his own side, to whom he had ceased to be serviceable. Meanwhile also, the Dutch Boers, taking advantage of the confusion, occupied a great part of Zululand, which they still hold. Indeed, they would long ago have taken it all, had not the English government, seeing the great misery to which its ever-changing policy had reduced the unhappy Zulus, assumed authority over the remainder of the country. From that day forward, there has been no more killing or trouble in British Zululand, which is ruled by Sir Melmoth Osborn, K.C.M.G., and the Queen has no more contented subjects than the Zulus, nor any who pay their taxes with greater regularity !

But the Zulus as a nation are dead, and never again will a great Impi, such as swept away our troops at Isandhlwana, be seen rushing down to war. Their story is but one scene in the vast drama which is being enacted in this generation, and which some of you who read these lines may live to see, not accomplished, indeed, but in the way of accomplishment—the drama of the building up of a great Anglo-Saxon empire in Africa—an empire that within the next few centuries may well become one of the mightiest in the world. We have made many and many a mistake, but still that empire grows ; in spite of the errors of the Home Government, the obstinacy of the Boers, the power of native chiefs, and the hatred of Portuguese, still it grows. Already it is about as big as Europe, and it is only a baby yet, a baby begotten by the genius and courage of individual Englishmen.

When the child has become a giant—yes, even in those far-off ages when it is a very old giant, a king among the nations—we may be sure that, from generation to generation, men will show their sons the mountain that was called Isandhlwana, or the place of the Little Hand, and a certain spot on the banks of the Buffalo River, and tell the tale of how beneath that hill the wild Zulus of the ancient times overwhelmed the forces of the early English settlers; of how, for a long night through, a few men of those forces held two grass-thatched sheds against their foe's savage might; and of how some miles away two heroes named Melville and Coghill died together whilst striving to save the colours of their regiment from the grasp of the victorious 'Children of Heaven.'

Now it may interest you to know that these last words are written with a pen that was found among the bones of the dead at Isandhlwana.

H. RIDER HAGGARD.

HOW LEIF THE LUCKY FOUND VINELAND THE GOOD

THIS is the story of the first finding of America by the Icelanders, nearly five hundred years before Columbus. They landed on the coast, and stayed for a short time; where they landed is uncertain. Thinking that it was in New England, the people of Boston have erected a statue of Leif in their town. The story was not written till long after Leif's time, and it cannot *all* be true. Dead men do not return and give directions about their burial as we read here. We have omitted a silly tale of a one-footed man. In the middle ages, people believed that one-footed men lived in Africa; they thought Vineland was near Africa, so they brought the fable into the Saga.

Hundreds of years before Columbus discovered America, there lived in Iceland a man named Eric the Red. His father had slain a man in Norway, and fled with his family to Iceland. Eric, too, was a dangerous man. His servants did mischief on the farm of a neighbour, who slew them. Then Eric slew the farmer, and also Holmgang Hrafn, a famous duellist, of whom the country was well rid. Eric was banished from that place, and, in his new home, had a new quarrel. He lent some furniture to a man who refused to restore it. Eric, therefore, carried off his goods, and the other pursued him. They fought, and Eric killed him. For this he was made an outlaw, and went sailing to discover new countries. He found one, where he settled, calling it Greenland, because, he said, people would come there more readily if it had a good name.

One Thorbiorn, among others, sailed to Greenland, but came in an unlucky time, for fish were scarce, and some settlers were drowned. At that day, some of the new comers were Christians, some still worshipped the old Gods, Thor and Woden, and practised magic. These sent for a prophetess to tell them what the end of their new colony would be. It is curious to know what a real witch was like, and how she behaved, so we shall copy the story from the old Icelandic book.

' When she came in the evening, with the man who had been sent to meet her, she was clad in a dark-blue cloak, fastened with a strap, and set with stones quite down to the hem. She wore glass beads around her neck, and upon her head a black lambskin hood, lined with white catskin. In her hands she carried a staff,

upon which there was a knob, which was ornamented with brass, and set with stones up about the knob. Circling her waist she wore a girdle of touchwood, and attached to it a great skin pouch, in which she kept the charms which she used when she was practising her sorcery. She wore upon her feet shaggy calfskin shoes, with long, tough latchets, upon the ends of which there were large brass buttons. She had catskin gloves upon her hands; the gloves were white inside and lined with fur. When she entered, all of the folk felt it to be their duty to offer her becoming greetings. She received the salutations of each individual according as he pleased her. Yeoman Thorkel took the sibyl by the hand, and led her to the seat which had been made ready for her. Thorkel bade her run her eyes over man and beast and home. She had little to say concerning all these. The tables were brought forth in the evening, and it remains to be told what manner of food was prepared for the prophetess. A porridge of goat's beestings was made for her, and for meat there were dressed the hearts of every kind of beast which could be obtained there. She had a brass spoon, and a knife with a handle of walrus tusk, with a double hasp of brass around the haft, and from this the point was broken. And when the tables were removed, Yeoman Thorkel approaches the prophetess Thorbiorg, and asks how she is pleased with the home, and the character of the folk, and how speedily she would be likely to become aware of that concerning which he had questioned her, and which the people were anxious to know. She replied that she could not give an opinion in this matter before the morrow, after that she had slept there through the night. And on the morrow, when the day was far spent, such preparations were made as were necessary to enable her to accomplish her soothsaying. She bade them bring her those women who knew the incantation which she required to work her spells, and which she called Warlocks ; but such women were not to be found. Thereupon a search was made throughout the house, to see whether anyone knew this [incantation]. Then says Gudrid, Thorbiorn's daughter : " Although I am neither skilled in the black art nor a sibyl, yet my foster-mother, Halldis, taught me in Iceland that spell-song, which she called Warlocks." Thorbiorg answered : " Then art thou wise in season ! " Gudrid replies ; " This is an incantation and ceremony of such a kind that I do not mean to lend it any aid, for that I am a Christian woman." Thorbiorg answers : " It might so be that thou couldst give thy help to the company here, and still be no worse woman than before ; however, I leave it with Thorkel to provide for my needs." Thorkel now so urged Gudrid that she said she must needs comply with his wishes. The women then made a ring round about, while Thorbiorg sat up on the spell-daïs. Gudrid then sang the song, so sweet and well, that no one remembered ever before to have heard the melody sung with so fair a voice as this. The sorceress thanked her for the song, and said : " She has indeed lured many spirits hither, who think it pleasant to hear this song, those who were wont to forsake us hitherto and refuse to submit themselves to us.   Many things are now revealed to me, which hitherto have been hidden, both from me and from others.   And I am able to announce that this period of famine will not endure longer, but the season will mend as spring approaches.   The visitation of disease, which has been so long upon you, will disappear sooner than expected." '

After this, Thorbiorn sailed to the part of Greenland where Eric the Red lived, and there was received with open arms.   Eric had two sons, one called Thorstein, the other Leif the Lucky, and it was Leif who afterwards discovered Vineland the Good, that is, the coast of America, somewhere between Nova Scotia and New England.   He found it by accident.   He had been in Norway, at the court of king Olaf, who bade him proclaim Christianity in Greenland.   As he was sailing thither, Leif was driven by tempests out of his course, and came upon coasts which he had never heard of, where wild vines grew, and hence he called that shore Vineland the Good.   The vine did not grow, of course, in Iceland.   But Leif had with him a German Tyrker, and one day, when they were on shore, Tyrker was late in joining the rest.   He was very much excited, and spoke in the German tongue, saying ' I have found something new, vines and grapes.'   Then they filled their boat full of grapes, and sailed away.   He also brought away some men from a wreck, and with these, and the message of the Gospel, he sailed back to Greenland, to his father, Eric the Red, and from that day he was named Leif the Lucky.   But Eric had no great mind to become a Christian, he had been born to believe in Thor and his own sword.

Next year Leif's brother, Thorstein, set out to find Vineland, and Eric, first burying all his treasures, started with him, but he fell from his horse, and broke his ribs, and his company came within sight of Ireland, but Vineland they did not see, so they returned to Ericsfirth in Greenland, and there passed the winter.

There was much sickness, and one woman died.   After her death she rose, and they could only lay her by holding an axe before her breast.   Thorstein, Eric's son, died also, but in the night he arose again and said that Christian burial should be given to men in consecrated ground.   For the manner had been to bury the dead in their farms with a long pole driven through the earth till it touched the breast of the corpse.   Afterwards the priest came, and poured holy water through the hole, and not till then, perhaps long after the death, was the funeral service held. After Thorstein rose and spoke, Christian burial was always used in Greenland. Next year came Karlsefni from Iceland, with two ships, and Eric received him kindly, and gave all his crew winter quarters. In summer nothing would serve Karlsefni but to search again for Vineland the Good. They took three ships and one hundred and sixty men, and south they sailed. They passed Flat Stone Land, where there were white foxes, and Bear Island, where they saw a bear, and Forest Land, and

a cape where they found the keel of a wrecked ship, this they named Keelness. Then they reached the Wonder Strands, long expanses of sandy shore. Now Karlsefni had with him two Scotch or Irish savages, the swiftest of all runners, whom King Olaf had given to Leif the Lucky, and they were fleeter-footed than deer. They wore only a plaid and kilt all in one piece, for the rest they were naked. Karlsefni landed them south of Wonder Strands, and bade them run south and return on the third day to report about the country. When they returned one carried a bunch of grapes, the other ears of native wheat (maize ?). Then they sailed on, passed an isle covered with birds' eggs, and a firth, which they called Streamfirth, from the tide in it.

Beyond Streamfirth they landed and established themselves there.

' There were mountains thereabouts. They occupied themselves exclusively with the exploration of the country. They remained there during the winter, and they had taken no thought for this during the summer. The fishing began to fail, and they began to fall short of food. Then Thorhall the Huntsman disappeared. They had already prayed to God for food, but it did not come as promptly as their necessities seemed to demand. They searched for Thorhall for three half-days, and found him on a projecting crag. He was lying there, and looking up at the sky, with mouth and nostrils agape, and mumbling something. They asked him why he had gone thither; he replied, that this did not concern anyone. They asked him then to go home with them, and he did so. Soon after this a whale appeared there, and they captured it, and flensed it, and no one could tell what manner of whale it was; and when the cooks had prepared it, they ate of it, and were all made ill by it. Then Thorhall, approaching them, says : " Did not the Red-beard (that is, Thor) prove more helpful than your Christ ? This is my reward for the verses which I composed to Thor the Trustworthy ; seldom has he failed me." When the people heard this, they cast the whale down into the sea, and made their appeals to God. The weather then improved, and they could now row out to fish, and thenceforward they had no lack of provisions, for they could hunt game on the land, gather eggs on the island, and catch fish from the sea.'

Next spring Thorhall the heathen left them, laughing at the wine which he had been promised, and sailed north. He and his crew were driven to Ireland, where they were captured and sold as slaves, and that was all Thorhall got by worshipping the Red Beard. Karlsefni sailed south and reached a rich country of wild maize, where also was plenty of fish and of game. Here they first met the natives, who came in a fleet of skin-canoes. 'They were swarthy men and ill-looking, and the hair of their heads was ugly. They had great eyes and were broad of cheek.'

The Icelanders held up a white shield in sign of peace, and the natives withdrew. They may have been Eskimo or Red Indians.

The winter was mild and open, but spring had scarce returned, when the bay was as full of native canoes ' as if ashes had been sprinkled over it.' They only came to trade and exchanged furs for red cloth, nor did they seem to care whether they got a broad piece of cloth or a narrow one. They also wanted weapons, but these Karlsefni refused to sell. The market was going on busily when a bull that Karlsefni had brought from Greenland came out of the wood and began to bellow, whereon the Skraelings (as they called the natives) ran ! Three weeks passed when the Skraelings returned in very great force, waving their clubs *against* the course of the sun, whereas in peace they waved them with it. Karlsefni showed a red shield, the token of war, and fighting began. It is not easy to make out what happened, for there are two sagas, or stories of these events, both written down long after they occurred. In one we read that the Skraelings were good slingers, and also that they used a machine which reminds one rather of gunpowder than of anything else. They swung from a pole a great black ball, and it made a fearful noise when it fell among Karlsefni's men. So frightened were they that they saw Skraelings where there were none, and they were only rallied by the courage of a woman named Freydis, who seized a dead man's sword and faced the Skraelings, beating her bare breast with the flat of the blade. On this the Skraelings ran to their canoes and paddled away. In the other account Karlsefni had fortified his house with a palisade, behind which the women waited. To one of them, Gudrid, the appearance of a white woman came ; her hair was of a light chestnut colour, she was pale and had very large eyes. 'What is thy name ? ' she said to Gudrid. ' My name is Gudrid ; but what is thine ? ' ' Gudrid ! ' says the strange woman. Then came the sound of a great crash and the woman vanished. A battle followed in which many Skraelings were slain.

It all reads like a dream. In the end Karlsefni sailed back to Ericsfirth with a great treasure of furs. A great and prosperous family in Iceland was descended from him at the time when the stories were written down. But it is said that Freydis who frightened the Skraelings committed many murders in Vineland among her own people.

The Icelanders never returned to Vineland the Good, though a bishop named Eric is said to have started for the country in 1121. Now, in the story of Cortés, you may read how the Mexicans believed in a God called Quetzalcoatl, a white man in appearance, who dwelt among them and departed mysteriously, saying that he would come again, and they at first took Cortes and his men for the children of Quetzalcoatl. So we may fancy if we please that Bishop Eric, or one of his descendants, wandered from Vineland south and west across the continent and arrived among the Aztecs, and by them was taken for a God.[1]

---

[1] The story is taken from the Saga of Eric the Red, and from the Flatey Book in Mr. Reeves's *Finding of Wineland the Good* (Clarendon Press, 1890). The discovery of Vineland was made about the year 1000. The saga of Eric the Red was written about 1300-1334, but two hundred years before, about 1134, Ari the learned mentions Vineland as quite familiar in his *Íslandingabók*. There are other traces of Vineland, earlier than the manuscript of the Saga of Eric the Red. Of course we do not know when that saga was first written down. The oldest extant manuscript of it belonged to one Hauk, who died in 1334.

THE ESCAPES OF CERVANTES

MOST people know of the terrible war, waged even down to the present century, between the Christian ships cruising about the Mediterranean and the dreaded Moors or Corsairs of the Barbary Coast. It was a war that began in the name of religion, the Crescent against the Cross; but, as far as we can learn from the records of both sides, there was little to choose in the way that either party treated the captives. A large number of these were chained to the oars of the galleys which were the ships of battle of the middle ages, and sometimes the oars were so long and heavy that they needed forty men to each. The rowers had food enough to give them the strength necessary for their work, and that was all, and the knowledge that they were exerting themselves for the downfall of their fellow-Christians, often of their fellow-countrymen, must have made their labour a toil indeed. Often it happened that a man's courage gave way and he denied his faith and his country, and rose to great honours in the service of the Sultan, the chief of the little kings who swarmed on the African coasts, The records of the Corsairs bristle with examples of these successful renegades, many of them captured as boys, who were careless under what flag they served, as long as their lives were lives of adventure.

All the captives were not, however, turned into galley slaves. Some were taken to the towns and kept in prisons called *bagnios*, waiting till their friends sent money to redeem them. If this was delayed, they were set to public works, and treated with great severity, so that their letters imploring deliverance might become yet more urgent. The others, known as the king's captives, whose ransom might be promptly expected, did no work and were kept apart from the rest.

It was on September 26, 1575, that Miguel Cervantes, the future author of 'Don Quixote,' fell into the hands of a Greek renegade

M

Dali Mami by name, captain of a galley of twenty-two banks of oars. Cervantes, the son of a poor but well-descended gentleman of Castile, had served with great distinction under Don John of Austria at the battle of Lepanto four years earlier, and was now returning with his brother Rodrigo to Spain on leave, bearing with him letters from the commander-in-chief, Don John, the Duke of Sesa, Viceroy of Sicily, and other distinguished men, testifying to his qualities as a soldier, 'as valiant as he was unlucky,' and recommending Philip II. to give him the command of a Spanish company then being formed for Italian service. But all these honours proved his bane. The Spanish squadron had not sailed many days from Naples when it encountered a Corsair fleet, and after a sharp fight Cervantes and his friends were carried captive into Algiers.

Of course the first thing done was to examine each man as to his position in life, and the amount of ransom he might be expected to bring, and the letters found upon Miguel Cervantes impressed them with the notion that he was a person of consequence, and capable of furnishing a large sum of money. They therefore took every means of ensuring his safety, loading him with chains, appointing him guards, and watching him day and night.

> ' Stone walls do not a prison make,
>   Nor iron bars a cage.'

Cervantes never lost heart a moment, but at once began to plan an escape for himself and his fellow-captives. But the scheme broke down owing to the treachery of the man in whom he had confided, and the Spaniards, particularly Cervantes, were made to suffer a stricter confinement than before. The following year the old Cervantes sent over what money he had been able to raise on his own property and his daughters' marriage portions for the ransom of his sons, by the hands of the Redemptorist Fathers, an Order which had been founded for the sole purpose of carrying on this charitable work. But when the sum was offered to Dali Mami he declared it wholly insufficient for purchasing the freedom of such a captive, though it was considered adequate as the ransom of the younger brother Rodrigo. Accordingly, in August 1577, Rodrigo Cervantes set sail for Spain, bearing secret orders from his brother Miguel to fit out an armed frigate, and to send it by way of Valencia and Majorca to rescue himself and his friends.

But even before the departure of Rodrigo, Cervantes had been laying other plans. He had, somehow or other, managed to make acquaintance with the Navarrese gardener of a Greek renegade named Azan, who had a garden stretching down to the sea-shore, about three miles east of Algiers, where Cervantes was then imprisoned. This gardener had contrived to use a cave in Azan's garden as a hiding place for some escaped Christians, and as far back as February 1577 about fifteen had taken refuge there, under the direction of Cervantes. How they remained for so many months undiscovered, and how they were all fed, no one can tell; but this part of the duty had been undertaken by a captive renegade called El Dorador, or the Gilder, to whom their secret had been confided.

Meanwhile, Rodrigo had proved faithful to his trust. He had equipped a frigate for sea, under the command of a tried soldier, Viana by name, who was familiar with the Barbary coast. It set sail at the end of September, and by the 28th had sighted Algiers. From motives of prudence the boat kept to sea till nightfall, when it silently approached the shore. The captives hailed it with joy, and were in the act of embarking, when a fishing craft full of Moors passed by, and the rescue vessel was forced to put to sea. Meanwhile, Cervantes and the fugitives in the cave had to return disheartened into hiding, and await another opportunity.

But once lost, the opportunity was gone for ever. Before any fresh scheme could be concerted, El Dorador had betrayed the hiding place of the Christians and their plan of escape to the cruel Dey or King Azan, who saw in the information a means to satisfy his greed. According to the law of the country, he was enabled to claim the escaped slaves as his own property (except Cervantes, for whom he paid 500 crowns), and with a company of armed men presented himself before the cave.

In this dreadful strait Cervantes' courage never faltered. He told the trembling captives not to fear, as he would take upon himself the entire responsibility of the plan. Then, addressing Azan's force, he proclaimed himself the sole contriver of the scheme, and professed his willingness to bear the punishment. The Turks were struck dumb at valour such as this, in the presence of the most dreadful torments, and contented themselves with ordering the captives into close confinement at the bagnio, hanging the gardener, and bringing Cervantes bound to receive his sentence from the Dey Azan himself.

The threats of impalement, torture, mutilation of every kind, which Cervantes well knew to be no mere threats, had no effect upon his faithful soul. He stuck to the story he had told, and the Dey, 'wearied by so much constancy,' as the Spanish historian says, ended by loading him with chains, and throwing him again into prison.

For some time he remained here, strictly and closely guarded, but his mind always active as to plans of escape. At last, however, he managed to enter into relations with Don Martin de Cordoba, General of Oran, by means of a Moor, who undertook to convey letters asking for help for the Spanish prisoners. But his ill fortune had not yet deserted him. The messenger fell into the hands of other Moors, who handed him over to Azan, and the wretched man was at once put to a cruel death by the Dey's orders. Curiously enough, the sentence of 2,000 lashes passed upon Cervantes was never carried into effect.

Disappointments and dangers only made Cervantes more determined to free himself or die in the attempt; but nearly two years dragged by before he saw another hope rise before him, though he did everything he could in the interval to soothe the wretched lot of his fellow-captives. This time his object was to induce two Valencia merchants of Algiers to buy an armed frigate, destined to carry Cervantes and a large number of Christians back to Spain, but at the last minute they were again betrayed, this time by a countryman, and again Cervantes took the blame on his own shoulders, and confessed nothing to the Dey.

Now it seemed indeed as if his last moment had come. His hands were tied behind him, and a cord was put round his neck; but Cervantes never swerved from the tale he had resolved to tell, and at the close of the interview found himself within the walls of a Moorish prison, where he lay for five months loaded with fetters and chains, and treated with every kind of severity, though never with actual cruelty.

All this time his mind was busy with a fresh scheme, nothing short of a concerted insurrection of all the captives in Algiers, numbering about 25,000, who were to overpower the city, and to plant the Spanish flag on its towers. His measures seem to have been taken with sufficient prudence and foresight to give them a fair chance of success, bold as the idea was, but treachery as usual caused the downfall of everything. Why, under such repeated provocation, the cruel Azan Aga did not put him to a frightful death it is hard to understand, but in his 'Captive's Story,' Cervantes himself bears testimony to the comparative moderation of the Dey's behaviour towards him. 'Though suffering,' he says, 'often, if not indeed always, from hunger and thirst, the worst of all our miseries was the sight and sound of the tortures daily inflicted by our master on our fellow-Christians. Every day he hanged one, impaled another, cut off the ears of a third; and all this for so little reason, or even for none at all, that the very Turks knew he did it for the mere pleasure of doing it; and because to him cruelty was the natural employment of mankind. Only one man did he use well, and that was a Spanish soldier, named Saavedra, and though this Saavedra had struck blows for liberty which will be remembered by Moors for many years to come, yet Azan never either gave him stripes himself, nor ordered his servants to do so, neither did he ever throw him an evil word; while we trembled lest for the smallest of his offences the tyrant would have him impaled, and more than once he himself expected it.' This straightforward account of matters inside the bagnio is the more valuable and interesting if we recollect that Cervantes' great-grandmother was a Saavedra, and that the soldier alluded to in the text was really himself. It is impossible to explain satisfactorily the sheathing of the tiger's claws on his account alone; did Cervantes exercise unconsciously a mesmeric influence over Azan? Did Azan ascribe his captive's defiance of death and worse than death to his bearing a charmed life? Or did he hold him to be a man of such consequence in his own country, that it was well to keep him in as good condition as Azan's greed would permit? We shall never know; only there remains Cervantes' emphatic declaration that during the five long years of his captivity no man's hand was ever lifted against him.

Meanwhile, having no more money wherewith to ransom his son, Rodrigo de Cervantes made a declaration of his poverty before a court of law, and set forth Miguel's services and claims. In March 1578, the old man's prayer was enforced by the appearance of four witnesses who had known him both in the Levant and in Algiers and could testify to the truth of his father's statement, and a certificate of such facts as were within his knowledge being willingly offered by the Duke of Sesa, the King, Philip II., consented to furnish the necessary ransom.

But the ill-fortune which had attended Cervantes in these past years seemed to stick to him now. Just when the negotiations were drawing to a conclusion, his father suddenly died, and it appeared as if the expedition of the Redemptorist Fathers would sail without him. However, his mother was happily a woman of energy, and after managing somehow to raise three hundred ducats on her own possessions, appealed to the King for help. This he appears to have granted her at once, and he gave her an order for 2,000 ducats on some Valencia merchandise; but with their usual bad luck they only ultimately succeeded in obtaining about sixty, which with her own three hundred were placed in the hands of the Redemptorist Fathers.

It was time : the fact that the term of Azan's government of Algiers had drawn to an end rendered him more than ever greedy for money, and he demanded for Cervantes double the price that he himself had paid, and threatened, if this was not forthcoming, to carry his captive on board his own vessel, which was bound for Constantinople. Indeed, this threat was actually put into effect, and Cervantes, bound and loaded with chains, was placed in a ship of the little squadron that was destined for Turkish waters. The good father felt that once in Constantinople, Cervantes would probably remain a prisoner to the end of his life, and made unheard of efforts to accomplish his release, borrowing the money that was still lacking from some Algerian merchants, and even using the ransoms that had been entrusted to him for other captives. Then at last Cervantes was set free, and after five years was able to go where he would and return to his native country.

His work however was not yet done. He somehow discovered that a Spaniard named Blanco de Paz, who had once before betrayed him, was determined, through jealousy, to have him arrested the moment he set foot in Spain, and to this end had procured a mass of false evidence respecting his conduct in Algiers. It is not easy to see what Cervantes could have done to incur the hatred of this man, but about this he did not trouble himself to inquire, and set instantly to consider the best way of bringing his schemes to naught. He entreated his friend, Father Gil, to be present at an interview held before the notary Pedro de Ribera, at which a number of respectable Christians appeared to answer a paper of twenty-five questions, propounded by Cervantes himself, as to the principal events of his five years of imprisonment, and his treatment of his fellow-captives. Armed with this evidence, he was able to defy the traitor, and to return in honour to his native land.

With the rest of his life we have nothing to do. It was not, we may be sure, lacking in adventure, for he was the kind of man to whom adventures come, and as his inheritance was all gone, he went back to his old trade, and joined the army which Philip was assembling to enforce his claim to the crown of Portugal. In this country as in all others to which his wandering life had led him, he made many friends and took notice of what went on around him. He was in all respects a man practical and vigorous, in many ways the exact opposite of his own Don Quixote, who saw everything enlarged and glorified and nothing as it really was, but in other ways the true counterpart of his hero in his desire to give help and comfort wherever it was needed, and to leave the world better than he found it.

THE WORTHY ENTERPRISE OF JOHN FOXE, AN ENGLISHMAN, IN DELIVERING TWO HUNDRED AND SIXTY-SIX CHRISTIANS OUT OF THE CAPTIVITY OF THE TURKS AT ALEXANDRIA, JANUARY 3, 1577

AMONG our English merchants it is a common thing to traffic with Spain, for which purpose, in 1563, there set out from Portsmouth a ship called the 'Three Half Moons,' with thirty-eight men on board, and well armed, the better to encounter any foes they might meet. Now, drawing near the Straits, they found themselves beset by eight Turkish galleys, so that it was impossible for them to fly, but they must either yield or be sunk. This the owner perceiving, manfully encouraged his company, telling them not to faint in seeing such a heap of their foes ready to devour them ; putting them in mind also that if it were God's pleasure to give them into their enemies' hands, there ought not to be one unpleasant look among them, but they must take it patiently; putting them in mind also of the ancient worthiness of their countrymen, who in the hardest extremities have always most prevailed. With other such encouragement they all fell on their knees, making their prayers briefly to God.

Then stood up Grove, the master, being a comely man, with his sword and target, holding them up in defiance against his enemies. Likewise stood up the owner, boatswain, purser, and every man well armed. Now also sounded up the trumpets, drums, and flutes, which would have encouraged any man, however little heart he had in him.

Then John Foxe, the gunner, took him to his charge, sending his bullets among the Turks, who likewise fired among the Christians, and thrice as fast. But shortly they drew near, so that the English bowmen fell to shooting so terribly among their galleys that there

were twice as many of the Turks slain as the whole number of the
Christians. But the Turks discharged twice as fast against the
Christians, and so long that the ship was very sorely battered and
bruised, which the foe perceiving, made the more haste to come
aboard. For this coming aboard many a Turk paid dearly with his
life, but it was all in vain, and board they did, where they found a
hot skirmish. For the Englishmen showed themselves men indeed,
and the boatswain was valiant above the rest, for he fought among
the Turks like a mad lion, and there was none of them that could

stand in his face; till at last there came a shot that struck him
in the breast, so that he fell down, bidding them farewell, and
to be of good comfort, and exhorting them rather to win praise by
death than to live in captivity and shame. This, they hearing,
indeed intended to have done, but the number and press of the
Turks was so great that they could not wield their weapons,
and so were taken, when they intended rather to have died,
except only the master's mate, who shrank from the fight like a
notable coward.

But so it was, and the Turks were victors, though they had little
cause of triumph. Then it would have grieved any hard heart to
see these infidels wantonly ill-treating the Christians, who were no

sooner in the galleys than their garments were torn from their backs, and they set to the oars.

I will make no mention of their miseries, being now under their enemies raging stripes, their bodies distressed with too much heat, and also with too much cold ; but I will rather show the deliverance of those who, being in great misery, continually trust in God, with a steadfast hope that He will deliver them.

Near the city of Alexandria, being a harbour, there is a ship-road, very well defended by strong walls, into which the Turks are accustomed to bring their galleys every winter, and there repair them and lay them up against the spring. In this road there is a prison, in which the captives and all those prisoners who serve in the galleys are confined till the sea be calm again for voyaging, every prisoner being most grievously laden with irons on his legs, giving him great pain. Into this prison, all these Christians were put, and fast guarded all the winter, and every winter. As time passed the master and the owner were redeemed by friends ; but the rest were left in misery, and half-starved—except John Foxe, who being a somewhat skilful barber, made shift now and then, by means of his craft, to help out his fare with a good meal. Till at last God sent him favour in the sight of the keeper of the prison, so that he had leave to go in and out to the road, paying a stipend to the keeper, and wearing a lock about his leg. This liberty six more had, on the same conditions ; for after their long imprisonment, it was not feared that they would work any mischief against the Turks.

In the winter of the year 1577, all the galleys having reached port, and their masters and mariners being at their own homes, the ships themselves being stripped of their masts and sails, there were in the prison two hundred and sixty-eight Christian captives, belonging to sixteen different nations. Among these were three Englishmen, one of them John Foxe, the others William Wickney and Robert Moore. And John Foxe, now having been thirteen or fourteen years under the bondage of the Turks, and being weary thereof, pondered continually, day and night, how he might escape, never ceasing to pray God to further his enterprise, if it should be to His glory.

Not far from the road, at one side of the city, there was a certain victualling-house, which one Peter Unticare had hired, paying a fee to the keeper of the prison. This Peter Unticare was a Spaniard, and also a Christian, and had been a prisoner about thirty years, never contriving any means to escape, but keeping himself quiet without being suspected of conspiracy. But on the coming of John Foxe they disclosed their minds to each other about their loss of liberty; and to this Unticare John Foxe confided a plan for regaining their freedom, which plan the three Englishmen continually brooded over, till they resolved to acquaint five more prisoners with their secret. This being done, they arranged in three more days to make their attempt at escape. Whereupon John Foxe, and Peter Unticare, and the other six arranged to meet in the prison on the last day of December, and there they told the rest of the prisoners what their intention was, and how they hoped to bring it to pass. And having, without much ado, persuaded all to agree, John Foxe gave them a kind of files, which he had hoarded together by means of Peter Unticare, charging them every man to be free of his fetters by eight o'clock on the following night.

The next night John Foxe and his six companions, all having met at the house of Peter Unticare, spent the evening mirthfully for fear of rousing suspicion, till it was time for them to put their scheme into execution. Then they sent Peter Unticare to the master of the road, in the name of one of the masters of the city, with whom he was well acquainted, and at the mention of whose name he was likely to come at once, desiring him to meet him there, and promising to bring him back again.

The keeper agreed to go with Unticare, telling the warders not to bar the gate, for he would come again with all speed. In the meantime the other seven had provided themselves with all the weapons they could find in the house, and John Foxe took a rusty old sword without a hilt, which he managed to make serve by bending the hand end of the sword instead of a hilt.

Now the keeper being come to the house, and seeing no light nor hearing any noise, straightway suspected the plot, and was turning back. But John Foxe, standing behind the corner of the house, stepped forth to him. He perceiving it to be John Foxe, said: ' O Foxe ! what have I deserved of thee that thou shouldest seek my death ? '

' Thou, villain,' quoth Foxe, ' hast been a blood-sucker of many a Christian's blood, and now thou shalt know what thou hast deserved at my hands ! '

Therewith he lifted up his bright shining sword, cleared of its ten years' rust, and struck him so strong a blow that his head was cleft asunder, and he fell stark dead to the ground. Thereupon Peter Unticare went in and told the rest how it was with the keeper, and at once they came forth, and with their weapons ran him through and cut off his head, so that no man should know who he was.

Then they marched towards the road, and entered it softly. There were six warders guarding it, and one of them asked who was there. Then quoth Foxe and his company, ' All friends ! '

But when they were within it proved contrary, for, quoth Foxe to his companions :

'My masters, here there is not a man to a man, so look you play your parts ! ' They so behaved themselves indeed that they had despatched those six quickly. Then John Foxe, intending not to be thwarted in his enterprise, barred the gate surely, and planted a cannon against it.

They entered the gaoler's lodge, where they found the keys of the fortress and prison by his bedside, and then they all got better weapons. In this chamber was a chest holding a great treasure, all in ducats, which Peter Unticare and two more stuffed into their garments, as many as they could carry. But Foxe would not touch them, saying that it was his liberty and theirs he sought, and not to make a spoil of the wicked treasure of the infidels. Yet these words did not sink into their hearts, though they had no good of their gain.

Now, having provided themselves with the weapons they needed, they came 'to the prison, and unlocked its gates and doors, and called forth all the prisoners, whom they employed, some in ramming up the gate, some in fitting up a galley which was the best in the road.

In the prison were several warders, whom John Foxe and his company slew ; but this was perceived by eight more Turks, who fled to the top of the prison, where Foxe and his company had to reach them by ladders. Then followed a hot skirmish, and John Foxe was shot thrice through his apparel, without being hurt ; but Peter Unticare and the other two, who had weighed themselves down with the ducats so that they could not manage their weapons, were slain.

Among the Turks there was one thrust through who fell from the top of the prison wall, and made such a crying out that the inhabitants of a house or two that stood near came and questioned him, and soon understood the case—how the prisoners were attempting to escape. Then they raised both Alexandria on the west side of the road, and a castle at the end of the city next to the road, and also another fortress on the north side of the road. And now the

prisoners had no way to escape but one that might seem impossible for them.

Then every man set to work, some to their tackling, some carrying arms and provisions into the galley, some keeping the enemy from the wall of the road. To be short, there was no man idle, nor any labour spent in vain; so that presently the galley was ready, and into it they all leaped hastily, and hoisted sail.

But when the galley had set sail, and was past the shelter of the road, the two castles had full power over it, and what could save it from sinking? The cannon let fly from both sides, and it was between them both.

Yet there was not one on board that feared the shot that came thundering about their ears, nor yet was any man scarred or touched. For now God held forth His buckler and shielded this galley, having tried their faith to the uttermost. And they sailed away, being not once touched with the glance of a shot, and were presently out of the reach of the Turkish cannon. Then might you see the Turks coming down to the waterside, in companies like swarms of bees, trying to make ready their galleys—which would have been a quick piece of work, seeing that they had in them neither oars, nor sails, nor anything else. Yet they carried them in, but some into one galley, some into another, for there was much confusion among them; and the sea being rough, and they having no certain guide, it was a thing impossible that they should overtake the prisoners. For they had neither pilot, mariners, nor any skilful master that was ready at this pinch.

When the Christians were safe out of the enemy's coast, John Foxe called to them all, telling them to fall down upon their knees, thanking God for their delivery, and beseeching Him to aid them to the land of their friends. Then they fell straightway to labouring at the oars, striving to come to some Christian country, as near as they could guess by the stars. But the winds were so contrary, now driving them this way, now that, that they were bewildered, thinking that God had forsaken them and left them to yet greater danger. And soon there were no victuals left in the galley; and the famine grew to be so great that in twenty-eight days there had died eight persons.

But it fell out that upon the twenty-ninth day, they reached the Isle of Candy, and landed at Gallipoli, where they were made much of by the Abbot and monks, and cared for and refreshed. They kept there the sword with which John Foxe had killed the keeper, esteeming it a most precious jewel.

Then they sailed along the cost to Tarento, where they sold the galley, and went on foot to Naples, having divided the price. But at Naples they parted asunder, going every man his own way, and John Foxe journeyed to Rome, where he was well entertained by an Englishman and presented to the Pope, who rewarded him liberally and gave him letters to the King of Spain. And by the King of Spain also he was well entertained, and granted twenty pence a day. Thence, desiring to return into his own country, he departed in 1579, and being come into England, he went into the Court, and told all his travel to the Council, who, considering that he had spent a great part of his youth in thraldom, extended to him their liberality, to help to maintain him in age—to their own honour and the encouragement of all true-hearted Christians.

. BARON TRENCK

MOST men who have escaped from prison owe their fame, not to their flight, but to the deeds which caused their imprisonment. It may, however, safely be asserted that few people out of his own country would have heard of Baron Trenck had it not been for the wonderful skill and cunning with which he managed to cut through the 'stone walls' and 'iron bars' of all his many 'cages.' He was born at Königsberg in Prussia in 1726, and entered the body-guard of Frederic II. in 1742, when he was about sixteen. Trenck was a young man of good family, rich, well-educated, and, according to his own account, fond of amusement. He confesses to having shirked his duties more than once for the sake of some pleasure, even after the War of the Austrian Succession had broken out (September 1744), and Frederic, strict though he was, had forgiven him. It is plain from this, that the King must have considered that Trenck had been guilty of some deadly treachery towards him, when in after years he declined to pardon him for crimes which after all the young man had never committed.

Trenck's first confinement was in 1746, when he was thrown into the Castle of Glatz, on a charge of corresponding with his cousin and namesake, who was in the service of the Empress Maria Theresa, and of being an Austrian spy. At first he was kindly treated and allowed to walk freely about the fortifications, and he took advantage of the liberty given him to arrange a plan of escape with one of his fellow-prisoners. The plot was, however, betrayed by the other man, and a heavy punishment fell on Trenck. By the King's orders, he was promptly deprived of all his privileges, and placed in a cell in one of the towers, which overlooked the ramparts lying ninety feet below, on the side nearest the town. This added a fresh difficulty to his chances of escape, as, in passing from the castle to the town, he was certain to be seen by many people. But no obstacles mattered to Trenck. He had money, and then, as now, money could do a great deal. So he began by bribing one of the officials about the prison, and the official in his turn bribed a soap-boiler, who lived not far from the castle gates, and promised to conceal Trenck somewhere in his house. Still, liberty must have seemed a long way off, for Trenck had only one little knife (*canif*) with which to cut through everything. By dint of incessant and hard work, he managed to saw through three thick steel bars, but even so, there were eight others left to do. His friend the official then procured him a file, but he was obliged to use it with great care, lest the scraping sound should be heard by his guards. Perhaps they wilfully closed their ears, for many of them were sorry for Trenck; but, at all events, the eleven bars were at last sawn through, and all that remained was to make a rope ladder. This he did by tearing his leather portmanteau into strips, and plaiting them into a rope, and as this was not long enough, he added his sheets. The night was dark and rainy, which favoured him, and he reached the bottom of the rampart in safety. Unluckily, he met here with an obstacle on which he had never counted. There was a large drain, opening into one of the trenches, which Trenck had neither seen nor heard of, and into this he fell. In spite of his struggles, he was held fast, and his strength being at last exhausted, he was forced to call the sentinel, and at midday, having been left in the drain for hours to make sport for the town, he was carried back to his cell.

Henceforth he was still more strictly watched than before, though, curiously enough, his money never seems to have been taken from him, and at this time he had about eighty louis left, which he always kept hidden about him. Eight days after his last attempt, Fouquet, the commandant of Glatz, who hated Trenck and all his family, sent a deputation consisting of the adjutant, an officer, and a certain Major Doo, to speak to the unfortunate man, and exhort him to patience and submission. Trenck entered into conversation with them for the purpose of throwing them off their guard, when suddenly he snatched away Doo's sword, rushed from his cell, knocked down the sentinel and lieutenant who were standing outside, and striking right and left at the soldiers who came flying to bar his progress, he dashed down the stairs and leapt from the ramparts. Though the height was great he, fell into the fosso without injury, and still grasping his sword. He scrambled quickly to his feet and jumped easily over the second rampart, which was much lower than the first, and then began to breathe freely, as he thought he was safe from being overtaken by the soldiers, who

N

would have to come a long way round. At this moment, however, he saw a sentinel making for him a short distance off, and he rushed for the palisades which divided the fortifications from the open country, from which the mountains and Bohemia were easily reached. In the act of scaling them, his foot was caught tight between the bars, and he was trapped till the sentinel came up, and after a sharp fight got him back to prison.

For some time poor Trenck was in a sad condition. In his struggle with the sentinel he had been wounded, while his right foot had got crushed in the palisades. Beside this, he was watched far more strictly than before, for an officer and two men remained always in his cell, and two sentinels were stationed outside. The reason of these precautions of course was to prevent his gaining over his guards singly, either by pity or bribery. His courage sank to its lowest ebb, as he was told on all sides that his imprisonment was for life, whereas long after he discovered the real truth, that the King's intention had been to keep him under arrest for a year only, and if he had had a little more patience, three weeks would have found him free. His repeated attempts to escape naturally angered Frederic, while on the other hand the King knew nothing of the fact which excused Trenck's impatience—namely, the belief carefully instilled in him by all around him that he was doomed to perpetual confinement.

It is impossible to describe in detail all the plans made by Trenck to regain his freedom, first because they were endless, and secondly because several were nipped in the bud. Still the unfortunate man felt that as long as his money was not taken from him his case was not hopeless, for the officers in command were generally poor and in debt, and were always sent to garrison work as a punishment. After one wild effort to liberate *all* the prisoners in the fortress, which was naturally discovered and frustrated, Trenck made friends with an officer named Schell, lately arrived at Glatz, who promised not only his aid but his company in the new enterprise. As more money would be needed than Trenck had in his possession, he contrived to apply to his rich relations outside the prison, and by some means—what we are not told—they managed to convey a large sum to him. Suspicion, however, got about that Trenck was on too familiar a footing with the officers, and orders were given that his door should always be kept locked. This occasioned further delay, as false keys had secretly to be made, before anything else could be done.

Their flight was unexpectedly hastened by Schell accidentally learning that he was in danger of arrest. One night they crept unobserved through the arsenal and over the inner palisade, but on reaching the rampart they came face to face with two of the officers, and again a leap into the fosse was the only way of escape. Luckily the wall at this point was not high, and Trenck arrived at the bottom without injury ; but Schell was not so happy, and hurt his foot so badly that he called on his friend to kill him, and to make the best of his way alone. Trenck, however, declined to abandon him, and having dragged him over the outer palisade, took him on his back, and made for the frontier. Before they had gone five hundred yards they heard the boom of the alarm guns from the fortress, while clearer still were the sounds of pursuit. As they knew that they would naturally be sought on the side towards Bohemia, they changed their course and pushed on to the river Neiss, at this season partly covered with ice. Trenck swam over slowly with this friend on his back, and found a boat on the other side. By means of this boat they evaded their enemies, and reached the mountains after some hours, very hungry, and almost frozen to death.

Here a new terror awaited them. Some peasants with whom they took refuge recognised Schell, and for a moment the fugitives gave themselves up for lost. But the peasants took pity on the two wretched objects, fed them and gave them shelter, till they could make up their minds what was best to be done. To their unspeakable dismay, they found that they were, after all, only seven miles from Glatz, and that in the neighbouring town of Wunschelburg a hundred soldiers were quartered, with orders to capture all deserters from the fortress. This time, however, fortune favoured the luckless Trenck, and though he and Schell were both in uniform, they rode unobserved through the village while the rest of the people were at church, and, skirting Wunschelburg, crossed the Bohemian frontier in the course of the day.

Then follows a period of comparative calm in Trenck's history. He travelled freely about Poland, Austria, Russia, Sweden, Denmark and Holland, and even ventured occasionally across the border into Prussia. Twelve years seem to have passed by in this manner, till in 1758 his mother died, and Trenck asked leave of the council of war to go up to Dantzic to see his family and to arrange his affairs. Curiously enough, it appears never to have occurred to him that he was a deserter, and as such liable to be arrested at any moment.

And this was what actually happened. By order of the King, Trenck was taken first to Berlin, where he was deprived of his money and some valuable rings, and then removed to Magdeburg, of which place Duke Ferdinand of Brunswick was the governor.

Here his quarters were worse than he had ever known them. His cell was only six feet by ten, and the window was high, with bars without as well as within. The wall was seven feet thick, and beyond it was a palisade, which rendered it impossible for the sentinels to approach the window. On the other side the prisoner was shut in by three doors, and his food (which was not only bad, but very scanty) was passed to him through an opening.

One thing only was in his favour. His cell was only entered once a week, so he could pursue any work to further his escape without much danger of being discovered. Notwithstanding the high window, the thick wall, and the palisade, notwithstanding too his want of money, he soon managed to open negotiations with the sentinels, and found, to his great joy, that the next cell was empty. If he could only contrive to burrow his way into that, he would be able to watch his opportunity to steal through the open door ; once free he could either swim the Elbe and cross into Saxony, which lay about six miles distant, or else float down the river in a boat till he was out of danger.

Small as the cell was, it contained a sort of cupboard fixed into the floor by irons, and on these Trenck began to work. After frightful labour he at last extracted the heavy nails which fastened the staples to the floor, and breaking off the heads (which he put back to avoid detection), he kept the rest to fashion for his own purposes. By this means he made instruments to raise the bricks.

On this side also the wall was seven feet thick, and formed of bricks and stones. Trenck numbered them as he went on with the greatest care, so that the cell might present its usual appearance before the Wednesday visit of his guards. To hide the joins, he scraped off some of the mortar, which he smeared over the place.

As may be supposed, all this took a very long time. He had nothing to work with but the tools he himself had made, which of course were very rough. But one day a friendly sentinel gave him a little iron rod, and a small knife with a wooden handle. These were treasures, indeed ! And with their help he worked away for six months at his hole, as in some places the mortar had become so hard that it had to be pounded like a stone.

During this time he enlisted the compassion of some of the

other sentinels, who not only described to him the lie of the country which he would have to traverse if he ever succeeded in getting out of prison, but interested in his behalf a Jewess named Esther Heymann, whose own father had been for two years a prisoner in Magdeburg. In this manner Trenck became the possessor of a file, a knife, and some writing paper, as the friendly Jewess had agreed to convey letters to some influential people both at Vienna and Berlin, and also to his sister. But this step led to the ruin, not only of Trenck, but of several persons concerned, for they were betrayed by an Imperial Secretary of Embassy called Weingarten, who was tempted by a bill for 20,000 florins. Many of those guilty of abetting Trenck in this fresh effort to escape were put to death, while his sister was ordered to build a new prison for him in the Fort de l'Etoile, and he himself was destined to pass nine more years in chains.

In spite of his fetters, Trenck was able in some miraculous way to get on with his hole, but his long labour was rendered useless by the circumstance that his new prison was finished sooner than he expected, and he was removed into it hastily, being only able to conceal his knife. He was now chained even more heavily than before, his two feet being attached to a heavy ring fixed in the wall, another ring being fastened round his body. From this ring was suspended a chain with a thick iron bar, two feet long at the bottom, and to this his hands were fastened. An iron collar was afterwards added to his instruments of torture.

Besides torments of body, nothing was wanting which could work on his mind. His prison was built between the trenches of the principal rampart, and was of course very dark. It was likewise very damp, and, to crown all, the name of ' Trenck ' had been printed in red bricks on the wall, above a tomb whose place was indicated by a death's head.

Here again, he tells us, he excited the pity of his guards, who gave him a bed and coverlet, and as much bread as he chose to eat; and, wonderful as it may seem, his health did not suffer from all these horrors. As soon as he got a little accustomed to his cramped position, he began to use the knife he had left, and to cut through his chains. He next burst the iron band, and after a long time severed his leg fetters, but in such a way that he could put them on again, and no one be any the wiser. Nothing is more common in the history of prisoners than this exploit, and nothing is more astonishing, yet we meet with the fact again and again in

their memoirs and biographies. Trenck at any rate appears to
have accomplished the feat without much difficulty, though he
found it very hard to get his hand back into his handcuffs. After
he had disposed of his bonds, he began to saw at the doors leading
to the gallery. These were four in number, and all of wood, but
when he arrived at the fourth, his knife broke in two, and the
courage that had upheld him for so many years gave way. He

opened his veins and lay down to die, when in his despair he
heard the voice of Gefhardt, the friendly sentinel from the other
prison. Hearing of Trenck's sad plight, he scaled the palisade,
and, we are told expressly, bound up his wounds, though we are
not told how he managed to enter the cell. Be that as it may, the
next day, when the guards came to open the door, they found
Trenck ready to meet them, armed with a brick in one hand, and a
knife, doubtless obtained from Gefhardt, in the other. The first

man that approached him, he stretched wounded at his feet, and thinking it dangerous to irritate further a desperate man, they made a compromise with him. The governor took off his chains for a time, and gave him strong soup and fresh linen. Then, after a while, new doors were put to his cell, the inner door being lined with plates of iron, and he himself was fastened with stronger chains than those he had burst through.

For all this the watch must have been very lax, as Gefhardt soon contrived to open communications with him again, and letters were passed through the window (to which the prisoner had made a false and movable frame) and forwarded to Trenck's rich friends. His appeal was always answered promptly and amply. More valuable than money were two files, also procured from Gefhardt, and by their means the new chains were speedily cut through, though, as before, without any apparent break. Having freed his limbs, he began to saw through the floor of his cell, which was of wood. Underneath, instead of hard rock, there was sand, which Trenck scooped out with his hands. This earth was passed through the window to Gefhardt, who removed it when he was on guard, and gave his friend pistols, a bayonet and knives to assist him when he had finally made his escape.

All seemed going smoothly. The foundations of the prison were only four feet deep, and Trenck's tunnel had reached a considerable distance when everything was again spoilt. A letter written by Trenck to Vienna fell into the hands of the governor, owing to some stupidity on the part of Gefhardt's wife, who had been entrusted to deliver it. The letter does not seem to have contained any special disclosure of his plan of escape, as the governor, who was still Duke Ferdinand of Brunswick, could find nothing wrong in Trenck's cell except the false window frame. The cut chains, though examined, somehow escaped detection, from which we gather either that the officials were very careless, or the carpenter very stupid. Perhaps both may have been the case, for as the Seven Years' War (against Austria) was at this time raging, sentinels and officers were frequently changed, and prison discipline insensibly relaxed. Had this not been so, Trenck could never have been able to labour unseen, but as it was, he was merely deprived of his bed, as a punishment for tampering with the window.

As soon as he had recovered from his fright and an illness which followed, he returned to his digging. It was necessary for him to bore under the subterranean gallery of the principal rampart, which was a distance of thirty-seven feet, and to get outside the foundation of the rampart. Beyond that was a door leading to the second rampart. Trenck was forced to work naked, for fear of raising the suspicions of the officials by his dirty clothes, but in spite of all his precautions and the wilful blindness of his guards, who as usual were on his side, all was at length discovered. His hole was filled up, and a year's work lost.

The next torture invented for him was worse than any that had gone before. He was visited and awakened every quarter of an hour, in order that he might not set to work in the night. This lasted for four years, during part of which time Trenck employed himself in writing verses and making drawings on his tin cups, after the manner of all prisoners, and in writing books with his blood, as ink was forbidden. We are again left in ignorance as to how he got paper. He also began to scoop out another hole, but was discovered afresh, though nothing particular seems to have been done to him, partly owing to the kindness of the new governor, who soon afterwards died.

It had been arranged by his friends that for the space of one year horses should be ready for him at a certain place, on the first and fifteenth of every month. Inspired by this thought, he turned to his burrowing with renewed vigour, and worked away at every moment when he thought he could do so unseen. One day, however, when he had reached some distance, he dislodged a large stone which blocked up the opening towards his cell. His terror was frightful. Not only was the air suffocating and the darkness dreadful, but he knew that if any of the guards were unexpectedly to come into his cell, the opening must be discovered, and all his toil again lost. For eight hours he stayed in the tunnel paralysed by fear. Then he roused himself, and by dint of superhuman struggles managed to open a passage on one side of the stone, and to reach his cell, which for once appeared to him as a haven of rest.

Soon after this the war ended with the Peace of Paris (1763), and Trenck's hopes of release seemed likely to be realised. He procured money from his friends, and bribed the Austrian Ambassador in Berlin to open negotiations on his behalf, and while these were impending he rested from his labours for three whole months. Suddenly he was possessed by an idea which was little less than madness. He bribed a major to ask for a visit from Duke

Ferdinand of Brunswick, again governor of Magdeburg, offering to disclose his passage, and to reveal all his plans of escape, on condition that the Duke would promise to plead for him with the King. This message never reached the Duke himself, but some officers arrived ostensibly sent by him, but in reality tools of the major's. They listened to all he had to say, and saw all he had to show, then broke their word, filled up the passage, and redoubled the chains and the watch.

Notwithstanding this terrible blow, Trenck's trials were drawing to an end. Whether Frederic's heart was softened by his brilliant victories, or whether Trenck's influential friends succeeded in making themselves heard, we do not know, but six months later he was set free, on condition that he never tried to revenge himself on any one, and that he never again should cross the frontiers of Saxony or Prussia.

THE ADVENTURE OF JOHN RAWLINS

IN the year 1621, one John Rawlins, native of Rochester, sailed from Plymouth in a ship called the 'Nicholas,' which had in its company another ship of Plymouth, and had a fair voyage till they came within sight of Gibraltar. Then the watch saw five sails that seemed to do all in their power to come up with the 'Nicholas,' which, on its part, suspecting them to be pirates, hoisted all the sail it could; but to no avail, for before the day was over, the Turkish ships of war—for so they proved to be—not only overtook the Plymouth ships, but made them both prisoners.

Then they sailed for Argier, which, when they reached, the English prisoners were sold as slaves, being hurried like dogs into the market, as men sell horses in England, and marched up and down to see who would give most for them. And though they had heavy hearts and sad countenances, yet many came to behold them, sometimes taking them by the hand, sometimes turning them round about, sometimes feeling their arms and muscles, and bargaining for them accordingly, till at last they were sold.

John Rawlins was the last who was sold, because his hand was lame, and he was bought by the very captain who took him, named Villa Rise, who, knowing Rawlins' skill as a pilot, bought him and his carpenter at a very low rate—paying for Rawlins seven pounds ten reckoned in English money. Then he sent them to work with other slaves: but the Turks, seeing that through Rawlins' lame hand he could not do so much as the rest, complained to their master, who told him that unless he could obtain a ransom of fifteen pounds, he should be banished inland, where he would never see Christendom again.

But while John Rawlins was terrified with this stern threat of Villa Rise, there was lying in the harbour another English ship that had been surprised by the pirates—the 'Exchange,' of Bristol. This ship was bought by an English Turk, who made captain of it another English Turk, and because they were both renegades, they concluded to have English and Dutch slaves to go in her. So it came about that, inquiring if any English slave were to be sold who could serve them as pilot, they heard of John Rawlins, and forthwith bought him of his master, Villa Rise.

By January 7 the ship left Argier, with, on board her, sixty-three Turks and Moors, nine English slaves, and a French slave, four Dutchmen, who were free, and four gunners, one English, and one Dutch renegade.

Now, the English slaves were employed for the most part under hatches, and had to labour hard, all of which John Rawlins took to heart, thinking it a terrible lot to be subject to such pain and danger only to enrich other men, and themselves to return as slaves. Therefore he broke out at last with such words as these :

' Oh, horrible slavery, to be thus subject to dogs ! Oh, Heaven strengthen my heart and hand, and something shall be done to deliver us from these cruel Mahometan dogs ! '

The other slaves, pitying what they thought his madness, bade him speak softly, lest they should all fare the worse for his rashness.

' Worse,' said Rawlins, ' what can be worse ? I will either regain my liberty at one time or another, or perish in the attempt ; but if you would agree to join with me in the undertaking, I doubt not but we should find some way of winning glory with our freedom.'

' Prithee be quiet,' they returned, ' and do not think of impossibilities, though, if indeed you could open some way of escape, so that we should not be condemned as madmen for trying as it were to pull the sun out of the heavens, then we would risk our lives ; and you may be sure of silence.'

After this the slavery continued, and the Turks set their captives to work at all the meanest tasks, and even when they laboured hardest, flogged and reviled them, till more and more John Rawlins became resolved to recover his liberty and surprise the ship. So he provided ropes with broad spikes of iron, and all the iron crows, with which he could, with the help of the others, fasten up the scuttles, gratings, and cabins, and even shut up the captain himself with his companions ; and so he intended to work the enterprise, that, at a certain watchword, the English being masters of the gunner-room and the powder, would either be ready to blow the Turks into the air, or kill them as they came out one by one, if by any chance they forced open the cabins.

Then, very cautiously, he told the four free Dutchmen of his plot, and last of all the Dutch renegades, who were also in the gunner-room; and all these consented readily to so daring an enterprise. So he fixed the time for the venture in the captain's morning watch.

But you must understand that where the English slaves were there always hung four or five iron crows, just under the gun carriages, and when the time came it was very dark, so that John Rawlins, in taking out his iron dropped it on the side of the gun, making such a noise that the soldiers, hearing it, waked the Turks and told them to come down. At this the boatswain of the Turks descended with a candle, and searched everywhere, making a great deal of stir, but finding neither hatchet nor hammer, nor anything else suspicious, only the iron which lay slipped down under the gun-carriages, he went quietly up again and told the captain what had happened, who thought that it was no remarkable thing to have an iron slip from its place. But through this John Rawlins was forced to wait for another opportunity.

When they had sailed further northward there happened another suspicious accident, for Rawlins had told his scheme to the renegade gunner, who promised secrecy by everything that could induce one to believe in him. But immediately after he left Rawlins, and was absent about a quarter of an hour, when he returned and sat down again by him. Presently, as they were talking, in came a furious Turk, with his sword drawn, who threatened Rawlins as if he would certainly kill him. This made Rawlins suspect that the renegade gunner had betrayed him; and he stepped back and drew out his knife, also taking the gunner's out of its sheath; so that the Turk, seeing him with *two* knives, threw down his sword, saying he was only jesting. But the gunner, seeing that Rawlins suspected him, whispered something in his ear, calling Heaven to witness that he had never breathed a word of the enterprise, and never would. Nevertheless, Rawlins kept the knives in his sleeve all night, and was somewhat troubled, though afterwards the gunner proved faithful and zealous in the undertaking.

All this time Rawlins persuaded the captain, who himself had little knowledge of seamanship, to steer northward, meaning to draw him away from the neighbourhood of other Turkish vessels. On February 6 they descried a sail, and at once the Turks gave chase, and made her surrender. It proved to be a ship from near Dartmouth, laden with silk. As it was stormy weather, the Turks did not put down their boat, but made the master of the conquered ship put down his, and come on board with five of his

men and a boy, while ten of the Turks' men, among whom were
one English and two Dutch renegades belonging to the conspiracy,
went to man the prize instead.

But when Rawlins saw this division of his friends, before they
could set out for the other ship, he found means to tell them plainly

that he would complete his enterprise either that night or the next,
and that whatever came of it they must acquaint the four English
left on the captured ship with his resolution, and steer for England
while the Turks slept and suspected nothing. For, by God's grace,
in his first watch he would show them a light, to let them know
that the enterprise was begun, or about to be begun.

So the boat reached the ship from Dartmouth; and next Rawlins told the captain and his men whom the Turks had sent down among the other prisoners of his design, and found them willing to throw in their lot with him.

The next morning, being February 7, the prize from Dartmouth was not to be seen—the men indeed having followed Rawlins' counsel and steered for England. But the Turkish captain began to storm and swear, telling Rawlins to search the seas up and down for her—which he did all day without success. Then Rawlins, finding a good deal of water in the hold, persuaded the captain, by telling him that the ship was not rightly balanced, to have four of the guns brought aft, that the water might run to the pump. This being done, and the guns placed where the English could use them for their own purpose, the final arrangement was made. The ship having three decks, those that belonged to the gunner-room were all to be there, and break up the lower deck. The English slaves, who belonged to the middle deck, were to do the same with that, and watch the scuttles. Rawlins himself prevailed with the gunner to give him as much powder as would prime the guns, and told them all there was no better watchword than, when the signal gun was heard, to cry:

' For God, and King James, and Saint George for England.'

Then, all being prepared, and every man resolute, knowing what he had to do, Rawlins advised the gunner to speak to the captain, that he might send the soldiers to the poop, to bring the ship aft, and, weighing it down, send the water to the pumps. This the captain was very willing to do; and so, at two o'clock in the afternoon the signal was given, by the firing of the gun, whose report tore and broke down all the binnacle and compasses.

But when the Turks heard this, and the shouts of the conspirators, and saw that part of ship was torn away, and felt it shake under them, and knew that all threatened their destruction—no bear robbed of her whelps was ever so mad as they, for they not only called us dogs, and cried in their tongue, ' The fortune of war! the fortune of war!' but they tried to tear up the planking, setting to work hammers, hatchets, knives, the oars of the boat, the boat hook, and whatever else came to hand, besides the stones and bricks of the cook-room, still trying to break the hatches, and never ceasing their horrible cries and curses.

Then Rawlins, seeing them so violent, and understanding that the slaves had cleared the decks of all the Turks and Moors underneath, began to shoot at them through different scoutholes, with their own muskets, and so lessened their number. At this they cried for the pilot, and so Rawlins, with some to guard him, went to them, and understood by their kneeling that they cried for

mercy and begged to come down. This they were bidden to do, but coming down one by one, they were taken and slain with their own curtleaxes. And the rest, perceiving this, some of them leapt into the water, still crying : ' The fortune of war ! ' and calling their foes English dogs, and some were slain with the curtleaxes, till the decks were well cleared, and the victory assured.

At the first report of the gun, and the hurly-burly on deck, the captain was writing in his cabin, and he came out with his curtle-axe in hand, thinking by his authority to quell the mischief. But when he saw that the ship was surprised, he threw down his curtle-axe, and begged Rawlins to save his life, telling him how he had redeemed him from Villa Rise, and put him in command in the ship, besides treating him well through the voyage. This Rawlins confessed, and at last consented to be merciful, and brought the captain and five more renegades into England.

When all was done, and the ship cleared of the dead bodies, John Rawlins assembled his men, and with one consent gave the praise to God, using the accustomed services on shipboard. And for want of books they lifted up their voices to God, as He put it into their hearts or renewed their memories. Then did they sing a psalm, and last of all, embraced one another for playing the men in such a deliverance, whereby their fear was turned into joy. That same night they steered for England, and arrived at Plymouth on February 13, and were welcomed with all gladness.

As for the ship from Dartmouth, that had arrived in Penzance on February 11, for the English had made the Turks believe that they were sailing to Argier, till they came in sight of England. Then one of the Turks said plainly *that the land was not like Cape Vincent*; but the Englishmen told them to go down into the hold, and trim more to windward, and they should see and know more to-morrow. Thereupon five of them went down very orderly, while the English feigned themselves asleep; but presently they started up, and nailed down the hatches, and so overpowered the Turks. And this is the story of this enterprise, and the end of John Rawlins' voyage.

THE CHEVALIER JOHNSTONE'S ESCAPE FROM CULLODEN

THE Chevalier Johnstone (or *de* Johnstone, as he preferred to call himself) was closely connected with the Highland army, hastily collected in 1745 for the purpose of restoring Charles Edward to his grandfather's throne. He was aide-de-camp to Lord George Murray, Generalissimo to the little force, and seems to have known enough of warfare to be capable of appreciating his commander's skill. He was also a captain in the regiment of the Duke of Perth, and later, when the petals of the White Rose were trampled under foot, he became an officer in the French service.

From his position, therefore, he was peculiarly fitted to tell the tale of those two eventful years, 1745 and 1746. Though only the son of a merchant, Johnstone was well connected, and, like many Scottish gentlemen of that day, had been bred in loyalty to the Jacobite cause. He was one of the first to join the Prince when he had reached Perth, and it was from the Prince himself that he received his company, after the fight at Prestonpans. His life was all romance, but the part on which it is our present purpose to dwell is the account he has left in his memoirs of his escape from the field of Culloden, and the terrible sufferings he went through for some months, till he finally made his way safely to Holland.

'The battle of Culloden,' he says,[1] ' was lost rather by a series of mistakes on our part than by any skilful manoeuvre of the Duke of Cumberland,' and every Scot in arms knew too well the doom that awaited him at the 'Butcher's' hands. The half-starved Highlanders were no match for the well-fed English troops, and when the day was lost, and the rout became general, each man sought to conceal himself in the fastnesses of the nearest mountains, and, as long as he put himself well out of reach, was not particular as to the means he took to purchase safety.

[1] P. 211.

Panics disclose strange and unexpected depths in men's minds, and Johnstone was in no respect superior to his fellows. 'Being no longer able to keep myself on my legs,' he relates,[1] 'and the enemy always advancing very slowly, but redoubling their fire, my mind was agitated and undecided whether I should throw away my life, or surrender a prisoner, which was a thousand times worse than death on the field of battle. All at once I perceived a horse, about thirty paces before me, without a rider. The idea of being yet able to escape gave me fresh strength and served as a spur to me. I ran and laid hold of the bridle, which was fast in

the hand of a man lying on the ground, whom I supposed dead; but, what was my surprise when the cowardly poltroon, who was suffering from nothing but fear, dared to remain in the most horrible fire to dispute the horse with me, at twenty paces from the enemy. All my menaces could not induce him to quit the bridle. Whilst we were disputing, a discharge from a cannon loaded with grape-shot fell at our feet, without however producing any effect upon this singular individual, who obstinately persisted in retaining the horse. Fortunately for me, Finlay Cameron, an officer in Lochiel's regiment, a youth of twenty years of age, six feet high,

[1] P. 215.

and very strong and vigorous, happened to pass near us. I called on him to assist me. "Ah Finlay," said I, "this fellow will not give me up the horse." Finlay flew to me like lightning, immediately

presented his pistol to the head of this man, and threatened to blow out his brains if he hesitated a moment to let go the bridle. The fellow, who had the appearance of a servant, at length yielded and took to his heels. Having obtained the horse, I attempted to mount him several times, but all my efforts were ineffectual, as I was without strength and completely exhausted. I called again on poor Finlay, though he was already some paces from me, to assist me to mount. He returned, took me in his arms, with as much ease as if I had been a child, and threw me on the horse like a loaded sack, giving the horse at the same time a heavy blow to make him set off with me. Then wishing that I might have the good fortune to make my escape, he bounded off like a roe, and was in a moment out of sight. We were hardly more than fifteen or twenty paces from the enemy when he quitted me. As soon as I found myself at the distance of thirty or forty paces, I endeavoured to set myself right on the horse, put my feet in the stirrups, and rode off as fast as the wretched animal could carry me.'

There is something peculiarly funny in the simplicity of this account of horse-stealing with violence! Why a man should be more of a coward who clings to his own property and only means of safety, than the person who deliberately deprives him of both, is not easy to see. But Johnstone never doubts for one moment that what he does is always right, and what anyone else does is always wrong, and he goes on complacently to remark that he probably 'saved the life of the poltroon who held the horse, in rousing him out of his panic fear, for in less than two minutes the English army would have passed over him.' [1]

The shelter which Johnstone made up his mind to seek was the castle of Rothiemurchus, the property of the Grant family, situ. ated in the heart of the mountains, and on the banks of the 'rapid Spey.' But his troubles were not so easily over. The English army barred the way, and Johnstone was forced to take the road to Inverness. Again he was turned from his path by the dreaded sight of the British uniform, and, accompanied by a Highlander whom he had met by chance, he took refuge in a small cottage in Fort Augustus. In spite of his peculiar views about courage, Johnstone was a man who generally managed to do whatever he had set his heart on. He had resolved to go to Rothiemurchus, and to Rothiemurchus he would go. At last he arrived there, but found, to his great disappointment, that the laird, his old friend, was away from home. In his place was his eldest son, who was urgent that Johnstone should surrender himself a prisoner, as Lord Balmerino had just done, by his advice, and under his escort.

[1] P. 217.

Johnstone replied that he would keep his liberty as long as he could, and when it was no longer possible, he would meet his fate with resignation. We all know the end to which poor Balmerino came, but Johnstone was more fortunate.

His brother-in-law, the son of Lord Rollo, had been made inspector of merchant ships in the town of Banff, and Johnstone fondly hoped that by his help he might obtain a passage to some foreign country. So he set off with three gentlemen of the name

of Gordon, who had also been staying at Rothiemurchus, and rested the first night at the house of a shepherd near the mountain of Cairngorm. Here he saw for the first time the stones which bear this name, and though he is flying for his life, he dwells with the delight of a collector on the beauty of the colours, and even persuades his friends to put off their departure for a day, in order that he may search for some specimens himself. He contrived, he tells us,[1] to find several beautiful topazes, two of which he had cut

---

[1] P. 229.

as seals, and presented to the Duke of York, brother of Prince Charles Edward.

Four days after leaving Rothiemurchus Banff was reached, and the fugitives were sheltered by a Presbyterian minister, who was a secret adherent of the Stuarts. Johnstone at once took the precaution of exchanging his laced Highland dress for that of an old labourer, 'quite ragged, and exhaling a pestilential odour,' due apparently to its having been used for many years 'when he cleaned the stables of his master.' In this unpleasant disguise, he entered the town of Banff, then garrisoned with four hundred English soldiers, and went straight to the house of a former acquaintance, Mr. Duff. After gaining admittance from the servant with some difficulty, he found with dismay that his brother-in-law was away from home, and he could not therefore carry out his plan of embarking, with his permission, on board one of the merchant ships. There seemed nothing for it, therefore, but for Johnstone to return at daybreak to the house of Mr. Gordon, where he had spent the previous night. At daybreak, however, he was roused by a fearful disturbance in the courtyard below, occasioned by the quarrels of some stray soldiers. For a moment he thought death was certain, but the soldiers had no suspicion of his presence in the house, and as soon as they had settled their affairs took themselves off elsewhere.

Mr. Rollo proved a broken reed, and the Chevalier found, after a few minutes' talk with his brother-in-law, that if he wished to reach the Continent he must not count on a passage in the merchant ships to help him. He therefore, after consultation with his friends, came to the conclusion that his best plan was to make for the Lowlands, and to this end he set out for Edinburgh as soon as possible. Of course this scheme was beset with difficulties and dangers of every kind. The counties through which he would be forced to pass were filled with Calvinists, inspired with deadly hatred of the Jacobite party. To escape their hands was almost certainly to fall into those of the soldiery, and over and above this, government passports were necessary for those who desired to cross the Firths of Forth and Tay.

But, nothing daunted, Johnstone went his way. He was passed in disguise from one house to another, well-fed at the lowest possible prices (he tells us of the landlady of a small inn who charged him threepence for 'an excellent young fowl' and his bed), till at last he found himself in the region of Cortachy, the country of the Ogilvies, who one and all were on the side of the Prince. At Cortachy he was quite secure, as long as no English soldiery came by, and even if they did, the mountains were full of hiding places, and there was no risk of treachery at home. Two officers who had served in the French army, Brown and Gordon by name, had sought refuge here before him, and lay concealed in the house of a peasant known as Samuel. They implored him not to run the risk of proceeding south till affairs had quieted down a little, and he agreed to remain at Samuel's cottage till it seemed less dangerous to travel south.

It would be interesting to know what was 'the gratification beyond his hopes' which Johnstone gave Samuel when they parted company some time after. It ought to have been something very handsome considering the risks which the peasant had run in his behalf, and also the fact that for several weeks Johnstone and his two friends had shared the scanty fare of Samuel and his family. They had 'no other food than oatmeal, and no other drink than the water of the stream which ran through the glen. We breakfasted every morning on a piece of oatmeal bread which we were enabled to swallow by draughts of water ; for dinner we boiled oatmeal with water, till it acquired a consistency, and we ate it with horn spoons ; in the evening, we poured boiling water on this meal in a dish, for our supper.'[1] Even this frugal diet could not be swallowed long in peace, for shortly after their arrival, Samuel's daughter, who lived at the mouth of the glen, came to inform her father that some English troops had been seen in the neighbourhood, and whenever there was any chance of their appearing in the glen Johnstone and his friends had to take refuge in the mountains.

One day this woman arrived with the news that the soldiery were hovering dangerously near, and had taken several notable prisoners. Upon this the fugitives decided to leave their shelter at daybreak the following morning and to make the best of their way to the Highlands, where they would be sure of finding some rocks and caverns to hide them from their foes.

This resolution once taken, they all went early to bed, and there Johnstone had a dream which he relates with many apologies for his superstition. He fancied himself in Edinburgh safe from the snares of his enemies, and with no fears for the future, and describing his adventures and escapes since the battle of Culloden to his old friend Lady Jane Douglas. The impression of peace and happiness and relief from anxiety was so strong that it remained

[1] P. 249.

with him after he woke, and after lying turning the matter over in
his mind for another hour, informed Samuel (who had come to
rouse him with the intelligence that his companions had already
set off for the mountains) that he had altered his plans and intended
to go straight to Edinburgh. In vain the old man argued and
entreated. Johnstone was determined, and that same evening he
set forth on horseback with Samuel for his guide, and made straight
for the nearest arm of the sea, which he describes, though quite
wrongly, as being only eight miles from Cortachy.

To reach this, they were obliged to pass through Forfar, a town
which, being a Calvinistic stronghold, the Chevalier can never
mention without an abusive epithet. But here poor Samuel, whose
nerves had doubtless been strained by the perpetual watching and
waiting of the last few weeks, was frightened out of his senses by
the barking of a dog, and tried to throw himself from his horse. At
this juncture, Johnstone, who knew that to be left without a guide
in this strange place meant certain death, interfered promptly.
' He was continually struggling to get down,' he says,[1] ' but I prevented him by the firm hold I had of his coat. I exhorted him to
be quiet; I reproached him; I alternately entreated and menaced
him; but all in vain. He no longer knew what he was about, and
it was to no purpose I assured him that it was only the barking of
a dog. He perspired at every pore, and trembled like a person in
an ague. Fortunately I had an excellent horse, and galloped
through Forfar at full speed, retaining always fast hold of his coat.
As soon as we were fairly out of the town, as no persons had come
out of their houses, poor Samuel began to breathe again, and made
a thousand apologies for his fears.'

As the day broke and they drew near Broughty Ferry, where
Johnstone intended to cross the Firth of Tay, the Chevalier dismounted, and being obliged to part from his horse, offered it as a
present to Samuel, who declined the animal from motives of
prudence. It was then turned loose in a field (the saddle and bridle
being first thrown down a well), and the wayfarers proceeded on
their way. Only a few minutes later, they were joined by an
acquaintance of Samuel's, who seems to have been of a curious turn
of mind, and cross-questioned him as to where he was going and
why. Samuel, with more readiness than could have been expected
from his recent behaviour, invented a story that sounded plausible
enough, explaining Johnstone to be a young man whom he had

[1] P. 257.

picked up on the road, and had taken into his service at low wages, owing to his want of a character. The stranger was satisfied, and after a prolonged drink they separated, when Samuel informed Johnstone that the man was one of the 'greatest knaves and cheats in the country,' and that they would assuredly have been betrayed if he had discovered who they were.

They arrived at the Ferry about nine in the morning, and by Samuel's advice, the Chevalier immediately sought the help of Mr. Graham, a gentleman of Jacobite family, then living at Duntroon. After a warm welcome from Mr. Graham, who gave him all the entertainment he could without the knowledge of his servants, a boat was engaged to convey him across the Firth about nine that night. Mr. Graham did not, however, dare to be his guide down to

the sea-shore, but gave him careful directions as to his following an old woman who had been provided for this purpose. But all Mr. Graham's precautions would have been useless, had not chance once more favoured the Chevalier. His protectress decided that it would be dangerous to allow him to loiter about the shore while the boat was getting ready for sea, so she told her charge to wait for her on the road on top of the hill, and she would return and fetch him when all was ready. Half an hour passed very slowly: the sun was sinking, and the Chevalier grew impatient. He left the road by which he had been sitting, and lay down in a furrow a few yards off, nearer the brow of the hill, so that he might perceive his guide at the earliest moment. Scarcely had he changed his quarters, than he heard the sound of horses, and peeping cautiously out, ' saw eight or ten horsemen pass in the very place he had just quitted.' No sooner were they out of sight, than the old woman arrived, trembling with fright. ' Ah ! ' she exclaimed in a transport of joy, ' I did not expect to find you here.' She then explained that the horsemen were English dragoons, and that they had so threatened the boatmen engaged by Mr. Graham that they absolutely refused to fulfil their compact. This was a terrible blow to the Chevalier, but he declined to listen to the old woman's advice and return for shelter to Mr. Graham, and after much persuasion, induced his guide to show him the way to the public-house by the sea-shore. Here he was welcomed by the landlady, whose son had been likewise ' out ' with the Prince, but neither her entreaties nor those of the Chevalier could move the boatmen from their resolution. They even resisted the prayers of the landlady's two beautiful daughters, till the girls, disgusted and indignant with such cowardice, offered to row him across themselves.

' We left Broughty Ferry,' he writes in his memoirs, ' at ten o'clock in the evening, and reached the opposite shore about mid-night.' He then took an affectionate leave of his preservers, and proceeded, footsore as he was, to walk to St. Andrews. At this time Johnstone seems to have felt more physically exhausted than at almost any other moment of his travels ; and it was only by dint of perpetually washing his sore and bleeding feet in the streams he passed, that he managed to reach St. Andrews towards eight o'clock. He at once made his way to the house of his cousin, Mrs. Spence, who, herself a suspected person, was much taken aback by the sight of him, and hastily sent a letter to a tenant farmer living near the town, to provide the fugitive with a horse which would carry him to Wemyss, a seaport town on the way to Edinburgh. The old University city does not appear to have made a favourable impression on the Chevalier. He declares that no town ' ever deserved so much the fate of Sodom and Gomorrah,' [1] and this, not from any particular wickedness on the part of the inhabitants, but because they were supposed to be Calvinists. However, his sentiments must have been confirmed when the farmer declined to take his horses out on a Sunday, and, lame as he was, Johnstone had no choice but to set out on foot for Wemyss. Halfway, he suddenly remembered that close by lived an old servant of his family, married to the gardener of Mr. Beaton, of Balfour. Here he was housed and fed for twenty hours, and then conducted by his host, a rigid Pres-

[1] P. 274.

byterian, to a tavern at Wemyss, kept by the mother-in-law of the gardener. By her advice they applied to a man named Salmon, who, though a rabid Hanoverian, could be trusted not to betray those who had faith in him. It was hard work to gain over Salmon, who was proof against bribery, but at last it was done. By his recommendation Johnstone was to lie till dawn in a cave near Wemyss (a place whose name means 'caves'), and with the first ray of light was to beg a passage to Leith from some men who were with Salmon part owners of a boat. In this cave, which, notwithstanding its narrow entrance, was deep and spacious, the Chevalier was glad to repose his weary bones. But, after dozing about an hour, he was 'awakened by the most horrible and alarming cries that ever were heard.'[1] His first thought was that Salmon had betrayed him, and he retreated to the interior of the cavern, cocked his pistol, and prepared to sell his life dearly. Soon, however, the swift movements accompanying the noise convinced him that it did not proceed from men, for 'sometimes the object was about my ears, and nearly stunned me, and, in an instant, at a considerable distance. At length I ceased to examine any more this horrible and incomprehensible phenomenon, which made a noise in confusion like that of a number of trumpets and drums, with a mixture of different sounds, altogether unknown to me.'

Effectually aroused by the whining of the owls and bats (for these, of course, were the authors of all this disturbance), Johnstone fixed his eyes on the sea to note the first entrance of the fishing boats into the harbour. He then went down to the shore and began to make the bargain as directed by Salmon, and the fishermen agreed to land him at Leith for half-a-crown. But alas! once more his hopes were blighted. He was in the act of stepping into the boat, when Salmon's wife appeared on the scene, and forbade her husband to go to Leith that day, still less to take a stranger there. Neither Salmon nor Johnstone dared insist, for fear of rousing the woman's suspicions, and after a short retreat in the cave in order to collect his thoughts, he returned to the tavern at Wemyss, to consult with the friendly landlady. Thanks to her, and with the help of one or two people to whom she introduced him, Johnstone at last arrived at the house of one Mr. Seton, whose son had formerly served with Johnstone in the army of the Prince. Here he remained eight days, vainly seeking to find a second man who could aid the fisherman who had already promised

---

[1] P. 295.

to put him across, though it does not appear why Johnstone, who had already observed [1] that he was able to row, did not take an oar when his own head was at stake.

[1] P. 271.

At last affairs were brought to a crisis, by rumours having got abroad of the presence of a fugitive on the coast. Things seemed in a desperate condition, when young Seton threw himself into the breach, and agreed to help Cousselain, the fisherman, to take the Chevalier to Leith. They were actually launching the boat when the inhabitants of the village, alarmed by the noise they made, raised a cry that a rebel was escaping, and the two oarsmen had barely time to conceal themselves without being discovered. However, in flat defiance of everyone's advice, and, as it turned out, in spite of the drunken state of Cousselain, Johnstone resolved to repeat the attempt in an hour's time, taking in the end, as he might have done at the beginning, his place at the oar. For a few moments they breathed freely; then the wind got up, and the waves, and, what was perhaps more dangerous, the drunken Cousselain, who had been placed in the bottom of the boat. 'We were obliged to kick him most unmercifully in order to keep him quiet,' observes Johnstone, 'and to threaten to throw him overboard if he made the least movement. Seton and myself rowed like galley slaves. We succeeded in landing, about six in the morning, on a part of the coast a league and a half to the east of Edinburgh,[1] near the battlefield of Gladsmuir.' Here he parted with his deliverers, tenderly embracing young Seton, and presenting to the 'somewhat sober' Cousselain a gratification beyond his hopes.

After taking a little of the food with which Mr. Seton had provided him, he determined to seek refuge for a few days with an old governess, Mrs. Blythe, wife of a small shipowner at Leith. Blythe himself was another of the many 'rigid Calvinists and sworn enemies of the house of Stuart' to whom Johnstone entrusted his safety during his wanderings, and never once had occasion to repent it. Mr. Blythe, indeed, combined the profession of Calvinist with that of smuggler, and had numerous hiding places in his house for the concealment of contraband goods, which would prove equally serviceable, as Johnstone told him, for 'the most contraband and dangerous commodity that he had ever had in his possession.'

Though Johnstone had reached the goal of his desires, his perils were by no means at an end. English soldiers visited the house, and could with difficulty be persuaded to admit the exemption pleaded by Mr. Blythe. In consequence of this event, Johnstone accepted the offer of an asylum made him by Lady Jane Douglas,

[1] P. 308.

in her place at Drumsheugh, half a league away. So his dream came true, and after all his wanderings he was safe with Lady Jane, telling the story of his adventures. He remained with her for two months, unknown to anyone but his hostess and the gardener, reading all day, and only taking a walk at night, when the household was in bed. At the end of that time, when Lady Jane and his father were of opinion that he might safely go to London, and thence abroad, fresh rumours as to his whereabouts began to arise, and fearing the immediate visit of a detachment of English soldiers, he was concealed for a whole day under a huge haycock, so overcome by the heat that he could hardly breathe, in spite of a bottle of water and another of wine, with which he was provided.

This measure, which after all was needless, for no soldiers came, was the last trial he had to undergo before leaving Scotland, and here we must part from him. In France, which he made his home, he became the friend of many eminent men, and was aide-de-camp in Canada to the Marquis de Montcalm. But the end of his life was sad, and he died in poverty.[1]

---

[1] From *Memoirs of the Chevalier de Johnstone.* Longmans. London, 1822. The Memoirs were written in French, and deposited in the Scots College at Paris. They were communicated to Messrs. Longman by Robert Watson, the adventurer, who, under Napoleon, was Principal of the Scots College. The Chevalier left a granddaughter, who corresponded on the subject of the Memoirs with Sir Walter Scott.

THE ADVENTURES OF LORD PITSLIGO

WHEN Prince Charles came to Scotland in 1745, to seek his grandfather's crown, no braver and no better man rode with him than Lord Pitsligo. He was now sixty-seven years of age, for he was born in 1678, ten years before James II. was driven out of England. As a young man he had lived much in France, where he became the friend of the famous Fénelon, author of 'Télémaque.' Though much interested in the doctrines of Fénelon, Lord Pitsligo did not change his faith, but remained a member of the persecuted Episcopal Church of Scotland. In France he met the members of the exiled Royal family, whom he never ceased to regard as his lawful monarchs, though Queen Anne, and later the First and Second Georges, occupied the throne of England. When the clans rose for King James, the son of James II., in 1715, Lord Pitsligo, then a man of twenty-seven, joined the forces under his kinsman, Lord Marr. His party was defeated, and he went abroad. He did not stay long with James in Rome, but was allowed to return to his estates in Scotland. Here he lived very quietly, beloved by rich and poor. But, in 1745, Prince Charles landed, and the old Lord believed it to be his duty to join him. He had, as he says, no keen enthusiasm for the Stuarts, but to his mind they were his lawful rulers. So aged was he, and so infirm, that, when he left a neighbour's house before setting out, a little boy brought a stool to help him to mount his horse. 'My little fellow, he said, ' this is the severest reproof I have yet met with, for presuming to go on such an expedition.' Lady Pitsligo in vain reminded him of the failure of 1715. 'There never was a bridal,' he replied, ' but the second day was the best.' The gentlemen of his county thought that they could not do wrong in following so learned and excellent a man, so they all mounted the white cockade and rode with him. He arrived just too late for the victory of Preston Pans. 'It seemed,' said an eye-witness, ' as if

religion, virtue, and justice were entering the camp under the appearance of this venerable old man.' When he wrote home, he said,
' I had occasion to discover the Prince's humanity, I ought to say
tenderness: this is giving myself no great airs, for he showed the

same dispositions to everybody.' In the fatigues of the campaign,
the Prince, who was young and strong, insisted on Lord Pitsligo's
using his carriage, while he himself marched on foot at the head of
his army.

After the defeat of Culloden, Lord Pitsligo hid among the moun-

tains, living on oatmeal, moistened with hot water. They had not
even salt to their brose; for, as one of the Highlanders said, ' Salt is
touchy,' meaning expensive. Yet these men, who could not even
buy salt, never betrayed their Prince for the great reward of thirty
thousand pounds, nor any of the other gentlemen in hiding. Possibly they did not believe that there was so much money in the
world. Lord Pitsligo had made up his mind not to go abroad again,
but to live or die among his own people. At one time he lay for
days hidden in a damp hole under a little bridge, and at other times
concealed himself in the mosses and moors. Here the lapwings,
flitting and crying above him, were like to have drawn the English
soldiers to his retreat. His wife gave him two great bags, like these

which beggars carried ; in these he would place the alms which were
given to him, and in this disguise he had many narrow escapes. Once
he saw some dragoons on the road behind him, but he was too old
and too ill to run. He was obliged to sit down and cough, and one
of the dragoons who were in search of him actually gave him some
money as they passed by, and condoled with him on the severity
of his cough.

Lord Pitsligo often hid in a cave on the coast of Buchan. Here
was a spring of water welling through the rock, and he carved a
little cistern for it, to pass the time. He was fed by a little girl,
too young to be suspected, who carried his meals from a neighbouring farm. One day he was sitting in the kitchen of the farm,
when some soldiers came in. and asked the goodwife to guide them

P

to Lord Pitsligo's cave. She said, 'That travelling body will go with you,' and Lord Pitsligo conducted the soldiers to his hiding place, left them there, and walked back to the farm. But the following adventure was perhaps his narrowest escape.

In March 1756, and of course long after all apprehension of a search had ceased, information having been given to the then commanding officer at Fraserburgh, that Lord Pitsligo was at that moment in the house of Auchiries, it was acted upon with so much promptness and secrecy, that the search must have proved successful but for a very singular occurrence. Mrs. Sophia Donaldson, a lady who lived much with the family, repeatedly dreamt on that particular night that the house was surrounded by soldiers. Her mind became so haunted with the idea, that she got out of bed, and was walking through the room in hopes of giving a different current to her thoughts before she lay down again, when, day beginning to dawn, she accidentally looked out at the window as she passed it in traversing the room, and was astonished at actually observing the figures of soldiers among some trees near the house. So completely had all idea of a search been by that time laid asleep, that she supposed they had come to steal poultry; Jacobite poultry-yards affording a safe object of pillage for the English soldiers in those days. Under this impression Mrs. Sophia was proceeding to rouse the servants, when her sister having awaked, and inquiring what was the matter, and being told of soldiers near the house, exclaimed, in great alarm, that she feared they wanted something more than hens. She begged Mrs. Sophia to look out at a window on the other side of the house, when not only soldiers were seen in that direction, but also an officer giving instructions by signals, and frequently putting his fingers on his lips, as if enjoining silence. There was now no time to be lost in rousing the family, and all the haste that could be made was scarcely sufficient to hurry the venerable man from his bed, into a small recess behind the wainscot of an adjoining room, which was concealed by a bed, in which a lady, Miss Gordon of Towie, who was there on a visit, lay, before the soldiers obtained admission. A most minute search took place. The room in which Lord Pitsligo was concealed did not escape: Miss Gordon's bed was carefully examined, and she was obliged to suffer the rude scrutiny of one of the party, by feeling her chin, to ascertain that it was not a man in a lady's night-dress. Before the soldiers had finished their examination in this room, the confinement and anxiety increased Lord Pitsligo's asthma so much, and his breath-

ing became so loud, that it obliged Miss Gordon, lying in bed, to
counterfeit and continue a violent coughing, in order to prevent the
high breathing behind the wainscot from being heard. It may
easily be conceived what agony she would suffer, lest, by overdoing
her part, she should increase suspicion, and in fact lead to a discovery. The *ruse* was fortunately successful. On the search
through the house being given over, Lord Pitsligo was hastily taken
from his confined situation, and again replaced in bed; and as soon

as he was able to speak, his accustomed kindness of heart made him
say to his servant, 'James, go and see that these poor fellows get
some breakfast, and a drink of warm ale, for this is a cold morning;
they are only doing their duty, and cannot bear me any ill-will.'
When the family were felicitating each other on his escape, he
pleasantly observed, 'A poor prize had they obtained it—an old
dying man!' That the friends who lived in the house,—the hourly
witnesses of his virtues, and the objects of his regard, who saw him

escape all the dangers that surrounded him, should reckon him the peculiar care of Providence, is not to be wondered at; and that the dream which was so opportune, as the means of preventing his apprehension, and probably of saving his life, was supposed by some of them at last to be a special interposition of Heaven's protecting shield against his enemies, need not excite surprise. This was accordingly the belief of more than one to their dying hour.

After some fifteen years, the English Government ceased to think Lord Pitsligo dangerous. He was allowed to live unmolested at the house of his son, where he died in 1762, in his eighty-fifth year. 'He was never heard to speak an ill word of any man living,' says one who knew him well, and who himself spoke many ill words of others.[1] Lord Pitsligo left a little book of 'Thoughts on Sacred Things,' which reminds those who read it of the meditations of General Gordon. His character, as far as its virtues went, is copied in the Baron Bradwardine, in Sir Walter Scott's novel of 'Waverley.'[2]

[1] Dr. King, of St. Mary's Hall, Oxford.
[2] From *Thoughts Concerning Man's Condition and Duties in this Life.* By Alexander, Lord Pitsligo. Edinburgh: Blackwood. 1854.

THE ESCAPE OF CÆSAR BORGIA FROM THE CASTLE OF MEDINA DEL CAMPO

CÆSAR BORGIA forms, with his father Pope Alexander VI., and his sister Lucrezia, one of a trio who have become a proverb for infamy of every kind. His father, Roderigo, was by birth a Spaniard, and by education a lawyer, in which profession he gained much distinction, till suddenly, with an impetuosity strange in a man who did everything by calculation, he threw up his legal career for that of a soldier. But the rough life was repugnant to one of his temperament, which demanded ease and luxury, so after a little active service, when his courage, during some sharp engagements, was proved beyond a doubt, he abandoned the army also, and retired to live in comfort on the large fortune lately bequeathed to him by his father.

It required some pressing on the part of his uncle, Calixtus III., recently made Pope, to induce him to leave his native land and his secular existence, for Italy and a Cardinalate. But no sooner did he occupy his new position, than a set of base qualities, which had hitherto lain dormant, suddenly developed themselves, and from this moment he became one of the cleverest and most successful hypocrites of his age.

It was in 1492, the year that saw the landing of Columbus in America, and the death of Lorenzo the Magnificent at Florence, that the Cardinal Borgia obtained, by means of huge bribes, his election to the Papal Throne, and took the name of Alexander VI. His first care was to establish (for his own credit's sake) order and security in Rome, and this done, he turned his thoughts to the aggrandisement of his family. For when Roderigo sailed for Italy he was shortly followed by his four children, Francis, Cæsar, Lucrezia and Geoffrey, and their mother Rosa Vanozza. All four, but more particularly Cæsar and Lucrezia, inherited in the highest degree their father's beauty, talents and wickedness. Honours of every kind were showered upon them, marriages made and unmade to suit the requirements of the moment, murders committed to ensure them wealth and possessions. For eleven years the roll of crime grew heavier day by day, till at last the chastisement came, and the

Borgias, who had invited several of the Cardinals to supper for the purpose of poisoning them and seizing on their revenues, were themselves
served with the draught they had intended for their guests.   The Pope
died after eight days, in mortal agony, but, owing to his having drunk
less of the wine, Cæsar slowly recovered, and resumed his old trade of
arms.   The talents which had made him one of the first captains in
Italy caused him to be the dread of all his enemies, and finally led to
his capture (by violation of a safe-conduct), at the hands of Gonsalvo de
Cordova, Captain of the Forces of Ferdinand of Spain.]

It was in June 1504 that Cæsar Borgia, General of the Church
and Duke of Romagna and Valentinois, was conducted to the
Castle of Medina del Campo in Spain.   For two years Cæsar waited
in prison, hoping that his old ally, Louis XII., whose cousin Mlle.
d'Albret he had married, would come to his assistance.   But he
waited in vain and his courage began to give way, when one day
something happened which proved to him that he had still one
friend left, his faithful Michelotto, a soldier of fortune who had followed him to Spain, and was now hidden in the neighbourhood of
the prison.   It was breakfast time, and Cæsar was in the act of
cutting his bread when he suddenly touched a hard substance, and
found a file, and a small bottle containing a narcotic, and a note
concealed in the loaf.   The note was from Michelotto, and informed Cæsar that he and the Count of Benevento would hide
themselves every night on the road between the castle and the
village, in company with three good horses, and that he must make
the best use he could of the file and the sleeping draught.[1]

Two years' imprisonment had weighed too heavily on Cæsar
for him to waste a single moment in trying to regain his freedom.
He, therefore, lost no time in beginning to work on one of the bars
of his window, which opened on an inside court, and soon contrived to cut through so far, that a violent shake would enable
him to remove it altogether.   But the window was nearly seventy
feet above the ground, while the only way of leaving the court
was by a door reserved for the governor alone, the key of which was
always carried about his person.   By day it was suspended from
his belt, by night it was under his bolster.   To gain possession of
this key was the most difficult part of the matter.

Now in spite of the fact that he was a prisoner, Cæsar had
invariably been treated with all the respect due to his name and
rank.   Every day at the dinner hour, he was conducted from the

---

[1] What follows is translated from Dumas.

room in which he was confined to the governor's apartments and
was received by him as an honoured guest. Don Manuel himself
was an old soldier who had served with distinction under Ferdinand,
and, while carrying out punctually his orders for Cæsar's safe custody, he admired his military talents, and listened with pleasure to
the story of his fights. He had often desired that Cæsar should
breakfast as well as dine with him, but, luckily for himself, the
prisoner, perhaps aided by some presentiment, had always refused
this favour. It was owing to his solitude that he was able to
conceal the instruments for his escape sent by Michelotto.

Now it happened that the very same day that he had received
them, Cæsar contrived to stumble, and twist his foot as he was returning to his room. When the hour of dinner came he tried to
go down, but declared that walking hurt him so much, that he
should be obliged to give it up, so the governor paid him a visit
instead, and found him stretched on his bed.

The next day Cæsar was no better; his dinner was ordered to
be served upstairs, and the governor paid him a visit as before. He
found his prisoner so dull and bored with his own company, that
he offered to come and share his supper. Cæsar accepted the offer
with gratitude and joy.

This time it was the prisoner who did the honours of the table,
and Cæsar was particularly charming and courteous in manner.
The governor seized the opportunity of putting some questions as
to his capture, and inquired, with the pride of a Castilian noble,
who set honour above all, what was the exact truth as to the way in
which Gonsalvo de Cordova and Ferdinand had broken their faith
with him. Cæsar showed every disposition to give him satisfaction
on this point, but indicated by a sign that he could not speak freely
before the valets. This precaution was so natural, that the governor
could not seem offended at it, and dismissed his attendants, so that
he and his companion remained alone. When the door was shut,
Cæsar filled his glass and that of the governor, and proposed the
king's health. The governor emptied his glass at once, and Cæsar
began his story, but he had hardly told a third of it, when in spite
of its exciting adventures, the eyes of his guest closed as if by magic,
and his head fell on the table in a deep sleep.

At the end of half-an-hour, the servants, not hearing any noise,
entered the room, and found the two boon companions, one on the
table and the other under it. There was nothing very unusual
about such an event to excite their suspicions, so they contented

themselves with carrying Don Manuel to his chamber and laying
Cæsar on his bed; they then locked the door with great care, leaving
the prisoner alone.

For a minute or two longer Cæsar lay still, apparently plunged

in a profound slumber, but when the sound of footsteps had completely died away, he softly raised his head, opened his eyes, and
moved towards the door, rather slowly it is true, but without seeming to feel any ill-effects from his accident on the previous day. He

stood still for a few seconds with his ear at the keyhole, then, raising himself, with a strange expression of triumph on his face, he
passed his hand over his forehead, and, for the first time since the
guards had left the room, breathed freely.

But there was no time to be lost, and without a moment's delay
he fastened the door from the inside as securely as it was fastened
without. He next extinguished his lamp, threw open his window,
and finished cutting through the bar. This done, he took off the
bandages tied round his leg, tore down the curtains, both of his
window and his bed, and made them into strips, adding to them
sheets, table cloths, napkins, and whatever else he could lay hands
on. At last he had a rope between fifty and sixty feet long, which
he secured firmly at one end to the bar next to the one that he had
sawn away, and mounting on the window-ledge, he began the most
dangerous part of his expedition in trusting himself to this frail
support. Happily, Cæsar was as strong as he was agile, and slid
down the whole length of the cord without accident; but when he
had reached the very end, in vain he tried to touch the earth with
his feet. The rope was too short.

Cæsar's position was terrible. The darkness of the night preventing his knowing how far he might be above the ground, and
his exertions had so fatigued him that he could not have gone back
even had he wished. There was no help for it, and, after muttering
a short prayer, he let go the rope, and fell, a distance of twelve or
fifteen feet.

The danger he had escaped was too great for the fugitive to
mind some slight bruises caused by his fall, so he jumped up, and
taking his bearings, made straight for the little door which stood
between him and freedom. When he reached it he felt in his pocket
for the key, and a cold sweat broke out on his face as he found it
was not there. Had he forgotten it in his room, or had he lost it
in his descent?

Collecting his thoughts as well as he could, he soon came to the
conclusion that it must have fallen out of his pocket as he climbed
down the rope. So he made his way a second time cautiously
across the court, trying to discover the exact spot where it might
be, by the aid of the wall of a cistern, which he had caught hold of
to raise himself from the ground. But the lost key was so small
and so insignificant, that there was little chance that he would ever
see it. However, it was his last resource, and Cæsar was searching
for it with all his might, when suddenly a door opened and the

night patrol came out, preceded by two torches. At first Cæsar
gave himself up for lost, then, remembering the water-butt that was
behind him, he at once plunged into it up to his neck, watching
with intense anxiety the movements of the soldiers who were advancing towards his hiding place. They passed him within a few
feet, crossed the court, and vanished through the door opposite ; but,
though all this had taken such a very short time, the light of the
torches had enabled Cæsar to distinguish the key lying on the
ground, and hardly had the gate closed on the soldiers when he was
once more master of his liberty.

Half-way between the castle and the village the Count of Benevento and Michelotto awaited him with a led horse. Cæsar flung
himself on its back and all three set out for Navarro, where, after
three days' hard riding, they found an asylum with the king, Jean
d'Albret, brother of Cæsar's wife.

THE KIDNAPPING OF THE PRINCES

*(The following story is adapted from Carlyle's
Essay, ' The Prinzenraub ')*

ABOUT the year 1455, one of the Electors of Saxony, Friedrich
der Sanftmütige (Frederick the Mild), quarrelled with a
certain knight named Konrad von Kaufungen. Friedrich had
hired Konrad, or Kunz as he was called, to fight for him in a war
against another Elector. In one of the battles, Kunz was taken
prisoner. To ransom himself he was obliged to pay 4,000 gold
gulden, for which he thought Friedrich ought to repay him. Friedrich refused to do so, as Kunz was not his vassal whom he was
bound to protect, but only a hired soldier who had to take all risks
on himself. Kunz was very angry, and threatened to revenge himself on the Elector, who took all his threats very calmly, saying to
him, ' Keep cool, Kunz ; don't burn the fish in the ponds.' But
Kunz was in bitter earnest. He went away to an old castle called
Isenburg in Bohemia, on the Saxon frontier, where he lived for some
time with his two squires, Mosen and Schönberg, plotting against
the Elector and his family. He had, moreover, bribed one of the
Elector's servants, Hans Schwalbe, to tell him all that was being
done in his castle of Altenburg. In July, Schwalbe sent word to
him that, on the seventh day of the month, the Elector and most cf
his followers were going away to Leipzig, and would leave the
Electress and his two boys, Ernst and Albrecht, guarded only by a
few servants, and these, he added, would probably spend the evening drinking in the town. Now the castle of Altenburg was built
on a steep hill, and one side of it overhung a precipice. As this
side was little guarded, Hans agreed to let down a rope-ladder from
one of the windows, and thus enable Kunz to get an entrance into
the castle. His plan then was to make his way to the sleeping
room of the two little princes, carry them off to his castle at Isen-

burg, and keep them till their father should grant his demands. Isenburg Castle was about a day's journey from the little town of Altenburg; so Kunz and his two squires, Mosen and Schönberg, and a few other men, started early on the 7th to ride to Altenburg, and when they reached it they hid themselves till nightfall. About midnight Kunz and his men went as quietly as possible to the foot of the cliff. Everyone seemed asleep in the castle, and outside no sound was to be heard but the stealthy tramp of the armed men. When they reached the rendezvous under the castle, Kunz gave his men their orders. Mosen, Schönberg, and three or four more were to come with him into the castle, and, when inside, to lock the doors of the Electress's and the servants' room, while the rest were to guard the gates in order that no one should escape to give the alarm. Each was to be ready when once the princes were secured to ride away for Isenburg as hard as possible.

Then Kunz whistled softly. He listened for a moment; another whistle answered his own, and a rope-ladder was slowly lowered from one of the windows. Kunz mounted it, and made his way to the room where the two little princes were sleeping under the charge of an old governess. He seized the eldest, a boy of fourteen, and carried him down the ladder, and Mosen followed with a second child in his arms. This boy kept calling out, 'I am not one of the princes; I am their playfellow, Count von Bardi. Let me go! Let me go!' Thereupon, telling the others to ride on with Prince Ernst in order to secure him, Kunz dashed up the ladder again, and ran to the princes' room, where he found little Prince Albrecht hiding under the bed. He caught him up and descended again with him. As he went, the Electress, roused by the boys' cries and finding her door bolted, rushed to the window and begged and implored him not to take her children.

'My husband shall grant all your demands, I swear to you,' she cried, 'only leave me my children!'

'Tell the Elector, Madam,' laughed Kunz, looking up, 'that I *can* burn the fish in the ponds!'

Then he mounted his horse, which his servant was holding, and away they rode as fast as the horses would carry them. They had not ridden many miles before the clang of bells broke on their ears. The alarm peal of the castle had awakened that of the town, and in a few hours every bell in every belfry in Saxony was ringing an alarm. The sun rose, and Kunz and his followers plunged deeper into the forest, riding through morasses and swamps, over rough and stony ground—anywhere to escape from the din of those alarm bells. At last the ride for dear life was nearly over; the band was within an hour's journey of the castle of Isenburg, when Prince Albrecht declared that he was dying of thirst.

'For the love of Heaven, give me something to drink, Sir Knight,' he implored.

Kunz bade the others ride on, and giving his squire his horse to hold he dismounted, lifted Albrecht down, and began looking for bilberries for him.

Whilst he was doing so, a charcoal-burner with his dog came up. He was much surprised to see such grand people in the forest, and asked,

'What are you doing with the young lord?'

'He has run away from his parents,' answered Kunz, impatiently. 'Can you tell me where bilberries are to be found here?'

'I do not know,' replied the charcoal-burner, still staring at the strangers.

Anxious to make him leave them, Kunz turned angrily round on him, and in doing so caught his spurs in the bushes, and fell flat on his face.

Albrecht caught hold of the charcoal-burner's arm.

'Save me!' he whispered eagerly. 'I am the Elector's son; this man has stolen me!'

The squire struck at the Prince with his sword, but the charcoal-burner warded aside the blow with his long pole, and felled the man to the ground. Kunz fought fiercely with him, but in answer to his summons for help, and attracted by the barking of the dog, a number of other charcoal-burners appeared on the scene to help their comrade, and Kunz was disarmed and taken prisoner. They marched him in triumph to the monastery of Grünheim, where he was secured in one of the cells, and in a few days was sent to Freiburg. On the 14th he was tried and condemned to death. It is said that a pardon was sent by the Elector, but if it were so it arrived too late, and Kunz was beheaded.

The rest of the robber-band with Prince Ernst did not fare much better. The alarm bells had aroused the whole country; six of the men were captured, and Mosen and the others with Prince Ernst took refuge in a cave near Zwickau. Not daring to venture out, and half starving for want of food, they lay there for three days in wretched plight. Then they learned accidentally from some woodmen, whose conversation they overheard, that Kunz had been

taken prisoner, had been tried, and by this time was in all probability beheaded.   As soon as they received this piece of intelligence,
they held a consultation and finally decided to send a message to
the Amtmann of Zwickau, offering to restore Prince Ernst if a free
pardon were granted to them, but threatening, if this was refused,
they would at once kill him.   Had they known that Kunz was
still alive, they might have stipulated for his pardon as well, but

believing him dead, they made no terms as regards his fate.   The
Amtmann had no choice but to accede to their demands when
their proposal reached him.   Prince Ernst was given up.   Mosen
and the rest fled away, nor were they ever heard of any more.

When the brave charcoal-burner, Georg Schmidt, was brought
before the Elector and his court, the Electress asked him how he
had dared to fight the robber-knight with no weapon but his pole.

'Madam,' he replied, 'I gave him a sound " drilling " with my
pole.'

All the court laughed, and thenceforward he was always called

Georg der Triller (the Driller), and his descendants took this name as their surname.   The only reward he would accept for his brave deed was leave for himself and his family to cut what wood they needed in the forest in which he lived.

The Electress and the two princes made a pilgrimage to the shrine at the monastery of Ebersdorf, and there in the church they hung up the coats which they and Kunz and the 'Triller' had worn on the memorable night when they were kidnapped, and there it is said they may be seen at this day.

THE CONQUEST OF MONTEZUMA'S EMPIRE ·

THE YOUTH OF CORTÉS

LONG ago, when Henry VIII. was King of England and Charles V. was King of Spain, there lived a young Spanish cavalier whose name was Hernando Cortés. His father, Don Martin Cortés, sent him to Salamanca when he was about fourteen years old, intending to have him educated as a lawyer. But Hernando cared nothing for books, and after wasting two years at college returned home, to the great annoyance of his parents, who were glad enough when, after another year of idleness, he proposed to go and seek his fortune in the New World so lately discovered by Columbus. An exploring expedition was just being fitted out, and Hernando Cortés had quite made up his mind to join it, when he unluckily fell from a high wall which he was climbing, and before he had recovered from his injuries the ships had sailed without him. Two more years did he remain at home after this misadventure, but at length, when he was nineteen years old, he joined a small fleet bound for the Indian Islands. The vessel in which he sailed was commanded by one Alonso Quintero, who, when they reached the Canary Islands, and all the other vessels were detained by taking in supplies, stole out of the harbour under cover of the night, meaning to reach Hispaniola before his companions, and so secure a better chance of trading. However, he met with a furious storm, and was driven back to the port with his ship dismasted and battered. The rest of the fleet generously consented to wait while his ship was being refitted, and after a short delay they set out again, but so soon as they neared the islands, the faithless Quintero again gave his companions the slip, but with no better success, for he met with such heavy gales that he entirely lost his reckoning, and for many days they tossed about helplessly, until one morning they were cheered by the sight of a white dove, which settled upon the rigging. Taking the direction of the bird's flight, they soon reached Hispaniola, where the captain had the satisfaction of finding all the other ships had arrived before him, and had sold all their cargoes. Cortés, as soon as he landed, went to see Ovando, the governor of the island, whom he had known in Spain, and presently was persuaded by him to accept a grant of land and settle down to cultivate it, though at first he said, 'I came to get gold, not to till the ground like a peasant.' So six years passed, during which the monotony of Cortés's life was only broken by occasional expeditions against the natives, in which he learned to endure toil and danger, and became familiar with the tactics of Indian warfare. At length, in 1511, when Diego Velasquez, the governor's lieutenant, undertook the conquest of Cuba, Cortés gladly accompanied him, and throughout the expedition made himself a favourite both with the commander and the soldiers. But when later on there arose discontent over the distribution of lands and offices, the malcontents fixed upon Cortés as the most suitable person to go back to Hispaniola, and lay their grievances before the higher authorities. This came to the ears of Velasquez, however, and he at once seized Cortés, whom he loaded with fetters and threw into prison. Luckily he soon succeeded in freeing himself from the irons, and letting himself down from the window took refuge in the nearest church, where he claimed the right of sanctuary. Velasquez, who was very angry at his escape, stationed a guard with orders to seize Cortés if he should leave the sanctuary, and this he was soon careless enough to do. As he stood outside the church an officer suddenly sprang upon him from behind, and made him prisoner once more. This time he was carried on board a ship which was to sail the next morning for Hispaniola, where he was to be tried, but again he managed to escape by dragging his feet through the rings which fettered them, and dropping silently over the ship's side into a little boat under cover of the darkness. As he neared the shore the water became so rough that the boat was useless, and he was forced to swim the rest of the way; but at last he got safely to land, and again took refuge in the church. After this he married a lady named Catalina Xuarez, and by the aid of her family managed to make his peace with Velasquez. Cortés now received a large estate near St. Jago, where he lived prosperously for some years, and even amassed a considerable sum of money. But at last news came of an exploring expedition which had set out in 1518 under Grijalva, the nephew of Velasquez. He had touched at various places on the Mexican coast, and had held a friendly conference with one cacique, or chief, who seemed desirous of collecting all the information he could about the Spaniards, and their motives in visiting Mexico, that he might transmit it to his master, the Aztec emperor. Presents were exchanged at this interview, and in return for a few glass beads, pins, and such paltry trifles, the Spaniards had received such a rich treasure of jewels and gold ornaments that the general at once sent back one of his ships under the command of Don Pedro de Alvarado to convey the spoil, and acquaint the governor of Cuba with the progress of the expedition, and also with all the information he had been able to glean respecting the Aztec emperor and his dominions. Now in those days nothing whatever was known about the interior of the country or of its inhabitants—it was as strange to the explorers as another planet.

The Wonders of Mexico

This was what they had to tell the governor. Far away towards the Pacific Ocean there stood, in a beautiful and most fertile valley, the capital of a great and powerful empire, called by its inhabitants ' Tenochtitlan,' but known to the Europeans only by its other name of ' Mexico,' derived from 'Mexitli,' the war-god of the Aztecs. These Aztecs seem to have come originally from the north, and after many wanderings to have halted at length on the south-western borders of a great lake, of which there were several in the Mexican valley. This celebrated valley was situated at a height of about 7,500 feet above the sea, and was oval in form, about 67 leagues in circumference, and surrounded by towering rocks, which seemed to be meant to protect it from invasion. It was in the year 1325 that the Aztecs paused upon the shore of the lake, and saw, as the sun rose, a splendid eagle perched upon a prickly pear which shot out of a crevice in the rock. It held a large serpent in its claws, and its broad wings were opened towards the rising sun. The Aztecs saw in this a most favourable omen, and there and then set about building themselves a city, laying its foundations upon piles in the marshy ground beside the lake, and to this day the eagle and the cactus form the arms of the Mexican republic.

The little body of settlers increased rapidly in number and power, and made their name terrible throughout the valley, in which various other tribes had long been settled, until at last they united them-

selves with the king of the Tezcucans, to aid him against a tribe
called the Tepanecs, who had invaded his territory. The allies were
completely successful, and this led to an agreement between the

states of Mexico, Tezcuco, and Tlacopan, that they should support
each other in all their wars, and divide all the spoils between them.
This alliance remained unbroken for over a hundred years and

under a succession of able princes the Aztec dominion grew, till at the coming of the Spaniards it reached across the continent, from the Atlantic to the Pacific Ocean. The Aztecs had many wise laws and institutions, and were indeed in some respects a highly civilised community. When their emperor died a new one was chosen from among his sons or nephews, by four nobles. The one preferred was obliged to have distinguished himself in war, and his coronation did not take place until a successful campaign had provided enough captives to grace his triumphal entry into the capital, and enough victims for the ghastly sacrifices which formed an important part of all their religious ceremonies. Communication was held with the remotest parts of the country by means of couriers, who, trained to it from childhood, travelled with amazing swiftness. Post-houses were established on the great roads, and the messenger bearing his despatches in the form of hieroglyphical paintings, ran to the first station, where they were taken by the next messenger and carried forward, being sent in one day a hundred or two hundred miles. Thus fish was served at the banquets of the emperor Montezuma which twenty-four hours before had been caught in the Gulf of Mexico, two hundred miles away. Thus too the news was carried when any war was going on, and as the messengers ran to acquaint the court with the movements of the royal armies, the people by the way knew whether the tidings were good or bad by the dress of the courier. But the training of warriors was the chief end and aim of all Aztec institutions. Their principal god was the god of war, and one great object of all their expeditions was the capture of victims to be sacrificed upon his altars. They believed that the soldier who fell in battle was transported at once to the blissful regions of the sun, and they consequently fought with an utter disregard of danger. The dress of the warriors was magnificent. Their bodies were protected by a vest of quilted cotton, impervious to light missiles, and over this the chiefs wore mantles of gorgeous feather-work, and the richer of them a kind of cuirass of gold or silver plates. Their helmets were of wood, fashioned like the head of some wild animal, or of silver surmounted by plumes of variously coloured feathers, sprinkled with precious stones, beside which they wore many ornaments of gold, and their banners were embroidered with gold and feather-work.

The Aztecs worshipped thirteen principal gods, and more than two hundred of less importance, each of whom, however, had his day of festival, which was duly observed. At the head of all stood the war-god, the terrible Huitzilopochtli, whose fantastic image was loaded with costly ornaments, and whose temples, in every city of the empire, were the most splendid and stately. The Aztecs also had a legend that there had once dwelt upon the earth the great Quetzalcoatl, god of the air, under whose sway all things had flourished and all people had lived in peace and prosperity ; but he had in some way incurred the wrath of the principal gods, and was compelled to leave the country. On his way he stopped at the city of Cholula, where a temple was dedicated to him, of which the great ruins remain to this day. When he reached the shores of the Mexican Gulf he embarked in his magic boat, made of serpents' skins, for the fabulous land of Tlapallan, but before he bade his followers farewell he promised that he and his descendants would one day come again. The Aztecs confidently looked forward to the return of their benevolent god, who was said to have been tall in stature, with a white skin, long dark hair, and a flowing beard, and this belief of theirs prepared the way, as you will presently see, for the success of Cortés.[1] The Mexican temples, or teocallis as they were called—which means ' Houses of God '—were very numerous, there being several hundreds of them in each of the principal cities. They looked rather like the Egyptian pyramids, and were divided into four or five stories, each one being smaller than the one below it, and the ascent was by a flight of steps at an angle of the pyramid. This led to a sort of terrace at the base of the second story, which passed quite round the building to another flight of steps immediately over the first, so that it was necessary to go all round the temple several times before reaching the summit. The top was a broad space on which stood two towers, forty or fifty feet high, which contained the images of the gods. Before these towers stood the dreadful stone of sacrifice, and two lofty altars on which the sacred fires burned continually. Human sacrifices were adopted by the Aztecs about two hundred years before the coming of the Spaniards. Rare at first, they became more and more frequent till at length nearly every festival closed with this cruel abomination. The unhappy victim was held by five priests upon the stone of sacrifice, while the sixth, who was clothed in a scarlet mantle, emblematic of his horrible office, cut open his breast with a sharp razor of ' itztli,' a volcanic substance as hard as flint, and tearing

[1] In 1121 Bishop Eric left Iceland for Vinland, part of America discovered by Leif the Lucky (1000-1002). Bishop Eric was heard of no more. Can he have reached the Aztecs, and been regarded as a god ?

out his heart, held it first up to the sun, which they worshipped, and then cast it at the feet of the god to whom the temple was devoted; and to crown the horror, the body of the captive thus sacrificed was afterwards given to the warrior who had taken him in battle, who thereupon gave a great banquet and served him up amid choice dishes and delicious beverages for the entertainment of his friends. When the great teocalli of Huitzilopochtli was dedicated in the year 1486, no less than 70,000 prisoners were thus sacrificed, and in the whole kingdom every year the victims were never fewer than 20,000, or, as some old writers say, 50,000. The Aztec writing was not with letters and words, but consisted of little coloured pictures, each of which had some special meaning. Thus a ' tongue ' denoted speaking, a ' footprint ' travelling, a ' man sitting on the ground ' an earthquake. As a very slight difference in position or colour intimated a different meaning, this writing was very difficult to read, and in the Aztec colleges the priests specially taught it to their pupils. At the time of the coming of the Spaniards there were numbers of people employed in this picture-writing, but unfortunately hardly any of the manuscripts were preserved; for the Spaniards, looking upon them as magic scrolls, caused them to be burned by thousands. In many mechanical arts the Aztecs had made considerable progress. Their ground was well culti-vated, they had discovered and used silver, lead, tin, and copper. Gold, which was found in the river-beds, they cast into bars, or used as money by filling transparent quills with gold dust. They also made many fantastic ornaments of gold and silver, and cast gold and silver vessels, which they carved delicately with chisels. Some of the silver vases were so large that a man could not encircle them with his arms. But the art in which they most delighted was the wonderful feather-work. With the gorgeous plumage of the tropical birds they could produce all the effect of a beautiful mosaic. The feathers, pasted upon a fine cotton web, were wrought into dresses for the wealthy, hangings for their palaces, and ornaments for their temples.

These then were the people of whom Grijalva sent back to Cuba a few vague reports, and these, and the accounts of the splendour of the treasure, spread like wildfire through the island. The governor having resolved to send out more ships to follow up these discoveries, looked about him for a suitable person to com-mand the expedition and share the expenses of it, and being re-commended by several of his friends to choose Hernando Cortés, he presently did so. Cortés had now attained his heart's desire, and at once began with the utmost energy to purchase and fit out the ships. He used all the money he had saved, and as much more as he could persuade his friends to lend him, and very soon he was in possession of six vessels, and three hundred recruits had enrolled themselves under his banner. His orders were, first, to find Grijalva and to proceed in company with him; then to seek out and rescue six Christians, the survivors of a previous expedition, who were supposed to be lingering in captivity in the interior; and to bear in mind, before all things, that it was the great desire of the Spanish monarch that the Indians should be converted to Christianity. They were to be invited to give their allegiance to him, and to send him presents of gold and jewels to secure his favour and protection. The explorers were also to survey the coast, acquaint themselves with the general features of the country, and to barter with the natives.

THE BEGINNING OF THE EXPEDITION

But before Cortés was ready to start, a jealousy and distrust of him took possession of the mind of Velasquez, so that he determined to entrust the command of the fleet to someone else. This came to the ears of Cortés, and he with great promptitude assembled his officers secretly, and that very night set sail with what supplies he was able to lay hands upon, his ships being neither ready for sea nor properly provisioned. When morning broke news was carried to Velasquez that the fleet was under weigh, and he rose hastily and galloped down to the quay. Cortés rowed back to within speaking distance.

' This is a courteous way of taking leave of me, truly,' cried the governor.

' Pardon me,' answered Cortés, ' time presses, and there are some things that should be done before they are even thought of.' And with that he returned to his vessel, and the little fleet sailed away to Macaca, where Cortés laid in more stores. This was on November 18, 1518. Shortly afterwards he proceeded to Trinidad, a town on the south coast of Cuba, where he landed, and setting up his standard, invited all who would to join the expedition, holding out to them great hopes of wealth to be gained. Volunteers flocked in daily, including many young men of noble family, who were attracted by the fame of Cortés. Among them were Pedro de Alvarado, Cristóval de Olid, Alonso de Avila, Juan Velasquez de Leon, Alonso Hernandez de Puertocarrero, and Gonzalo de Sandoval, of all of whom you will hear again before the story is finished. Finally, in February 1519, when all the reinforcements were assembled, Cortés found he had eleven vessels, one hundred and ten mariners, five hundred and fifty-three soldiers, and two hundred Indians. He also had sixteen horses, ten large guns, and four lighter, which were called falconets. Cortés, before embarking, addressed his little army, saying that he held out to them a glorious prize, and that if any among them coveted riches, he would make them masters of such as their countrymen had never dreamed of; and so they sailed away for the coast of Yucatan.

The first thing that happened was that they were overtaken by a furious tempest, and Cortés was delayed by looking after a disabled vessel, and so was the last to reach the island of Cozumel. Here he found that Alvarado, one of his captains, had landed, plundered a temple, and by his violence caused the natives to fly and hide themselves inland.

Cortés, much displeased, severely reprimanded his officer, and, by the aid of an interpreter, explained his peaceful intentions to two Indians who had been captured. Then he loaded them with presents, and sent them to persuade their countrymen to return, which they presently did, and the Spaniards had the satisfaction of bartering the trifles they had brought for the gold ornaments of the natives. Next Cortés sent two ships to the opposite coast of Yucatan, where they were to despatch some Indians inland, to seek for and ransom the Christian captives, of whom he had gained some tidings from a trader, and while they were gone he explored the island, and induced the natives to declare themselves Christians by the very summary method of rolling their venerated idols out of their temple, and setting up in their stead an image of the Virgin and Child. When the Indians saw that no terrible consequences followed, they listened to the teaching of the good priest, Father Olmedo, who accompanied the expedition, though it is probable that they did not, after all, understand much of his instruction. After eight days the two ships came back, but with no news of the captives, and Cortés sorrowfully decided that he could wait no longer. He accordingly took in provisions and water, and set sail again, but before they had gone far one of the ships sprang a leak, which obliged them to put back into the same port. It was lucky that they did, for soon after they landed a canoe was seen coming from the shore of Yucatan, which proved to contain one of the long-lost Spaniards, who was called Aguilar. He had been for eight years a slave among the natives in the interior, but his master, tempted by the ransom of glass-beads, hawk-bells, and such treasures, had consented to release him. When he reached the coast the ships were gone, but owing to the fortunate accident of their return, he found himself once more among his countrymen. Cortés at once saw the importance of having him as an interpreter, but in the end he proved to be of more use to the explorers than could have been at first imagined.

Again the fleet set out, and coasted along the Gulf of Mexico till they reached the mouth of the Rio de Tabasco. Here Cortés landed, but found that the Indians were hostile, and were drawn up in great force against him. However, after some hard fighting the Spaniards were victorious, and having taken possession of the town of Tabasco, Cortés sent messengers to the chiefs saying that if they did not at once submit themselves he would ravage the country with fire and sword. As they had no mind for any more fighting they came humbly, bringing presents, and among them thirty slaves, one of whom, a beautiful Mexican girl named Malinche, was after-wards of the utmost importance to the expedition. She had come into the possession of the cacique of Tabasco through some traders from the interior of the country, to whom she had been secretly sold by her mother, who coveted her inheritance. Cortés now re-embarked his soldiers and sailed away to the island of San Juan de Uloa, under the lee of which they anchored, and soon saw the light pirogues of the Indians coming off to them from the mainland. They brought presents of fruit and flowers, and little ornaments of gold which they gladly exchanged for the usual trifles. Cortés was most anxious to converse with them, but found to his disappointment that Aguilar could not understand their dialect. In this dilemma he was informed that one of the slaves was a Mexican, and could of course speak the language. This was Malinche, or as the Spaniards always called her, 'Marina.' Cortés was so charmed with her beauty and cleverness that he made her his secretary, and kept her always with him; and she very soon learned enough Spanish to interpret for him without the help of Aguilar. But at first they were both necessary, and by their aid Cortés learned that his visitors were subjects of Montezuma, the great Aztec emperor, and were governed by Tenhtlile, one of his nobles. Cortés having ascertained that there was abundance of gold in the interior, dismissed them, loaded with presents, to acquaint their governor with his desire for an interview. The next morning he landed on the mainland with all his force. It was a level sandy plain, and the troops employed themselves in cutting down trees and bushes to provide a shelter from the weather; in this they were aided by the natives, who built them huts with stakes and earth, mats and cotton carpets, and flocked from all the country round to see the wonderful strangers. They brought with them fruits, vegetables, flowers in abundance, game, and many dishes cooked after the fashion of the country; and these they gave to, or bartered with, the Spaniards. The next day came Tenhtlile, the governor, with a numerous train, and was met by Cortés, and conducted to his tent

with great ceremony. All the principal officers were assembled, and after a ceremonious banquet at which the governor was regaled with Spanish wines and confections, the interpreters were sent for and a conversation began. Tenhtlile first asked about the country of the strangers, and the object of their visit. Cortés replied that he was the subject of a powerful monarch beyond the seas, who had heard of the greatness of the Mexican emperor, and had sent him with a present in token of his goodwill, and with a message which he must deliver in person. He concluded by asking when he could

be admitted into Montezuma's presence. To this the Aztec noble
replied haughtily,

'How is it that you have been here only two days, and demand
to see the emperor?'

Then he added that he was surprised to hear that there could
be another monarch as powerful as Montezuma, but if it were so
his master would be happy to communicate with him, and that he
would forward the royal gift brought by the Spanish commander,
and so soon as he had learned Montezuma's will would inform him
of it. Tenhtlile then ordered his slaves to bring forward the
present for the Spanish general. It consisted of ten loads of fine
cotton, several mantles of gorgeous feather-work, and a wicker
basket of golden ornaments. Cortés received it with due acknow-
ledgments, and in his turn ordered the presents for Montezuma to
be brought forward. These were an armchair richly carved and
painted, a crimson cloth cap with a gold medal, and a quantity of
collars, bracelets, and other ornaments of cut-glass, which in a
country where glass was unknown were as valuable as real gems.
The Aztec governor observed a soldier in the camp in a shining
gilt helmet, and expressed a wish that Montezuma should see it, as
it reminded him of one worn by the god Quetzalcoatl. Cortés
declared his willingness that the helmet should be sent, and begged
that the emperor would return it filled with the gold dust of the
country, that he might compare its quality with that of his own.
He also said that the Spaniards were troubled with a disease of
the heart, for which gold was a sure remedy. In fact, he made his
want of gold very clear to the governor. While these things were
passing Cortés observed one of Tenhtlile's attendants busy with a
pencil, and on looking at his work he found it was a sketch of the
Spaniards, their costumes, weapons, and all objects of interest being
correctly represented both in form and colour. This was the celebrated picture-writing, and the governor said that this man was
drawing all these things for Montezuma, as he would get a much
better idea of their appearance thus. Cortés thereupon ordered
out the cavalry, and caused them to go through their military
exercises upon the firm wet sands of the beach; and the appearance
of the horses—which were absolutely unknown in Mexico—filled
the natives with astonishment, which turned to alarm when the
general ordered the cannon to be fired, and they saw for the first
time the smoke and flame, and beheld the balls crashing among
the trees of the neighbouring forest and reducing them to splinters.

Nothing of this sort was lost upon the painters, who faithfully recorded every particular, not omitting the ships—the 'water-houses,' as they called them—which swung at anchor in the bay. Finally, the governor departed as ceremoniously as he had come, leaving orders with his people to supply the Spanish general with all he might require till further instructions should come from the emperor.

In the meantime the arrival of the strangers was causing no small stir in the Mexican capital. A general feeling seems to have prevailed that the Return of the White God, Quetzalcoatl, was at hand, and many wonderful signs and occurrences seemed to confirm the belief.

In 1510 the great lake of Tezcuco, without tempest, earthquake, or any visible cause, became violently agitated, overflowed its banks, and, pouring into the streets of Mexico, swept away many buildings by the fury of its waters. In 1511 one of the towers of the great temple took fire, equally without any apparent cause, and continued to burn in defiance of all attempts to extinguish it. In the following years three comets were seen, and not long before the coming of the Spaniards a strange light broke forth in the east, resembling a great pyramid or flood of fire thickly powdered with stars : at the same time low voices were heard in the air, and doleful wailings, as if to announce some strange, mysterious calamity. A lady of the Royal house died, was buried, and rose again, prophesying ruin to come. After the conquest she became a Christian.

Montezuma, terrified at these apparitions, took counsel of Nezahualpilli, King of Tezcuco, who was a great proficient in astrology ; but far from obtaining any comfort from him, he was still further depressed by being told that all these things predicted the speedy downfall of his empire. When, therefore, the picture-writings showing the Spanish invaders reached Montezuma, they caused him great apprehension, and he summoned the kings of Tezcuco and Tlacopan to consult with them as to how the strangers should be received. There was much division of opinion, but finally Montezuma resolved to send a rich present which should impress them with a high idea of his wealth and grandeur, while at the same time he would forbid them to approach the capital. After eight days at the most, which however seemed a long time to the Spaniards, who were suffering from the intense heat of the climate, the embassy, accompanied by the governor Tenhtlile, reached the camp, and presented to Cortés the magnificent treasure sent by Montezuma. One of the two nobles had been sent on account of his great likeness to the picture of Cortés which the Aztec painter had executed for Montezuma. This resemblance was so striking that the Spanish soldiers always called this chief 'the Mexican Cortés.' After the usual ceremonious salutes, the slaves unrolled the delicately wrought mats and displayed the gifts they had brought. There were shields, helmets, and cuirasses embossed with plates and ornaments of pure gold, with collars and bracelets of the same precious metal, sandals, fans, plumes, and crests of varieg ted feathers wrought with gold and silver thread and sprinkled with pearls and precious stones. Also imitations of birds and animals in wrought or cast gold and silver of exquisite workmanship; and curtain coverlets and robes of cotton, fine as slik—of rich and varied hues—interwoven with feather-work that rivalled the most delicate painting. There were more than thirty loads of cotton cloth, and the Spanish helmet was returned filled to the brim with grains of gold. But the things which excited the most admiration were two circular plates of gold and silver as large as carriage-wheels. One, representing the sun, was richly carved with plants and animals, and was worth fifty-two thousand five hundred pounds. The Spaniards could not conceal their rapture at this exhibition of treasure which exceeded their utmost dreams; and when they had sufficiently admired it the ambassadors courteously delivered their message, which was to the effect that Montezuma had great pleasure in holding communication with so powerful a monarch as the King of Spain, but he could not grant a personal interview to the Spaniards; the way to his capital was too long and too dangerous. Therefore the strangers must return to their own land with the gifts he had sent them. Cortés, though much vexed, concealed his annoyance and expressed his sense of the emperor's munificence. It made him, he said, only the more desirous of a personal interview, so that he felt it was impossible that he should present himself again before his sovereign without having accomplished this great object of his journey. He once more requested them to bear this message to their master, with another trifling gift. This they seemed unwilling to do, and took their leave repeating that the general's wish could not be gratified. The soldiers were by this time suffering greatly from the heat, surrounded as they were by burning sands and evil-smelling marshes, and swarms of venomous insects which tormented them night and day. Thirty of their number died, and the discomfort of the rest was greatly increased by the indifference of the natives, who no longer brought them such abundant supplies, and demanded an immense price for what they did provide. After ten days the Mexican envoys returned, bearing another rich present of stuffs and gold ornaments, which, though not so valuable as the first, was yet worth three thousand ounces of gold. Beside this there were four precious stones, somewhat resembling emeralds, each of which they assured the Spaniards was worth more than a load of gold, and was destined as a special mark of respect for the Spanish monarch, since only the nobles of Mexico were allowed to wear them. Unfortunately, however, they were of no value at all in Europe. Montezuma's answer was the same as before. He positively forbade the strangers to approach nearer to his capital, and requested them to take the treasure he had bestowed upon them, and return without delay to their own country. Cortés received this unwelcome message courteously, but coldly, and turning to his officers exclaimed, ' This is a rich and powerful prince indeed, yet it shall go hard but we will one day pay him a visit in his capital.' Father Olmedo then tried to persuade the Aztec chiefs to give up their idol-worship, and endeavoured by the aid of Marina and Aguilar to explain to them the mysteries of his own faith, but it is probable that he was not very successful. The chiefs presently withdrew coldly, and that same night every hut was deserted by the natives, and the Spaniards were left without supplies in a desolate wilderness. Cortés thought this so suspicious that he prepared for an attack, but everything remained quiet.

The general now decided to remove his camp to a more healthy place a little farther along the coast, where the ships could anchor and be sheltered from the north wind. But the soldiers began to grumble and be discontented, and to say that it was time to return with their spoil, and not linger upon those barren shores until they had brought the whole Mexican nation about their ears. Fortunately at this juncture five Indians made their appearance in the camp, and were taken to the general's tent. They were quite different from the Mexicans in dress and appearance, and wore rings of gold and bright blue gems in their ears and nostrils, while a gold leaf, delicately wrought, was attached to the under lip. Marina could not understand their language, but luckily she found that two of them could speak in the Aztec tongue. They explained that they came from Cempoalla, the chief town of a tribe called the Totonacs, and that their country had been lately conquered by the

Aztecs, whose oppressions they greatly resented. They also said that the fame of the Spaniards had reached their master, who had sent to request them to visit him in his capital. It is easy to imagine how eagerly Cortés listened to this communication, and how important it was to him. Hitherto, as he knew absolutely nothing of the state of affairs in the interior of the country, he had supposed the empire to be strong and united. Now he saw that the discontent of the provinces conquered by Montezuma might be turned to his own advantage, and that by their aid he might hope to succeed in his cherished scheme of subduing the emperor himself. He therefore dismissed the Totonacs with many presents, promising soon to visit their city. Then with his usual energy and diplomacy he turned upon the immediate difficulties which beset him—the discontent of the soldiers, the jealousy of some of his officers, and the fact that he had no warrant for his ambitious plans in the commission that he had received from Velasquez. By tact and cunning he managed to settle everything as he wished, and set to work to establish a colony in the name of the Spanish sovereign, and appointed his chief friend Puertocarrero to be one of its magistrates, and Montejo, who was a friend of Velasquez, to be the other. The new town was called Villa Rica de Vera Cruz, ' The rich town of the True Cross,' and, as you see, its governors and officials were appointed before a single house was built. To them Cortés then resigned the commission which he had received from Velasquez, and the council, which consisted chiefly of his own friends, immediately reappointed him to be captain-general and chief justice of the colony, with power to do practically just as he liked. Of course this caused a great commotion in the opposing party, but Cortés put the leaders into irons and sent them on board one of the ships, while he sent the soldiers on a foraging expedition into the surrounding country. By the time these returned with supplies they had altered their minds, and joined their companions in arms, pledging themselves to a common cause, while even the cavaliers on board the ship came to the same conclusion, and were reconciled to the new government, and were from that time staunch adherents to Cortés.

Peace being thus restored, the army set out to march northwards to the place where it had been decided to build the town. They crossed a river in rafts and broken canoes which they found upon its bank, and presently came to a very different scene from the burning sandy waste, which they had left. The wide plains were covered with green grass, and there were groves of palms, among which the

Spaniards saw deer and various wild animals, and flocks of phea-
sants and turkeys. On their way they passed through a deserted
village, in the temples of which they found records in the picture-
writing, and also, to their horror, the remains of sacrificed victims.
As they proceeded up the river they were met by twelve Indians,
sent by the cacique of Cempoalla to show them the way to his town.
The farther they went the more beautiful did the country become.
The trees were loaded with gorgeous fruits and flowers, and birds
and butterflies of every hue abounded. As they approached the
Indian city they saw gardens and orchards on each side of the road,
and were met by crowds of natives, who mingled fearlessly with the
soldiers, bringing garlands of flowers, in which they specially de-

lighted, to deck the general's helmet and to hang about the neck
of his horse. The cacique, who was tall and very fat, received
Cortés with much courtesy, and assigned to the army quarters in
a neighbouring temple, where they were well supplied with provisions, and the general received a present of gold and fine cotton.
But in spite of all this friendliness he neglected no precautions,
stationing sentinels, and posting his artillery so as to command the
entrance. The following morning Cortés paid the cacique a visit
at his own residence, and, by the aid of Marina, a long conference
was held in which the Spanish general gained much important information, and promised to aid the Totonacs against Montezuma,
and prevent him from carrying off their young men and maidens
to be sacrificed to his gods. The following day the army marched

off again to the town of Chiahuitztla, which stood like a fortress on a crag overlooking the gulf. Though the inhabitants were alarmed at first, they soon became friendly, and the chiefs came to confer with Cortés and the cacique of Cempoallo, who had accompanied him, carried in a litter. Just then there was a stir among the people, and five men entered the market-place where they were standing. By their rich and peculiar dress they seemed to belong to a different race : their dark glossy hair was tied in a knot at the top of the head, and they carried bunches of flowers in their hands. Their attendants carried wands, or fans, to brush away the flies and insects from their lordly masters. These persons passed the Spaniards haughtily, scarcely deigning to return their salutations, and they were immediately joined by the Totonac chiefs, who seemed anxious to conciliate them by every sort of attention. The general, much astonished, inquired of Marina what this meant, and she replied that these were Aztec nobles empowered to receive tribute for Montezuma.

Soon after the chiefs returned in dismay, saying that the Aztecs were very angry with them for entertaining the Spaniards without the emperor's permission, and had demanded twenty young men and maidens to be sacrificed to the gods as a punishment. Cortés was most indignant at this insolence, and insisted that the Totonacs should not only refuse the demand, but should also seize the Aztec nobles, and throw them into prison. This they did, but the Spanish general managed to get two of them freed in the night, and brought before him. He then very cunningly made them believe that he regretted the indignity that had been offered them, and would help them to get away safely, and the next day would do his best to release their companions. He also told them to report this to Montezuma, assuring him of the great respect and regard in which he was held by the Spaniards. Then he sent them away secretly to the port, and they were taken in one of the vessels, and landed safely at a little distance along the coast. The Totonacs were furious at the escape of some of their prisoners, and would at once have sacrificed the remainder, had not Cortés expressed the utmost horror at the idea, and sent them on board one of the ships for safe keeping, whence he very soon allowed them to join their companions. This artful proceeding had, as we shall presently see, just the effect it was meant to have upon Montezuma. By order of Cortés, messengers were now sent to all the other Totonac towns, telling them of the defiance that had been shown to the emperor, and bidding

R

them also refuse to pay the tribute. The Indians soon came flocking into Chiahuitztla to see and confer with the powerful strangers, in the hope of regaining liberty by their aid, and so cleverly had Cortés managed to embroil them with Montezuma, that even the most timid felt that they had no choice but to accept the protection of the Spaniards, and make a bold effort for the recovery of freedom.

Cortés accordingly made them swear allegiance to the Spanish sovereign, and then set out once more for the port where his colony was to be planted. This was only half a league distant, in a wide and fruitful plain, and he was not long in determining the circuit of the walls, and the site of the fort, granary, and other public buildings. The friendly Indians brought stone, lime, wood, and bricks, and in a few weeks a town rose up, which served as a good starting-point for future operations, a retreat for the disabled, a place for the reception of stores, or whatever might be sent to or from the mother-country, and was, moreover, strong enough to overawe the surrounding country. This was the first colony in New Spain, and was hailed with satisfaction by the simple natives, who could not foresee that their doom was sealed when a white man set his foot upon their soil.

While the Spaniards were still occupied with their new settlement they were surprised by another embassy from Mexico. When the account of the imprisonment of the royal collectors first reached Montezuma, his feelings of fear and superstition were swallowed up in indignation, and he began with great energy to make preparations for punishing his rebellious vassals, and avenging the insult offered to himself. But when the Aztec officers liberated by Cortés reached the capital and reported the courteous treatment they had received from the Spanish commander, he was induced to resume his former timid and conciliatory policy, and sent an embassy consisting of two young nephews of his own and four of his chief nobles to the Spanish quarters. As usual they bore a princely gift of gold, rich cotton stuffs, and wonderful mantles of feather embroidery. The envoys on coming before Cortés presented this offering, with the emperor's thanks to him for the courtesy he had shown to the captive nobles. At the same time Montezuma expressed his surprise and regret that the Spaniards should have countenanced the rebellion. He had no doubt, he said, that Cortés and his followers were the long-looked-for strangers, and therefore of the same lineage as himself. From deference to them he would spare the

Totonacs while they were present, but the day of vengeance would come. Cortés entertained the Indians with frank hospitality, taking care, however, to make such a display of his resources as should impress them with a sense of his power. Then he dismissed them with a few trifling gifts and a conciliatory message to the emperor, to the effect that he would soon pay his respects to him in his capital, when all misunderstanding between them would certainly be adjusted. The Totonacs were amazed when they understood the nature of this interview; for, in spite of the presence of the Spaniards, they had felt great apprehension as to the consequence of their rash act, and now they felt absolutely in awe of the strangers who even at a distance could exercise such a mysterious influence over the terrible Montezuma.

Not long after the cacique of Cempoalla appealed to Cortés to aid him against a neighbour with whom he had a quarrel. The general at once marched to support him with a part of his force, but when they reached the hostile city they were received in a most friendly manner, and Cortés had no difficulty in reconciling the two chiefs to one another. In token of gratitude the Indian cacique sent eight noble maidens, richly decked with collars and ornaments of gold, whom he begged the general to give as wives to his captains. Cortés seized the opportunity of declaring that they must first become Christians, and be baptized, since the sons of the Church could not be allowed to marry idolaters. The chief replied that his gods were good enough for him, and that he should at once resent any insults offered to them, even if they did not avenge themselves by instantly destroying the Spaniards. However, the general and his followers had seen too much already of the barbarous rites of the Indian religion and its horrible sacrifices. Without hesitation they attacked the principal teocalli, whereupon the cacique called his men to arms, the priests in their blood-stained robes rushed frantically about among the people, calling upon them to defend their gods, and all was tumult and confusion. Cortés acted with his usual promptitude at this crisis. He caused the cacique and the principal inhabitants and the priests to be taken prisoners, and then commanded them to quiet the people, threatening that a single arrow shot at the Spaniards should cost them their lives. Marina also represented the madness of resistance, reminding the cacique that if he lost the friendship of the strangers, he would be left alone to face the vengeance of Montezuma. This consideration decided him: covering his face with his hands, he exclaimed that the gods would avenge their own wrongs. Taking advantage of this tacit consent, fifty soldiers rushed up the

stairway of the temple, and dragging the great wooden idols from their places in the topmost tower, they rolled them down the steps of the pyramid amid the groans of the natives and the triumphant shouts of their comrades, and then burnt them to ashes. The Totonacs, finding that their gods were unable to prevent or even punish this profanation of their temple, now believed that they were indeed less to be feared than the Spaniards, and offered no further resistance. By Cortés's orders the teocalli was then thoroughly purified, and an altar was erected, surmounted by a great cross hung with garlands of roses, and Father Olmedo said Mass before the Indians and Spaniards, who seem to have been alike impressed by the ceremony. An old disabled soldier, named Juan de Torres, was left to watch over the sanctuary and instruct the natives in its services, while the general, taking a friendly leave of his Totonac allies, set out once more for Villa Rica, to finish his arrangements before departing for the capital. Here he was surprised to find that a Spanish vessel had arrived in his absence, having on board twelve soldiers and two horses, a very welcome addition to the tiny army. Cortés now resolved to execute a plan of which he had been thinking for some time. He knew very well that none of his arrangements about the colony would hold good without the Spanish monarch's sanction, and also that Velasquez had great interest at court, and would certainly use it against him. Therefore he resolved to send despatches to the emperor himself, and such an amount of treasure as should give a great idea of the extent and importance of his discoveries. He gave up his own share of the spoil, and persuaded his officers to do the same, and a paper was circulated among the soldiers, calling upon all who chose to resign the small portion which was due to them, that a present worthy of the emperor's acceptance might be sent home. It is only another proof of the extraordinary power which Cortés had over these rough soldiers, who cared for nothing but plunder, that not a single one refused to give up the very treasure which he had risked so much to gain.

These are some of the wonderful things that were sent. Two collars made of gold and precious stones. Two birds made of green feathers, with feet, beaks, and eyes of gold, and in the same piece with them animals of gold resembling snails. A large alligator's head of gold. Two birds made of thread and feather-work, having the quills of their wings and tails, their feet, eyes and the ends of their beaks of gold, standing upon two reeds covered with gold, which are raised on balls of feather-work and gold embroidery, one white and the other yellow, with seven tassels of feather-work hanging from each of them. A large silver wheel, also bracelets, leaves, and five shields of the same metal. A box of feather-work embroidered on leather, with a large plate of gold weighing seventy ounces in the midst. A large wheel of gold with figures of strange animals on it, and worked with tufts of leaves, weighing three thousand eight hundred ounces. A fan of variegated feather-work with thirty-seven rods plated with gold. Sixteen shields of precious stones, with feathers of various colours hanging from their rims, and six shields each covered with a plate of gold, with something resembling a mitre in the centre. Besides all this there was a quantity of gold ore, and many pieces of richly embroidered cotton cloth and feather-work. He accompanied this present with a letter to the emperor in which he gave an account of all his adventures and discoveries, and ended by beseeching him to confirm his authority, as he was entirely confident that he should be able to place the Castilian crown in possession of this great Indian empire. He also sent four slaves, who had been rescued from the cage in which were kept the victims about to be sacrificed, and some Mexican manuscripts.

Very soon after the departure of the treasure-ship Cortés discovered that there was a conspiracy among some of his followers, who either did not like the way the general arranged matters, or else were terrified at the prospect of the dangerous campaign that was before them. They had seized one of the ships, and got provisions and water stored, and were on the eve of setting sail for Cuba, when one of their number repented of the part he had taken in the plot, and betrayed it to Cortés, who at once took measures for the arrest of the ringleaders, two of whom were afterwards hanged. This affair showed the general that there were some among his followers who were not heart and soul in the expedition, and who might therefore fail him when he most needed them, and might also cause their comrades to desert if there was any chance for them to escape. He therefore determined to take the bold step of destroying the ships without the knowledge of his army. Accordingly, he marched the whole army to Cempoalla, and when he arrived there he told his plan to a few of his devoted adherents, who entirely approved of it. Through them he persuaded the pilots to declare the ships unseaworthy, and then ordered nine of them to be sunk, having first brought on shore their sails, masts, iron, and all movable fittings. When the news of this proceeding reached Cempoalla, it caused the deepest consternation among the Spaniards, who felt themselves betrayed and abandoned, a mere handful of men arrayed against a great and formidable empire, and cut off from all chance of escape. They murmured loudly, and a serious mutiny was threatened. But Cortés, whose presence of mind never deserted him, managed to reassure them, and to persuade them that he had only done what was really best for everyone; and he so cunningly dwelt upon the fame and the treasure which they were on the eve of gaining, that not one of them accepted the offer which he made to them of returning to Cuba in the only remaining ship. Their enthusiasm for their leader revived, and as he concluded his speech they made the air ring with their shouts of 'To Mexico! To Mexico!'

THE MARCH TO MEXICO

While he was still at Cempoalla, news came to Cortés from Villa Rica that four strange ships were hovering off the coast, and that they refused to respond to repeated signals made to them by Don Juan de Escalante, who was in command of the garrison left in the town. This greatly alarmed Cortés, who was continually dreading the interference of his enemy, the governor of Cuba. He rode hastily back to Villa Rica, and, almost without stopping to rest, pushed on a few leagues northwards along the coast, where he understood the ships were at anchor. On his way he met with three Spaniards just landed from them, and learned that they belonged to a squadron fitted out by Francisco de Garay, who had landed on the Florida coast a year before, and had obtained from Spain authority over the countries he might discover in its neighbourhood. Cortés saw he had nothing to fear from them, but he did wish he could have induced the crews of the ships to join his expedition. The three men he easily persuaded, but those who remained on board feared treachery, and refused to send a boat ashore. Finally, by a stratagem, Cortés succeeded in capturing three or four more, out of a boat's crew who came to fetch their comrades, and with this small party of recruits he returned to Cempoalla. On August 16, 1519, Cortés bade farewell to his hospitable Indian friends, and set out for Mexico. His force consisted of about four hundred foot and fifteen horse, with seven pieces of artillery, and in addition to these he had obtained from the cacique of Cempoalla thirteen hundred warriors, and a thousand porters to carry the baggage and drag the guns. During the first day the army marched through the 'tierra caliente,' or hot region. All around them fruit and flowers grew in the wildest profusion, as indeed they did all the year round in that wonderful climate; the air was heavy with perfume, and bright birds and insects abounded. But after some leagues' travel, over roads made nearly impassable by the summer rains, they began to ascend gradually, and at the close of the second day they reached Xalapa, from which they looked out over one of the grandest prospects that could be seen anywhere. Down below them lay the hot region with its gay confusion of meadows, streams, and flowering forests, sprinkled over with shining Indian villages, while a faint line of light upon the horizon told them that there was the ocean they had so lately crossed, beyond which lay their country, which many of them would never see again. To the south rose the mighty mountain called 'Orizaba,' in his mantle of snow, and in another direction the Sierra Madre, with its dark belt of pine-trees, stretched its long lines of shadowy hills away into the distance. Onward and upward they went, and on the fourth day they arrived at the strong town of Naulinco. Here the inhabitants entertained them hospitably, for they were friendly with the Totonacs, and Cortés endeavoured, through Father Olmedo, to teach them something about Christianity. They seem to have listened willingly, and allowed the Spaniards to erect a cross for their adoration, which indeed they did in most of the places where they halted. The troops now entered upon a rugged, narrow valley, called 'the Bishop's Pass,' and now it began to be terribly cold, the snow and hail beat upon them, and the freezing wind seemed to penetrate to their very bones. The Spaniards were partly protected by their armour, and their thick coats of quilted cotton, but the poor Indians, natives of the hot region and with very little clothing, suffered greatly, and indeed several of them died by the way. The path lay round a bare and dreadful-looking volcanic mountain, and often upon the edge of precipices three thousand feet in depth. After three days of this dreary travelling the army emerged into a more genial climate; they had reached the great tableland which spreads out for hundreds of miles along the crests of the Cordilleras, more than seven thousand feet above the sea-level. The vegetation of the torrid and temperate regions had of course disappeared, but the fields were carefully cultivated. Many of the crops were unknown to the Spaniards, but they recognised maize and aloes, and various kinds of cactus. Suddenly the troops came upon what seemed to be a populous city, even larger than Cempoalla, and with loftier and more substantial buildings, of stone and lime. There were thirteen teocallis in the town, and in one place in the suburbs one of the Spaniards counted the stored-up skulls of a hundred thousand sacrificed victims. The lord of the town ruled over twenty thousand vassals ; he was a tributary to Montezuma,

and there was a strong Mexican garrison in the place. This was probably the reason of his receiving Cortés and his army very coldly, and vaunting the grandeur of the Mexican emperor, who could, he declared, muster thirty great vassals, each of whom commanded a hundred thousand men. In answer to the inquiries of Cortés, he told him about Montezuma and his capital. How more than twenty thousand prisoners of war were sacrificed every year upon the altars of his gods, and how the city stood in the midst of a great lake, and was approached by long causeways connected in places by wooden bridges, which when raised cut off all communication with the country—and many other strange things which were not of a kind to reassure the minds of the Spaniards. They hardly knew whether to believe the old cacique or not, but at any rate the wonders they heard made them, as one of their cavaliers said, 'only the more earnest to prove the adventure, desperate as it might appear.'

The natives were also very curious to know about the Spaniards, their horses and dogs, and strange weapons, and Marina in answering their questions took care to expatiate upon the exploits and victories of her adopted countrymen, and to state the extraordinary marks of respect they had received from Montezuma. This had its effect upon the cacique, who presently sent the general some slaves to make bread for the soldiers, and supplied them with the means of refreshment and rest, which they needed so much after their toilful march.

The army rested in this city four or five days, and even at the end of the last century the Indians would still point out the cypress tree under the shelter of which the conqueror's horse had been tied. When the journey was resumed, the way was through a broad green valley, watered by a splendid river and shaded by lofty trees. On either side of the river an unbroken line of Indian dwellings extended for several leagues, and on some rising ground stood a town which might contain five or six thousand inhabitants, commanded by a fortress with walls and trenches. Here the troops halted again, and met with friendly treatment.

In their last halting-place Cortés had been advised by the natives to take the route to the ancient city of Cholula, the inhabitants of which were a mild race, subjects of Montezuma, and given to peaceful arts, who were likely to receive him kindly. But his Cempoallan allies declared that the Cholulans were false and perfidious, and counselled him to go to Tlascala, a valiant little republic which had managed to maintain its independence against the arms of Mexico. The tribe had always been friendly with the Totonacs, and had the reputation of being frank, fearless, and trustworthy. The Spanish general decided to try and secure their goodwill, and accordingly despatched four of the principal Cempoallans with a gift, consisting of a cap of crimson cloth, a sword and a cross-bow, to ask permission to pass through their country, expressing at the same time his admiration of their valour, and of their long resistance of the Aztecs, whose pride he, too, was determined to humble. Three days after the departure of the envoys the army resumed its march, lingering somewhat by the way in hopes of receiving an answer from the Indian Republic. But the messengers did not return, which occasioned the general no little uneasiness. As they advanced the country became rougher and the scenery bolder, and at last their progress was arrested by a most remarkable fortification. It was a stone wall nine feet high and twenty feet thick, with a parapet a foot and a half broad at the top, for the protection of those who defended it. It had only one opening in the centre, made by two semicircular lines of wall overlapping each other for the space of forty paces, and having a passage-way between, ten paces wide, so contrived as to be perfectly commanded by the inner wall. This fortification, which extended for more than two leagues, rested at either end on the bold, natural buttresses of the chain of mountains. It was built of immense blocks of stone nicely laid together without cement, and from the remains that still exist it is easy to imagine what its size and solidity must have been. This singular structure marked the limits of Tlascala, and was intended, the natives said, as a barrier against Mexican invasions. The soldiers paused amazed, and not a little apprehensive as to their reception in Tlascala, since a people who were capable of such a work as that would indeed prove formidable should they not be friendly. But Cortés, putting himself at the head of his cavalry, shouted, 'Forward, soldiers; the Holy Cross is our banner, and under that we shall conquer.' And so they marched through the undefended passage, and found themselves in Tlascala.

The Tlascalan people belonged to the same great family as the Aztecs, and had planted themselves upon the western shore of Lake Tezcuco at about the same period—at the close of the twelfth century. There they remained many years, until they had, for some reason, incurred the displeasure of all the surrounding tribes, who combined to attack them, and a terrible battle took place. Though the Tlascalans were entirely victorious, they were so disgusted by this state of things that they resolved to migrate, and the greater number of them finally settled in the warm and fruitful valley overshadowed by the mountains of Tlascala. After some years the monarchy was divided, first into two, then four separate states, each with its own chief, who was independent in his own territory, and possessed equal authority with the other three in all matters concerning the whole republic, the affairs of which were settled by a council consisting of the four chiefs and the inferior nobles. They were an agricultural people, and the fertility of their new country was signified by its name—'Tlascala' meaning the land of bread. Presently their neighbours began to be envious of their prosperity, and they were frequently obliged to defend themselves against the Cholulans, and were always successful. But when Axayacatl, king of the Aztecs, sent demanding the same tribute and obedience from them which the other people of the country paid him, threatening, if they refused, to destroy their cities, and give their land to their enemies, they answered proudly, 'Neither they nor their forefathers had ever paid tribute or homage to a foreign power, nor ever would pay it. If their country was invaded, they knew how to defend it.'

This answer brought upon them the forces of the Mexican monarch, and a pitched battle was fought in which the republic was again victorious, but from that time hostilities never ceased between the two nations, every captive was mercilessly sacrificed, and the Tlascalan children were trained from the cradle to hate the Mexicans with a deadly hatred. In this struggle the Tlascalans received valuable support from a wild and warlike race from the north, called the Otomies. Some of them settled in the republic, and having proved themselves courageous and faithful, were entrusted with the defence of the frontier. After Montezuma became emperor of Mexico greater efforts than before were made to subdue Tlascala. He sent a great army against it, commanded by his favourite son, but his troops were defeated and his son killed. Enraged and mortified, Montezuma made still greater preparations and invaded the valley with a terrific force. But the Tlascalans withdrew to the recesses of the hills, and watching their opportunity, swept down upon the enemy and drove them from their territory with dreadful slaughter. Nevertheless they were greatly harassed by these constant struggles with a foe so superior to themselves in numbers and resources. The Aztec armies lay between them and the coast, cutting off all possibility of obtaining any supplies. There were some things, as cotton, cacas, and salt, which they were unable to grow or manufacture, of which they had been deprived for more than fifty years, and their taste was so much affected by this enforced abstinence that they did not get used to eating salt with their food for several generations after the conquest. This was the state of affairs in Tlascala when the

Spaniards reached it, and it is easy to see how important it was to Cortés to form an alliance with it, but that was not an easy thing to do.

The Tlascalans had heard about the Christians and their victorious advance, but they had not expected that they would come their way. So they were much embarrassed by the embassy demanding a passage through their territories. The council was assembled, and a great difference of opinion was found among its members. Some believed that these were the white-skinned, bearded men whose coming was foretold, and at all events they were enemies to Mexico, and might help them in their struggle against it. Others argued that this could not be : the march of the strangers through the land might be tracked by the broken images of the Indian gods, and desecrated temples. How could they be sure that they were not friends of Montezuma ? They had received his embassies, accepted his gifts, and were even now on their way to his capital in company with his vassals. This last was the opinion of an aged chief, one of the four rulers of the republic. His name was Xicotencatl, and he was nearly blind, for he was over a hundred years old. He had a son of the same name as himself, an impetuous young man, who commanded a powerful force of Tlascalans and Otomies on the eastern frontier where the great fortification stood. The old chief advised that this force should at once fall upon the Spaniards. If they were conquered they would be at the mercy of the Tlascalans, but if by any mischance his son should fail, the council could declare that they had nothing to do with the attack, laying the whole blame of it upon the young Xicotencatl. Meantime the Cempoallan envoys were to be detained under pretence of assisting at a religious sacrifice. By this time, as we know, Cortés and his gallant band had passed the rocky rampart, from which, for some reason or other, the Otomie guard was absent. After advancing a few leagues he saw a small party of Indians, armed with sword and buckler, who fled at his approach. He made signs for them to halt, but they only fled the faster.

The Spaniards spurred their horses, and soon succeeded in over-taking them, when they at once turned, and, without showing the usual alarm at the horses and strange weapons of the cavaliers, attacked them furiously. The latter, however, were far too strong for them, and they would soon have been cut to pieces had not a body of several thousand Indians appeared, coming quickly to their rescue. Cortés seeing them, hastily despatched a messenger to hurry up his infantry. The Indians, having discharged their missiles, fell upon the little band of Spaniards, striving to drag the riders from their horses and to tear their lances from their grasp. They brought one cavalier to the ground, who afterwards died of his wounds, and they killed two horses, cutting their necks through with one blow of their formidable broadswords. This was a most serious loss to Cortés, whose horses were so important, and so few in number.

The struggle was a hard one, and it was with no small satisfaction that the Spaniards saw their comrades advancing to their aid. No sooner had the main body reached the field of battle, than, hastily falling into position, they poured such a volley from their muskets and cross-bows as fairly astounded the enemy, who made no further attempt to continue the fight, but drew off in good order, leaving the road open to the Spaniards, who were only too glad to get rid of their foes and pursue their way. Presently they met two Tlascalan envoys, accompanied by two of the Cempoallans. The former, on being brought to the general, assured him of a friendly reception in the capital, and declared the late assault upon the troops to have been quite unauthorised. Cortés received his message courteously, pretending to believe that all was as he said. As it was now growing late the Spaniards quickened their pace, anxious to reach a suitable camping-ground before nightfall, and they chose a place upon the bank of a stream, where a few deserted huts were standing. These the weary and famishing soldiers ransacked in search of food, but could find nothing but some animals resembling dogs, which, however, they cooked and ate without ceremony, seasoning their unsavoury repast with the fruit of the Indian fig, which grew wild in the neighbourhood. After several desperate battles with the Tlascalans, Cortés finally won a great victory.

The next day—as he usually did after gaining a battle—the Spanish commander sent a new embassy to the Tlascalan capital, making as before professions of friendship, but this time threatening that if his offers were rejected he would visit their city as a conqueror, razing their house to the ground and putting every inhabitant to the sword. Of course this message was given to the envoys by the aid of the Lady Marina, who became day by day more necessary to Cortés, and who was, indeed, generally admired for her courage and the cheerfulness with which she endured all the hardships of the camp and raised the drooping spirits of the soldiers, while by every means in her power she alleviated the miseries of her own countrymen. This time, the ambassadors of

Cortés received a respectful hearing from the deeply dejected council of Tlascala, for whom nothing remained but to submit. Four principal caciques were chosen to offer to the Spaniards a free passage through the country, and a friendly reception in the capital. Their friendship was accepted, with many excuses for the past, and the chiefs were further ordered to touch at the camp of Xicotencatl, the Tlascalan general, and require him to cease hostilities and furnish the white men with a plentiful supply of provisions.

While the Tlascalan envoys were still in the camp came a fresh

embassy from Montezuma. Tidings had been sent to him of each step in the progress of the Spaniards, and it was with great satisfaction that he had heard of their taking the road to Tlascala, trusting that if they were mortal men they would find their graves there. Great was his dismay, therefore, when courier after courier brought him news of their successes, and how the most redoubtable warriors had been scattered by this handful of strangers. His superstitious fears returned with greater force than ever, and in his alarm and uncertainty he despatched five great nobles of his court, attended by two hundred slaves, to bear to Cortés a gift consisting of three thousand ounces of gold and several hundred robes of cotton and feather-work. As they laid it at his feet they said that they had come to offer Montezuma's congratulations upon his victories, and to express his regret that he could not receive them in his capital, where the numerous population was so unruly that he could not be answerable for their safety. The merest hint of the emperor's wishes would have been enough to influence any of the natives, but they made very little impression upon Cortés; and, seeing this, the envoys proceeded, in their master's name, to offer tribute to the Spanish sovereign, provided the general would give up the idea of visiting the capital. This was a fatal mistake, and a most strange one for such a brave and powerful monarch to make, for it amounted to an admission that he was unable to protect his treasures. Cortés in replying expressed the greatest respect for Montezuma, but urged his own sovereign's commands as a reason for disregarding his wishes. He added that though he had not at present the power of requiting his generosity as he could wish, he trusted ' to repay him at some future day with good works.' You will hear before long how he kept his word.

The Mexican ambassadors were anything but pleased at finding the war at an end and a firm friendship established between their mortal enemies and the Spaniards, and the general saw with some satisfaction the evidences of a jealousy between them, which was his surest hope of success in undermining the Mexican empire. Two of the Aztecs presently returned to acquaint Montezuma with the state of affairs; the others remained with the Spaniards, Cortés being willing that they should see the deference paid to him by the Tlascalans, who were most anxious for his presence in their city.

The city of Tlascala lay about six leagues away from the Spanish camp, and the road led through a hilly region, and across a deep ravine over which a bridge had just been built for the passage of the army; they passed some towns by the way, where they were received with the greatest hospitality. The people flocked out to meet them, bringing garlands of roses, with which they decorated the Spanish soldiers, and wreathed about the necks of their horses. Priests in their white robes mingled with the crowd, scattering clouds of incense from their censers, and thus escorted the army slowly made its way through the gates of the city of Tlascala. Here the press became so great that it was with difficulty that a passage was cleared for it. The flat housetops were crowded with eager spectators, while garlands of green boughs, roses, and honeysuckle were thrown across the streets, and the air was rent with songs and shouts and the wild music of the national instruments. Presently the procession halted before the palace of the aged

Xicotencatl, the father of the general, and Cortés dismounted from his horse, that the blind old man might satisfy his natural curiosity respecting him, by passing his hand over his face. He

s

then led the way to a spacious hall, where a banquet was served to the whole army, after which, quarters were assigned to them in a neighbouring teocalli, the Mexican ambassadors being, at the desire of Cortés, lodged next to himself that he might the better protect them in the city of their foes.

For some days the Spaniards were feasted and entertained in four quarters of the city, which was really like separate towns divided from one another by high walls, in each of which lived one of the rulers of the republic, surrounded by his own vassals. But amid all these friendly demonstrations the general never for a moment relaxed the strict discipline of the camp, and no soldier was allowed to leave his quarters without special permission. At first this offended the Tlascalan chiefs, as they thought it showed distrust of them. But when Cortés explained that this was only in accordance with the established military system of his country, they began to think it admirable, and the young Xicotencatl proposed, if possible, to imitate it. The Spanish commander now turned his thoughts to the converting of the Tlascalans; but as they refused to part with their own gods, though they were willing enough to add the God of the Christians to their number, he took the advice of the wise Father Olmedo, and abandoned the idea for the time. However, a cross was erected in one of the great squares, and there the Spaniards held their religious services unmolested, and it happened, strangely enough, that they had scarcely left the city when a thin, transparent cloud settled like a column upon the cross, wrapping it round, and continuing through the night to shed a soft light about it. This occurrence did more for the conversion of the natives than all the preaching of Father Olmedo. Several of the Indian princesses were now baptized, and given in marriage to the officers of Cortés. One, who was the daughter of Xicotencatl, became the wife of Alvarado, who was always a great favourite with the Tlascalans. From his gay manners, joyous countenance, and bright golden hair, he gained the nickname of ' Tonatiuh,' or the ' Sun,' while Cortés, who hardly ever appeared anywhere without the beautiful Marina, was called by the natives ' Malinche,' which you will remember was her Indian name. While all this was happening, came yet another embassy from Montezuma, loaded as usual with costly gifts. This time he invited the Spaniards to visit him in his capital, assuring them that they would be welcome. Further, he besought them to enter into no alliance with the base and barbarous Tlascalans, but he invited them to take the route of the friendly city of Cholula, where arrangements were being made, by his orders, for their reception. The Tlascalans were much concerned that Cortés should propose to go to Mexico, and what they told him fully confirmed all the reports he had heard of the power and ambition of Montezuma, of the strength of his capital, and the number of his soldiers. They warned him not to trust to his gifts and his fair words, and when the general said that he hoped to bring about a better understanding between the emperor and themselves, they replied that it was impossible; however smooth his words, he would hate them at heart. They also heartily protested against the general's going to Cholula. The people, they said, though not brave in the open field, were crafty; they were Montezuma's tools, and would do his bidding. That city, too, was specially under the protection of the god Quetzalcoatl, and the priests were confidently believed to have the power of opening an inundation from the foundations of his shrine, which should overwhelm their enemies in the deluge, and lastly, though many distant places had sent to testify their goodwill, and offer their allegiance, Cholula, only six leagues distant, had done neither. This consideration weighed more with the general than either of the preceding ones, and he promptly despatched a summons to the city demanding a formal tender of its submission. It was not long before deputies arrived from Cholula profuse in expressions of goodwill and invitations to visit their city; but the Tlascalans pointed out that these messengers were below the usual rank of ambassadors, which Cortés regarded as a fresh indignity. He therefore sent a new summons, declaring that if they did not at once send a deputation of their principal men he would treat them as rebels to his own sovereign, the rightful lord of these realms. This soon brought some of the highest nobles to the camp, who excused their tardy appearance, by saying that they had feared for their personal safety in the capital of their enemies. The Tlascalans were now more than ever averse to the projected visit. A strong Aztec force was known to be near Cholula, and the city was being actively prepared for defence. Cortés, too, was disturbed by these circumstances, but he had gone too far to recede without showing fear, which could not fail to have a bad effect on his own men, as well as on the natives. Therefore, after a short consultation with his officers, he decided finally to take the road to Cholula. This ancient city lay six leagues to the south of Tlascala, and was most populous and flourishing. The inhabitants excelled in the art of working in metals and manufacturing cotton cloth and delicate pottery, but were indisposed to war, and less distinguished for courage than for cunning. You will remember that it was in this place that the god Quetzalcoatl had paused on his way to the coast, and in his honour a tremendous pyramid had been erected, probably by building over a natural hill, and on the top of this rose a gorgeous temple, in which stood an image of the god bedecked with gold and jewels. To this temple pilgrims flocked from every corner of the empire, and many were the terrible sacrifices offered there, as, indeed, in all the other teocallis, of which there were about four hundred in the city. On the day appointed, the Spanish army set out for Cholula, followed by crowds of citizens, who admired the courage displayed by this little handful of men in proposing to brave the mighty Montezuma in his own territory. An immense body of warriors had offered to join the expedition, but Cortés thought it wise to accept only six thousand, and even these he left encamped at some distance from Cholula, because the caciques of that city, who came out to meet the Spaniards, objected to having their mortal enemies brought within its walls. As the troops drew near the town they were met by swarms of men, women, and children, all eager to catch a glimpse of the strangers, whose persons, horses, and weapons were equally objects of intense curiosity to them. They in their turn were struck by the noble aspect of the Cholulans, who were much superior in dress and general appearance to the other tribes they had encountered. An immense number of priests swinging censers mingled with the crowd, and, as before, they were decorated with garlands and bunches of flowers, and accompanied by gay music from various instruments. The Spaniards were also struck by the width and cleanliness of the streets and the solidity of the houses. They were lodged in the court of one of the many teocallis, and visited by the great nobles of the city, who supplied them plentifully with all they needed, and at first paid them such attentions as caused them to believe that the evil apprehensions of the Tlascalans had been merely suspicion and prejudice. But very soon the scene changed. Messengers came from Montezuma, who shortly and pleasantly told Cortés that his approach occasioned much disquietude to their master, and then conferred apart with the Mexicans who were still in the Spanish camp, presently departing, and taking one of them away with them. From this time the Cholulans visited the Spanish quarters no more, and when invited to do so excused themselves, saying they were ill. Also, the supply of provisions ran short, and they said it was because maize was scarce. Naturally, Cortés became very uneasy at this change, and his alarm was increased by the reports of the Cempoallans, who told him that in wandering about the city they had seen several streets barricaded, and in some places holes had been dug, and a sharp stake planted upright in each, and branches strewn to conceal them, while the flat roofs of the houses were being stored with stones and other missiles. Some Tlascalans also came in from their camp to inform him that a great sacrifice, mostly of children, had been held in a distant quarter of the town, to secure the aid of the gods in some intended enterprise, and numbers of the people had taken their wives and children out of the city.

These tidings confirmed the worst suspicions of Cortés, but just then the Lady Marina made a discovery which changed his doubts into certainty. The wife of one of the Cholulan caciques had taken a great fancy to the Mexican girl, and continually urged her to visit her house, hinting mysteriously that she would in this way escape a great danger which threatened the Spaniards. Marina pretended to be delighted with this proposal, and glad of the chance of escaping from the white men, and by degrees she thus won the confidence of the Cholulan, who presently revealed the whole plot to her. It originated, she said, with the Aztec emperor, who had bribed the caciques of Cholula, her husband among the number, to assault the Spaniards as they marched out of the city, and to throw them into confusion all sorts of obstacles had been placed in their way. A force of twenty thousand Mexicans was already quartered near the city to support the Cholulans, and the Spaniards would, it was confidently expected, fall an easy prey to their united enemies. A sufficient number of them were to be reserved to be sacrificed in Cholula, and the rest led in fetters to the capital of Montezuma. While this conversation was taking place, Marina was making a show of collecting and packing up such dresses and jewels as she was to take with her to the house of her new friend. But after a while she managed to slip away without exciting her suspicion, and, rushing to the general, told him all. Cortés at once caused the cacique's wife to be seized, and she repeated to him the same story that she had told to Marina. He was most anxious to gain further particulars of the conspiracy, and accordingly induced two priests, one of them a person of much influence, to visit his quarters, where by courteous treatment and rich presents he got from them a complete confirmation of the report. The emperor had been in a state of pitiable vacillation since the arrival of the Spaniards. His first orders had been that they should be kindly received, but on consulting his oracles anew he had obtained for answer that Cholula would be the grave of his enemies, and so positive of success were the Aztecs, that they had already sent into the city numbers of the poles with thongs attached to them with which to bind the prisoners. Cortés now dismissed the priests, bidding them observe the strictest secrecy, which, indeed they were likely to do for their own sakes. He also requested that they would induce some of the principal caciques to grant him an interview in his quarters. When they came he gently rebuked them for their want of hospitality, and said that the Spaniards would burden them no longer, but would leave the city early the next morning. He also asked that they would supply him with two thousand men to carry his artillery and baggage. The chiefs, after some consultation, agreed to this as being likely to favour their own plans. Then he sent for the Mexican ambassadors, and acquainted them with his discovery of the plot, saying that it grieved him much to find Montezuma mixed up in so treacherous an affair, and that the Spaniards must now march as enemies against a monarch they had hoped to visit as a friend. The ambassadors, however, asserted their entire ignorance of the conspiracy, and their belief that Montezuma also knew nothing of it. The night that followed was one of intense anxiety; every soldier lay down fully armed, and the number of sentinels was doubled; but all remained quiet in the populous city, and the only sounds which reached their ears were the hoarse cries of the priests who, from the turrets of the teocallis, proclaimed through their trumpets the watches of the night.

With the first streak of morning light Cortés was on horseback, directing the movements of his little band, part of which he posted in the great square court. A strong guard was placed at each of the three gates, and the rest had charge of the great guns which were outside the enclosure, and so placed as to command the roads which led to the teocalli. The arrangements were hardly completed before the Cholulan caciques appeared, bringing a larger body of porters than had been demanded. They were marched at once into the square, which was, as we have seen, completely lined by the Spanish troops. Cortés then took the caciques aside, and sternly and abruptly charged them with the conspiracy, taking care to show that he knew every detail. The Cholulans were thunderstruck, and gazed with awe upon the strangers who seemed to have the power of reading their most secret thoughts. They made no attempt to deny the accusation, but tried to excuse themselves by throwing the blame on Montezuma. Cortés, however, declared with still more indignation that such a pretence would not serve them, and that he would now make such an example of them as should be a warning to the cities far and near, and then the fatal signal—the firing of a gun—was given, and in an instant every musket and crossbow was levelled at the unhappy Cholulans as they stood crowded together in the centre. They were completely taken by surprise, having heard nothing of what was going forward, and offered hardly any resistance to the Spanish soldiers, who followed up the discharge of their pieces by rushing upon them with their swords and mowing them down in ranks as they stood.

While this dreadful massacre was going on the Cholulans from outside, attracted by the noise, began a furious assault upon the Spaniards, but the heavy guns opened fire upon them and swept them off in files as they rushed on, and in the intervals of reloading the cavalry charged into their midst. By this time the Tlascalans had come up, having by order of Cortés bound wreaths of sedge about their heads that they might be the more easily distinguished from the Cholulans, and they fell upon the rear of the wretched townsmen, who, thus harassed on all sides, could no longer maintain their ground. They fled, some to the near buildings, which were speedily set on fire, others to the temples. One strong body headed by the priests got possession of the great teocalli. There was, as you remember, a tradition that if part of the wall was removed the god would send a flood to overwhelm his enemies. Now the Cholulans strove with might and main, and at last succeeded in wrenching away a few stones, but dust, not water, followed. In despair they crowded into the wooden turrets which surmounted the temple, and poured down stones, javelins, and burning arrows upon the Spaniards as they came swarming up the steps. But the fiery shower fell harmlessly upon the steel head-pieces of the soldiers, and they used the blazing shafts to set fire to the wooden towers, so that the wretched natives either perished in the flames or threw themselves headlong from the parapet. In the fair city, lately so peaceful and prosperous, all was confusion and slaughter, burning and plundering. The division of spoil was greatly simplified by the fact that the Tlascalans desired wearing-apparel and provisions far more than gold or jewels; they also took hundreds of

prisoners, but these Cortés afterwards induced them to release.
The work of destruction had gone on for some hours before the
general yielded to the entreaties of the Cholulan chiefs who had
been saved from the massacre, and of the Mexican envoys, and
called off his men, putting a stop as well as he could to further violence.   Two of the caciques were also permitted to go to their
countrymen with offers of pardon and protection to all who would
return to their obedience, and so by degrees the tumult was appeased.   Presently Cortés helped the Cholulans to choose a successor
to their principal cacique, who was among the slain, and confidence
being thus restored the people from the country round began to
flock in, the markets were again opened, and the ordinary life of
the city resumed, though the black and smouldering ruins remained
to tell the sad tale of the massacre of Cholula.   This terrible vengeance made a great impression upon the natives, and none trembled more than the Mexican monarch upon his throne among the
mountains.   He felt his empire melting away from him like a
morning mist, for some of the most important cities, overawed by
the fate of Cholula, now sent envoys to the Spanish camp tendering
their allegiance, and trying to secure the favour of the conqueror
by rich gifts of gold and slaves.   Again did Montezuma seek counsel from his gods, but the answers he obtained were far from reassuring, and he determined to send another embassy to Cortés to
declare that he had nothing to do with the conspiracy at Cholula.
As usual the envoys were charged with a splendid present of golden
vessels and ornaments, and among other things were artificial birds,
made in imitation of turkeys with plumage of worked gold; there
were also fifteen hundred robes of delicate cotton cloth.   The emperor's message expressed regret for the late catastrophe, and denied
all knowledge of the plot which had, he said, brought a retribution
upon its authors which they richly deserved; and he explained the
presence of the Aztec force in the neighbourhood by saying that
there was a disturbance that had to be quelled.   More than a fortnight had passed since the Spaniards entered Cholula, and the
general had, after the city was once more restored to order, tried to
induce the people to give up their false gods, but this they would
not do willingly.   However, he seized upon the great teocalli of
which all the woodwork had been burned, and built a church of the
stone that remained, and he opened the cages in which the wretched
victims about to be sacrificed were imprisoned, and restored them
to liberty, and then he thought it time to begin the march to Mexico

once more. So the allied army of Spaniards and Tlascalans set out upon their journey through luxuriant plains and flourishing plantations, met occasionally by embassies from different towns, anxious to claim the protection of the white men, and bringing rich gifts of gold to propitiate them. They passed between the two enormous mountain peaks, Popocatapetl, 'the hill that smokes,' and Iztaccihuatl, 'the white woman,' and presently encountered a blinding snow-storm, from which they found shelter in one of the large stone buildings, put up by the Mexicans for the use of travellers and couriers, and here they encamped for the night. The next morning they reached the top of a range of hills where

progress was comparatively easy, and they had not gone far when, turning sharply round the shoulder of a hill, they saw spread out before them the lovely Mexican valley. The clearness of the air enabled them to see distinctly the shining cities, the lakes, woods, fields and gardens, and in the midst of all the fair city of Mexico rose as it were from the waters of the great lake, with its towers and temples white and gleaming, and behind it the royal hill of Chapoltepec, the residence of the Mexican kings, crowned with the very same gigantic cypress trees which to this day fling their broad shadows across the land. The Spaniards gazed in rapture over the gay scene, exclaiming, 'It is the promised land!' but presently the evidences of a power and civilisation so far superior to anything they had yet encountered disheartened the more timid among them, they shrank from the unequal contest, and begged to be led back again to Vera Cruz. But this was not the effect produced upon Cortés by the glorious prospect. His desire for treasure and love of adventure were sharpened by the sight of the dazzling spoil at his very feet, and with threats, arguments, and entreaties he revived the drooping spirits of his soldiers, and by the aid of his brave captains succeeded in once more rousing them to enthusiasm, and the march down the slope of the hill was gaily resumed.

With every step of their progress the woods became thinner, and villages were seen in green and sheltered nooks, the inhabitants of which came out to meet and welcome the Spaniards. Everywhere Cortés heard with satisfaction complaints of the cruelty and injustice of Montezuma, and he encouraged the natives to rely on his protection, as he had come to redress their wrongs. The army advanced but slowly, and was soon met by another embassy from the emperor, consisting of several Aztec lords bringing a rich gift of gold, and robes of delicate furs and feathers, and offering four loads of gold to the general, and one to each of his captains, with a yearly tribute to the Spanish sovereign, if they would even then turn back from Mexico. But Cortés replied that he could not answer it to his sovereign if he were to return without visiting the emperor in his capital. The Spaniards came in the spirit of peace as Montezuma would see for himself; but should their presence prove burdensome to him, it would be very easy for them to relieve him of it.

This embassy had been intended to reach the Spaniards before they crossed the mountains, and the dismay of the Atzec emperor was great when he learned that it had failed, and that the dreaded strangers were actually on their march across the valley. They were so utterly unlike anything he had ever known before, these strange beings, who seemed to have dropped from another planet, and by their superior knowledge and more deadly weapons overcome the hitherto unconquerable nations, though a mere handful of men in comparison to the swarms of his own countrymen. He felt himself to be the victim of a destiny from which nothing could save him. All peace, power, and security seemed to be gone from him, and in despair he shut himself up in his palace, refusing food, and trying by prayers and sacrifices to wring some favour from his gods. But the oracles were dumb. Then he called a council of his chief nobles, but a great difference of opinion arose amongst them. Cacama, the emperor's nephew, king of Tezcuco, counselled him to receive the Spaniards courteously as ambassadors of a foreign prince, while Cuitlahua, his brother, urged him to muster his forces and then and there drive back the invaders, or die in the defence of his capital. But Montezuma could not rouse himself for this struggle. He exclaimed in deep dejection, ' Of what avail is resistance when the gods have declared themselves against us ? Yet I mourn for the old and infirm, the women and children, too feeble to fight or fly. For myself and the brave men around me, we must face the storm as best we may ! '' and he straightway sent off a last embassy, with his nephew at its head, to meet the Spaniards and welcome them to Mexico. By this time the army had reached the first of the towns built on piles driven into the lake, and were delighted with its fine stone houses, with canals between them instead of streets, up and down which boats passed continually, laden with all kinds of merchandise. Though received with great hospitality, Cortés still was strictly on his guard, and neglected no precaution for the security of his men. Before he left this place a messenger came, requesting him to wait for the arrival of the king of Tezcuco, who very soon afterwards appeared, borne in a palanquin richly decorated with plates of gold and precious stones, having pillars curiously wrought which supported a canopy of green plumes. He was accompanied by a numerous retinue of nobles and inferior attendants, and when he came into the presence of Cortés he descended from his palanquin and advanced towards him, his officers sweeping the ground before him as he did so.

The prince was a handsome young man, erect and dignified ; he made the usual Mexican salutation to people of high rank, touching the earth with his right hand and raising it to his head, and said that he came as the representative of Montezuma to bid the Spaniards welcome to Mexico, and presented the general with three pearls of uncommon size and lustre. Cortés embraced him, and in return threw over his neck a chain of cut glass. After this exchange of courtesies, and the most friendly and respectful assurances on the part of Cortés, the Indian prince withdrew, leaving the Spaniards much impressed by his superiority in state and bearing to anything they had before seen in the country.

Resuming their march along the southern shore of Lake Chalco, through splendid woods, and orchards glowing with unknown fruits, the army came at length to a great dyke or causeway four or five miles long, which divided the Lake. Chalco from Xochicalco on the west.   It was a lance in breadth at the narrowest part, and in some places wide enough for eight horsemen to ride abreast, and was solidly built of stone and lime.   As they passed along it they saw multitudes of Indians darting up and down the lake in their light pirogues, eager to catch a glimpse of the strangers, and they were amazed at the sight of the floating islands, covered with flowers and vegetables and moving like rafts over the waters.   All round the margin, and occasionally far out in the lake, they saw little towns and villages half buried in foliage; and the whole scene seemed to them so new and wonderful that they could only compare it to the magical pictures of the old romances.   Midway across the lake the army halted at the town of Cuitlahuae, which was not large, but was remarkable for the beauty of its buildings.   The curiosity of the Indians increased as the Spaniards proceeded, and they clam-bered up the causeway and lined the sides of the road, so that the troops were quite embarrassed by them, and Cortés was obliged to resort to commands, and even menaces, to clear a passage.   He found, as he neared the capital, a considerable change in the feeling shown towards the government, and heard only of the pomp and magnificence of Montezuma, and nothing of his oppressions.   From the causeway the army descended on a narrow point of land which lay between the two lakes, and crossing it reached the royal residence of Iztapalapan.

This place was governed by the emperor's brother, who, to do greater honour to Cortés, had invited the neighbouring lords to be present at his reception, and at the banquet which followed. The Spaniards were struck with admiration, when, after the usual ceremonies had been gone through, and a gift of gold and costly stuffs had been presented, they were led into one of the gorgeous halls of the palace, the roof of which was of odorous cedar-wood, and the stone walls tapestried with brilliant hangings.   But, indeed, this was only one of the many beautiful things which they saw in this fairy city.   There were gardens cunningly planted, and watered in every part by means of canals and aqueducts, in which grew gor-geous flowers and luscious fruits.   There was an aviary filled with all kinds of birds, remarkable for the brilliancy of their plumage and the sweetness of their songs.   But the most elaborate piece of work was a huge reservoir of stone full of water and stocked with all kinds of fish, and by this all the fountains and aqueducts were supplied.   In this city of enchantment the army rested for the night, within sight of the capital into which Cortés intended to lead them on the morrow.

THE OCCUPATION OF MEXICO.

With the first faint streak of dawn, on the morning of November 8, 1519, the Spanish general was astir and mustering his followers, and as the sun rose above the eastern mountains he set forth with his little troop of horsemen as a sort of advanced guard, the Spanish infantry followed, then the baggage, and finally the dark files of the Tlascalan warriors. The whole number cannot have amounted to seven thousand, of which less than four hundred were Spaniards. For a short distance the army kept along the narrow tongue of land between the lakes, and then entered upon the great dyke which crosses the salt waters of Lake Tezcuco to the very gates of the capital. It was wide enough all the way for ten horsemen to ride abreast, and from it the Spaniards could see many towns and villages—some upon the shores of the lake, some built upon piles running far out into its waters. These cities were evidently crowded with a thriving population, and contained many temples and other important buildings which were covered with a hard white stucco glistening like enamel in the sunshine. The lake was darkened with a swarm of canoes filled with Indians who were eager to gaze upon the strangers, and here and there floated those fairy islands of flowers which rose and fell with every undulation of thé water, and yet were substantial enough to support trees of a considerable size. At the distance of half a league from the capital they encountered a solid fortification, like a curtain of stone, which was built across the dyke. It was twelve feet high, and had a tower at each end, and in the centre a battlemented gateway through which the troops passed. This place was called the Fort of Xoloc, and was afterwards occupied by Cortés in the famous siege of Mexico. Here they were met by several hundred Aztec chiefs in their gay and fanciful costume. Some of them wore broad mantles of delicate feather embroidery, and collars and bracelets of turquoise mosaic with which fine plumage was curiously mingled, while their ears, underlips, and sometimes even their noses, were adorned with pendants of precious stones, or crescents of fine gold. After the usual formal salutations, which caused some delay, the march was resumed, and the army presently reached a wooden drawbridge which crossed an opening in the dyke, meant to serve as an outlet for the water, should it for any reason rise beyond its usual height. As they left this bridge behind them the Spaniards felt that they were indeed committing themselves to the mercy of Montezuma, who might, by means of it, cut them off from communication with the country, and hold them prisoners in his capital. They now beheld the glittering retinue of the emperor emerging from the great street which led through the heart of the city. Amidst a crowd of Indian nobles, preceded by three officers of state bearing golden wands, they saw the royal palanquin, blazing with burnished gold. It was borne on the shoulders of nobles, and over it a canopy of gorgeous feather-work, powdered with jewels and fringed with silver, was supported by four attendants, also of high rank, who were barefooted and walked with a slow, measured pace, with their eyes bent upon the ground. As soon as the procession had come within a short distance of the Spaniards the emperor descended from his palanquin, and advanced under the canopy, leaning upon the arms of his nephew and his brother. The ground before him was strewn with cotton tapestry by his attendants, and the natives who lined the sides of the causeway bent forward with their eyes fixed upon the ground as he passed, whilst some of the humbler class prostrated themselves before him. Montezuma wore the usual broad girdle and square cloak of the finest cotton, on his feet were sandals with soles of gold, and leathern thongs ornamented with the same metal. Both cloak and sandals were sprinkled with pearls and precious stones, principally emeralds, and the green 'chalchivitl,' which was more highly esteemed by the Aztecs than any jewel. On his head he wore only a plume of royal green feathers, a badge of his military rank. He was at this time about forty years of age, and was tall and thin, and of a lighter complexion than is usual among his countrymen; he moved with dignity, and there was a benignity in his whole demeanour which was not to have been anticipated from the reports of his character which had reached the Spaniards. The army halted as Montezuma drew near, and Cortés dismounted and advanced to meet him with a few of the principal cavaliers. The emperor received him with princely courtesy, and expressed his satisfaction at seeing him in his capital. Cortés responded by the most profound expressions of respect and gratitude for all Montezuma's munificence to the Spaniards; he then hung round the emperor's neck a chain of coloured crystal, making at the same time a movement as if to embrace him, but was restrained by the two Aztec lords, who were shocked at the idea of such presumption. Montezuma then appointed his brother

MONTEZUMA GREETS THE SPANIARDS

to conduct the Spaniards to their quarters in the city, and again entering his litter was borne off amid prostrate crowds in the same state in which he had come. The Spaniards quickly followed, and with colours flying and music playing entered the southern portion of the city of Mexico. The great wide street facing the causeway stretched for some miles in nearly a straight line through the centre of the city. In the clear atmosphere of the tableland it was easy to see the blue mountains in the distance beyond the temples, houses, and gardens which stood on either side of it. But what most impressed the Spaniards was the swarm of people who thronged every street, canal, and roof, and filled every window and doorway. To the Aztecs it must indeed have been a strange sensation when they beheld the fair-faced strangers, and for the first time heard their well-paved streets ringing under the iron tramp of the horses —those unknown animals which they regarded with superstitious terror. But their wonder changed to anger when they saw their detested enemies, the Tlascalans, stalking through their city with looks of ferocity and defiance.

As they passed along the troops frequently crossed bridges which spanned some of the numerous canals, and at length they halted in a wide open space, near the centre of the city, close to the huge temple of the war-god. Facing the western gate of the temple enclosure stood a range of low stone buildings, spreading over a large extent of ground, once a palace belonging to the emperor's father. This was to be the lodging of the Spaniards. Montezuma himself was waiting in the courtyard to receive them. Approaching Cortés he took from one of his slaves a massive collar, made of the shells of a kind of crawfish much prized by the Indians, set in gold, and connected by heavy golden links; from this hung eight finely-worked ornaments, each a span long, made to resemble the craw-fish, but of fine gold. This gorgeous collar he hung round the neck of the general, saying : ' This palace belongs to you, Malinche ' (this was the name by which he always addressed him), ' and your brethren. Rest after your fatigues, for you have much need to do so ; in a little while I will visit you again.' So saying, he withdrew with his attendants. The general's first care was to inspect his new quarters. The rooms were of great size, and afforded accommodation for the whole army—the Tlascalans probably encamping in the outer courts. The best apartments were hung with draperies of gaily coloured cotton, and the floors were covered with mats or rushes. There were also low stools carved from single pieces of

T

wood, and most of the rooms had beds made of the palm-leaf, woven into a thick mat, with coverlets, and sometimes canopies of cotton. The general, after a rapid survey, assigned his troops their respective quarters, and took as vigilant precautions for security as if he expected a siege; he planted his cannon so as to command the approaches to the palace, stationed sentinels along the walls, and ordered that no soldier should leave his quarters under pain of death. After all these precautions he allowed his men to enjoy the banquet prepared for them. This over, the emperor came again, attended by a few nobles; he was received with great deference by Cortés, and with Marina's aid they conversed, while the Aztecs and the cavaliers stood around in respectful silence. Montezuma made many inquiries concerning the country of the Spaniards, its sovereign, and its government, and especially asked their reasons for visiting Mexico. Cortés replied that they had desired to see its great monarch, and to declare to him the true faith professed by the Christians. The emperor showed himself to be fully acquainted with all the doings of the Spaniards since their landing, and was curious as to their rank in their own country; he also learned the names of the principal cavaliers, and their position in the army. At the conclusion of the interview the Aztecs brought forward a gift of cotton robes, enough to supply every man, even including the Tlascalans, and gold chains and ornaments, which were distributed in profusion among the Spaniards. That evening Cortés ordered a general discharge of artillery, and the noise of the guns and the volumes of smoke filled the superstitious Aztecs with dismay, reminding them of the explosions of the great volcano.

On the following morning he asked permission to return the emperor's visit, and Montezuma sent officers to conduct the Spaniards to his presence.

On reaching the hall of audience the Mexican officers took off their sandals, and covered their gay attire with mantles of 'nequen;' a coarse stuff made from the fibres of the aloe, and worn only by the poorest classes; for it was thus humbly that all, excepting the members of his own family, approached the sovereign. Then with downcast eyes and formal obeisance they ushered the Spaniards into the royal presence. They found Montezuma surrounded by a few of his favourite chiefs, and were kindly received by him; and Cortés soon began upon the subject uppermost in his thoughts, setting forth as clearly as he could the mysteries of his faith, and assuring Montezuma his idols would sink him in perdition. But the emperor only listened calmly, and showed no sign of being con-vinced. He had no doubt, he said, that the god of the Spaniards was good, but his own gods were good also ; what Cortés told him of the creation of the world was like what he had been taught to believe. It was not worth while to discuss the matter farther. He added that his ancestors were not the original possessors of his land, but had been led there by the great Being, who, after giving them laws, and ruling over them for a time, had withdrawn to the region where the sun rises, declaring on his departure that he or his descendants would some day come again and reign. The wonderful deeds of the Spaniards, their fair faces, and the quarter whence they came all showed that they were his descendants. If Montezuma had resisted their visit to his capital, it was because he had heard that they were cruel, that they sent the lightning to consume his people, or crushed them to pieces under the hard feet of the ferocious animals on which they rode. He was now con-vinced that these were idle tales, that the Spaniards were kind and generous,—mortals indeed, but of a different race from the Aztecs, wiser, and more valiant. You, too, he added with a smile, have per-haps been told that I am a god and dwell in palaces of gold and silver. But you see it is false : my houses, though large, are of wood and stone ; and as to my body, he said, baring his tawny arm, you see it is flesh and bone like yours. It is true that I have a great empire inherited from my ancestors, lands, and gold and silver, but your sovereign beyond the waters is, I know, the rightful lord of all. I rule in his name. You, Malinche, are his ambassador ; you and your brethren shall share these things with me. Rest now from your labours. You are here in your own dwellings, and everything shall be provided for your subsistence. I will see that your wishes shall be obeyed in the same way as my own. Cortés, while he encouraged the idea that his own sovereign was the great Being, as Montezuma believed, assured him that his master had no desire to interfere with his authority otherwise than, out of concern for his welfare, to effect his conversion, and that of his people, to Christianity. Before the emperor dismissed his visitors, rich stuffs and orna-ments of gold were distributed among them, so that the poorest soldier received at least two heavy collars of gold, and on their homeward way they could talk of nothing but the generosity and courtesy of the Indian monarch. But the general was harassed by many anxious thoughts. He had not been prepared to find so much luxury, civilisation, and power. He was in the heart of a great capital which seemed like an extensive fortification, with its dykes and drawbridges, where every house might be converted into a castle. At a nod from the sovereign all communication with the rest of the country might be cut off, and the whole warlike population be at once hurled upon himself and his handful of followers, and against such odds of what avail would be his superior science? As to the conquest of the empire, now he had seen the capital, it must have seemed to him a more doubtful enterprise than ever; but at any rate his best policy was to foster the superstitious reverence in which he was held by both prince and people, and to find out all he could about the city and its inhabitants. To this end he asked the emperor's permission to visit the principal public buildings, which was readily granted, Montezuma even arranging to meet him at the great temple. Cortés put himself at the head of his cavalry, and, followed by nearly all the Spanish foot, set out under the guidance of several caciques sent by Montezuma. They led him to the great teocalli near their own quarters. It stood in the midst of a vast space which was surrounded by a wall of stone and lime about eight feet high, ornamented on the outer side by raised figures of serpents, which gave it the name of the 'Coatepantli,' or 'wall of serpents.' This wall was pierced by huge battlemented gateways, opening upon the four principal streets of the city, and over each gate was a kind of arsenal filled with arms and warlike gear. The teocalli itself was of the usual pyramidal shape, and five stories high, coated on the outside with hewn stones. The ascent was by flights of steps on the outside, and Cortés found two priests and several caciques waiting to carry him up them as they had just carried the emperor; but the general declined this compliment, preferring to march up at the head of his men. On reaching the great paved space at the summit, the first thing they saw was the stone on which the unhappy victims were stretched for sacrifice; at the other end of the platform stood two towers, each three stories high, the lower story being of stone, the two upper of carved wood. In these stood the images of the gods, and before each stood an altar upon which blazed the undying fires, the putting out of which was supposed to portend so much woe to the nation. Here also was the huge drum, made of serpents' skins, struck only on extraordinary occasions, when it sent forth a melancholy sound that could be heard for miles—a sound of woe to the Spaniards in after times. Montezuma, attended by a high priest, came forward to receive Cortés. After conferring with the priests the emperor conducted the

CORTES IN THE TEMPLE OF HUITZILOPOCHTLI

Spaniards into the building, which was adorned with sculptured figures; at one end was a recess, with a roof of timber richly carved and gilt, and here stood a colossal image of Huitzilopochtli, the war-god. His countenance was hideous ; in his right hand he held a bow, and in his left a bunch of golden arrows, which a mystic legend connected with the victories of his people. A huge serpent of pearls and precious stones was coiled about his waist, and costly jewels were profusely sprinkled over his person. On his left foot were the delicate feathers of the humming-bird, from which, singularly enough, he took his name, while round his neck hung a chain of gold and silver hearts, as an emblem of the sacrifice in which he most delighted. Indeed, even at that moment three bleeding human hearts lay upon the altar before him. The next sanctuary was dedicated to Tezcatlipoca, who, they believed, had created the earth and watched over it. He was represented as a young man, and his image of polished black stone was garnished with gold plates and ornaments, among which was a shield burnished like a mirror, in which he was supposed to see reflected all the doings of the world ; and before this shrine also lay five hearts in a golden platter. From the horrors of this place the Spaniards gladly escaped into the open air, and Cortés said, turning to Montezuma, 'I do not understand how a great and wise prince like you can put faith in such evil spirits as these idols. If you will but permit us to erect here the true cross, and place the images of the Blessed Virgin and her Son in your sanctuaries, you will soon see how your false gods will shrink before them.' Montezuma was greatly shocked at this speech. 'These,' said he, ' are the gods who have led the Aztecs on to victory since they were a nation, and who send us the seed time and harvest. Had I thought you would have offered them this outrage I would not have admitted you into their presence.' Cortés then took his leave, expressing concern for having wounded the feelings of the emperor, who remained to expiate, if possible, the crime of having exposed the shrines of his gods to such profanation by the strangers. On descending into the court the Spaniards took a leisurely survey of the other buildings in the enclosure ; there were several other teocallis, but much smaller ones, in which the Spaniards saw implements of sacrifice and many other horrors. And there was also a great mound with a timber framework upon its summit, upon which were strung hundreds of thousands of skulls—those of the victims who had been sacrificed. Schools, granaries, gardens, and fountains filled up the remainder of the enclosed space, which seemed a complete city in itself, containing a mixture of barbarism and civilisation altogether characteristic of the Aztec nation. The next day the Spaniards asked permission to convert one of the halls in their palace into a chapel where they might hold the services of their church. The request was granted, and while the work was in progress some of them discovered what seemed to be a door recently plastered over. As there was a rumour that Montezuma kept the treasures of his father in this palace, they did not scruple to gratify their curiosity by removing the plaster and forcing open the door which it concealed, when they beheld a great hall filled with rich and beautiful stuffs, articles of curious workmanship of various kinds, gold and silver in bars or just as it had been dug from the earth, and many jewels of great value. ' I was a young man,' says one of the Spaniards who was allowed a sight of the treasure, ' and it seemed to me that all the riches of the world were in that room.'

By Cortés' order the wall was built up again, and strict injunctions were given that the discovery should be kept a profound secret. The Spaniards had now been a week in Mexico, and the general's anxieties increased daily. Cortés resolved upon a bold stroke. Calling a council of his officers, he laid his difficulties before them, and, ignoring the opinion of some who advised an immediate retreat, he proposed to march to the royal palace and by persuasion or force to induce Montezuma to take up his abode in the Spanish quarters. Once having obtained possession of his person, it would be easy to rule in his name by allowing him a show of sovereignty, until they had taken measures to secure their own safety and the success of their enterprise. A pretext for the seizure of the emperor was afforded by a circumstance which had come to the ears of Cortés while he was still in Cholula. Don Juan de Escalante, who had been left in charge of the Spanish settlement at Vera Cruz, had received a message from an Aztec chief called Quanhpopoca declaring his desire to come in person and tender his allegiance to the Spaniards, and requesting that four soldiers might be sent to protect him through the country of an unfriendly tribe. This was not an uncommon request, and the soldiers were sent, but on their arrival two of them were treacherously murdered by the Aztec; the others escaped, and made their way back to the garrison. The commander at once marched with fifty of his men and some thousands of

Indians to take vengeance upon the cacique, and though his allies fled before the Mexicans, the few Spaniards stood firm, and by the aid of their firearms made good the field against the enemy. Unfortunately, seven or eight of them were killed, including Escalante himself, and the Indians who were taken prisoners declared that the whole proceeding had been by Montezuma's orders. One of the Spaniards fell into the hands of the enemy, but soon died from his wounds. He happened to be a very big man of ferocious appearance, and when his head was sent to Montezuma, the Aztec emperor gazed upon it with a shudder, and commanded that it should be taken out of the city, and not offered at the shrine of any of his gods. He seemed to see in those terrible features a prophecy of his sure destruction. The bolder spirits among the cavaliers approved of the general's plan, and the next day, having asked an audience of Montezuma, Cortés made the necessary arrangements for his enterprise. The principal part of his force was drawn up in the courtyard; one detachment was stationed in the avenue leading to the palace, to prevent any attempt at rescue by the citizens. Twenty-five or thirty soldiers were ordered to drop in at the palace by twos and threes, as if accidentally, and he took with him five cavaliers on whose coolness and courage he could rely.

That they should all be in full armour excited no suspicion; it was too common an occurrence. The Spaniards were graciously received by the emperor, who by the aid of interpreters held a gay conversation with them, and as usual presented them with gold and jewels. He paid Cortés the compliment of offering him one of his daughters in marriage—an honour which was respectfully declined, on the ground that he already had one wife. But as soon as the general saw that his soldiers had all come upon the scene he abruptly changed his tone, and accused the emperor of being the author of the treacherous proceedings on the coast. Montezuma listened in surprise, and declared that such an act could only have been imputed to him by his enemies. Cortés pretended to believe him, but said that Quanhpopoca and his accomplices must be sent for that they might be dealt with after their deserts. Montezuma agreed, and, taking his royal signet from his wrist, gave it to one of his nobles, with orders to show it to the Aztec governor and require his immediate presence in the capital, and in case of his resistance to call in the aid of the neighbouring towns. When the messenger had gone, Cortés assured the emperor that he was now convinced of his innocence in the matter, but that it was necessary that his own sovereign should be equally convinced of it. Nothing would promote this so much as for Montezuma to transfer his residence to the palace occupied by the Spaniards, as this would show a condescension and personal regard for them which would absolve him from all suspicion. The emperor listened to this proposal with profound amazement, exclaiming with resentment and offended dignity :

' When was it ever heard that a great prince like myself willingly left his own palace to become a prisoner in the hands of strangers ? '

Cortés declared that he would not go as a prisoner, but would be simply changing his residence. ' If I should consent to such degradation,' he cried, ' my subjects never would.'

When further pressed, he offered one of his sons and two of his daughters as hostages, so that he might be spared this disgrace. Two hours passed in this fruitless discussion, till Velasquez de Leon, impatient of the long delay, and seeing that to fail in the attempt must ruin them, cried out, ' Why do we waste words on this barbarian ? Let us seize him, and if he resists plunge our swords into his body ! ' The fierce tone and menacing gesture alarmed the emperor, who asked Marina what the angry Spaniard said. She explained as gently as she could, beseeching him to accompany the white men, who would treat him with all respect and kindness, while if he refused he would but expose himself to violence, perhaps to death.

This last appeal shook the resolution of Montezuma ; looking round for support and sympathy, he saw only the stern faces and mail-clad forms of the Spaniards, and felt that his hour had indeed come. In a scarcely audible voice he consented to accompany them, and orders were given for the royal litter to be brought. The nobles who bore and attended it could hardly credit their senses, but now Montezuma had consented to go pride made him wish to appear to go willingly. As the royal retinue marched dejectedly down the avenue, escorted by the Spaniards, the people ran together in crowds, declaring that the emperor had been carried off by force, and a tumult would have arisen had not he himself called out to them to disperse, since he was of his own accord visiting his friends, and on reaching the Spanish quarters he sent out his nobles to the mob with similar assurances, bidding them all return to their homes.

He was received with ostentatious respect by the Spaniards, and chose the apartments which pleased him best, which were speedily furnished with tapestry, featherwork, and all other Indian luxuries.

He was attended by his own household, and his meals were served with the usual pomp and ceremony, while not even the general himself approached him without due obeisance, or sat down in his presence uninvited. Nevertheless it was but too clear to his people that he was a prisoner, for day and night the palace was guarded by sixty sentinels in front and sixty in the rear, while another body was stationed in the royal antechamber. This was the state of affairs when Quanhpopoca arrived from the coast. Montezuma received him coldly, and referred the matter to Cortés, who speedily made an end of it by condemning the unhappy chief and his followers to be burnt to death. The funeral piles were erected in the courtyard before the palace, and were made of arrows, javelins, and other weapons drawn by the emperor's permission from those stored round the great teocalli. To crown these extraordinary proceedings, Cortés, just before the executions took place, entered the emperor's apartments, followed by a soldier bearing fetters in his hands. Sternly he again accused Montezuma of having been the original contriver of the treacherous deed, and said that a crime which merited death in a subject must in some way be atoned for even by a king, whereupon he ordered the soldier to fasten the fetters upon Montezuma's ankles, and after coolly waiting until it was done turned his back and quitted the room.

The emperor was speechless under this last insult, like one struck down by a heavy blow. But though he offered no resistance low moans broke from him, which showed the anguish of his spirit. His faithful attendants did their utmost to console him, holding his feet in their arms, and trying to keep the irons from touching him by inserting their own robes; but it was not the bodily discomfort that so afflicted him, but the feeling that he was no more a king, and so utterly broken in spirit was he that when Cortés came after the execution had taken place, and with his own hands unclasped the irons, Montezuma actually thanked him as if for some great and unmerited favour. Not long after the Spanish general expressed his willingness that the emperor should if he wished return to his own palace, but Montezuma declined the offer, doubtless fearing to trust himself again to the haughty and ferocious chieftains, who could not but despise the cowardly proceedings of their master, so unlike the usual conduct of an Aztec monarch. Montezuma often amused himself with seeing the Spanish troops go through their exercises, or with playing at some of the national games with Cortés and his officers. A favourite one was called 'totoloque,' played with golden balls, which were thrown at a golden target, and the emperor always staked precious stones or ingots of gold, and won or lost with equal good-humour, and indeed it did not much matter to him, since if he did win he gave away his gains to his attendants.   But while Montezuma thus resigned himself without a struggle to a life of captivity, some of his kinsmen were

feeling very differently about the matter, and especially his nephew Cacama, lord of the Tezcuco, and second in power to Montezuma himself.

This prince saw with alarm and indignation his uncle's abject submission to the Spaniards, and endeavoured to form a league with the other chiefs to rescue him out of their hands.   But they, from jealousy, declined to join him, declaring themselves unwilling to do anything without the emperor's sanction. These plots came to the ears of Cortés, who wished at once to march upon Tezcuco and stamp out this spark of rebellion, but Montezuma dissuaded him. He therefore sent a friendly message of expostulation, which met with a haughty response, and to a second message asserting the supremacy of the King of Spain Cacama replied that ' he acknowledged no such authority. He knew nothing of the Spanish sovereign or his people, nor did he wish to know anything of them.' When Montezuma sent to him to come to Mexico that this difference might be adjusted, he answered that he understood the position of his uncle, and that when he did visit the capital it would be to rescue it, as well as the emperor himself and their common gods, from bondage, to drive out the detested strangers who had brought such dishonour on their country. This reply made Cortés very angry ; but Montezuma, anxious to prevent bloodshed, begged him still to refrain from declaring war against Cacama, saying that it would be better to obtain possession of him personally, which he could easily do by means of several Tezcucan nobles who were in his own pay. So Cacama was enticed by these faithless chiefs into a villa overhanging the lake, where he was easily overpowered and forced into a boat, which speedily brought him to Mexico. Cortés promptly fettered and imprisoned him, while Montezuma declared that he had by his rebellion forfeited his kingdom and appointed his brother—a mere boy—to reign in his stead. Now Cortés felt himself powerful enough to demand that Montezuma and all his nobles should formally swear allegiance to the Spanish sovereigns, and accordingly the emperor assembled his principal caciques and briefly stated to them the object for which he had summoned them.

' You all know,' said he, ' our ancient tradition—how the great Being, who once ruled over the land, declared that he would one day return and reign again. That time has now arrived. The white men have come from the land beyond the ocean, where the sun rises, sent by their master to reclaim the obedience of his ancient subjects. I am ready, for my part, to acknowledge his authority. You have been faithful vassals of mine all the years that I have sat upon the throne of my fathers ; I now expect that you will show me a last act of obedience, by acknowledging the great king beyond the waters to be your lord also, and that you will pay him tribute as you have hitherto done to me.' As he spoke the tears fell fast down his cheeks. and his nobles were deeply affected by the sight of his distress. Many of them, coming from a distance, and not having realised what was taking place in the capital, were filled with astonishment on beholding the voluntary abasement of their master, whom they had reverenced as the all-powerful lord of the whole country. His will, they told him, was their law now as ever, and if he thought the sovereign of the strangers was the ancient lord of their country, they were willing to swear allegiance to him as such. Accordingly the oaths were administered with all due solemnity, and a full record of the proceedings was drawn up by the royal notary to be sent to Spain. Cortés now seemed to have accomplished most of the great objects of his expedition, but towards the conversion of the natives he had made no progress, and still the horrible sacrifices took place day by day. The general could bear it no longer, but told the emperor that the Christians could not consent to hold the services of their religion shut in within the narrow walls of the garrison. They wished to spread its light abroad and share its blessings with the people. To this end they requested that the great teocalli should be given up to them as a fit place where their worship might be conducted in the presence of the whole city. Montezuma listened in consternation.

'Malinche,' said he, 'why will you push matters to an extremity that must surely bring down the vengeance of our gods and stir up an insurrection among my people, who will never endure this profanation of their temple?'

Cortés, seeing that he was much agitated, pretended that the demand had come from his followers, and that he would endeavour to persuade them to be contented with one of the sanctuaries of the teocalli. If that were not granted, they should be obliged to take it by force and to throw down the idols in the face of the city. Montezuma, still greatly disturbed, promised to confer with the priests, and in the end the Spaniards were allowed to take possession of one of the sanctuaries, in which, when it had been purified, an altar was raised, surmounted by a crucifix and the image of the Virgin; its walls were decorated with garlands of fresh flowers, and an old soldier was stationed to watch over it. Then the whole army moved in solemn procession up the winding ascent of the pyramid, and mass was celebrated by Father Olmedo and another priest, while the Aztecs looked on with mingled curiosity and repugnance. For a nation will endure any outrage sooner than that which attacks its religion, and this profanation touched a feeling in the natives which the priests were not slow to take advantage of.

Soon the Spaniards noticed a change in Montezuma. He was grave instead of cheerful, and avoided their society. Many conferences went on between him and the priests and nobles, at which even Orteguilla, his favourite page, was not allowed to be present. Presently Cortés received a summons to appear before the emperor, who told him that his predictions had come to pass, his gods were offended, and threatened to forsake the city if the sacrilegious strangers were not driven from it, or sacrificed on their altars as an expiation. 'If you have any regard for your safety,' he continued, ' you will leave the country without delay. I have only to raise my finger, and every Aztec in the land will rise against you.'

Cortés knew well enough that this was true, but, concealing his dismay, he replied that he should much regret to leave the capital so precipitately, especially when he had no ships to take him back to his own country. He should also regret that if he quitted it under these circumstances he should be driven to taking the emperor with him. Montezuma was evidently troubled by this last suggestion, and finally offered to send workmen to the coast to build ships under the direction of the Spaniards, while he restrained the impatience of his people with the assurance that the white men would leave their land as soon as they were ready. This was accordingly done, and the work went forward at Vera Cruz with great apparent alacrity, but those who directed it took care to interpose as many delays as possible, while Cortés hoped in the meantime to receive such reinforcements from Spain as should enable him to hold his ground. Nevertheless the whole aspect of affairs in the Spanish quarters was utterly changed; apprehension had taken the place of security, and as many precautions were observed as if the garrison was actually in a state of siege. Such was the unpleasant state of affairs when, in May 1520, six months after his arrival in the capital, Cortés received tidings from the coast which caused him greater alarm than even the threatened insurrection of the Aztecs. The jealous governor of Cuba was sending an expedition to attack Cortés.

It was the news of the arrival of this fleet at the place where he had himself landed at first that had caused Cortés so much consternation, for he at once suspected that it was sent by his bitter enemy the governor. The commander of this second expedition, who was called Narvaez, having landed, soon met with a Spaniard from one of the exploring parties sent out by Cortés. This man related all that had occurred since the Spanish envoys left Vera Cruz, the march into the interior, the furious battles with the Tlascalans, the occupation of Mexico, the rich treasures found in it, and the seizure of Montezuma, 'whereby,' said the soldier, 'Cortés rules over the land like its own sovereign, so that a Spaniard may travel unarmed from one end of the country to the other without insult or injury.'

Narvaez and his followers listened in speechless amazement to this marvellous report, and the leader waxed more and more indignant at the thought of all that had been snatched from Velasquez, whose adherent he was. He now openly proclaimed his intention of marching against Cortés and punishing him, so that even the natives who had flocked to this new camp comprehended that these white men were enemies of those who had come before. Narvaez proposed to establish a colony in the barren, sandy spot which Cortés had abandoned, and when informed of the existence of Villa Rica, he sent to demand the submission of the garrison. Sandoval had kept a sharp eye upon the movements of Narvaez from the time that his ships had first appeared upon the horizon, and when he heard of his having landed he prepared to defend his post to the last extremity. But the only invaders of Villa Rica were a priest named Guevara and four other Spaniards, who formally addressed Sandoval, pompously enumerating the services and claims of Velasquez, taxing Cortés with rebellion, and finally demanding that Sandoval should tender his submission to Narvaez. That officer, greatly exasperated, promptly seized the unlucky priest and his companions, and, remarking that they might read the obnoxious proclamation to the general himself in Mexico, ordered them to be bound like bales of goods upon the backs of sturdy porters and placed under a guard of twenty Spaniards, and in this way, travelling day and night, only stopping to obtain relays of carriers, they came within sight of the capital at the end of the fourth day.

Its inhabitants were already aware of the fresh arrival of white men upon the coast. Indeed Montezuma had sent for Cortés and told him there was no longer any obstacle to his leaving the country, as a fleet was ready for him, and in answer to his astonished inquiries, had shown him a picture map sent him from the coast, whereon the Spaniards, with their ships and equipments, were minutely depicted. Cortés pretended to be vastly pleased by this intelligence, and the tidings were received in the camp with firing of cannon and other demonstrations of joy, for the soldiers took the newcomers for a reinforcement from Spain. Not so Cortés, who guessed from the first that they came from the governor of Cuba. He told his suspicions to his officers, who in turn informed the men; but, though alarm succeeded their joy, they resolved to stand by their leader come what might. When Sandoval's letter acquainting him with all particulars was brought to Cortés, he instantly sent and released the bewildered prisoners from their ignominious position, and furnished them with horses to make their entry into the capital, where, by treating them with the utmost courtesy and loading them with gifts, he speedily converted them from enemies into friends, and obtained from them much important information respecting the designs of Narvaez and the feelings of his army. He gathered that gold was the great object of the soldiers, who were evidently willing to co-operate with Cortés if by so doing they could obtain it. Indeed, they had no particular regard for their own leader, who was arrogant, and by no means liberal. Profiting by these important hints, the general sent a conciliatory letter to Narvaez, beseeching him not to unsettle the natives by a show of animosity, when it was only by union they could hope for success, and declaring that for his part he was ready to greet Narvaez as a brother in arms, to share with him the fruits of conquest, and, if he could produce a royal commission, to submit to his authority. Of course Cortés knew well enough that he had no such commission to show. Soon after the departure of Guevara he resolved to send a special envoy of his own, and chose Father Olmedo for the task, with instructions to converse privately with as many of the officers and soldiers as he could with a view to securing their goodwill; and to this end he was also provided with a liberal supply of gold. During this time Narvaez had abandoned his idea of planting a colony on the sea-coast, and had marched inland and taken up his quarters at Cempoalla. He received the letter of Cortés with scorn, which changed to stern displeasure when Guevara enlarged upon the power of his rival and urged him to accept his friendly offers. But the troops, on the other hand, listened with greedy ears to the accounts of Cortés, his frank and liberal manners, and the wealth of his camp, where the meanest soldier could stake his ingot and his chain of gold at play, and where all revelled in plenty. And when Father Olmedo arrived, his eloquence and his gifts soon created a party in the interest of Cortés. This could not go on so secretly as not to excite ·

the suspicions of Narvaez, and the worthy priest was sent back to his master, but the seed which he had sown was left to grow.

Narvaez continued to speak of Cortés as a traitor whom he intended to punish, and he also declared he would release Montezuma from captivity and restore him to his throne. It was rumoured that the Aztec monarch had sent him a rich gift, and entered into correspondence with him. All this was observed by the watchful eye of Sandoval, whose spies frequented his enemy's camp, and he presently sent to Cortés saying that something must speedily be done to prevent Villa Rica from falling into the hands of the enemy, and pointing out that many of the Indians, from sheer perplexity, were no longer to be relied upon.

The general felt that it was indeed time to act, but the situation was one of great difficulty. However, he marched against Narvaez, defeated and captured him, embodied his forces, and set out on his return to Mexico, where he had left Alvarado in command.

On his march he received a letter from Alvarado, which conveyed the startling news that the Mexicans were up in arms and had assaulted the Spanish quarters, that they had overwhelmed the garrison with a torrent of missiles, which had killed some and wounded many, and had burned some brigantines which Cortés had built to secure a means of retreat, and it ended by imploring him to hasten to the relief of his men if he would save them or keep his hold on the capital. This was a heavy blow to Cortés, but there was no time for hesitation. He laid the matter fully before his soldiers, and all declared their readiness to follow him.

On June 24, 1520, the army reached the same causeway by which they had before entered the capital; but now no crowds lined the roads, and no pirogues swarmed upon the lake; a death-like stillness brooded over the scene. As they marched across Cortés ordered the trumpets to sound, and their shrill notes were answered by a joyful peal of artillery from the beleaguered fortress. The soldiers quickened their pace, and all were soon in the city once more. But here the appearance of things was far from reassuring. In many places they saw the smaller bridges had been taken away; the town seemed deserted, and the tramp of the horses awakened melancholy echoes in the deserted streets. When they reached the palace the great gates were speedily thrown open, and Cortés and his party were eagerly welcomed by the garrison, who had much to tell and to hear. Of course the general's first inquiry was as to the origin of the tumult, and this was the story he heard.

The Aztec festival called 'The incensing of Huitzilopochtli' was about to be celebrated, in which, as it was an important one, nearly all the nobles took part. The caciques asked the permission of Alvarado to perform their rites in the teocalli which contained the chapel of the Spaniards, and to be allowed the presence of Monte-zuma. This latter request was refused, but he consented to their using the teocalli provided they came unarmed and held no human sacrifice. Accordingly, on the day appointed the Aztecs assembled to the number of at least six hundred. They wore their magnificent gala costumes, with mantles of featherwork sprinkled with precious stones, and collars, bracelets, and ornaments of gold. Alvarado and his men, fully armed, attended as spectators, and when the hapless natives were engaged in one of their ceremonial dances, they fell upon them suddenly, sword in hand. Then followed a great and dreadful slaughter. Unarmed, and taken unawares, the Aztecs were hewn down without resistance. Those who attempted to escape by climbing the wall of serpents were speared ruthlessly, till presently not one of that gay company remained alive ; then the Spaniards added the crowning horror to their dreadful deed by plundering the bodies of their murdered victims. The tidings of the massacre flew like wildfire through the capital, and every long-smothered feeling of hostility burst forth in the cry that arose for vengeance. The city rose in arms to a man and almost before the Spaniards could secure themselves in their defences, they were assaulted with desperate fury : some of the assailants attempted to scale the walls, others succeeded in partially undermining and setting fire to the works. It is impossible to say how the attack would have ended, but the Spaniards entreated Montezuma to interfere, and he, mounting the battlements, conjured the furious people to desist from storming the fortress out of regard for his safety. They so far respected him that they changed their opera-tions into a regular blockade, throwing up works round the palace to prevent the egress of the Spaniards, and suspending the market so that they might not obtain any supplies, and then they sat down to wait sullenly till famine should throw their enemies into their hands.

The condition of the besieged was gloomy enough. True their provisions still held out, but they suffered greatly from want of water, that within the enclosure being quite brackish, until a fresh spring was suddenly discovered in the courtyard. Even then the fact that scarcely a man had escaped unwounded, and that they had no prospect before them but a lingering death by famine, or one more dreadful still upon the altar of sacrifice, made their situation a very trying one. The coming of their comrades was therefore doubly welcome. As an explanation of his atrocious act, Alvarado declared that he had but struck the blow to intimidate the natives and crush an intended rising of the people, of which he had received information through his spies.

Cortés listened calmly till the story was finished, then exclaimed with undisguised displeasure, ' You have done badly. You have been false to your trust. Your conduct has been that of a mad-man ! ' And so saying, he turned and left him abruptly, no doubt bitterly regretting that he had entrusted so important a command to one whose frank and captivating exterior was but the mask for a rash and cruel nature. Vexed with his faithless lieutenant, and embarrassed by the disastrous consequences of his actions, Cortés for the first time lost his self-control, and allowed his disgust and irritation to be plainly seen. He treated Montezuma with haughty coldness, even speaking of him as ' this dog of a king ' in the presence of his chiefs, and bidding them fiercely go tell their master and his people to open the markets, or he would do it for them to their cost. The chiefs retired in deep resentment at the insult, which they comprehended well enough from his look and gesture, and the message lost nothing of its effect in transmission. By the suggestion of Montezuma, Cortés now released his brother Cuitlahua, thinking he might allay the tumult and bring about a better state of things. But this failed utterly, for the prince, who was bold and ambitious, was bitterly incensed by the injuries he had received from the Spaniards. Moreover, he was the heir presumptive to the crown, and was welcomed by the people as a substitute for the captive Montezuma. So being an experienced warrior, he set him-self to arrange a more efficient plan of operations against the Spaniards, and the effect was soon visible. Cortés, meanwhile, had so little doubt of his ability to quench the insurrection that he said as much in the letter that he wrote to the garrison of Villa Rica informing them of his safe arrival in the capital. But his messenger had not been gone half-an-hour before he returned breathless with terror, and covered with wounds, saying that the city was in arms, the drawbridges were raised, and the enemy would soon be upon them.

Surely enough before long a hoarse, sullen roar arose, becoming louder and louder, till from the parapet surrounding the enclosure the great avenues that led to it could be seen dark with masses of warriors rolling on in a confused tide towards the fortress, while at the same time the flat roofs of the neighbouring houses were suddenly covered, as if by magic, with swarms of menacing figures, brandishing their weapons—a sight to appal the stoutest heart.

FIGHTING IN MEXICO.

When notice was given of the approach of the Aztecs, each man was soon at his post, and prepared to give them a warm reception. On they came, rushing forward in dense columns, each with its gay banner, and as they neared the enclosure they set up the hideous yell or shrill whistle used in fight, which rose high above the sound of their rude musical instruments. They followed this by a tempest of stones, darts, and arrows, which fell thick as rain on the besieged, and at the same time those upon the roofs also discharged a blinding volley. The Spaniards waited until the foremost column was within fire, and then, with a general discharge of artillery, swept the ranks of their assailants, mowing them down by hundreds. The Mexicans for a moment stood aghast, but soon rallying swept boldly forward over the prostrate bodies of their comrades : a second and third volley checked them and threw their ranks into disorder, but still they pressed on, letting off clouds of arrows, while those on the house-tops took deliberate aim at the soldiers in the courtyard. Soon some of the Aztecs succeeded in getting close enough to the wall to be sheltered by it from the fire of the Spaniards, and they made gallant efforts to scale the parapet, but only to be shot down, one after another, as soon as their heads appeared above the rampart. Defeated here, they tried to effect a breach by battering the wall with heavy pieces of timber, but it proved too strong for them, and then they shot burning arrows among the temporary buildings in the courtyard. Several of these took fire, and soon a fierce conflagration was raging, which was only to be checked by throwing down part of the wall itself, and thus laying open a formidable breach. This was protected by a battery of heavy guns, and a file of arquebusiers, who kept up an incessant volley through the opening. All day the fight raged with fury, and even when night came, and the Aztecs suspended operations according to their usual custom, the Spaniards found but little repose, being in hourly expectation of an assault. Early the next morning the combatants returned to the charge. Cortés did not yet realise the ferocity and determination of the Mexicans, and thought by a vigorous sortie he would reduce them to order, and, indeed, when the gates were thrown open, and he sallied out, followed by his cavalry, supported by a large body of infantry and Tlascalans, they were taken by surprise and retreated in some confusion behind a barricade which they had thrown up across the street.

But by the time Cortés had ordered up his heavy guns and demolished the barrier they had rallied again, and though, when the fight had raged all day, Cortés was, on the whole, victorious, still he had been so harassed on all sides by the battalions of natives who swarmed in from every side street and lane, by those in canoes upon the canal, and by the showers of huge stones from those upon the house-tops, that his losses had been severe. Earlier in the day he had caused a number of houses to be burned to rid himself of some of his tormentors, but the Aztecs could probably better afford to lose a hundred men than the Spaniards one, and the Mexican ranks showed no signs of thinning. At length, exhausted by toil and hunger, the Spanish commander drew off his men, and retreated into his quarters, pursued to the last by showers of darts and arrows; and when the Spaniards re-entered their fortress, the Indians once more encamped round it; and though through the night they were inactive, still they frequently broke the stillness with menacing cries and insults.

' The gods have delivered you into our hands at last ! ' they said. ' Huitzilopochtli has long cried for his victims. The stone of sacrifice is ready—the knives are sharpened. The wild beasts in the palace are roaring for their feast.' These taunts, which sounded dismally in the ears of the besieged, were mingled with piteous lamentations for Montezuma, whom they entreated the Spaniards to deliver up to them. Cortés was suffering much from a severe wound and from his many anxieties, and he determined to induce Montezuma to exert his authority to allay the tumult. In order to give greater effect to his appearance he put on his imperial robes. His mantle of blue and white was held by a rich clasp of the precious ' chalchivitl,' which with emeralds of uncommon size, set in gold, also ornamented other portions of his dress. His feet were shod with golden sandals, and upon his head he wore the Mexican diadem. Surrounded by a guard of Spaniards and preceded by a golden wand, the symbol of sovereignty, the Indian monarch ascended the central turret of the palace. His presence was instantly recognised by the people, and a magical change came over the scene: the clang of the instruments and the fierce cries of the assailants ceased, and many in the hushed throng knelt or prostrated themselves, while all eyes were turned with eager expectation upon the monarch whom they had been taught to regard with slavish awe. Montezuma saw his advantage, and in the presence of his awe-struck people felt once more a king. With his former calm authority and confidence he addressed them :

' Why do I see my people here in arms against the palace of my fathers ? Is it that you think your sovereign a prisoner, and wish to release him ? If so you have done well ; but you are mistaken. I am no prisoner. The strangers are my guests. I remain with them only for choice, and can leave them when I will. Have you come to drive them from the city ? That is unnecessary ; they will depart of their own accord if you will open a way for them. Return to your homes then. Lay down your arms. Show your obedience to me, whose right it is. The white men shall go back to their land, and all shall be well again within the walls of Mexico.'

As Montezuma declared himself the friend of the detested strangers a murmur of contempt ran through the multitude. Their rage and desire for vengeance made them forget their ancient reverence, and turned them against their unfortunate monarch.

' Base Aztec,' they cried, 'woman, coward ! The white men have made you a woman, fit only to weave and spin.'

A chief of high rank brandished a javelin at Montezuma, as these taunts were uttered, and in an instant the place where he stood was assailed with a cloud of stones and arrows. The Spaniards, who had been thrown off their guard by the respect shown by the people on their lord's appearance, now hastily interposed their shields, but it was too late : Montezuma was wounded by three of the missiles, one of which, a stone, struck him on the head with such violence that he fell senseless to the ground. The Mexicans, shocked at their own sacrilegious act, set up a dismal cry, and dispersed panic-stricken until not one of all the host remained in the great square before the palace. Meanwhile, the unhappy king was borne to his own apartments, and as soon as he recovered from his insensibility the full misery of his situation broke upon him. He had tasted the last bitterness of degradation. He had been reviled and rejected by his people. Even the meanest of the rabble had raised their hands against him, and he had nothing left to live for. In vain did Cortés and his officers endeavour to soothe the anguish of his spirit and encourage him to hope for better things. Montezuma answered not a word. His wounds, though dangerous, need not have proved fatal had he not refused all remedies, tearing off the bandages as often as they were applied, and maintaining all the while a determined silence. He sat motionless, with downcast eyes, brooding over his humiliation; but from this painful scene the Spanish general was soon called away by the new dangers which threatened the garrison.

Opposite to the Spanish quarters stood the great teocalli of Huitzilopochtli, rising to a height of nearly a hundred and fifty feet, and thus completely commanding the palace occupied by the Spaniards. A body of five or six hundred Mexicans, many of them nobles and warriors of the highest rank, now took possession of the teocalli, whence they discharged such a tempest of arrows upon the garrison that it was impossible for any soldier to show himself for an instant outside his defences without great danger, while the Mexicans themselves were completely sheltered. It was absolutely necessary that they should be dislodged, and Cortés entrusted the task to his chamberlain Escobar, giving him a hundred men for the purpose. But after making three desperate attempts, in which he was repulsed with considerable loss, this officer returned unsuccessful, and Cortés determined to lead the storming party himself, though he was suffering much from a wound which disabled his left hand. He made the arm serviceable, however, by strapping his shield to it, and thus prepared sallied forth at the head of three hundred chosen cavaliers and several thousand of the Indian allies. In the courtyard of the temple a body of Mexicans was drawn up to oppose him, and he charged them briskly, but the horses could not keep their footing on the slippery pavement, and many of them fell. Hastily dismounting the Spaniards sent the animals back to their quarters, and then, renewing the assault, had little difficulty in dispersing the Indians and securing a passage to the teocalli. And now began a great and terrible struggle. You will remember that the huge pyramid-shaped teocalli was built in five divisions, growing smaller and smaller, till at the top you came out upon a square platform, crowned only by the two sanctuaries in which stood the images of the Aztec gods. You will also remember that the only ascent was by flights of stone steps on the outside, one above another, and that it was

MONTEZUMA ASSAILED BY MISSILES

necessary between each flight to pass by a kind of terrace, right round the building, so that a distance of nearly a mile had to be traversed before reaching the top. Cortés sprang up the lower stairway, followed by Alvarado, Sandoval, Ordaz, and the other gallant cavaliers, leaving a strong detachment to hold the enemy in check at the foot of the temple. On every terrace as well as on the topmost platform the Aztec warriors were drawn up to dispute his passage. From their elevated position they showered down heavy stones, beams, and burning rafters, which thundering along the stairway overturned the ascending Spaniards and carried desolation through their ranks. The more fortunate, eluding or springing over these obstacles, succeeded in gaining the first terrace, where they fell upon their enemies and compelled them to give way, and then, aided by a brisk fire from the musketeers below, they pressed on, forcing their opponents to retreat higher and higher, until at last they were glad to take shelter on the broad summit of the teocalli. Cortés and his companions were close behind them, and the two parties soon found themselves face to face upon this strange battle-field, engaged in mortal combat in the presence of the whole city, while even the troops in the courtyard ceased hostilities, as if by mutual consent, and watched with breathless interest the issue of the struggle.

The Spaniards and Mexicans closed with the desperate fury of men who have no hope but in victory. Quarter was neither asked nor given, and to fly was impossible. The edge of the platform was unprotected by parapet or battlement, and many of the combatants, as they struggled together, were seen to roll over the edge of the precipice, locked in a death-grip. Cortés himself but narrowly escaped this frightful fate. Two powerful warriors had seized upon him, and were dragging him violently towards the side of the pyramid, when, by sheer strength, he tore himself from their grasp and hurled one of them over the brink with his own arm.

The battle raged unceasingly for three hours. The number of the Mexicans was double that of the Spaniards, but the armour of the latter and their skill as swordsmen outweighed the odds against them. Resistance grew fainter and fainter on the side of the Aztecs. The priests, who had run to and fro among them with streaming hair and wild gestures, encouraging and urging them on, were all slain or captured. One by one the warriors fell dead upon the blood-drenched pavement, or were hurled from the dizzy height, until at last the wild struggle ceased, and the Spaniards stood alone upon the field of battle. Their victory had cost them dear, for forty-five of their comrades lay dead, and nearly all the remainder were more or less seriously wounded; but there was no time for regrets. The victorious cavaliers rushed to the sanctuaries to find that the cross and the image of the Virgin had disappeared from the one they had

appropriated, and that in the other, before the grim figure of Huitzi-lopochtli, lay the usual offering of human hearts, possibly those of their own countrymen! With shouts of triumph the Spaniards tore the hideous idol from its niche, and in the sight of the horror-stricken Aztecs hurled it down the steps of the teocalli, and, after having set fire to the sanctuaries, descended joyfully into the court-yard.

Passing through the ranks of the Mexicans, who were too much dismayed by all they had witnessed to offer any resistance, they reached their own quarters in safety, and that very night they followed up the blow they had struck by sallying forth into the sleeping town and burning three hundred houses. Cortés now hoped that the natives were sufficiently subdued to be willing to come to terms with him. He therefore invited them to a parley, and addressed the principal chiefs, who had assembled in the great square, from the turret before occupied by Montezuma. As usual, Marina interpreted for him, and the Indians gazed curiously at their countrywoman, whose influence with the Spanish general was well known. Cortés told them that they must now know how little they had to hope from their opposition to the Spaniards. They had seen their gods trampled in the dust, their altars destroyed, their dwellings burned, and their warriors falling on all sides. 'All this,' he continued, 'you have brought upon yourselves by your rebellion. Yet, for the sake of the affection felt for you by the sovereign you have treated so unworthily, I would willingly stay my hand if you will lay down your arms and return once more to your obedience. But if you do not,' he concluded, 'I will make your city a heap of ruins, and leave not a soul alive to mourn over it.'

But the Spanish commander did not yet understand the character of the Aztecs if he thought to intimidate them by menaces. It was true, they replied, that he had destroyed their temples, broken in pieces their gods, and massacred their countrymen. Many more doubtless were yet to fall under their terrible swords. But they were content so long as for every thousand Mexicans they could shed the blood of a single white man. 'Look out,' they said, 'upon our streets and terraces. See them still thronged with warriors as far as your eyes can reach. Our numbers are scarcely diminished by our losses. Yours, on the contrary, are lessening hour by hour. Your provisions and water are failing. You are perishing from hunger and sickness; you must soon fall into our hands. *The bridges are broken down and you cannot escape!* There will be too few of you left to glut the vengeance of our gods.' With this they discharged a volley of arrows, which compelled the Spaniards to beat a speedy retreat from the turret. The fierce answer of the Aztecs filled the besieged with dismay.

The general himself, pressed by enemies without and factions within, was, as usual, only roused to more energetic action by a situation which would have paralysed any ordinary mind. He calmly surveyed his position before deciding what course he would pursue. To retreat was hazardous, and it mortified him cruelly to abandon the city in which he had so long been master and the rich treasure which he had secured, with which he had hoped to propitiate the King of Spain. To fly now was to acknowledge himself further than ever from the conquest and to give great opportunity to his enemy, the Governor of Cuba, to triumph over him. On the other hand, with his men daily diminishing in strength and numbers, with the stock of provisions so nearly exhausted that one small daily ration of bread was all the soldiers had, with the breaches in his fortifications widening every day and his ammunition nearly gone, it was manifestly impossible to hold the place much longer against the enemy. Having reached this conclusion, the next difficulty was to decide how and when it would be well to evacuate the city. He tried to fight his way out, but he failed, and when night fell the Mexicans dispersed as usual, and the Spaniards, tired, famished, and weak from their wounds, slowly re-entered the citadel, only to receive tidings of a fresh misfortune. Montezuma was dead. 'The tidings of his death,' says the old Spanish chronicler, 'were received with real grief by every cavalier and soldier in the army who had had access to his person, for we all loved him as a father, and no wonder, seeing how good he was.'

Montezuma's death was a real misfortune for the Spaniards. While he lived there was still a possibility of his influence with the natives being of use to them. Now that hope was gone. The Spanish commander showed all respect for his memory. His body, arrayed in its royal robes, was laid upon a bier, and borne on the shoulders of those nobles who had remained with him to the last to his subjects in the city, whose wailings over it were distinctly heard by the Spaniards; but where he was buried, and with what honours, they never knew.

The Spanish general now called a council to decide as speedily as possible the all-important question of the retreat. It was his intention to fall back upon Tlascala, and once there to arrange according to circumstances his future operations. There was some difference of opinion as to the hour of departure; but owing to the predictions of a soldier named Botello, who pretended to be able to read the stars, and who announced that to leave the city at night would be for the good of his comrades, though he himself would meet his death through it, it was decided that the fortress should be abandoned that very night. After events proved that Botello's prophecy was unfortunately only true as far as he himself was concerned.

The general's first care was to provide for the safe conveyance of the treasure. The soldiers had most of them converted their share into gold chains or collars which could be easily carried about their persons. But the royal fifth, with that of Cortés himself and his principal officers, was in bars and wedges of solid gold.

That belonging to the crown was now given in charge to the royal officers, with the strongest horse to carry it, and a special guard for its protection. But much treasure belonging to the crown and to private individuals was necessarily abandoned, and the precious metal lay in shining heaps upon the floors of the palace. ' Take what you will of it,' said Cortés to the soldiers ; ' better you should have it than those Mexican hounds. But be careful not to overload yourselves : he travels safest who travels lightest.' His own wary soldiers took heed to his counsel, taking few treasures, and those of the smallest size. But the troops of Narvaez thought that the very mines of Mexico lay open before them, and the riches for which they had risked so much were within their reach at last. Rushing upon the spoil, they loaded themselves with all they could possibly carry or stow away.

Cortés next arranged the order of march. The van consisted of two hundred Spanish foot, commanded by Sandoval, with twenty other cavaliers. The rest of the infantry formed the rear-guard under Alvarado and De Leon, while the general himself took charge of the centre, some of the heavy guns, the baggage, the treasure, and the prisoners, among whom were a son and two daughters of Montezuma, Cacama, and several nobles. The Tlascalans were pretty equally divided among the three divisions. The general had previously superintended the construction of a portable bridge to be laid across the open canals. This was entrusted to the care of an officer named Magarino and forty men, all pledged to defend the passage to the last extremity. Well would it have been if three such bridges had been made, but the labour would have been great and the time was short. At midnight all was ready, and after a solemn mass had been celebrated by Father Olmedo, the Spaniards for the last time sallied forth from the ancient fortress, the scene of so much suffering and of such great courage.

The Night of Horror.

The night was dark, and a fine rain fell steadily. The vast square before the palace was deserted, as indeed it had been since the death of Montezuma, and the Spaniards made their way across it as noiselessly as possible, and entered the great street of Tlacopan. Though to their anxious eyes every dark lane and alley seemed to swarm with the shadowy forms of their enemies, it was not really so, and all went well until the van drew near the spot where the street opened upon the causeway. Before the bridge could be adjusted across the uncovered breach the Mexican sentinels stationed there fled, raising the alarm as they went. The priests from the summits of the teocallis heard them, and sounded their shells, while the huge drum upon the desolate temple of the war-god sent forth its solemn sound, which—heard only in seasons of calamity—vibrated through every corner of the capital. The Spaniards saw that there was no time to be lost; the bridge was fitted with all speed, and Sandoval rode across first to try its strength, followed by the first division, then came Cortés with the baggage and artillery, but before he was well over, a sound was heard as of a stormy wind rising in a forest. Nearer and nearer it came, and from the dark waters of the lake rose the plashing noise of many oars. Then a few stones and arrows fell at random among the hurrying troops, to be followed by more and more, ever thicker and faster, till they became a terrible blinding storm, while the air was rent with the yells and war-cries of the enemy, who seemed to be swarming in myriads over land and lake.

The Spaniards pushed on steadily, though the Mexicans, dashing their canoes against the sides of the causeway, clambered up and broke in upon their ranks. The soldiers, anxious only to make their escape, simply shook them off, or rode over them, or with their guns and swords drove them headlong down the sides of the dyke again. But the advance of such a body of men necessarily took time, and the leading files had already reached the second gap in the causeway before those in the rear had cleared the first. They were forced to halt, though severely harassed by the fire from the canoes, which clustered thickly round this opening, and many were the urgent messages which were sent to the rear, to hurry up the bridge. But when it was at length clear, and Magarino and his sturdy followers endeavoured to raise it, they found to their horror that the weight of the artillery and the horses passing over it had jammed it firmly into the sides of the dyke; and it was absolutely immovable. Not till many of his men were slain and all wounded did Magarino abandon the attempt, and then the dreadful tidings spread rapidly from man to man, and a cry of despair arose. All means of retreat were cut off; they were held as in a trap. Order and discipline were at an end, for no one could hope to escape except by his own desperate exertions. Those behind pressed forward, trampling the weak and wounded under foot, heeding not friend or foe. Those in front were forced over the edge of the gulf, across which some of the cavaliers succeeded in swimming their

horses, but many failed, or rolled back into the lake in attempting to ascend the opposite bank. The infantry followed pell-mell, heaped one upon the other, frequently pierced by the Aztec arrows, or struck down by their clubs, and dragged into the canoes to be reserved for a more dreadful death. All along the causeway the battle raged fiercely.

The Mexicans clambered continually up the sides of the dyke, and grappled with the Spaniards, till they rolled together down into the canoes. But while the Aztec fell among friends, his unhappy antagonist was secured, and borne away in triumph to the sacrifice.

z

The struggle was long and deadly, but by degrees the opening in the causeway was filled up by the wreck of the waggons, guns, rich bales of stuffs, chests of solid ingots, and bodies of men and horses which had fallen into it; and over this dismal ruin those in the rear were able to reach the other side. Cortés had found a place that was fordable, and, halting halfway across, had vainly endeavoured to check the confusion, and lead his followers safely to the opposite bank. But his voice was lost in the wild uproar; and at length, attended by a few trusty cavaliers, he pushed forward to the front. Here he found Sandoval and his companions, halting before the last breach, trying to cheer on the soldiers to attempt the crossing; but, though not so beset with enemies as the last, it was wide and deep, and the men's resolution failed them. Again the cavaliers set the example, by plunging into the lake. Horse and foot followed, swimming or clinging to the manes and tails of the horses. Those fared best, as the general had predicted, who travelled lightest, and many were, the unfortunate wretches, who, weighed down by the fatal treasure, were buried with it at the bottom of the lake. Cortés, with a few others, still kept in advance, leading the miserable remnant off the causeway. The din of battle was growing faint in the distance, when the rumour reached them that, without speedy succour, the rearguard must be utterly overwhelmed. It seemed a desperate venture, but the cavaliers, without thinking of the danger, turned their horses, and galloped back to the relief of their comrades. Swimming the canal again, they threw themselves into the thick of the fray. The first gleam of morning light showed the hideous confusion of the scene; the masses of combatants upon the dyke were struggling till the very causeway seemed to rock, while as far as the eye could see, the lake was covered with a dense crowd of canoes full of warriors. The cavaliers found Alvarado unhorsed, and, with a mere handful of followers, defending himself against an overwhelming tide of the enemy, who by this time possessed the whole rear of the causeway, and received constant reinforcements from the city. The Spanish artillery, which had done good service at first, had been overthrown, and utterly confounded by the rush from the back. In the general ruin, Cortés strove by a resolute charge to give his countrymen time to rally, but it was only for a moment: they were speedily borne down by the returning rush. The general and his companions were forced to plunge into the lake once more, though with their numbers reduced this time, and Alvarado stood for an instant upon the brink, uncertain what to do. There was no time to be lost. He was a tall and powerful man. Setting his long lance firmly on the wreck which strewed the lake, he gave a mighty leap which landed him in safety upon the opposite bank. Aztecs and Tlascalans looked on in amazement at this almost incredible feat, and a general shout arose. ' This is truly the Tonatiuh—the Child of the Sun.' To this day, the place is called ' Alvarado's Leap.' Cortés now rode to the front,

where the troops were straggling miserably off the fatal causeway. Most fortunately, the attention of the Aztecs was diverted by the rich spoil that strewed the ground, and their pursuit ceased, so that the Spaniards passed unmolested through the village of Popotla. There the Spanish commander dismounted from his weary steed, and sitting down on the steps of an Indian temple, looked mournfully on while the broken files dragged slowly past. It was a piteous spectacle. The cavalry, many of them dismounted, were mingled with the infantry, their shattered mail dripping with the salt ooze, and showing through its rents many a ghastly wound; their firearms, banners, baggage, artillery, everything was gone. Cortés, as he looked sadly on their thin, disordered ranks, sought in vain many a familiar face, and missed more than one trusty comrade who had stood by his side through all the perils of the conquest; and accustomed as he was to conceal his emotions, he could bear it no longer, but covered his face with his hands, while he wept tears of anguish. It was, however, some consolation to him that Marina had been carried safely through the awful night by her faithful guards. Aguilar was also alive, and Martin Lopez, who had built two boats for him in Mexico, as well as Alvarado, Avila, Sandoval, Olid, and Ordaz.

But this was no time to give way to vain regrets. Cortés hastily mounted again and led his men as speedily as possible through Tlacopan, and, as soon as he reached the open country, endeavoured to bring his disorganised battalions into something like order. The broken army, half-starved, moved slowly towards the coast. On the seventh morning the army reached the mountain range which overlooks the plains of Otumba. All the day before, parties of the enemy had hovered round, crying vindictively, 'Hasten on. You will soon find yourselves where you cannot escape!' Now, as they climbed the steep hillside, Cortés realised what this meant, for his scouts came back reporting that a powerful body of Aztecs was encamped upon the other side waiting for them, and truly enough, when they looked down into the valley, they saw it filled with a mighty host of warriors who had been gathered together by Cuitlahua, and stationed at this point to dispute the passage of the Spaniards. Every chief of importance had taken the field with his whole array. As far as the eye could reach extended a moving mass of glittering shields and spears, mingled with the banners and bright feather-mail of the caciques, and the white cotton robes of their followers. It was a sight to dismay the stoutest heart among the Spaniards, and even Cortés felt that his last hour was come. But since to escape was impossible, he disposed his little army to the best advantage, and prepared to cut his way through the enemy or perish in the attempt. He gave his force as broad a front as possible, protecting it on each flank with his cavalry, now reduced to twenty horsemen, who were instructed to direct their long lances at the faces of the enemy, and on no account to lose their hold of them. The infantry were to thrust, not strike, with their swords, and above all to make for the leaders of the enemy, and then, after a few brave words of encouragement, he and his little band began to descend the hill, rushing, as it seemed, to certain destruction. The enemy met them with the usual storm of stones and arrows, but when the Spaniards closed with them, their superiority became apparent, and the natives were thrown into confusion by their own numbers as they fell back from the charge. The infantry followed up their advantage, and a wide lane was opened in the ranks of the enemy, who receded on all sides as if to allow them a free passage. But it was only to return with fresh fury, and soon the little army was entirely surrounded, standing firmly, protected on all sides by its bristling swords and lances, like an island in the midst of a raging sea. In spite of many gallant deeds and desperate struggles, the Spaniards found themselves, at the end of several hours, only more deeply wedged in by the dense masses of the enemy. Cortés had received another wound, in the head, his horse had fallen under him, and he had been obliged to mount one taken from the baggage train. The fiery rays of the sun poured down upon the nearly exhausted soldiers, who were beginning to despair and give way, while the enemy, constantly reinforced from the rear, pressed on with redoubled fury. At this critical moment the eagle eye of Cortés, ever on the watch for any chance of arresting the coming ruin, descried in the distance a chief, who, from his dress and surroundings, he knew must be the commander of the Aztec forces. He wore a rich surcoat of feather-work, and a gorgeous plume of jewelled feathers floated from his helmet, while above this, and attached to his back between the shoulders, showed a golden net fastened to a short staff—the customary symbol of authority for an Aztec commander. Turning quickly round to Sandoval, Olid, Alvarado, and Avila who surrounded him, he cried, pointing to the chief, ' There is our mark ! Follow and support me ! ' And shouting his war-cry he plunged into the thickest of the press. Taken by surprise the enemy fell back ; those who could not escape were trampled under his horse's feet, or pierced by his long lance ; the cavaliers followed him closely ; in a few minutes they were close to the Aztec chief, and Cortés hurled him to the ground with one stroke from his lance ; a young cavalier named Juan de Salamanca hastily dismounted and slew him where he lay, and tearing away his banner presented it to the Spanish general. The cacique's guard, overpowered by this sudden onset, fled precipitately, and

their panic spread to the other Indians, who, on hearing of the death
of their chief, fought no more, but thought only of escape. In their
blind terror they impeded and trampled down their own comrades,
and the Spaniards, availing themselves fully of the marvellous turn
affairs had taken, pursued them off the field, and then returned to
secure the rich booty they had left behind them.

Cortés reached Tlascala in safety, and at once began to prepare
his revenge on the Mexicans, aided by reinforcements of a few
Spaniards from Vera Cruz. Gunpowder had also to be manufac-

tured, and a cavalier named Francio Montaño undertook the perilous
task of obtaining sulphur for the purpose from the terrible volcano of
Popocatepetl. He set out with four comrades, and after some days
journeying, they reached the dense forest which covered the base
of the mountain, and forcing their way upward, came by degrees to
a more open region. As they neared the top the track ended, and
they had to climb as best they could over the black glazed surface
of the lava, which, having issued from the crater in a boiling flood,
had risen into a thousand odd forms wherever it met with any
obstacle, and continually impeded their progress. After this they

arrived at the region of perpetual snow, which increased their difficulties, the treacherous ice giving way at every step, so that

many times they narrowly escaped falling into the frozen chasms that yawned all round them. At last, however, they reached the mouth of the crater, and, crawling cautiously to the very edge, peered down into its gloomy depths. At the bottom of the abyss, which seemed to them to go down into the very heart of the earth, a lurid flame burned sullenly, sending up a sulphureous steam, which cooling as it rose, fell again in showers upon the sides of the cavity. Into this one of the brave explorers had to descend, and when they had cast lots the choice fell upon Montaño himself. His preparations were soon made, and his companions lowered him in a basket into the horrible chasm to a depth of four hundred feet, and there as he hung, he scraped the sulphur from the sides of the crater, descending again and again until he had procured enough for the wants of the army, with which they returned triumphantly to Tlascala. Meanwhile the construction of the ships went forward prosperously, and by Christmas, in the year 1520, there was no longer any reason to delay the march to Mexico.

While all these preparations were being made, some changes had taken place among the Aztecs. Cuitlahua had suddenly died after reigning four months, and Guatemozin his nephew had been chosen in his stead. This young prince had married one of Montezuma's daughters. He was handsome and valiant, and so terrible that his followers trembled in his presence. He had a sort of religious hatred of the Spaniards, and prepared manfully to meet the perils which he saw threatening his country, for by means of spies he had kept a watch upon the movements of the Spaniards, and had discovered their intention of besieging the capital. Cortés, upon reviewing his army, found that his whole force fell little short of six hundred men, of whom forty were cavalry, and eighty arque-busiers and cross-bowmen. The rest were armed with sword, target, and the long copper-headed pikes, which had been made specially by the general's directions. There were also nine cannons of moderate size, but the supply of powder was but indifferent. Cortés published a code of strict regulations for the guidance of his men before they set out, and addressed them as usual with stirring words, touching all the springs of devotion, honour, and ambition in their hearts, and rousing their enthusiasm as only he could have done. His plan of action was to establish his headquarters at some place upon the Tezcucan lake, whence he could cut off the supplies from the surrounding country, and place Mexico in a state of blockade until the completion of his ships should enable him to begin a direct assault. The most difficult of the three ways into the valley was the one Cortés chose; it led right across the moun-

tain chain, and he judged wisely that he would be less likely to be
annoyed by the enemy in that direction. Before long the army
halted within three leagues of Tezcuco, which you will remember
was upon the opposite shore of the lake to Mexico, and somewhat
further north. Up to this time they only had had a few slight
skirmishes with the Aztecs, though beacon fires had blazed upon
every hill-top, showing that the country was roused. Cortés thought
it very unlikely that he would be allowed to enter Tezcuco, which
was now reigned over by Coanaco, the friend and ally of Guatemozin.
But the next morning, before the troops were well under arms,
came an embassy bearing a golden flag, and a gift for Cortés, and
imploring him to spare Coanaco's territories, and to take up his
quarters in his capital. Cortés first sternly demanded an account
of the Spaniards who, while convoying treasure to the coast, had
been slain by Coanaco just when Cortés himself was retreating to
Tlascala. The envoys declared at once that the Mexican emperor
alone was to blame; he had ordered it to be done, and had received
the gold and the prisoners. They then urged that to give them
time to prepare suitable accommodation for him, Cortés should not
enter Tezcuco until the next day; but disregarding this he marched
in at once, only to find the place deserted, and Coanaco well on his
way across the lake to Mexico. The general, however, turned this
to his own advantage by assembling the few persons left in the city,
and then and there electing a brother of the late sovereign to be
ruler in his place, and when a few months later he died, he was
succeeded by Ixtlilxochitl, son of Negahualpilli, who, always a friend
of the Spaniards, now became their most valuable ally, and by the
support of his personal authority and all his military resources, did
more than any other Aztec chieftain to rivet the chains of the
strangers round the necks of his own countrymen.

THE SIEGE AND SURRENDER OF MEXICO

The city of Tezcuco, which lay about half a league from the
shore of the lake, was probably the best position Cortés could have
chosen for the headquarters of the army. His first care was to
strengthen the defences of the palace in which they were lodged,
and next to employ eight thousand Indian labourers in widening a
stream, which ran towards the lake, so that when the ships arrived
they might be put together in Tezcuco, and floated safely down to
be launched upon it. Meanwhile many of the places in the neigh-

bourhood sent in their submission to Cortés, and several noble
Aztecs fell into his hands. These men he employed to bear a
message to Guatemozin, in which he deprecated the necessity of
the present hostilities, and declared himself willing to forget the
past, inviting the Mexicans by a timely submission to save their
capital from the horrors of a siege. But every man in Mexico was
determined to defend it to the uttermost, and this appeal produced
no effect. The general now turned his attention to securing all the
strong places upon the lake. Iztapalapan was the first; the attacking party, after a sharp struggle, succeeded in entering the town;
many of the inhabitants fled in their canoes, but those who remained
were massacred by the Tlascalans in spite of all Cortés could do to
restrain them. Darkness set in while the soldiers were eagerly
loading themselves with plunder; some of the houses had been set
on fire, and the flames lighted up the scene of ruin and desolation.
Suddenly a sound was heard as of the rush of the incoming tide—
and Cortés with great alarm realised that the Indians had broken
down the dykes, and that before long the low-lying ground upon
which the town stood would be under water. He hastily called off
his men and retreated, the soldiers, heavily laden, wading with
difficulty through the flood which gained fast upon them. As they
left the burning city behind them they could no longer find their
way, and sometimes plunged into deep water where many of the
allies, unable to swim, were carried away and drowned. When
morning dawned they were harassed by the enemy, who hovered
round and discharged volleys of arrows and stones, so that it was
with no small satisfaction that they presently found themselves
once more within the walls of Tezcuco. Cortés was greatly disappointed at this disastrous end of an expedition which had begun so
well, but after all the fate of Iztapalapan produced a good effect,
and many more towns sent to tender their allegiance, amongst
others Otumba and Chalco, which was a place of great importance.
Cortés also managed to induce the tribes, who though friendly to
him were hostile to one another, to forget their feuds and combine
against Mexico, and to this wise policy he owed much of his future
success.

News now came from Tlascala that the ships were ready,
and Sandoval was despatched with a considerable guard to bring
them to Tezcuco. On his way he was to stop at Zoltepec, where
the massacre of the Spaniards had taken place, to find out and
punish all who had had a hand in the matter; but when they got

there the inhabitants had fled. In the deserted temples they had the horror of finding many traces of the fate of their comrades; for beside their arms and clothing, and the hides of their horses, the heads of several soldiers were found suspended as trophies of victory; while traced in charcoal upon the wall in one building were the words, in the Spanish language, 'In this place the unfortunate Juan Juste, with many others of his company, was imprisoned.' It was fortunate that the inhabitants had fled, for they would have met with but scant mercy from the Spaniards, who were full of indignation at the thought of the horrible doom which had overtaken their companions. Sandoval now resumed his march to Tlascala, but before he could reach it, the convoy appeared transporting the ships through the mountain passes. Retaining twenty thousand of the warriors as a guard, the Spanish captain dismissed the rest, and after four laborious days Cortés and his garrison had the joy of welcoming them safe within the walls of Tezcuco. It was not long before the general once more sallied forth to reconnoitre the capital, and by the way to chastise certain places which had sent him hostile messages. After an exciting struggle Xaltocan and three other towns were taken, and a considerable quantity of gold and food fell into the hands of the victors. Marching on, the general found himself before Tlacopan, through whose streets he had hurried in consternation at the end of the night of horror. It was his intention to occupy the town, which he did after a sharp fight, just before nightfall, and the next morning, seeing the enemy in battle array on the open ground before the city, he marched out against them and routed them utterly. The Aztecs fled into the town, but were driven through its streets at the point of the lance, and compelled once more to abandon it, after which the Tlascalans pillaged and set fire to the houses, much against the will of Cortés, but they were a fierce race, and sometimes dangerous to friends as well as foes. After six days the general went back to Tezcuco, and for some time things went on as before, with many skirmishes and expeditions against the towns garrisoned by the Mexicans. Sandoval took several strongholds which threatened the security of Chalco, and all the while the work upon the canal was going rapidly forward, and the ships were nearing completion in spite of three attempts made by the enemy to burn them. Just at this time came the welcome news that three vessels had arrived at Villa Rica, with two hundred men on board well provided with arms and ammunition, and with seventy or eighty horses, and the new comers soon made their way to Tezcuco, for the roads to the port were now safe and open.

In April 1521, Cortés started once more to scour the country with a large force, passing quite round the great lakes, and exploring the mountain regions to the south of them. Here he came upon Aztec forces intrenched in strong towns, often built like eagles' nests upon some rocky height, so that to take them was a work of great difficulty and danger. Once he found himself before a city which it was absolutely necessary to subdue, but he was separated from it by a cleft in the solid rock of no great width, but going sheer down thousands of feet. The bridges which generally crossed it had been broken down at the approach of the Spaniards, and as they stood there, unable to advance, the enemy's archers as usual kept up a steady fire, to which they were unavoidably exposed. The general sent a party to seek a passage lower down, but they met with no success until they came to a spot where two large trees, growing one on either side of the ravine, interlaced their branches overhead, and by this unsteady and perilous bridge one of the Tlascalans ventured to cross. His example was soon followed, and one by one about thirty Spaniards and some more of the natives crawled across, swinging dizzily above the abyss. Three lost their hold and fell, but the rest alighted in safety on the other side and attacked the Aztecs, who were as much amazed at their sudden appearance as if they had dropped from the clouds. Presently a temporary bridge was contrived by which the remainder of the force managed to cross also, and before long the town was taken, and the trembling caciques appeared before Cortés, throwing the blame of their resistance upon the Mexicans, and promising submission for the future.

The general then continued his march across the eastern shoulder of the mountain, descending finally upon Xochimilco, which was built partly upon the lake like Mexico itself, and was approached by causeways, which, however, were of no great length. It was in the first attack upon this town that Cortés was as nearly as possible taken prisoner by the Aztecs. He had thrown himself into the thick of the fight with his usual bravery, and was trying to resist an unexpected rush of the enemy, when his horse stumbled and fell, he himself received a severe blow upon the head before he could rise, and was seized and dragged off in triumph by several Indians. At this moment a Tlascalan saw his danger and sprang furiously upon his captors, trying to tear him from their grasp. Two Spaniards also rushed to the rescue, and between them the Aztecs were forced to quit their hold of the general, who lost no time in regaining his saddle, and laying about him with his good sword as vigorously as before. After a terrible struggle the enemy was driven out, and Cortés took possession of the city. As it was not yet dusk he ascended the principal teocalli to reconnoitre the surrounding country, and there beheld a sight which could but cause him grave anxiety. The lake was covered with rapidly approaching canoes full of warriors, while inland Indian squadrons were marching up in dense columns. Xochimilco was but four leagues from the capital, and at the first tidings of the arrival of the Spaniards, Guatemozin had mustered a strong force and marched to its relief. Cortés made all possible preparations for the defence of his quarters, but not until the next day did the Mexicans attack him, and then the battle raged long and with varying success; but in the end Spanish discipline prevailed, and the natives were routed with such dreadful slaughter that they made no further attempt to renew the conflict. The city yielded a rich hoard of plunder, being well stored with gold and feather-work, and many other articles of use or luxury, so that when the general mustered his men upon the neighbouring plain before resuming his march, many of them came staggering under the weight of their spoil. This caused him much uneasiness, since their way would be through a hostile country; but seeing that the soldiers were determined to keep what they had so hardly won, he contented himself with ordering the baggage to be placed in the centre guarded by part of the cavalry, and having disposed the rest to the best advantage, they once more set forth, at the last moment setting fire to the wooden buildings of Xochimilco, which blazed furiously, the glare upon the water telling far and wide the fate that had befallen it. Resting here and there, and engaging in many skirmishes with the Aztecs who followed them up, furious at the sight of the plunder which was being carried away by the invaders, the army presently completed the circuit of the lakes, and reached Tezcuco, to be greeted with the news that the ships were fully rigged and the canal completed, so that there was no longer any reason to delay their operations against Mexico.

It was a triumphant moment when the vessels were launched, and reached the lake in good order. Cortés saw to their being properly armed and manned, and then reviewed the rest of his forces, and summoned his native allies to furnish their promised levies at once.

The general's plan of action against Mexico was to send Sandoval with one division to take possession of Iztapalapan at the southern end of the lake, while Alvarado and Olid were to secure Tlacopan and Chapoltepec upon its western shore, and at the latter place destroy the aqueduct, and so cut off the supply of fresh water from Mexico. This they did successfully, and in several days of fierce fighting breach after breach was carried, and the Spaniards penetrated the city as far as the great teocalli, driving the natives before them, while the Tlascalans in the rear filled up the gaps in the dyke as well as they could, and brought up the heavy guns. Cortés and his men now pushed their way into the inclosure of the temple, and some of them rushed to the top, so lately the scene of their terrible battle, and there found a fresh image of the war-god. Tearing away the gold and jewels with which it was bedecked, they hurled it and its attendant priests over the side of the pyramid, and hastened down to the assistance of their comrades, who were by this time in a most perilous position, the Aztecs having rallied and attacked them furiously. Indeed it seemed likely to go hard with them, for they were driven helplessly back down the great street in utter confusion and panic ; but the timely arrival of a small body of cavalry created a diversion in their favour, and Cortés managed to turn them once more and drive the enemy back into the enclosure with much loss. As it was by this time evening, he retreated in good order to Xoloc. Though this affair caused some consternation among the Mexicans, they speedily opened the canals and built up the ramparts again, so that when Cortés renewed the attack the whole scene had to be gone through as before. When they had once gained the street, however, they found it much easier to advance, the Tlascalans having on the last occasion pulled down many of the houses on either side. This time Cortés had determined to destroy some of the cherished buildings of the Mexicans, and began by setting fire to his old quarters, the palace of Axayacatl, and then the palace of Montezuma on the other side of the great square. The sight so maddened the natives that the Spaniards had some ado to make good their retreat, and few reached their camp that night unwounded. The Aztec emperor for his part made frequent sallies against the Spaniards both by land and upon the lake, sometimes with considerable success. At first he managed to obtain supplies of food in canoes, under cover of the darkness, but by degrees the large towns on the mainland, seeing the Mexicans unable to defend themselves, gave in their allegiance to the Spaniards, and then starvation began to be felt in the unhappy city. In spite of everything, however, all offers of terms from Cortés were steadily refused.

At this juncture, the general was persuaded by some of his officers that it would be well for two of the divisions to unite, and occupy the great market-place in the heart of the town, and so at a given time they marched along their respective causeways and entered the city. Strict orders were given by Cortés that as they advanced every opening in the causeways should be filled up and made secure. The attack began, and the enemy, taken apparently by surprise, gave way and fell back; on rushed the Spaniards by every street, eager to reach the appointed meeting place. Only the general suspected that the enemy might be purposely luring them on to turn upon them when they were hopelessly involved. Taking a few men with him, he hastily proceeded to see for himself if the way was clear should a retreat become necessary, and found, as he had feared, that all had been too eager to be in the front to attend to this most important duty. In the first street he traversed was a huge gap, twelve feet wide, and at least as many deep, full of water, for it connected two canals. A feeble attempt had been made to fill this up with beams and rubbish, but it had been left before any good had been done. Worse than all Cortés saw that this breach was freshly made, and that his officers had probably rushed headlong into a snare laid by the enemy. Before his men could do anything towards filling up the trench, the distant sounds of the battle changed into an ever-increasing tumult, the mingled yells and war cries, and the trampling of many feet grew nearer, and at last, to his horror, Cortés beheld his men driven to the edge of the fatal gulf, confused, helpless, surrounded by their foes. The foremost files were soon hurried over the edge, some trying to swim across, some beaten down by the struggles of their comrades, or pierced by the darts of the Indians. In vain with outstretched hands did Cortés try to rescue his soldiers from death, or worse still from capture; he was soon recognised, and six of the enemy tried to seize and drag him into a canoe. It was only after a severe struggle, in which he was wounded in the leg, that he was rescued by his brave followers. Two were killed in the attempt, while another was taken alive as he held the general's horse for him to mount. In all, sixty

Spaniards were captured on this fatal day, and it was only when
the rest reached their guns in the open space before the causeway
that they were able to rally and beat back the Aztecs. The other
division had fared equally ill, and were moreover in great anxiety
as to the fate of Cortés, who was reported to have been killed.
When they once more reached their quarters, Sandoval, though
badly wounded, rode into the camp of Cortés to learn the truth, and
had a long and earnest consultation with him over the disaster,
and what was next to be done. As he returned to his camp he was
startled by the sound of the great drum on the temple of the war-
god, heard only once before during the night of horror, and looking
up he saw a long file of priests and warriors, winding round the
terraces of the teocalli. As they came out upon the platform at the
top he perceived, with rage and despair, that his own countrymen
were about to be sacrificed with the usual ghastly ceremonies.
The camp was near enough to the city for the white skins of the
victims and their unavailing struggles to be distinctly seen by
their comrades, who were nevertheless powerless to help them, and
their distress and fury may be imagined.

For five days the horrible scenes went on, the Mexicans feasting,
singing, and dancing, while their priests predicted that in eight
days the war-god, appeased by these sacrifices, would overwhelm
their enemies and deliver them into their hands. These prophecies
had a great effect upon the native allies of Cortés, who withdrew
from him in immense numbers. But the general treated their
superstition with cheerful contempt, and only bargained with the
deserters to remain close by and see what would happen. When
the ninth day came, and the city was still seen to be beset on
every side, they ceased to believe in the oracle, and returned, with
their anger against the Mexicans rekindled, and their confidence
in the Spaniards greatly strengthened. At this time another vessel
loaded with stores and ammunition touched at Vera Cruz, and her
cargo was seized and sent on to Cortés by the governor. With his
strength thus renewed the Spanish general resumed active operations. This time not a step was taken in advance without securing
the entire safety of the army, once and for all, by solidly building
up the dykes, filling every canal, and pulling down every house,
so that slowly and by degrees a bare open space was made, which
took in more and more of the town, till at last the unhappy Aztecs,
after many desperate sallies, were shut into the portion of the city
which lay between the northern and western causeways. Here

famine and pestilence did their awful work unchecked. The ordinary articles of food were long exhausted, and the wretched people ate moss, insects, grass, weeds, or the bark of trees. They had no fresh water. The dead were unburied, the wounded lay in misery, yet all the endeavours of Cortés to induce Guatemozin and his chiefs to submit were useless. Though the two divisions of the army had proceeded with their work of destruction until they could join their forces, and seven-eighths of the city lay in ruins, though the banner of Castile floated undisturbed from the smouldering remains of the sanctuary on the teocalli of the war-god, still the Aztecs defied the conquerors, and fiercely rejected their overtures of peace.

Hundreds of famishing wretches died every day, and lay where they fell, for there was no one to bury them. Familiarity with the spectacle made men indifferent to it. They looked on in dumb despair waiting for their own turn to come. There was no complaint or lamentation, but deep, unutterable woe. In the midst of this appalling misery Guatemozin remained calm and courageous, and as firmly resolved not to capitulate as at the beginning of the siege. It is even said that when Cortés persuaded a noble Aztec prisoner to bear his proposals for a treaty to the emperor, Guatemozin instantly ordered him to be sacrificed. The general, who had suspended hostilities for several days hoping for a favourable answer to his message, now resolved to drive him to submission by a general assault, and for that purpose led his men across the dreary waste of ruins to the narrow quarter of the city into which the wretched Mexicans had retreated. But he was met by several chiefs, who, holding out their emaciated arms, exclaimed, ' Why do you delay so long to put an end to our miseries ? Rather kill us at once that we may go to our god Huitzilopochtli, who waits to give us rest from our sufferings ! '

Cortés, moved by the piteous sight, replied that he desired not their death but their submission. ' Why does your master refuse to treat with me,' he said, 'when in a single hour I can crush him and all his people ? ' Then once more he sent to demand an interview with Guatemozin. This time the emperor hesitated, and agreed that next day he would meet the Spanish general. Cortés, well satisfied, withdrew his force, and next morning presented himself at the appointed place in the great square, where a stone platform had been spread with mats and carpets and a banquet made ready. But after all Guatemozin, instead of coming himself, sent his nobles.

Y

Cortés, though greatly disappointed, received them courteously, persuading them to partake of the feast he had prepared, and dismissing them with a supply of provisions for their master and a renewed entreaty that he would next day come in person. But though he waited for three hours beyond the time appointed, neither the emperor nor his chiefs appeared, and the general heard that the Mexicans were preparing to resist an assault. He delayed no longer, but ordering Sandoval to support him by bringing up the ships and directing his big guns against the houses near the water, he marched at once into the enemy's quarters. The Mexicans set up a fierce war-cry, and with their usual spirit sent off clouds of arrows and darts; but the struggle soon became a hand-to-hand one; and weakened by starvation and hemmed in as they were the unhappy Aztecs had no chance against their foes. After a scene of indescribable horror, which appalled even the soldiers of Cortés, used as they were to war and violence, the Spanish commander sounded a retreat and withdrew to his quarters, leaving behind him forty thousand corpses and a smouldering ruin. Through the long night that followed all was silent in the Mexican quarter. There was neither light nor movement. This last blow seemed to have utterly stunned them. They had nothing left to hope for. In the Spanish camp, however, all was rejoicing at the prospect of a speedy termination to the wearisome campaign. The great object of Cortés was now to secure the person of Guatemozin, and the next day, which was August 13, 1521, he led his forces for the last time across the black and blasted ruin which was all that remained of the once beautiful city. In order to give the distressed garrison one more chance, he obtained an interview with the principal chiefs and reasoned with them about the conduct of their emperor.

' Surely,' he said, ' Guatemozin will not see you all perish when he can so easily save you.' But when he had with difficulty prevailed upon them to urge the king to confer with him, the only answer they could bring was that Guatemozin was ready to die where he was, but would hold no communication with the Spanish commander. ' Go then,' replied the stern conqueror, 'and prepare your countrymen for death. Their last moment is come.' Still, however, he postponed the attack for several hours; but the troops were impatient at the delay, and a rumour spread that Guatemozin was preparing to escape by the lake. It was useless to hesitate: the word was given, and the terrible scene that ensued repeated the horrors of the day before. While this was going forward on shore

numbers of canoes pushed off across the lake, most of them only to
be intercepted and sunk by the Spanish ships, which beat down
upon them, firing to right and left. Some few, however, under
cover of the smoke, succeeded in getting into open water. Sandoval
had given particular orders that his captains should watch any boat
that might contain Guatemozin, and now two or three large canoes
together attracted the attention of one named Garci Holguin, who
instantly gave chase, and with a favourable wind soon overtook the
fugitives, though they rowed with the energy of despair. As his

men levelled their guns at the occupants of the boat one rose
saying, 'I am Guatemozin; lead me to Malinche; I am his prisoner.
But let no harm come to my wife and followers.'

Holguin took them on board, and then requested that the
emperor would order the people in the other canoes to surrender.
'There is no need,' he answered sadly, 'they will fight no longer
when they see their prince is taken.' And so it was, for when the
news of his capture reached the shore the Mexicans at once ceased
to defend themselves. It seemed as if they had only gone on so

long to give their sovereign a better chance of escape. Cortés, who had taken up his station on the flat roof of one of the houses, now sent to command that Guatemozin should be brought before him, and he came, escorted by Sandoval and Holguin, who each claimed the honour of having captured him. The conqueror, who was, as usual, accompanied by the Lady Marina, came forward with dignified courtesy to receive his noble prisoner. The Aztec monarch broke the silence saying, ' I have done all I could to defend myself and my people. I am now reduced to this state. Deal with me, Malinche, as you will.' Then laying his hand on a dagger which hung from the belt of Cortés, he added, ' Better despatch me at once with this and rid me of life.'

' Fear not,' answered the conqueror. ' You shall be treated with honour. You have defended your capital like a brave warrior, and a Spaniard knows how to respect valour even in an enemy.' He then sent for the queen, who had remained on board the Spanish ship, and after ordering that the royal captives should be well cared for and supplied with all they needed, he proceeded to dispose of his troops. Olid and Alvarado drew off their divisions to their quarters, leaving only a small guard in the wasted suburbs of the pestilence-stricken city, whilst the general himself, with Sandoval and the prisoners, retired to a town at the end of the southern causeway. That night a tremendous tempest arose, such as the Spaniards had never before witnessed, shaking to its foundations all that remained of the city of Mexico. The next day, at the request of Guatemozin, the Mexicans were allowed to leave the capital, and for three days a mournful train of men, women, and children straggled feebly across the causeways, sick and wounded, wasted with famine and misery, turning often to take one more look at the spot which was once their pleasant home. When they were gone the conquerors took possession of the place and purified it as speedily as possible, burying the dead and lighting huge bonfires in the deserted streets. The treasure of gold and jewels found in it fell far short of the expectation of the Spaniards, the Aztecs having probably buried their hoards or sunk them in the lake on purpose to disappoint the avarice of their enemies. Cortés, therefore, to his eternal disgrace, caused Guatemozin to be tortured; but fire and cord could not wring the secret of the treasure from this illustrious prince. In later days Cortés hanged Guatemozin, on pretence of a conspiracy. Cortés, having no further need for his native allies, now dismissed them with presents and flattering speeches, and they departed well pleased, loaded with the plunder of the Mexican houses, which was despised by the Spanish soldiers. Great was the satisfaction of the conquerors at having thus brought the long campaign successfully to an end. Cortés celebrated the event by a banquet as sumptuous as circumstances would permit, and the next day, at the request of Father Olmedo, the whole army took part in a solemn service and procession in token of their thankfulness for victory.

Thus, after a siege of nearly three months, in which the beleaguered Mexicans showed a constancy and courage under their sufferings which is unmatched in history, fell the renowned capital of the Aztecs, and with its fall the story of the nation comes to an end.

The Aztec empire fell by its own sin. The constant capture of men from neighbouring states as victims for sacrifice had caused the Aztecs to be hated; thus Cortés obtained the aid of the Tlascalans, but for which even his courage and energy would have been of no avail. He deserted Marina when she ceased to be useful, and gave her as a wife to one of his followers.

ADVENTURES OF BARTHOLOMEW PORTUGUES,
A PIRATE

A CERTAIN pirate, born in Portugal, and from the name of his country called Bartholomew Portugues, was cruising from Jamaica in his boat (in which he had only thirty men and four small guns) near the Cape de Corrientes, in the island of Cuba. In this place he met with a great ship bound for the Havana, well provided, with twenty great guns and threescore and ten men, passengers and mariners. This ship he assaulted, but found strongly defended by them that were on board. The pirate escaping the first encounter, resolved to attack her more vigorously than before, seeing he had sustained no great damage hitherto. This resolution he boldly performed, renewing his assaults so often that after a long and dangerous fight he became master of the great vessel, having lost only ten men, and had four wounded.

Having possessed themselves of such a ship, and the wind being contrary for returning into Jamaica, the pirates resolved to steer towards the Cape of St. Anthony, on the western side of the isle of Cuba, there to repair themselves and take in fresh water, of which they had great necessity at the time.

Being now very near the cape above mentioned, they unexpectedly met with three great ships that were coming from New Spain, and bound for the Havana. By these, not being able to escape, were easily retaken both ship and pirates. Thus they were all made prisoners through the sudden change of fortune, and found themselves poor, oppressed, and stripped of all the riches they had won.

Two days after this misfortune there happened to arise a huge and dangerous tempest, which separated the ships one from another. The great vessel in which the pirates were arrived at Campeche, where many considerable merchants came to salute and welcome the captain. These knew the Portuguese pirate as one who had committed innumerable crimes upon these coasts, not only murders and robberies, but also lamentable burnings, which those of Campeche still preserved very fresh in their memory.

The next day after their arrival the magistrates of the city sent several of their officers to demand and take into custody the prisoners from on board the ship, with intent to punish them according to their deserts. Yet fearing lest the captain of the pirates should escape out of their hands on shore (as he had formerly done, being once their prisoner in the city before), they judged it more convenient to leave him safely guarded on board the ship for the present. In the meanwhile they caused a gibbet to be erected, whereon to hang him the very next day, without any other form of trial than to lead him from the ship to the place of punishment.

The rumour of this tragedy was presently brought to the ears of Bartholomew Portugues, and he sought all the means he could to escape that night. With this design he took two earthen jars, in which the Spaniards usually carry wine from Spain to the West Indies, and he stopped them very well, intending to use them for swimming, as those who are unskilled in that art do a sort of pumpkins in Spain, and in other places they use empty bladders. Having made this necessary preparation, he waited for the night when all should be asleep, even the sentry that guarded him. But seeing he could not escape his vigilance, he secretly purchased a knife, and with the same gave him a stab that suddenly deprived him of life and the possibility of making any noise. At that instant Bartholomew Portugues committed himself to the sea, with those two earthen jars before mentioned, and by their help and support, though never having learned to swim, he reached the shore. Having landed, without any delay he took refuge in the woods, where he hid himself for three days without daring to appear, not eating any food but wild herbs.

Those of the city failed not the next day to make diligent search for him in the woods, where they concluded him to be. This strict search Bartholomew Portugues watched from the hollow of a tree, wherein he lay concealed. Seeing them return without finding what they sought for, he adventured to sally forth towards the coast of Golfotriste, forty leagues distant from the city of Campeche. Here he arrived within a fortnight after his escape from the ship, in which time, as also afterwards, he endured extreme hunger, thirst, and fear of falling again into the hands of the Spaniards.

For during all this journey he had no provision but a small calabash with a little water; neither did he eat anything but a few shellfish, which he found among the rocks nigh the seashore. Besides this, he was compelled to pass some rivers, not knowing

well how to swim. Being in this distress, he found an old board which the waves had thrown upon the shore, in which there stuck a few great nails. These he took, and with no small labour whetted against a stone, until he made them sharp like knives. With these, and no other instruments, he cut down some branches of trees, which he joined together with twigs and osiers, and as well as he could made a boat, or rather a raft, with which he crossed over the rivers. Thus he reached the Cape of Golfotriste, as was said before, where he happened to find a certain vessel of pirates who were great comrades of his own, and were lately come from Jamaica.

To these pirates he instantly related all his misfortunes, and asked of them a boat and twenty men to return to Campeche and assault the ship that was in the river, from which he had escaped fourteen days before. They readily granted his request, and equipped him a boat with the said number of men. With this small company he set forth for the execution of his design, which he bravely performed eight days after he separated from his comrades; for being arrived at the river of Campeche, with undaunted courage he assaulted the ship before mentioned. Those that were on board were persuaded that Bartholomew's was a boat from the land that came to bring goods, and therefore were not on their defence. So the pirates assaulted them without any fear of ill success, and in a short space of time compelled the Spaniards to surrender.

Being now masters of the ship, they immediately weighed anchor and set sail, determining to fly from the port, lest they should be pursued by other vessels. This they did with extreme joy, seeing themselves possessors of such a brave ship—especially Bartholomew Portugues, their captain, who now, by a second turn of fortune's wheel, was become rich and powerful again, who had been so lately in that same vessel a poor miserable prisoner, and condemned to the gallows. With this plunder he designed to do great things, for he had found in the vessel a great quantity of rich merchandise. Thus he continued his voyage towards Jamaica for four days. But coming nigh to the isle of Pino, on the south side of the island of Cuba, fortune suddenly turned her back once more, never to show him her countenance again; for a horrible storm arising at sea caused the ship to split against the rocks, and it was totally lost, and Bartholomew, with his companions, escaped in a canoe.

In this manner he arrived in Jamaica, where he remained but a short time, till he was ready to seek his fortune anew. But from that day of disaster it was always ill-luck with him.

THE RETURN OF THE FRENCH
FREEBOOTERS [1]

IN January, 1688, the daring band of French pirates who, sometimes alone, sometimes in company with English captains, had
been cruising in the South Seas, resolved to return to St. Domingo
with all the treasure they had won from the Spaniards. But it
was manifest that this return would be a matter of great difficulty.
They had not one seaworthy vessel left in which to set out for a
long voyage, and, with forces exhausted by the frightful hardships
they had gone through in the past years, they had to pass through
a country peopled by Spaniards —cowardly, indeed, but innumerable,
and only longing for revenge on the reckless crew that had plundered so many of their rich ships and towns. Moreover, provisions
were scarce among the Spaniards themselves, and it seemed likely
that the freebooters, in their passage, would find scant entertainment. But they were determined to risk everything, and having
prayed, and sunk their canoes that the Spaniards might make no
use of them, they set out on their journey. What followed is thus
recounted by one of their party, Raveneau de Lussan :—

The Spaniards, having been warned of our approach, employed
every means they could think of for our destruction, burning all
the provisions before us, setting fire to the prairies we entered, so
that we and our horses were almost stifled, and continually blocking
our way with great barricades of trees. About three hundred of
them formed themselves into a kind of escort, and morning and
evening diverted us with the sound of trumpets, but never dared
to show their faces.

A detachment of our men were always set to fire into woods
and thickets, to find out if a Spanish ambush were concealed there.

[1] 'The return of the French Freebooters from the South Sea, by the mainland, in
1688.' Written by Sieur Raveneau de Lussan, one of the party, taken from his *Journal
du voyage fait à la Mer du Sud avec les flibustiers de l'Amérique en* 1684 *et années suivantes.*
Paris. 1689.

On January 9 we reached an opening in the forest where we could see a good way before us, and therefore did not fire. But we had been looking in front for what was really on both sides of us, for in the bushes right and left the Spaniards were crouching, and presently they let fly on us so suddenly that only half the guard had time to fire back, and two of our men were killed on the spot.

On the 10th we found another ambush, where we surprised our

enemies, who took to flight, abandoning their horses, which became our property.

On the 11th, as we drew near Segovia, we found yet another ambuscade, which we forced to retire, and passed into the town, ready to fight our best—for we thought that here the Spaniards might make a great effort to expel us. But they only discharged their muskets at us now and then from the shelter of the pine-wood above the town, into which they had fled. But we found nothing to eat, for they had burned all the provisions.

On the 13th, having left Segovia, we climbed a hill which looked like a good place to camp, and we saw opposite us, on a mountain slope from which only a narrow valley divided us, twelve to fifteen hundred horses, which for some time we took for cattle pasturing there. Rejoicing in the prospect of good cheer, we sent forty men to make sure, and when they came back they told us that what we had taken for cattle were horses, ready saddled, and that in the same place they had found three intrenchments a pistol shot from each other, which, rising by degrees to about the middle of the mountain slope, entirely barred the way which we meant to travel the next day. These intrenchments commanded the river which ran the length of the valley, into which it was absolutely necessary for us to descend, there being no other way. They saw a man who, having discovered them, threatened them with a bare cutlass.

This grievous news was a bitter disappointment to us, especially the loss of our supposed cows, for we were perishing with hunger. But we had to take courage and find out how to leave this place—and without delay, for the Spaniards, who were assembling from all the country round, would fall upon our little troop, which must be overwhelmed, if we waited for them. The means were not easy to find, and perhaps escape would have seemed impossible, except to our reckless band, who had hitherto succeeded in nearly all our exploits. But ten thousand men could not have crossed that guarded valley without being cut off entirely, both by reason of the number of the Spaniards and the position they occupied.

Men alone could have gone round without crossing the valley, but we could find no way round for the horses and baggage. For the country on each side was nothing but a thick forest, without the trace of a path, all precipices and ravines, and choked with a multitude of fallen trees. And even had we found a way of escape through so many obstacles, it was indispensable to fight the Spaniards sooner or later, if they were ever to let us alone !

There was only one thing to be done—to cross these woods, rocks, and mountains, however inaccessible they seemed, and surprise our enemies, taking advantage of the place by coming upon them from above, where they certainly would not expect us. As to our prisoners, horses, and baggage, since through all our march a troop of three hundred Spaniards had been dogging our steps without daring to approach, we would leave eighty men to guard them—enough to beat four times as many Spaniards.

At nightfall we set out, leaving our eighty men, with orders to the sentinels to fire and beat the retreat and the diane at the usual times, to make the three hundred Spaniards who lurked near us think that we had not left the camp. If we were successful we would send back messengers with the good news, but if, an hour after the firing ended, none of us returned, they were to escape how they could.

All being arranged, we prayed in a low voice, not to be heard by the Spaniards, and set out by the moonlight, two hundred men of us, through this country of rocks, woods, and frightful precipices, where we went leaping and climbing, our feet seeming to be much less use to us than our hands and knees.

On the 14th, at the break of day, when we had already gained a great height, and were climbing on in profound silence, with the Spanish intrenchments to our left, we saw a sentry party, which, thanks to the fog—always thick in this country till ten o'clock in the morning—did not discover us. When it had passed we went straight to the place where we had seen it, and we found that there was really a road there. This, when we had halted half an hour to take breath, we followed, guided by the voices of the Spaniards, who were at matins. But we had only gone a few steps when we found two sentinels, very far advanced, on whom we were forced to fire, which warned the Spaniards, who dreamed of nothing less than our coming upon them from above, since they only expected us from below. So those who guarded the intrench-ment—about five hundred men—being taken at a disadvantage when they thought they had all the advantage on their side, were so terribly frightened that, when we fell upon them all at once, they vanished from the place in an instant, and escaped into the thick fog.

This unexpected assault so utterly upset their plans that the men in the second intrenchment all passed into the lowest one, where they prepared to defend themselves. We fought them a whole hour, under cover of the first intrenchment, which we had taken, and which commanded them, being higher up the mountain side. But as they would not yield we fancied our shots must have missed, since the fog hindered us from seeing our foes distinctly, so, resolved to waste no more powder, we went down, and fell right on the spot whence they had been firing. Then we assailed them furiously, and at sight of our weapons close upon them—which hitherto the fog had concealed—they left everything, and fled into the road below the intrenchments. Here they fell into their own trap; for, thinking it was the only road we could possibly come by, they had cut down trees and blocked it up, and their way being stopped, we could fire upon them from their intrenchment without once missing aim.

At last, seeing the river in the ravine running down with blood, and tired of pursuing the fugitives, we spared the few remaining Spaniards. After we had chanted the ' Te Deum,' sixty of us went to tell those left in the camp of the victory which Heaven had vouchsafed to us. We found them on the point of giving battle to the three hundred Spaniards, who had already (on finding out their weakness) sent a message to them by an officer to tell them that it was hopeless for them to expect to cross the valley, and to offer terms of peace. To which our men replied that were there as many Spaniards as the blades of grass in the prairie they would not be afraid, but would pass through in spite of them, and go where they liked!

The officer, being just dismissed with this message when we arrived, shrugged his shoulders with astonishment when he saw us safe back again, and mounted on the horses of his comrades of the intrenchments. He rode off with the news to his troop, whom we presently fired upon, to rid them altogether from their desire to follow in our wake. Unfortunately for them they had not time to mount their horses, so after a brief conflict, in which a great number of them fell, we let the rest go, though we kept their horses. Then, with our baggage, we joined those of our men who had stayed to guard the intrenchments. In both these combats we had only two men slain and four wounded.

Continuing our journey, we passed one more Spanish intrenchment, where, since the news of our victory had gone before us, we found no resistance. At last, on the sixteenth day of our march, we reached the river which we had been seeking eagerly, by whose means we meant to gain the sea into which it flowed.

At once we entered the woods which are on its banks, and everyone set to work in good earnest to cut down trees, in order to construct *piperies*, with which to descend the river. The reader may perhaps imagine that these piperies were some kind of comfortable boat to carry us pleasantly along the stream, but they were anything but this. We joined together four or five trunks of a kind of tree with light floating wood, merely stripping off their bark, and binding them, instead of cord, with a climbing plant growing in those forests, and embracing the trees like ivy, and when these structures, each large enough to hold two men (and in appearance something like huge wicker baskets) were completed, vessels and crew were ready.

The safest plan was to stand upright in them, armed with long poles to push them off from the rocks, against which the fierce current every moment threatened to dash them. As it was, they

sank two or three feet deep in the water, so that we were nearly always immersed up to our waists.

This river rises in the mountains of Segovia, and falls into the sea at Cape Gracia á Dios, after having flowed for a long distance, with frightful rapidity, among an infinite number of huge rocks, and between the most terrible precipices imaginable. We had to pass more than a hundred cataracts great and small, and there were three which the most daring of us could not look at without turning giddy with fear, when we saw and heard the water plunging from such a height into those horrible gulfs.

Everything was so fearful that only those who have experienced it can imagine it; as for me, though I shall all my life have my memory full of pictures of the perils of that voyage, it would be impossible for me to give any idea of it which would not be far below the reality.

We let ourselves go with the current, so rapid that often, in spite of our resistance, it bore us into foaming whirlpools, where we were engulfed with our pieces of wood. But happily before the greatest cataracts, and also just beyond them, there was a basin of calm water, which made it possible for us to gain the bank, drawing our piperies after us. Then, taking out of them whatever valuables we had there, we descended with these, leaping from rock to rock till we had reached the foot of the cataract. Then one of us would return and throw the piperies, which we had left behind, down into the flood—and we below caught them as they descended. Sometimes, indeed, we failed to catch them, and had to make new ones.

When we first set out we voyaged all together, that in case of accident we might come to each other's aid. But in three days, being out of all danger of the Spaniards, we began to travel separately, since a piperie dashed against the rocks had often been prevented from freeing itself by other piperies which the current hurled against it. It was arranged for those who descended first, when they came to an especially dangerous rapid, to hoist a little flag at the end of a stick, not to warn those behind of the cataract, since they could hear it nearly a league away, but to mark the side on which they ought to land. This plan saved a number of lives, nevertheless many others were lost.

The bananas which we found on the river bank were almost our only nourishment, and saved us from dying of hunger; for, though there was plenty of game, our powder and weapons were all wet and spoiled, so that we could not hunt.

Some days after we had begun to descend the river, as we were travelling separate, several freebooters who had lost all their spoils in gambling were guilty of most cruel treachery. Having gone in advance, these villains concealed themselves behind some rocks commanding the river, in front of which we all had to pass, and as everyone was looking after himself, and we descended unsuspiciously, at some distance from each other—for the reasons already given— they had time to fix upon and to massacre five Englishmen, who possessed greater shares of booty than the rest of us. They were completely plundered by these assassins, and my companion and I · found their dead bodies on the shore. At night, when we were encamped on the river bank, I reported what we had seen, and the story was confirmed both by the absence of the dead Englishmen and of their murderers, who dared not come back to us, and whom we never saw again.

On the 20th of February we found the river much wider, and there were no more cataracts. When we had descended some leagues further it was very fine, and the current was gentle, and seeing that the worst of our perils were over, we dispersed into bands of forty each to make canoes, in which we might safely complete our voyage down the river.

On the 1st of March, by dint of great diligence, having finished four canoes, a hundred and twenty of us embarked, leaving the others, whose canoes were still incomplete, to follow.

On the 9th we reached the mouth of the river in safety, and lived there among the mulattos and negroes who inhabit the coast, till an English boat, touching there, took on board fifty of us, of whom I was one. On the 6th of April, without any other accident, we arrived at our destination, ·St. Domingo.

PRINTED BY
SPOTTISWOODE AND CO., NEW-STREET SQUARE
LONDON